THE UNTOLD STORY OF
ISAAC ZANE
WHITE EAGLE
OF THE WYANDOTS

Other Books by the Author

Wilderness War on the Ohio

In Their Own Words

Place of the Skull

The White Indians

Captives and Kin in the Ohio Country

THE UNTOLD STORY OF
ISAAC ZANE
WHITE EAGLE
OF THE WYANDOTS
BY ALAN FITZPATRICK

Fort Henry Publications
Wheeling, West Virginia

The Untold Story of Isaac Zane White Eagle of the Wyandots
Copyright © 2021 by Alan Fitzpatrick

All rights reserved. No part of this book may be reproduced or transmitted in any form or by any means without written permission of the author.

Cover image, "Isaac Zane, The White Eagle of the Wyandots"

All artwork by the author.

To the memory of Isaac Zane and the hundreds of 'White Indians' who were adopted and assimilated into Native society, and chose to never come back.

Contents

Foreword	ix
Introduction	xi
Chapter One: The Great Wagon Road	1
Chapter Two: The South Potomac Valley	15
Chapter Three War Comes to the Valley	27
Chapter Four Bemino Strikes Back	39
Chapter Five Pontiac's Uprising	55
Chapter Six Captured by the Wyandot	71
Chapter Seven The Clan Mothers	87
Chapter Eight The Training Begins	101
Chapter Nine The Shaman	115
Chapter Ten War with the Cherokee	129
Chapter Eleven Isaac Becomes a Father	143
Chapter Twelve War with the Long Knives	157
Chapter Thirteen The Gathering Clouds of War	173
Chapter Fourteen Ambush at Fort Henry	189
Chapter Fifteen Attack on Fort Randolph	203
Chapter Sixteen The Enemy Prisoners	219
Chapter Seventeen To Remove the Black Coats	237

Chapter Eighteen The Battle of Upper Sandusky	251
Chapter Nineteen An Uneasy Peace	267
Chapter Twenty Fallen Timbers and Beyond	281
Epilogue	*297*
Isaac Zane Descendants	*301*
Bibliography	*303*

Foreword

There is a truth that I've heard spoken over and over in regards to history. "To the victors go the spoils of war, and the privilege of writing the history." To me, the meaning is clear in regards to this story I'm about to tell. When you are defeated in war, you are likely to lose everything you possess; your home, your land, your possessions, your culture, your life, and even your ability to speak about what happened. Nowhere is this truth more evident than the wars fought in America between Europeans and the indigenous Native tribes, from the time of the arriving Pilgrims to Wounded Knee and beyond. Sadly, there is another saying that goes hand-in-hand with the first that is equally relevant to this work. "The victors will always be the judge of what's written, and the vanquished the accused. Always."

These two simple truths are my reason for writing the story of Isaac Zane. Native people did not have an opportunity to tell their side of the "Indian Wars" story, or that of the many adopted "White Indians," because they were the vanquished. American historians writing about the terrible "frontier border wars" over the years have depicted Natives of that long, bloody conflict from the collective mindset of the victors. Natives are portrayed in history as inhuman red-skinned soul-less savages, who had no legitimate right to defend their lands from White invasion. Dispossessing them of everything was justified because Natives were considered less than human; a scourge to be eliminated. Thus, anyone who sided with

Natives, as in the case of the "White Indians" like Isaac Zane, was equally savage, having "gone over to the Injun Enemy."

This is the harsh reality that Isaac Zane was thrust into in 1763 during Pontiac's Uprising. As a child, Isaac was taken captive by Wyandot warriors on a raid into the South Potomac Valley. Isaac was torn from his family in one of the countless acts of a frontier war fought over possession of land. The facts surrounding that precipitous moment were simply unknown to historians. No one knew what happened to Isaac. No one knew if he was taken captive, and if so where he was taken, or who exactly were his Native captors. They didn't leave their calling card. As a result, what little has been written about Isaac by White people has been imaginative, fictitious history told by people free to indulge in their prejudices. Unfortunately, with the passage of time, fiction has become reality as writer upon succeeding writer took what was said as fact.

This, then is the untold unvarnished story of Isaac Zane in the context in which he lived. I could not have written this without the Native Wyandot side to his story. It has not been previously told because it never would have been believed by the English-speaking victors or their descendants of that terrible time. This is the story of the boy Isaac Zane who was captured in war, adopted into a Native-American family, clan, and tribe, and became completely assimilated as a Wyandot warrior, though his birth parents were White.

This is also the compelling story of someone, who like hundreds of other "White Indians," chose not to come back to colonial society when given the chance. To understand Isaac Zane is to understand the Wyandot Nation of that 18th century time. Consequently, today's Wyandotte Nation historian, archivist, story-teller, and author, Lloyd Devine, has been vitally instrumental for my understanding of Isaac Zane. I have chosen a historical narrative format to tell his story. Virtually nothing exists to quote from in colonial archives. I have referenced heavily from Lloyd's two books, adding the following abbreviations: "On the Back of a Turtle" is LD-BOT, and "That Time is Gone" is LD-TTIG for easier referencing and reading. I am deeply grateful to Lloyd Devine for all that he has done in sharing Wyandot heritage and history, which is the story of his descendants too.

Introduction

This book is about the untold story of Isaac Zane, the youngest of five Zane brothers and one sister born on the frontier of 18th century colonial America. We know from recorded colonial history a great deal about all of the Zane brothers except Isaac. Collectively, Isaac's older brothers and sister Betty played a role in founding the frontier settlement at what would become Wheeling, Virginia for which they are known. Equally so, they were in some ways each responsible for opening up the wilderness of the Ohio Country for exploration, settlement, and eventual assimilation into the young republic of the United States. The Zanes lived their adult lives in a time of tumultuous conflict between the Native American tribes who called the Ohio Country their home, and the European people of the seaboard English colonies who were intent on crossing the mountain barriers to claim Native land as their own. Those subsequent years of unrelenting war touched each of the lives of the Zanes, but none greater than that of their youngest brother. Isaac Zane was captured by the Wyandot during Pontiac's War in 1763, and disappeared at a time when "Injuns" were a hated and despised alien culture that had to be eradicated to fulfil the promise of "manifest destiny." War of ethnic cleansing proportions was the instrument used to accomplish that aim.

More than forty years of constant wilderness warfare resulted as the colonial frontier moved westward. That warfare included atrocities committed by both sides of the conflict bent on "scorching the earth" of their adversaries. However, during those forty years of war, almost 3,000 White captives were taken prisoner by Native war parties. Colonial frontiersmen, on the other hand, took no Native captives, killing every man, woman, and child that fell into their hands, excepting a few held as hostages. Captives of Natives were brought back to respective villages deep in the Ohio Country for assimilation, for ransom, for trade, or to exact vengeance. It is estimated that almost two thousand of these captives never returned to the colonial frontier during the intermittent periods of peace. Isaac Zane was one of them. Colonial authorities presumed these missing captives had been killed, and wrote them off as dead because they hadn't returned. The facts we now know is that they were not dead. Family members of the missing did not know where their loved ones were taken. Consequently, they feared the worst fate for them, believing Natives to be heartless, cruel, subhuman savages, having no more humane-ness than the wolf or panther.

Rather, writers perpetuated the deeply racist belief by today's standards that White people were dispossessing Natives of their land because Natives weren't legitimate owners of it. Natives, as people of color in the 18th century, were considered nothing more than "deer in the woods," as a Lenape Delaware friend of mine recently told me. The result is that the history of the wars was written from the context of the invader's mindset. Always. Typically, when a savage "Injun" killed a White man, it was called murder, or a massacre. But when a White man killed a Native, he was a hero who was cheered on to kill more. So, it was inconceivable that prisoners taken by the Natives were actually alive. It was equally impossible to believe that a White person being held captive by savages could and would turn their backs on their own people, and chose to stay with Natives rather than return to White society. Those few captives who were known to have assimilated, like the notorious Simon Girty, were considered traitors, turncoats, renegades, and savages themselves, often referred to as, "White Indians."

However, the reality is that no one knew what happened to captives once taken to Native villages. Nor did post-war writers have any real clue either. They portrayed the few known "White Indians" in their writings with the same racist view towards all people of color at the time. However, this prejudice was not equally applied in written history to Isaac Zane because he was not known or believed to have become a "White Indian." There was no definitive word about Isaac Zane for over twenty years, since the time Isaac had been taken in a Wyandot raid in 1763 at the age of nine. Simply, he was presumed dead, until 1785 when his name is mentioned in the colonial records at the Treaty of McIntosh by American Indian Commissioner Richard Butler. Isaac was 31 years old.

Isaac Zane was barely literate when he was captured. He wrote very little during his lifetime as an adopted and assimilated Wyandot so we don't know what he thought. Most White people who met him late in life at his home in Zane's Field, Ohio knew nothing about his prior life as a Wyandot warrior. Fearing retribution against his Native mixed-race family, Isaac, as a man in his late fifties, was careful to not bring up his Wyandot connection. Isaac had entered Wyandot society at a time when Wyandot culture was at the peak of its ascendancy in the Ohio Country. In his lifetime, he lived long enough to see its heart-breaking dissolution due to unrelenting warfare, disease, alcoholism, and loss of homeland due to the people streaming into Ohio as settlers. Isaac knew that he had fought against some of these settlers, and killed their kin in battle, so he kept his other life a secret. Consequently, first impressions written about him by White people who met him in his late life were positive. He was described as friendly and helpful from the few who described encountering him after the "Indian" wars were over. And from those few recollections, American writers took it upon themselves to construct fanciful characterizations of Isaac Zane, perhaps in their own images. Today, we call this the history of wishful thinking. The amateur historian, General Robert Kennedy, was one source of creating much of the fanciful image of Isaac Zane in his 1907 writing for the Ohio Magazine. Kennedy never bothered to verify with research the things he claimed.

Some perpetuated untruths were that the Zane brothers of the South Potomac Valley attended public schools in Moorefield when they were children when in fact there was no Moorefield in 1763 and schools would not come to exist for years to come. Kennedy, and others, claimed that Isaac returned to Virginia in 1772 to become a leader in the Virginia House of Burgesses from 1773-1774 before returning to the Wyandot. Actually, that particular Isaac Zane was a brother to William Zane, Isaac's father. Isaac was said to be the first White settler in the Upper Mad River Valley who built a fort there. The implication was that Isaac was protecting himself from Native attack, which is beyond fanciful. He built a simple log cabin on land given to him by the Wyandot as the wars were all but over in Ohio. At the heart of the false claims is that Isaac Zane was a White man who retained his White man identity while married to a beautiful Wyandot Indian maiden. This was erroneously deduced from a mis-read quote attributed to Isaac, in which he purportedly said that "he would never raise his tomahawk against the Big Knife," meaning White people. Historians capitalized on this original document from William Wilson in 1776, believing Isaac to be a pacifist. In truth, a careful read of the words reveals that an unnamed Wyandot chief who was also present made the statement, and not Isaac.

However, the real Isaac Zane was adopted and raised by the Wyandot who were the most militant of all the tribes of the Ohio Country. It was impossible for a boy in the Wyandot culture, adopted or otherwise, to abstain from training to become a warrior, much like a youth raised in Greek Sparta. The only path open for a young man to gain full status in Wyandot society was by proving himself in war. That culture would never have allowed Isaac to be a pacifist. Isaac was adopted into a loving, caring Wyandot family who cherished him. This was, and has been, an impossible circumstance for White people then, and even now, to accept as true. More so, Isaac married Myeerah, who was the only child and daughter of the Wyandot War Captain, Tarhe the Crane. Tarhe would not have allowed his daughter to marry any man, White or Wyandot, who was not a proven warrior. It just could not have happened. Isaac went where Tarhe went during his adult life, and when Tarhe went to war, so did Isaac. American apologists have never been able to understand or accept that fact. Consequently, they have created a false myth about Isaac that has lasted to this day; the mistaken belief that Isaac Zane never went to war against White people.

Little is known about Isaac for many reasons. He did not write about it, nor did the Wyandot leave a record in written English. Also, American post-war writers knew nothing about Native adoption and assimilation, as it was outside their realm of thinking, meaning outside their biased paradigm concerning who and what Native people were to them. What happened to Isaac Zane after he was captured? No one on the colonial frontier actually knew. They thought he was dead. This then, is the untold story of Isaac Zane, called The White Eagle of the Wyandot, as told not from fanciful story, but from the place where Isaac was taken to in 1763, the Wyandot Nation.

Chapter One
The Great Wagon Road

William entered the Quaker meeting room with his new wife, Nancy Anna Nolan. Anna, as she liked to be called, had a worried look on her face that did little to conceal her fear of what was about to soon happen. William tightly clasped her hand and whispered in her ear not to worry. He already knew what the Elders of the Newton Creek Quaker ministry near Gloucester in West Jersey were about to tell him.[1] At the moment, they were cloistered in the room behind the assembled congregation. William had no intention of concealing his simmering anger at the verdict which was about to be presented in response to his recent marriage to Anna in Philadelphia. William had defied church edict and married a woman from outside the Quaker beliefs and that was forbidden. The coming judgement was strictly perfunctory. William was about to be chastised for his violation by excommunication from the Society of Friends and ostracized and shunned by all family and friends for as long as he remained married to Anna.[2]

---

1 William Zane's family lived in a Quaker community some distance up Newton Creek which lay across the river from Philadelphia, PA in an area then called West Jersey. The community had been founded by Robert Zane, William's grandfather, in the early 1680's.

2 William Zane married Nancy Anna Nolan in a ceremony in Philadelphia, PA in 1742, at which time he was excommunicated from the Newton Creek Quakers and ostracized.

William cast a look around the dimmed room as he waited for the Elders to enter. He could not see his sisters Margaret and Hannah but could hear them softly sobbing in the rear of the congregation as they were comforted by their husbands.[3] William, now thirty years of age, recalled he had stood here once before in 1729, as a young man of seventeen, grasping the hand of his first wife, a Lenni Lenape Native maiden named in English, White Sparrow, whom he had met at the nearby Minisink Munsee Lenape village.[4] She, too, was no Quaker, however allowances were made by the Elders at Newton Creek then. That was because the head Elder happened to be William's father, Nathaniel, the son of Robert Zane, who was the founder of the Newton Creek mission. William's grandfather had come from Ireland and laid claim to the land on Newton Creek that could be subdivided for Quaker settlers. Because of his family's work, an exception was made in William's favor, even though Nathaniel, William's father, had been dead less than a year[5] when William and White Sparrow approached the Quaker council.

The terms presented then to William were not harsh in his mind. However, William did not grasp the severity of what was demanded of his Native spouse. White Sparrow would have to leave her people and come live with William in the Quaker community. In addition, she would, by necessity, need to take the English name Mary and give up her pagan beliefs. In addition, she would have to learn the English language so that she could study to become a Quaker. It had been a hard pill to swallow for White Sparrow as her family Wolf Clan ties ran deep. She had already incurred the wrath of the Clan Mothers of her village, including her mother. However, with William's own

---

3 William was the youngest of eight children (some references estimate ten) born to Nathaniel Zane and Grace Rakestraw. Margaret was born in 1698, Abigail in 1700, Joseph in 1702, Hannah in 1704, Jonathan in 1706, Ebenezer in 1708, Isaac in 1711 and William was born on November 26, 1712.

4 There is some documental evidence that William married a Native Lenni Lenape (Delaware) woman in 1729 when he was seventeen years of age. Her name is not recorded and no children are noted from the marriage. What happened to that marriage is not known, however it had ended some time before 1742 when he married Nancy Anna Nolan.

5 Nathaniel Zane, William's father, died in Newton, Gloucester, on February 20, 1724, at the age of 53.

mother's blessing, the two were married at Newton Creek and they settled into the community of Friends. However, it did not take long for problems to arise between them. White Sparrow made many trips to her mother's people, often not returning for days. She found the Quaker religion completely alien to her own beliefs as she struggled to master the new language, and at the same time teach William the Lenape tongue. After five years, White Sparrow broke with William and returned to her people. The marriage had produced no children. William's mother, Grace, believed that Mary had received a potion from her Lenape mother that prevented pregnancy.

The marriage breakup had been difficult for William. He made many trips to White Sparrow's village to attempt to reconcile with her, to no avail. William came to realize that the Quaker views on life, meaning the White Man's life, and that of the Native Lenape were too far apart for him and White Sparrow to overcome, or so he told himself. White Sparrow was adamant that he must leave her alone and never return. William finally decided he needed to depart Newton Creek for a while and seek some freedom from his past. So, he crossed the Delaware River to the growing community of Philadelphia in the Pennsylvania Colony. It was while he was there that he met Anna, a recent arrival from Berkeley, Virginia with her family. Anna was two years younger than William, and a Protestant by faith. That mattered little to William, as he had all but turned his back on his Quaker upbringing since the divorce. However, in the winter of 1741, William's mother, Grace died at the age of 67.[6] With her gone, he had no more ties to the Quaker community that would vouch for him. In the spring of 1742, William and Anna married in a Protestant church in Philadelphia as witnessed by her family, but unknown to William's siblings. William brought his new wife to the Newton community, not seeking consideration from the Elders which he knew was not possible. He had come to fulfil another more pressing need, which was to say goodbye to his brothers and sisters. William, with his new wife, was intent on leaving for the Valley of Virginia.

While in Philadelphia, William learned from his two older brothers, Isaac and Ebenezer, that land was available for settlers to claim

---

6 Grace Rakestreet Zane, born 6-7-1674 and died 12-8-1741.

in the mountains of western Virginia Colony ever since the negotiations with the Haudenosaunee were about to be finalized. It would be called the Treaty of Lancaster, and soon the terms of the treaty would be made known in Pennsylvania and New Jersey. William listened to the stories that Isaac and Ebenezer told him upon their return from the western lands across the Potomac River. The Native Confederacy of Six Nations who called themselves Haudenosaunee, which meant the People of the Longhouse, lived far to the north in the outreaches of New York Colony. They had, at one time in the mid-1600's, laid claim to all the wilderness lands to the west and south of the rugged mountains in New York, Pennsylvania, and Virginia, by right of conquest. A treaty had been agreed upon in 1722 that recognized the Blue Ridge Mountains of western Virginia as the boundary that prevented White colonial settlement. However, Virginia Colony and the British Crown had been unable to keep settlers from crossing that mountain barrier and settling in the Blue Ridge Valley called Shenandoah in the 1730's which angered the Haudenosaunee Confederacy, who colonials called Iroquois. To prevent outright war, the Virginia government sought a Treaty with the Natives in an attempt to outright buy the land that was in dispute.[7]

Ebenezer and Isaac urged William to seek his fortune on the wilderness frontier as soon as he could gather his belongings and prepare his new wife for the arduous trip. They intended on going back as soon as possible. Isaac, William's brother, wished to find available land close to the Potomac River in what was soon to be called Frederick County of Virginia. Ebenezer, on the other hand, was going to leave his family behind and help Isaac get a land claim, and then return. He had already purchased a lot of land from his uncle Robert Zane, on December 21, 1742 that was located in Newton. He and Isaac wanted William to accompany them and see for himself the Valley of Virginia. The Treaty negotiations with the Natives was being held in Lancaster. Even though it had not been finalized as yet,[8] both men were sure that it would be, as were hundreds of others who

---

7 Treaty of Lancaster, military wikia.org/wiki/Treaty_of_Lancaster

8 The treaty that was finally hammered out on July 4, 1744, had several missteps along the way as far as what the final determination of the new

were making preparations to gather their possessions and head west. It was an opportunity not to be found again, both brothers remarked to William to convince him. However, they had discovered on their last trip to the Shenandoah Valley that most of the valuable farm and timber lands had already been taken surreptitiously by squatting settlers from Virginia who as yet had no deeds to their claims. There was another valley, they heard, just as fertile as the Shenandoah. It was to the west over the crest of the mountain ridge running the length of the Shenandoah Valley that Virginia Colony was about to claim. To reach it, they would only have to follow the Indian trail that once was a buffalo trace across the mountain. Men returning from having seen the valley were calling it the Great South Potomac Valley, rather than the Native name of Wappacomo.[9]

Ebenezer related to William that the Lenape, called Delaware, and Shawnee warriors used the South Potomac Valley of Virginia primarily as a hunting ground. They were often known to travel from their villages in Pennsylvania to the valley and set up temporary camps through the summer and fall months to accumulate meat and furs. Ebenezer had seen evidence of cleared fields that Natives used for planting corn and squash. He had been told by Isaac Van Meter and his brother Jacob, two of the first White men to see the valley, that the warriors used the main trail that led to the southern Carolinas as a warpath against the Cherokee and Catawba, their ancestral enemies. Since the recent influx of settlers into the Shenandoah Valley, the Great Indian Warpath had been all but abandoned in favor of the South Potomac Warpath that led in the same direction. The fields that had once been cultivated by yearly burning of brush and trees had mostly been left to fallow. Now those old fields were being eagerly claimed by settlers as their own. Ebenezer related that he learned that the Lenape and

---

boundary line was to be agreed upon, which was the crest of the Allegheny mountains where the watershed flowed to the eastern rivers, like the Potomac.

9 Wappacomo was apparently a name used by all of the northern Native tribes of the 18th century who travelled the length of the South Branch of the Potomac River along a north to south trail that led to the southern tribes like the Cherokee and Catawba with whom they were at perpetual war. Wappacomo means South Branch.

Shawnee were not happy about the Haudenosaunee Iroquois laying claim to the land they did not live on that they now wished to sell to Virginia Colony. Neither tribe had been invited to Lancaster which further disgruntled them. However, Ebenezer did not think it would be a problem for the Zanes and others, because someone else from England was preparing to intervene in the same valley in question.

Word reached Pennsylvania and New Jersey from England that an Englishman named Lord Fairfax was coming to America to legitimize his legal royal claim to the land west of the Virginia tidewaters. Fairfax, Ebenezer learned, had inherited a huge land grant from English King Charles II called the Northern Neck Grant. The land of Fairfax's was wilderness stretching from the boundary of the head springs of the Rappahannock River in Virginia west across the mountains to the beginnings of the north branch of the Potomac River, wherever that might be. Fairfax's grant included the valley of the South Potomac. Fairfax, Ebenezer learned, had come from England to Virginia in 1735 to defend his claim to the land and prepare for surveyors to find and fix the actual boundaries.[10] What all of this meant to the Zanes, Ebenezer explained to his two brothers, "Fairfax is soon to return to hire surveyors. The law I've heard quoted by the Van Meters is that anyone who is already residing on the land with a claim of no more than four hundred acres has legal right to it that Fairfax must uphold. Anything else is his to carve up as he wishes. We need to get there and soon if we are to secure a claim for William, and maybe something for ourselves."

It was only a matter of a few weeks that the three brothers were ready to leave. Goodbyes were said to the remaining Zane family, including their heartbroken sisters who understood that their brothers had to make their own way regardless of the sisters' desire to not see them leave. Hannah told William that before

---

10 Lord Fairfax had to defend his royal claim against the colony of Virginia who saw the huge land claim as an infringement of their colonial right to the land in question which authorities believed stretched all the way to the Pacific Ocean. Virginia knew that Fairfax intended on settling people on his land to his own benefit and not that of Virginia Colony which had similar interests.

their mother died, she had said that she wished William to have a gift from her. Grace was sure her deceased husband would have granted William this gift, now that William had made his mind up to leave Newton Creek. She wanted William to take one of her negro slaves with him. She said she knew the slave would be of great help for William for overcoming the many hardships ahead in building a home, raising a family, and turning the virgin ground for farming. "I want you to have Luther, William. He's a strong young boy with a good back and he works hard. It will ease my mind to release him from me here in Newton as you know how many of our Brethren frown upon keeping slaves. Take him, William, he's young and he's yours to keep."[11]

William procured a horse and a small wagon for his wife and their meager possessions. Ebenezer said goodbye to his wife Mary and their five young children, the eldest being Elnathan aged twelve. Brother Isaac and his wife Sarah used a wagon of their own to haul their possessions and four children with all their luggage, tools, and guns that could be carried. Luther would travel in the wagon with William and Anna. They set out the short distance to the ferry across the Delaware River to Philadelphia town, taking a short detour to the Lenape village where William's former wife lived. To William's surprise, the Lenape village was gone. It had been abandoned. The Native people there were said to have dispersed to more distant villages up the Susquehanna River Valley. They had left to join their clan relations who were moving across the mountains to the far west in the Ohio Country.[12] William pondered for a moment, deep in thought. "Where had White Sparrow gone?"

---

11 The name of the personal slave of William's is not known, nor is there any history of him, however, on a visit to his sons at the settlement in Wheeling in 1777, William wrote a letter to the commander at Fort Pitt saying that, "the negro carried off by the Indians (during the Wyandot raid of 1763) had deprived him of means of support and he requested General Hand to secure the return of this man if the Indians make peace."

12 This migration movement from New Jersey was part of the continuing expulsion of the Lenape people from their ancestral land prior to the coming of Europeans in the mid 1600's.

8 | THE UNTOLD STORY OF ISAAC ZANE

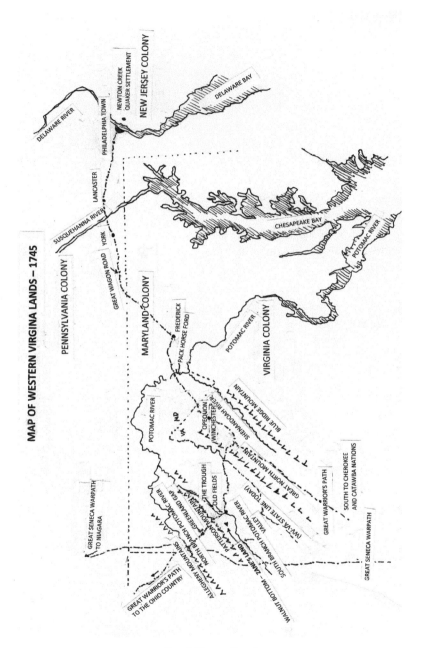

Great Wagon Road

The Zanes crossed the Delaware River by ferry which took them directly to the town of Philadelphia which the three brothers had often visited. From there, they headed west along a well-used rutted road called by everyone the King's Road. It was the beginning of what people named the Great Wagon Road that wound its way to the town of Lancaster, a distance of nearly seventy miles. Lancaster was bustling as the Zanes passed through it. There were residents, settlers, hunters, and fur traders clogging the streets. In addition, the Haudenosaunee Iroquois diplomats and their families were present for the treaty negotiations, as well as their counterparts from the colonial government. It was a sight for William to behold, and one he would never forget. Of particular interest were the many carpenters hard at work in their shops on the edge of town building the huge freight wagons called Conestoga's that needed four to six horses to pull them.

The next leg of the journey was along the trail heading out of Lancaster to the newly-founded town of York. The rough road William learned was following an ancient trail that the Lenape said was created by migrating buffalo.[13] Along the way, the brothers discovered that they had to wait their turn to cross the wide Susquehanna River by ferry as there were many other settlers moving west already ahead of them. The problem was that the river height was fluctuating enough that the ferry could not always be poled across the river if the depth was too shallow. In fact, it took them several days until they crossed and more time to travel to the village of York. From there, William noted that the wagon road turned towards the southwest and followed the Monocacy River in the valley of the same name. The trail was leading to the crossroads of Indian paths that met at a place that Ebenezer said was being called the settlement of Frederick in what was believed to be in the Colony of Maryland. From there, it would not be far to the Potomac River and the doorway to the Valley of Virginia.

---

13 These buffalo belonged to an eastern sub-species of buffalo that ranged east of the Mississippi River until their extinction by 1770 from over-hunting and loss of habitat.

The Zanes arrived at the Potomac River exhausted from the arduous travel. On the banks of the river, the Zanes, and other settlers like themselves had to make a decision to either pay a ferryman named Sam Taylor to ferry them across the Potomac, or continue on upstream to a natural ford where the river widened, and was thus shallow enough that a man could walk across. There was no need for discussion among the brothers; their resources for making payment were dwindling the longer they travelled on the wagon trail as they had to buy food. The upstream natural river ford was several miles out of their way, Ebenezer noted to Isaac and William. For everyone involved it would have to be the place to cross. When they reached the river shallows crossing, it turned out to be not as easy as they anticipated. The Potomac was high from heavy rain runoffs in the mountains to the west. Crossing the river was treacherous. There were places where the water partially flooded the wagons and their contents, causing needless worry among the women and children. Nonetheless, they were successful in crossing and all breathed a sigh of relief on reaching the south shore.

On the other side, they stopped to rest for the day and join other travelers on the road who were doing the same. Ebenezer and Isaac recognized from among the men sitting around a nearby cooking fire a man named John Van Meter[14] who had already staked a claim in the South Potomac Valley. John had his son with him named Jacob, as well as his brother Isaac. "Well, it's been a while since I've seen you two boys," John called out. "Come on and join us, and bring the young'uns and wives with you." Then turning to the river crossing, John pointed out, "I bet you didn't know they call that the Pack Horse Ford. I'm the one who gave it its name some years ago before there was ever a road of sorts here. Why, the buffalo and elk discovered it way back in the real olden times. It was the herds crossing the river at the shallows that made

---

14 John Van Meter was one of the first White men east of the Shenandoah Mountains to visit the valley of the South Branch of the Potomac River. John returned with his brother Isaac to begin laying claims to many areas making him a wealthy land owner. It is believed that an earlier White man, named John Lederer had seen the valley from a distance in late 1670.

a path either way. When I first saw it back in 1725, I was traveling with a Shawnee war party.[15] I had been trading with them and it had been a good trading season so they invited me to go along with them. Soon we were on our way first up the Shenandoah Valley war path and then the south branch of the Potomac to lift us some Catawba scalps in the Carolinas. And we did," John boasted with a hearty laugh. "Its beautiful country I expect all of you are headed towards. The Shawanese call the river Wappacomo and Wappatomack."

John's brother Isaac spoke to him in a language that William didn't recognize, which caught William's attention. "Perhaps it's Dutch," William thought to himself. Isaac van Meter said to John, "You boast too much, brother. Don't let them know how much land we own and what we've petitioned for, for Christ sakes."[16] John turned to the Zanes and asked, "Do you know the Dutch language? Back in Salem, New Jersey where we're from, they call me Jan Joosten Van Meter. That's my Dutch name but the Shawnee prefer to call me Joosten. It's hard not to laugh when I hear them saying 'Joosten, Joosten.' Why, me and Rutledge and Cockburn who were the first to tramp the valley should have the rights to own all of it, with the blessing of all the Natives who are claiming rights to the valley too. Then we could sell it to you folks," Van Meter guffawed. "If it wasn't for this English fella named Fairfax[17] who thinks he owns every damn thing here as far as you can see just

---

15 John Van Meter was a trader to the Shawnee and Delaware who were on friendly terms with him. He was also a horse breeder and kept a quantity of stallions, geldings, mares and foals which his son Jacob inherited upon his father's death on August 13, 1745 at the age of 62.

16 The Van Meter brothers had petitioned Virginia for the rights to 20,000 acres of land each in what would come to be called, Frederick County near the juncture of the Shenandoah and Potomac Rivers. In 1730, that petition was granted.

17 John is referring to Lord Fairfax of England who inherited from an original grant by English King Charles II a vast quantity of land west of established Virginia called the Fairfax Grant or the Northern Neck grant which included all of the lands draining the watershed east of the crest of the Allegheny Mountains. Thus, the valley of the South Branch of the Potomac was part of Fairfax's grant and ultimate ownership.

because some past king in England told him so.[18] Why he's never been down the valley like I have. Doesn't want to get his shoes muddied in the creek over thar," John pointed to the Potomac with a hearty laugh. "So, we all best be getting on our way in the morning and take care of business once we get to the South Potomac before this Lord Fairfax catches up with us and divests us of everything."

It turned out to be providential for the Zanes that they happened upon the Van Meters. John invited the three brothers to leave their wives, children, and possessions at a frontier cabin he and his brother owned in the little settlement that was located not far from the ford at the northern end of the Shenandoah River Valley.[19] John Van Meter and other early traders and explorers had followed the well-worn Native path from the Potomac ford to the spot where the Shawnee often camped and rested on their way up the valley to hunt or make war with the southern tribes. The Shawnee called the spot Opequon. A handful of Quakers putting up cabins were calling the place Frederick's Town. "Your kin will be safe and sound at Opequon. The Shawnee have abandoned the place. Too many White people settling around their camping site and moving down the Shenandoah Valley looking for land to claim. Oh, once in a while a war party or a bunch of their hunters will pass through, but that's getting more and more rare. Where we'll see them is in the South Potomac Valley once we get there. Some Shawnee are still planting crops in the cleared field that their ancestors created some time ago. We're headed there, in fact. I've called the place Old Fields.[20] It's ripe pickings for those who want to farm because the Injuns have cleared the trees and brush and turned the soil for who knows how long, even though there's no village."

---

18 Fairfax was laying claim to approximately 5 million acres of land in his proprietary grant from the King.

19 That settlement would grow to become a town called Winchester, officially founded two years later in 1744.

20 Old Fields was located at the north end of the South Branch of the Potomac Valley near the river. It lay just south of the start of the river gorge bounded by two impassible mountains that was called The Trough.

John Van Meter explained to the Zanes why the wives and children needed to stay at Opequon with the Van Meter kin. "The wagon road south out of Opequon is passable but rugged. However, once we reach the Warrior's path headed west across what the Natives call the Great North Mountain[21] that borders the entire western length of the Shenandoah Valley, it's not possible to take a wagon up that path and over the top to the other side. We'll take your horses and our string of laden packhorses for the trip over the mountains. Then at some point, we'll come back and fetch the families and possessions that we will need to take across on horseback. Me and Isaac already have cabins built near Old Fields where the Warrior's Path will take us. Maybe you boys with your negro can find some land you like and make your tomahawk claim to it before bringing the wives and young'uns." All of what John Van Meter said to William and his brothers sounded fine. It was evident that John had taken a liking to them and was willing to help them get established. If he had any other motive, they were sure to find out once they got there.

---

21 The Great North Mountain is the name for the seventy five mile long mountain ridge to the west of the Shenandoah Valley which ran parallel to the Blue Ridge Mountain on the other side of the valley.

Chapter Two
The South Potomac Valley

The trip across the Great North Mountain was grueling. The Van Meters had the Zanes help with the string of pack horses heavily loaded with trade goods and supplies that they were taking across the mountain to the South Potomac. The trip of about forty miles was going to take several days, the Van Meters said, due to the switchbacks near the top. At first, the path followed the old buffalo trace that wound its way up and down the crenulations of Great North Mountain. It would have been wide enough for a wagon at this point but soon the trace narrowed to no wider than a couple of pack horses. For generations Natives had followed the trace that led to their Old Fields camp. Great North Mountain was not one simple elevation but a series of gradually rising ridges that made up the wide mountain barrier for many miles. Near the crest, the Van Meters and Zanes came upon a cabin in a clearing where the Cacapon River that flowed to the Potomac was met by Trout Creek. The place had been built by William Warden and his family who had claimed all the surrounding rugged land on the top of Great North Mountain. It was a resting point that Ebenezer and Isaac had been to before.

In the days that followed, William began to see the horizon opening ahead as they descended the trail. He marveled at the view of the South Branch of the Potomac Valley from the final crest of the mountain ridge. It appeared to be a beautiful expanse of gently rolling hills that bordered the river on both sides by at least a mile or more. In the far distance, William could see the next mountain barrier arising to the west that the Van Meters were calling Patterson Mountain. Beyond that, lay another mountain ridge that was barely visible. Van Meter pointed out that the Warrior Path they were now on in fact climbed the next mountain range called Patterson's after passing Old Fields, and that path went on towards the setting sun. Jan had been as far as the first valley now called Patterson Creek Valley. He was told by the Shawnee that the path ran all the way to the Ohio Country, far to the west which White men had never seen. Soon they were approaching the cleared area of several acres that still showed evidence of Shawnee hunting shelters and crop cultivation. That is why it was called Old Fields, William was told.

The forty odd mile trip ended at the expanse of cleared land that had two cabins built on it. As they approached the cabins, William could see several White men hailing the Van Meters. However, someone else caught his attention. Ebenezer pointed out to William a group of seven Native warriors sitting around a fire. One of the warriors, their spokesman or War Captain as Ebenezer called him, approached the Van Meters. John called out to the bronzed Native. "Why if it isn't my old friend Bemino[22] who is here to welcome me. I'm glad to see you alive and well." Ebenezer commented to William, "Keep an eye on what is about to happen. I met this Delaware the last time I was here. He's a wily sort of

---

22 Bemino was a Lenape War Captain and son of a famous Delaware chief named Netawatwees, a principal chief of the Lenape Unami Turtle Clan. Bemino belonged to the Wolf Clan of his mother. His father, Netawatwees would eventually move from the Delaware Valley and settle west in the Ohio Country where he would establish a new Lenape village on the Tuscarawas River. Whites would begin to call him Chief Newcomer and his Native town called Newcomer's Town. Bemino, his son, was a medicine man and war leader, born in the Delaware River Valley and a lifelong antagonist of the White invasion of Lenape lands. He would later in life take the English name of John Killbuck Sr., and his son, Gelelemend would be known as John Killbuck Jr. who would support the Americans in the Revolutionary War.

individual, not to be mistaken for a fool, and I suspect he has something in mind that he's about to confront the Van Meters with, who are no fools themselves. It's a game of cat and mouse they'll play."

The Native spoke in crude English. "Well, Old Joost, I had plenty of time to get here to greet you. I could smell you Dutch on the other side of the mountain," said Bemino in a mixture of Delaware and English phrases while pointing to the North Mountain, and spitting. "I see you have brought more trespassing squatters to my father's land again. One part of me thinks I should do something about this outrage. But tell me, Joost, what are you going to do for me today that will persuade me not to kill all of you and take your horses with all the goods?" John Van Meter never skipped a beat in his reply. "Come my friend, and bring your fellows with you. I have a large twist of tobacco and a small keg of rum. Let's all have a drink and a good smoke." John motioned to Jacob to get the goods in question from the packs while the Zanes took care of unsaddling the horses. As the large party took their ease and passed around the keg of rum and several pipes of aromatic tobacco, Van Meter invited the Zanes to join them, advising his nervous companions to put aside their muskets. "There is no need for those guns," he scolded. "We're in the company of our Lenape dear friends."

William studied Bemino intently, trying to discern who this warrior really was. All of the conversation between the Van Meters and Bemino was now conducted mostly in the Lenape language which William could largely understand but his brothers could not. Bemino fit the part in William's mind of a ruthless War Captain of his warriors. He was tall, lithe, and muscular, and had an air of authority about him that his own men obviously respected. William had no doubt that if Bemino had given the order for the White men to be immediately killed, that Bemino's warriors would have carried it out without hesitation. It gave William a shiver to realize that Bemino was speaking with an element of menacing truth in his words. Indeed, this was Indian land without a doubt and the Zanes were trespassers and squatters from Bemino's point of view. The Whites in the valley were only alive because of

Bemino's good graces. It was different in New Jersey where White people, including many Quakers, looked down their noses upon the Delaware people with derision. "It is different here," William intuited to himself. "Bemino is looking down his nose at us as interlopers."

"My friend, Bemino. Of course, I have not forgotten you and your people here. I've brought gifts for all of you and I can trade some of the necessities you need for your excursion hunting or making war, of course, on credit." Bemino listened intently but remained silent. Van Meter continued, sensing that he had not touched upon the real things on Bemino's mind that gifts couldn't assuage. "Bemino, my friend, I know that you have a quarrel with settlers like these boys the Zanes coming here, but your quarrel is not with me or them. We are only here because our King across the Blue Ridge has commanded us to come here due to what has happened in Lancaster town and what is about to be transacted. Your unfaithful and devious brothers the Iroquois have sold these lands they surreptitiously claim as their own to our King. I know that they did not consult you or your father's people in this deal. You live here, and hunt here, and go where you wish. It is with the Iroquois that you have been wronged. It is the Iroquois who claim to own this land to do with as they wish by the rights of conquest that happened a long time ago when they made war against the Susquehannock. It is the Iroquois who are not friends and who have lied to you, not us."

Bemino looked up from the fire and stared most intently at John Van Meter without saying a word for the longest time which alarmed William. He wasn't sure if the Indian had been offended and intended to react violently. Finally, Bemino spoke. "What you say is true Old Joost. Your words are true, but cut me deeply with their meaning. There are no Iroquois here with us for me to shake them. These Iroquois are charlatans and liars and I do not fear their wrath when they speak of the time when they held all the lands and the peoples in their tight clenched hand. But as you say, that was a long time ago. The men who come for gold coin and presents at Lancaster are not warriors who speak with authority.

They are old men whose threats are empty. That is all true, Old Joost. But all your fine words that I always hear from you change nothing too. I look about and I see no Seneca raising their hatchets. Where is the Mohawk? I see only you, Old Joost. And your people. And every time you leave and return, you bring more settlers with you. And I know as sure as we sit here and drink to our friendship again, that the trickle of settlers will soon become a torrent." With that, Bemino stood up and spoke to his men to prepare to leave. "We soon go to hunt scalps and captives of the Cherokee, Old Joost. Make sure we have our presents before we leave, my friend."

William discovered that there were several settlers in the valley who claimed land ahead of Fairfax's surveyors. It was widely known that Lord Fairfax would be forced to honor any land claims within the boundaries of his proprietary land called the Northern Neck of Virginia Grant that were established before Fairfax had it properly and legally surveyed. Fairfax would have to uphold these claims that would bring him no income in quitrents.[23] However, surveyors had already been hired by Fairfax and the dispute over the exact boundaries in the wilderness were nearing a resolution. It would not be long before Fairfax's men entered the valley and set about surveying lots. The Van Meters said that Fairfax intended to have the surveyors mark off subdivided manors in the South Potomac Valley and Patterson Valley to the west. Once done, Fairfax would encourage an influx of settlers from New Jersey and Pennsylvania to occupy lots and pay leases to those lands for twenty-one years, or in some cases, outright sales to the potential settler. The annual fee for the tenant would be set at 25 shillings per hundred acres. All in all, it was a lucrative business opportunity that Fairfax had devised, and one that the Van Meters privately wished to duplicate in the new Frederick County bordering the Potomac.

Consequently, many of the handful of men that the Zanes were soon to meet had claimed more than one acreage in different

---

23 By the terms of the royal patent Fairfax was required to leave undisturbed those inhabitants who held valid colonial grants to land that was settled before the establishment of his own official land title in 1745. What would come into question in the future was whether or not the persons had their land claim officially recognized by Virginia by a recorded document.

areas and often outside what they estimated to be Fairfax's Manor boundary line but still within the Proprietary. James and Jonathan Cockburn,[24] were already claiming land in the valley, along with James Rutledge, John Howard, James Walker, and others. Some, like Jonathan Coburn, held claims both within and without the perceived Fairfax manor, but none of these claims were officially recorded. This was because in the valley there was nothing but undeveloped wilderness with no official Virginia presence in 1744. All of this had to be digested by the Zanes before any decision on land could be made for William, and of course, a tour of the valley would be necessary in the upcoming days. Jonathan Coburn was of particular help in that matter as he had already explored the side valleys of the South Potomac. He knew where the best opportunities existed, having claimed all that he could for himself already.

Coburn wisely pointed out to the Zanes that the unclaimed land close to the river, while much of it being excellent ground for farming like Old Fields, was undoubtedly within the boundaries of one of Fairfax's Manors. Thus, any claims to it could be outright disputed by Fairfax who would demand yearly rent, and possibly leasing only, and not outright ownership. Coburn suggested to the Zanes that they consider claiming land along one of the streams still within the greater South Branch Valley but to the west above Old Fields. Such land would be readily accessible by the Native path that climbed the hills and minor valleys in proximity to the top of Patterson Mountain. It was an idea that seemed very reasonable. By the time the Zanes made the trip with Coburn, William had already explored much of the valley on his own from the Trough Narrows north of Old Fields all the way south to the mouth of the South Branch Fork entering the South Branch River, near where Conrad Moore was building a cabin.[25]

---

24 Pronounced Coburn and Coben. Also, these names come from research done by Charles Morrison in "Early Fairfax Land Grants and Leases Along the South Branch of the Potomac," published in "West Virginia History," Volume XXXVIII October 1976, pp. 1-22.

25 Conrad Moore would provide the name of the settlement around his home that became the current site of Moorefield, West Virginia.

The Zanes, with Coburn, made their way from Old Fields slowly up the rolling hills on horseback, following the path the Natives call the Warrior's Trail. It was plain to see that the wide path was traveled by both beast and men by the many footprints that had worn a depression in the soil. Less than a mile up the trail, Coburn pointed to a narrow side path on the left next to a small stream of water flowing into the creek[26] that bordered the Warrior's Path. They turned their horses onto the barely visible side path that wound its way through a dense walnut forest paralleling the small stream.[27] Coburn noted to the Zanes the rolling hills on either side of the stream would make suitable farmland once cleared. "We're sitting slightly above the South Branch Valley and I'm sure out of the way of Fairfax's leased lands once he has them surveyed. I've called it Walnut Bottom. The only other settlers up here are just me at this point." Coburn pointed in the direction of the Trough in the distance saying, "I've got a piece up here next to the Trough. That's it."[28]

William, with Ebenezer's help, decided to cut a tomahawk claim along the creek that Coburn called Walnut Bottom. Isaac was not sure that he wanted to do so. Privately, William's brother Isaac was considering a deal that he had talked over with the Van Meters concerning a piece of land he might purchase from them back in what was called Frederick County in the vicinity of Opequon. He assured his two brothers that he would stay long enough to help erect a rudimentary cabin for William before all three of them returned to Isaac's family and William's wife still living with the Van Meter's kin now that the weather was beginning to turn colder. Word reached William from Opequon that

---

26 Today that creek is called Anderson Run Creek and the road that follows the Warrior's Path is called Old Fields Road.

27 That small stream today is called Walnut Bottom Creek and Run.

28 The exact location of the land claims of the three Zane brothers is not exactly known. In "Virginia Northern Neck Grants, Vol. II, 1742-45, a reference is made to a Jonathan Coben (misspelling for Coburn) and a William Zane having land on Walnut Bottom Run surveyed by John Moffat. In Morrison's account, he lists William Zane and Ebenezer Zane having claims "Near Old Fields" with no further explanation.

his wife, Anna, was ill with the morning sickness. Apparently, she was pregnant, and William, to his surprise, was to become a father. It was with that impetus that William, Ebenezer, Isaac, and Luther finished a spacious cabin and headed back over the Great North Mountain to spend the winter at Opequon. Along the way, they met many Native hunting parties coming and going along the same trails the Zanes and other settlers were using. Once at Opequon, Ebenezer said goodbye and left for Philadelphia, while Isaac with his family consulted with the Van Meters for a claim close to Opequon.

The years 1745 and 1746 came and went quickly in the South Potomac Valley with many developments. William had brought Anna over the mountains and was now living in their newly-constructed log home on Walnut Bottom. Anna had given birth to a son they named Silas on March 7, 1745 and a second son, Ebenezer, was born on October 7, 1747, whom they named after William's brother. To everyone's surprise, they received word that "Old Joost" John van Meter had died in September 1745 at the age of 62, leaving all his land and possessions to his surviving children but primarily to Jacob.[29] In 1745, the Privy Council in London ruled in favor of Fairfax's claim to the extant boundaries of his land grant over the counterclaim of Virginia. The headsprings of the Rappahannock River and that of the North Branch of the Potomac[30] were acknowledged and the survey was begun. Fairfax himself was heard to have returned to Virginia from England to oversee the surveying and plotting of his manors planned for the South Branch of the Potomac and beyond to Patterson's Creek.

By 1747, the Treaty of Lancaster was finalized with the Haudenosaunee or Iroquois Confederacy as it was known to Whites, legitimatizing the sale of lands east of the crest of the Allegheny Mountains where the waters flowed eastwardly to the

---

29 John Van Meter, born in Kingston, New York in 1683, died August 13, 1745 in Opequon.

30 The location of the headspring of the North Branch of the Potomac was identified and marked by surveyors and an engraved stone placed there, called the Fairfax Stone, which today can be found a couple of miles east of Route 219 just north of Thomas, West Virginia.

William Zane

Atlantic Ocean, thus opening it up for settlement. James Genn and his party of surveyors hired by Fairfax arrived in the South Branch of the Potomac Valley in late March of 1747 once the weather broke. While the surveyors worked to divide the land of the South Branch of the Potomac and Patterson Creek Valley into two manors comprising many lots for Fairfax, William concentrated on clearing his land on Walnut Bottom with Luther to help. Anna cared for their two young sons, Silas and Ebenezer. They put in enough food from hunting to winter over. By the late spring of 1748, Fairfax's tenants began arriving in the valley to occupy lots. It was with the coming of new settlers from Pennsylvania and even New Jersey that William learned of the death of his brother Ebenezer, who passed away in Philadelphia in late April.[31] William's brother Isaac visited William in the summer of 1749 just as another son of William and Anna was born. They named the baby after William's brother Jonathan who was said to be living in Philadelphia, according to Isaac who frequently made trips back to New Jersey. Isaac and his wife Sarah had put down roots near Opequon which was now being called Winchester. They had a total of eleven children but two had died in infancy.

In 1751, Anna gave birth to a fourth boy who they named Andrew. With their homestead firmly established, William was able to make a small profit at farming on the land he and Luther had cleared over the preceding years. William, at age 39, felt that the monumental task of clearing and building was beginning to take its toll on him, with more and more body aches and pains to account for. William began to look for other possible land acquisitions outside of Fairfax's Manors that he could possibly sell for profit, thus making his life easier. One of the trips he made with Luther was on horseback following the Warrior's Path that passed nearby and took them over the first ridge to the west called Patterson's Mountain to the valley of Patterson's Creek. There, Fairfax already had his surveyors lay out the Patterson Creek Manor covering both sides of the creek that made its way north

---

31 Ebenezer Zane, brother of William, born December 7, 1708 and died April 29, 1758 in Philadelphia.

to join the Potomac. In that manor were thirty-one lots. William could see from the heights above the valley that settlers were already arriving and taking up lease claims. However, William discounted looking any further for land outside the manor as the distance from his home on Walnut Bottom was plainly too far.

It was in the early winter of 1753, after a difficult pregnancy, that Anna Zane, now thirty-eight, gave birth to another son who William named after his brother Isaac.[32] It came at a time when there was troubling news reaching the South Branch of the Potomac settlements. Alarming reports concerning the French to the far north arrived from several sources, including Bemino and his Lenape and Shawnee friends. More news came to the valley from Lancaster and Williamsburg that the French in Canada's New France were intent on claiming the land west of the Allegheny Mountains in what was called the Ohio Country for the King of France. It was said that the Governor of Virginia had sent an emissary with a message to the French who were somewhere west of the mountains to order them to leave at once. Soon after William heard of this, Bemino and a band of warriors came down the Warrior's Path on their way south up the South Potomac Valley. William spoke to him in English, and the latest news Bemino brought was disconcerting.

Bemino had recently been across the mountains in the Ohio Country. In fact, he had seen and heard from the French. They were telling all Natives that they were coming to build a fort at the Forks of the Ohio River, and planned to trade with the Natives and drive any English back across the mountains and out of their lands that belonged to the Native people in New France. They had many soldiers in White Coats,[33] and they did not honor any English claims or English traders. The French were calling all Natives to support them as they wished to trade only for furs with Natives. The French men declared that they were not like the English whom they said wanted to take all Native lands for themselves. "What do

---

32 Isaac Zane, son of William and Anna Nolan Zane, was born November 26, 1753.

33 The French Marine troops of Canada wore a White regimental coat.

you think of that?" asked Bemino. "Look around you here. This was once my valley to hunt and fish and raise some corn. But how can my people do that now with you here? I can see the truth of what the King of the Canadas says right here. You are English. You have taken a piece of our land and have nothing to offer my people in return but your rum traders who bring us whiskey, steal our furs, and debauch our women. The French are making promises to end this English tyranny. My father Netawatwees is moving across the mountains to the Ohio Country to live with the French and I may soon go to." William thought about the Lenape's words for a long time after he left. "Yes, he is right." William thought to himself. He remembered his Quaker upbringing and the favorable attitude of most Quakers towards Native people. And most of all at that moment, William fondly remembered White Sparrow. "Coming to his senses, William asked himself, "Where would I and the others here go even if we wanted to? We have put down roots here. This is our home now, come what may."

Chapter Three
War Comes to the Valley

William learned in early August of the following year, 1754, that an attempt by Virginia to force the French to leave for Canada had failed. A skirmish, and then a battle had been fought over the mountains. Regretfully, the Virginian Englishman named George Washington had been surrounded and forced to surrender by the French and their Indian allies.[34] The shocking result was that the French and the English were now at war which was bound to affect everyone in America if peace was not restored. At the moment that seemed impossible, from what William had heard. Soon word reached the South Potomac Valley that the King of England was sending a British army to America to resolve the dispute by force of arms with New France over ownership of the lands across the mountains called the Ohio Country. So, it came as no surprise to William when he heard that the British army had arrived in February of 1755 in Hampton, Virginia under the command of General Edward Braddock. Braddock's army numbered 2,100 men of arms. Braddock planned to march that army up the main Potomac Valley to Cumberland before heading over the mountains to the Forks of the Ohio to attack the fort the French had built there.[35] At the behest

---

34 The Battle of Fort Necessity took place on July 3, 1754 at a spot called by Native people "The Great Meadows" in southwestern Pennsylvania.

35 French Fort Duquesne.

of the colonial government of Virginia, Braddock was requesting civilian wagoneers be hired to haul the massive guns, provisions, and baggage. Wagoneers would be drawn from the surrounding areas and paid in hard coin for the use of their wagons and horses during the expedition which was to begin in late May.

William thought it over long and hard. He had a wagon and two horses necessary to pull a heavy load. However, the thought of leaving Anna alone with four young children to take care of dissuaded him from going. Too, William knew that the long list of daily farm chores was more than Luther could handle himself. Silas was ten years old and capable of taking care of the animal stock that they had accumulated. However, the other four boys, Ebenezer, Jonathan, Andrew and Isaac were too young for William to be gone for any length of time. In spite of needing the hard coin, and the assurance by the British officials that wagoneers would only be gone a short time till the whole affair was settled, there was something about the expedition that loomed in William's mind that worried him. It was the impression that Bemino had left upon him during their last encounter. Bemino implied that the French in the Ohio Country were intent on enlisting the help of Native allies who knew the ways of wilderness war which British regulars, no matter how many were sent, did not. And what troubled William the most, is that since word reached the Potomac Valley of Braddock's upcoming campaign, William had not seen one Native, either Shawnee or Lenape, traversing the valley. The question vexed him. "Where was Bemino who never missed his seasonal coming and goings," William asked himself.

Far to the north in the Canadas, at the far-flung western post of French Detroit which was situated along the river that joined the two great lakes, Huron and Erie, the French commandant and his officers were satisfied with the results of their Grand Council with their French Native allies in the spring of 1755. Captain Daniel Beaujeu commanded both Fort Niagara and Fort Detroit outposts. He prepared to leave Detroit on orders from Quebec to take possession of the new fort built at the forks of the Ohio, called Fort Duquesne, at the first possible moment. Beaujeu would be accompanied by a contingent of French Marines de Troop as well as many warriors from the Great Lakes region supplemented by "couriers de bois."[36] Warriors were making ready for battle from the Chippewa, Ottawa, Pottawatomi, and Wyandot nations. Their grievances with the English were many. Fighting the English would not only satisfy their complaints but aid their French brothers at Detroit, many of whom were their own kin by marriage. Too, Natives heard that a Red Coat army was assembling in Virginia intent on driving out the French and taking the lands of the Ohio Country for their own. All past squabbles with the local French and each other were put aside to meet the coming war with the English. It was decided that Anastase, a Huron war chief from Lorette village in Quebec, would command all of the Native warriors in the battles to come.

Across the river from Detroit, the Wyandot village of Maquaqua was bustling with activity. Warriors readied themselves for the trip to the Ohio Country by shaving their heads except for a scalp lock of hair left on the crown. Too, they were checking their muskets, gunpowder, lead ball, and hatchets. The women prepared dried corn and pemmican for the warriors to carry with them as hunting would, by necessity, be near impossible. The warriors would travel the paths to the Forks of the Ohio with haste. In one lodge, a 14-year-old boy named Tarhe consulted with his father, seeking permission from him to accompany the party of Wyandot warriors preparing to depart for war. Tarhe, who had been born in the village close to Detroit, was the son of a woman of the Porcupine Clan. Thus, he was becoming a warrior of that same clan, unlike that of his father.[37] Tarhe's name was unique among the Porcupine

---

36 The name means "runners of the woods" and is used to describe fur traders allied with the French who were of mixed blood with Natives and engaged in the trade of animal furs with the tribes primarily of the Great Lakes region.

37 The exact place of Tarhe's birth is not known, nor is the Wyandot name of his mother and father. It is said he was born in or about 1742. A Wyandot child, male or female, took their clan affiliation from their mother, not father. So Tarhe's father would have his own name given to him by his own clan and not that of his wife.

Clan because his name was not clan property. Due to his unusual height as a child, his name meant "At the Tree."[38] Tarhe argued with his father that he had been preparing for this day to prove himself as a warrior. He was tall, lean, and muscular. Even at his young age he had demonstrated an ability to master the bow and arrow with great accuracy. Tarhe had bested all other boys of his age, and some older, at games of strength and cunning. He was almost as tall as his father, and Tarhe believed himself to be a warrior in every way except for the opportunity to prove himself in battle. To that end, his father was proud of his son, and would not deny him the opportunity that every Wyandot boy-to-become-a-man yearned for.[39]

By the 22nd of June, more than 150 Wyandot warriors were ready to leave for the Ohio Country. Tarhe was one of them. Boys as young as age ten could go to war, according to tribal tradition.[40] Tarhe would accompany the warriors of his Porcupine Clan which would include his father and several kin warriors of his own clan. Ensign Francois de Baileul and a company of French Marines would accompany the Wyandots who would join with the Ojibwa warriors recently arrived from the upper Great Lakes. The Ottawa and Pottawatomie numbering over 150 warriors had already left two days prior with Beaujeu. Tarhe carried with him his bow and arrow quiver, a neck knife, and a wooden war club tucked into his sash for weapons. He had replaced all of the flint arrowheads with metal cut from discarded worn-out cooking pots as a final preparation. Soon the Native warriors on the trails to the south-

---

38 "At the Tree" meaning of the name Tarhe was a personification of "the tree," alluding to his height.

39 Wyandot society was very martial-oriented for males, who at a very early age began training at skills used in hunting and warfare with enemies. Proving oneself in war was a way for a male to elevate his status in the clan and tribe. He not only gained recognition as a warrior status, but made himself eligible to seek a mate. A male could go to war as young as ten years old.

40 From a very early age, a Wyandot boy began his training as a warrior by first learning to master the bow and arrow for hunting, and then accompanying hunting parties where some of the tactics of hunting were the elements of Native warfare. LD-TTIG- page 148.

Young Wyandot Warrior Tarhe

east would join a fighting force of between six and seven hundred total fighting men from twenty nations who were arriving and setting up camp outside the French Fort Duquesne. There, they were greeted by Captain Daniel Beaujeu and advised to set up temporary camp among the others outside the walls. All in all, it was a sight to behold for Tarhe who had never seen so many warriors gathered together speaking so many diverse tongues, most of which he did not understand.

In the South Potomac Valley, several men with horses and wagons decided to join the Braddock expedition for the money that was promised. William watched as they left together over the trail to the east that had become a wagon road since his arrival in the valley in 1744. William wondered to himself if he had made the right decision to forgo the very lucrative paying proposition. He knew his family was in need of so many things that farming could not as yet provide. However, Anna and his young children depended upon William more than his desire to earn a temporary wagoner's wage. William heard that Braddock and his officers passed through Winchester on May 3rd as they headed west to join the army. That army included about 1,470 soldiers in addition to civilian contractors, wagoneers, washer women, cooks, and camp followers. All the talk throughout the valley was that the British would soon drive away the French at their fort across the mountains and hopefully allow Virginia to expand its land for settlement westward if all went well. That was a thought William kept in the back of his mind. While his land and home on Walnut Bottom Run was outside the Fairfax Manor boundaries and thus his by clear title, the soil was more stony and thinner than that in the valley below him. William had to work hard to till and coax crops out of it.

Messages regularly arrived from Winchester with news on the progress of Braddock's expedition. Slowly, the army snaked its way to the northwest over the Allegheny Mountains across a road that was cut by engineers working in the forefront of the advance. There was nothing of note to be concerning for the tenants and landowners of the South Potomac until an alarming commotion reached William's ears on the 18th of July. William and Luther were working in the fields when they heard two quick musket shots coming from the direction of Conrad Moore's home[41] a couple of miles south of Old Fields. Since such a sound could carry for miles, it caught William's attention and subsequent curiosity to find out what was happening. Leaving Luther, William rode a horse down the old Warrior's Path to Moore's. On the way, he met a rider approaching with news of what happened. "There's been a battle, alright, between Braddock and the French but the worst has happened. Braddock's entire force has been wiped out by the French and their allied savages, almost to the last man. Braddock, in fact, is dead. Everything was lost to the Indians. All the cannon, horses, guns, ammunition, and wagons fell into the hands of the Indians. Those men from the valley who went along to serve as wagoneers; most of them are dead too. It's too horrible to even comprehend, I'm told by those from Winchester who heard and seen the survivors passing through. Hundreds of men went to their deaths. All cut to pieces by the red devils."

William was shocked. In the days ahead he would learn more of the details of the disaster. More than five hundred soldiers were dead and over four hundred wounded, some so grievous that they would not survive the month. It was a stunning loss for the British that no one thought could happen. William heard that George Washington, the Virginian who commanded the provincial Virginia Regiment, had survived the battle. Washington managed to get the mortally wounded Braddock off the field and to a place on the retreat where Braddock died and was buried. Rumors were circulating that the annihilation of two regiments of the British army did not bode well for the civilian frontier which many people said was now left defenseless. The French, if they desired to attack Williamsburg as the next step in the war that had seemed so far away, could do so with nothing to stop them. No one had thought that possible until now. As the days turned into the early weeks of

---

41 Conrad Moore built a home at the juncture of the South Branch of the South Potomac Creek and the South Branch main course. Many years later, the town of Moorefield would take its name from settler Conrad and those people who lived around him in a semi-community.

autumn, more and more rumors from Pennsylvania colony to the north spoke of Indian war parties lurking about. A dread began to creep into William's mind that he dared not consider. What if the apparent abandoned Warrior Path close to his home was used again, this time by hostile warriors. What bothered William most of all, was recalling Bemino's words that last time they spoke.

Word reached the valley in mid-September that George Washington, the 23-year old survivor of Braddock's defeat, was appointed colonel of the Virginia Regiment and commander-in-chief of the military forces of Virginia. That brought no relief to the settlers on the South Potomac. Everyone was worried that the war would come to them sooner or later. From Fort Cumberland to the north they heard that Indian war parties were roaming the adjacent valleys attacking isolated families. Already William had seen several families pack their belongings and abandon their cabins as they rushed to reach the safety of Winchester. By mid-September panic gripped everyone still remaining in the valley. Word reached them of a Lenape raid on the settlement of Penn's Creek in Pennsylvania that occurred on October 16th. All the inhabitants, it was said, were either massacred or taken away as prisoners. The thought of it made William think of Bemino again, and that the raid could have been Bemino's handiwork. Soon after, it was reported that Washington was marching with one hundred men directly to Fort Cumberland to attempt to stabilize the South Potomac frontier. The onset of cold weather had the effect of quelling the Indian raids. Everyone guessed that the Indians had returned to their villages to hunt and prepare for winter quarters.

The respite allowed William and everyone else still in the valley to take in their harvest without distress. While that was happening, Washington had two forts built by his men in Patterson Creek Valley over the mountain to the west, in response to the Indian attacks in that area close to the mouth of Patterson Creek on the Potomac.[42] Soon after the new year, Washington ordered

---

42 Fort Ashby was the name of the fort in question. The other fort, far up Patterson Creek was called Fort Cocke, named after Captain William Cocke who built it on his land with the help of his ranger company.

Captain Thomas Waggener to take his company and proceed from Fort Cumberland to the South Branch of the Potomac Valley. Washington wanted Waggener to build two forts there above the narrows of the South Potomac called The Trough. Waggener arrived with his men late in January whereupon he called together the remaining settlers in the valley, including William. Waggener wanted everyone to discuss the location of the forts that he would eventually garrison with his men once they were built. He needed to find the best locations to protect everyone if Indian raiders should attack the valley. The forts, an upper and a lower on the South Branch of the Potomac, would be constructed of palisaded logs. Waggener made it clear that he expected the help of the settlers working with his own men to get the forts raised before spring.

It was agreed by everyone that the first fort should be located at or near Old Fields close to the Indian trails. One trail headed north through the Trough narrows and the other branched west over Patterson Mountain. A site on Henry Van Meter's property was chosen and work commenced. It would soon be called Waggener's Lower Fort.[43] William divided his time between caring for Anna who had bouts of sickness, tending to his children, and helping with the fort construction. It was decided that the other fort should be located more than five miles upriver to be able to protect the many settlers living in the valley between the two points. At a place called "Butter-milk" by the settlers, work was begun in earnest as the weather was turning milder and the dread of Indian attacks increasing day by day. In late March, William's brother Isaac arrived from Winchester with a wagon and coaxed William to let him take Anna and the children back with him to Winchester for their own safety. He had already heard of French and Indian attacks all across the isolated cabins of the Susquehanna River Valley. It was not a hard decision for William to make. Isaac had brought with him one of his own negress slaves named Peggy to help William and Luther with the daily cooking and washing. With that, William said goodbye to Anna and the children and promised to come and get them once the alarms of the frontier war were finally over.

---

43 In 1757, the fort was renamed Fort Pleasant.

William and Luther proceeded with the spring planting of corn, vegetables, and wheat. Meanwhile, word was reaching the valley of the resumption of Indian raids to the north from the Potomac River into mid-Pennsylvania. Waggener's soldiers supplemented with some militia seemed to be acting as a strong deterrent to Indian war parties. However, the situation was not the same in the Patterson Creek Valley where several homes were attacked with terrible results. Some settlers had been killed and their homes burnt. By late June, it was reported that Fort Ashby had repulsed a sizable Native force as had Fort Cocke, though no settlers remained in the valley. Everyone living there had fled their homes for points east. One morning in late April, Luther went to the pen to let the hogs out and came running back to the cabin. "Mr. Will, Mr. Will, there's been somebody walking around the horse shed during the night. I can see their footprints everywhere," blurted out Luther. William quickly investigated and came to the conclusion that the footprints had been made by Indians, and not White men as there were no boot or shoe heel impressions. Shocked, William grabbed his musket, shot pouch, and powder horn and saddled his horse all the while giving instructions to Luther to saddle the others, and skedaddle with Peggy as quickly as possible for Van Meter's.

William rode the quarter mile to the old Indian Path. Along the way he could see the footprints of many more warriors who had recently passed during the night. He spurred his horse up the trail to a point where he could see for a short distance towards the final rise of Patterson Mountain. It was there that he smelled smoke likely coming from old man Williams[44] home who lived a short distance beyond on the upper reach of Patterson Creek. Fearing to go any further, William turned his horse down the Warrior's Path and headed towards Old Fields. There, he met Luther and Peggy who had arrived safely. There was no need to inform the settlers gathered at Van Meter's. A party of eighteen of Waggener's men, most of them members of the Virginia Regiment and veteran survivors of Braddock's defeat, had just left on horseback towards the

---

[44] Vincent Williams was besieged in his home, killed, and his body cut to pieces by warriors and displayed at his home.

old Indian trail leading north into the Trough Gorge in pursuit of two warriors who had fired on Waggener's Fort before disappearing. Hearing this, William realized that Waggener's men did not know that there were more than two warriors close by and he felt compelled to try to warn them. However, by the time he reached the trail into the Trough, he realized he was too late.

Waggener's men had dismounted and gone on by foot since they could not take their horses further on the narrow winding path. As William approached the point where the path entered the deep defile, he could hear gunfire echoing from the heavily wooded gorge mixed with the war whoops of what sounded like dozens of Natives punctuated by the yells of Waggener's men which was coming closer and closer. It was evident to William that Waggener's men had walked into an ambush in which they were severely outnumbered. The shooting was constant and Isaac could hear the screams of men who had been hit. What was left of Waggener's men were attempting to fight their way out of the Trough and get to the horses. But the horses had already been taken by warriors who had fallen in behind the militiamen once the ambush had been sprung. William was aghast. With great difficulty, the survivors emerged from the trail carrying three wounded men with them, and leaving behind seven dead for the Natives to scalp and mutilate. War had come to the valley with a fury and the outcome had been disastrous.[45]

Several of the men who had fought in the battle with what was believed upwards of sixty Lenape warriors told William that they recognized Bemino as the leader of the Natives. They had seen him directing the warriors once the battle unfolded. Now, it was evident to everyone in the valley that no one was safe anywhere in their cabins. Remaining settlers rushed families to the protection of either one of Waggener's two forts, as did William. He was not about to take another chance up on Walnut Bottom. William knew that it

---

45 The ambush would become called, "The Battle of the Trough." The exact date is not recorded, but it occurred in March or April, 1756. The colonials numbered between 16-18 men, while the number of Lenape warriors is not known, but some estimates put their numbers as high as 60. Bemino is credited with leading the Native warriors and devising the ambush.

had probably been Bemino who had stealthily walked his property, intentionally leaving his footprints for William to find and inspire terror. William knew that the wily War Captain would not grant him another chance if he stubbornly refused to abandon his cabin. Reluctantly, William and Luther returned briefly to bring what possessions they could along with some livestock back to Waggener's Lower Fort with the help of a couple of neighbors who stood at the ready with loaded muskets. Everyone wondered when and where the savages would strike next. Silence gripped the ambush survivors the next day as the remains of those men killed in the Trough were recovered and buried. No where could an Indian be seen, and many wished to believe that they had left the way they came.

Then, on April 18th Bemino and his warriors struck again in a well-planned ambush. This time, the ambush was set along the Cacapon River several miles to the north near Fort Edward, one of the other frontier forts that Washington had the Virginia Regiment build. Bemino lured Captain Mercer and a company of his men numbering nearly sixty out of the fort in pursuit of a small band of Natives who had killed two soldiers outside the fort. Along the path that bordered the Cacapon River, Bemino intentionally left a trail of cornmeal at the place he wanted to ambush Mercer's approaching men. On a given signal, Bemino's warriors fired pointblank from ambush into the unsuspecting men, killing Mercer and sixteen others outright. The combined Lenape and Shawnee warriors immediately rushed in, as they had at Braddock's defeat and at the Trough. There, the warriors finished off the wounded and chased down the fleeing remnants of Mercer's force.[46] From that point on, Bemino's warriors, flushed with success, went on an unopposed rampage throughout the South Branch of the Potomac valley burning cabins and attacking anyone they came upon outside of the forts. Bemino made sure that all settler livestock were killed in an attempt to drive the settlers out permanently one way or another.

---

46 Bemino, later in life known as Killbuck Sr., recalled the battle and described to Whites in the Ohio Country that only six of Mercer's men escaped. The battle would come to be called, "Battle of Great Cacapon" also known as "Mercer's Massacre."

Chapter Four
Bemino Strikes Back

Gradually, the British fortunes of war in the colonies began to shift in their favor by early 1758. Because of the success of the British blockade of French shipping to Canada, Fort Duquesne at the Forks of the Ohio was not receiving adequate provisions, ammunition, reinforcements, and most important of all, trade goods and gifts for its Native allies. Consequently, the French and Indian raids into Pennsylvania and Virginia frontier settlements began to taper off by the end of 1757. Nonetheless, before winter set in, William, with many other remaining settlers, managed to make their way out of the valley and over the Great North Mountain to the Shenandoah wagon road that took them to Winchester. There, William found the bustling town of Winchester overcrowded with refugees like himself from all parts of western Virginia and even Pennsylvania. William was reunited with Anna and the children in a joyous reunion. He found them staying with William's brother, Isaac,[47] now serving in the Virginia local militia defending Winchester from French and Indian attack. By early April, word reached Winchester from Carlisle, Pennsylvania that the British intended to mount a second expedition to capture and destroy French Fort Duquesne as soon as the weather improved. Carlisle

---

47 Isaac Zane, brother to William, is not to be confused with William's son, Isaac.

was the staging area for an army of 6,000 men commanded by Brigadier General John Forbes. And as the weather improved, there were no reported incidents of Indian raids in the South Potomac Valley by Waggener's men garrisoned in the forts there.

William decided to bring Anna and the children with Luther and Peggy back to the homestead on Walnut Bottom. He was not alone. Other neighbors wished to see what was still standing on their properties in the valley. If all was well, they would prepare to plant now that the Indian raids had ceased. William and family got no farther than Warden's fort on the crest of North Mountain when a rider from the valley reached them with word of what had just happened. There had been a devastating Indian attack thirty miles to the south of Conrad Moore's block-house home up the South Fork of the South Potomac River that met the main branch at Moore's. A trail there followed the South Fork Creek to a settlement with a fort that a fellow named Seybert had built with his neighbors when war had broken out. There had been almost forty settlers inside the stockade when they were attacked by a large party of Lenape and Shawnee. The Natives were led by Bemino who called out in English to the defenders to surrender themselves, and in return, he promised he would spare their lives. Once the gates were opened, the warriors rushed in and captured and bound everyone. More than a dozen of the captives who were adult men were taken outside and immediately tomahawked and scalped, including Seybert himself. Many of the remaining captives who were women and children were missing and believed taken by the Indians back to their villages somewhere to the west. A man named Robinson had hid and managed to escape. The day before, another nearby militia stockade called Fort Upper Tract, was attacked and burned.[48] The twenty-two rangers in that company commanded by Captain James Dunlap were all killed without anyone escaping.

---

48 The attack on Fort Upper Tract was called a massacre. It occurred suddenly on April 27, 1758. Details of the capture of the fort are not known, as no one survived to record what happened. The warriors involved were led by Bemino, and it was this party that attacked Fort Seybert the next day.

Bemino's Ambush is Sprung

William and the others decided unanimously that the best course of action would be to turn around and retreat to the safety of Winchester considering this new development. William Warden believed that though the raids and subsequent destruction of the two forts had been a devastating blow, both raids occurred far to the south where there was little hope of intervention by nearby troops. That was not the case where Warden was situated, so close to the more populated northern part of the valley. Warden encouraged those in William's party to fort up with him in his blockhouse and rest for a few days before continuing on. William Zane could not be persuaded and turned around and headed back. Anna was feeling unusually weak and William was worried about her. It was only on the trip back that she confided to William that she was pregnant once again. William rejoiced for two reasons. Perhaps this time she would give birth to a girl after having five boys. The other reason was that William was glad he had made the right decision in light of her admission.

To the south in the valley, Bemino, with his Lenape warriors held a council with the Shawnee who had accompanied him. The Shawnee War Captain had met privately with his men beforehand. The Shawnee had decided that they would return home now to the Ohio Country. They had taken many Enemy scalps and were eager to bring their captives back to their village Clan Mothers for adoption or ransom. Too, before the forts were burned, all the warriors replenished their ammunition and food with what was found inside the cabins. In addition, each warrior had managed to claim some articles of loot for themselves. Consequently, the Shawnee and Lenape parted ways, jubilant at their recent successes. The Shawnee would take the Warrior's Path that would bypass the Whites at Waggener's two forts and cross Patterson Mountain to join with the path coming from Old Fields.[49] But Bemino had one last score to settle with the Whites before he headed home. Many years ago, the

---

49 That path was one of many that crisscrossed the Allegheny Mountains to reach the Ohio Country. The route the Shawnee took left the South Branch of the Potomac near what is now Petersburg, WV and merged with the trail from Old Fields at a juncture just west of Greenland Gap, WV.

Scotsman named William Warden had insulted Bemino by boasting that he had 400 acres of the Lenape's finest lands for his own without paying a rabbit skin for it. Bemino had not forgotten the White man's arrogance. So, it was only a few days after the Zane family departed that Bemino's warriors surprised Warden at his home, catching him and his oldest son out in the open. Wounded by a musket shot, the last thing that Warden saw was a laughing Bemino standing over him before the Native sunk his hatchet in the forty-two-year old man's head. The stockaded home was ransacked, and it too burned to the ground. Satisfied that his revenge had been taken, Bemino turned for home in the Ohio Country to pay his father, Netawatwees, a visit. He had the satisfaction of knowing that the burned-out home of Warden would serve as a great reminder to those Whites who wished to re-settle on Lenape ancestral land.[50]

To William, everything he heard from people arriving in the valley from Winchester was that the war with the French was all but over. That was because far to the north in Canada a British army had invaded New France. The successful siege and capitulation of French Fort Niagara was completed, and Fort Duquesne had fallen to Forbes. All of that meant that Indian attacks in the South Potomac Valley finally ceased. There had been no sightings of warriors anywhere in 1759. The trip back across Great North Mountain had been uneventful other than passing the grim reminder of Warden's burned-out home, and knowing the suffering the war had brought to so many people. "We're luckier than most," William said to Anna as they descended the wagon road that would take them past Van Meter's and then to their land on Walnut Bottom. "We survived the war unhurt and you're about to bring a new child into this world to cherish." To their complete surprise, the home that William and Luther had built was still standing along with the crude animal barn. It was badly in need of repairs but William breathed a sigh of relief that he would not have

---

50 An exact date of the attack on Warden has not been found recorded, other than it occurred in the spring of 1758 and was likely connected to the two previous attacks further south in the valley. It is also believed that another man by the name of Taff was also killed along with Warden and his son.

to start building a cabin from scratch like some of his neighbors. The fields were overgrown and needed plowed for the upcoming planting. William was glad that Silas, aged fourteen, and Eb, aged twelve, would be able to help him with all that needed done. Even Jonathan, aged ten, would be old enough to do his share of the work at the labor-intensive tasks.

With all the devastation done to so many in the valley by Bemino and his Lenape warriors, William often wondered why Bemino had not killed him when the opportunity arose on that fateful night when everyone was asleep inside the cabin. "Was it because I could speak Lenape to him? Or was it something about my having had a Lenape wife, White Sparrow, at one time?" William pondered to himself. He figured he most likely would never know. With more settlers than ever coming to the valley, and animosities towards the Natives still fresh in everyone's minds who had relatives killed or missing, Bemino would not be able to show his face again with impunity. What jarred William's mind from his musings while working the field one day was Peggy calling him to the cabin. Anna had gone into labor and delivered the family a baby girl. William gazed down at the newborn bundled baby daughter they agreed they would call Elizabeth.[51]

However, all was not well with Anna. After bearing six children on the frontier under harsh conditions, Anna, now at the age of forty-four, was in ill-health and did not seem to be recovering from the birth of Elizabeth. To make matters worse, Anna soon found that she was unable to nurse the baby. Fortunately, Peggy the slave-girl was also a nanny and able to produce breast-milk. William's brother, Isaac, recognized the plight that his brother was in with respect to Anna's health. He could see that she had not been well for a long time. Before William and the family left for the South Potomac Valley, Isaac bequeathed to William the

---

51 Elizabeth Zane, the youngest of William and Anna's six children was born July 19th 1759 in the South Potomac Valley. This is the Elizabeth "Betty" Zane who would make a run for the gunpowder during the last siege of Fort Henry in September 1782. Some sources give her birthdate as 1765, but that seems unlikely as her mother had already passed away by then.

slave Peggy. Isaac figured William would sorely need Peggy to tend to Anna if she took a turn for the worse. Unfortunately, that is what happened. Through the winter of 1760, William watched his wife slowly waste away until she became bedridden. Finally, in the spring of 1761, Nancy Anna Nolan Zane died in their cabin on Walnut Bottom.[52] Peggy said that Anna had died of consumption.[53] William and the family were devastated. He had lost a wife, and his six children had lost their mother whom the five boys truly loved. What grieved him most was the thought that baby Elizabeth would never remember or know of her mother's tender embrace. After a final goodbye, Anna was buried on the hill overlooking the homestead so that the boys and baby Elizabeth would know their mother was always looking over them.

Far to the north from where William grieved, at a Wyandot village across the river from Detroit, Tarhe, now aged seventeen, listened intently to the tribal orators from the different clans as they took their turn to express their sentiments in the council longhouse. It was now November of 1760 and the war between the English and the French was over. The French had been defeated and Canada was now put into the hands of the victorious English whom the Wyandot had no love for. The question at hand now under discussion was what to do. Word had reached Detroit that an English army was on its way across Lake Erie to take command of Detroit. Would the English Captain try to punish the Wyandot for supporting the French? As Tarhe listened to the intense discussion he heard the chiefs take their time reviewing what had happened over the course of the past few years. A council much like this one had been held in the same longhouse around the council fire to discuss what to do several years ago.

Tarhe remembered the council talk then. The French officers from Detroit had not been invited to that council. The French

---

[52] The most reliable reference is that Anna died sometime in 1761 in the South Potomac Valley, although some genealogical sources claim her death was as late as 1764. The place of her burial is unknown.

[53] The exact cause of Anna's death is not known. The 18th century common illness called consumption was in fact tuberculosis.

commander urgently petitioned the Wyandot War Captains to support their departure with the remaining Lake Indians to relieve the English siege of French Fort Niagara, which was increasingly dire. It was apparent to all that the French dominancy of Canada was rapidly crumbling. The heady days after Braddock's defeat were but a memory now, the Sachems related. Gone were the dozens of captured horses, the ammunition, the muskets, and kegs of provisions that were brought to the Wyandot villages as tribute to the overwhelming victory. The hard winters combined with the increasing inability of the French at Detroit to supply their needs while Wyandot warriors were afield had become problematic. The British, the Sachems reasoned, had cut off the supply ships arriving to the East and nothing more was coming to Detroit from Montreal. "The smell of defeat is in the air," one of the headmen said, which Tarhe recalled, as he remembered.

The consensus of the Wyandot War Captains and Village Chiefs was that their nation had bled enough for the French cause. While there was some dissension among clan leaders along clan lines, most of the headmen agreed to remain neutral in the outcome, considering that the English numbered more than 6,000 soldiers besieging Niagara. More importantly, word had privately reached the Wyandot from the Niagara area that the Haudenosaunee, or Iroquois, were largely siding with William Johnson, who was a war leader of the British siege. If called upon by the French, the Iroquois intended to state their neutrality. But if the French were defeated, they planned to cut the Frenchmen to pieces and share in the plunder of the fort, once it fell. The Wyandot would not fight or interfere with the Iroquois under any circumstances. It had been the Haudenosaunee Confederacy that had allowed the Wyandot people to settle at Detroit and in the Ohio Country[54] at the turn of the century. These were all good reasons to wait it out and see which of the two White men's nations would prevail. A small group of warriors would leave for Niagara under the War Chief named Aghstaghregck to fight for the French, as it was their

---

54 Particular to the south side of Lake Erie from Sandusky on the lake to Upper Sandusky plains.

right to do.⁵⁵ Tarhe wished that he could go as well, but his Clan Mother forbade it.

Soon, Tarhe learned that it was a good thing that most of the Wyandot warriors did not go to Niagara. The fort fell to the British and their Iroquois allies, and in a short time, all of French Canada surrendered. Now, all that was left was for the British to take possession of the French western posts, including Detroit. Word finally reached Detroit that a British force of Rangers were headed across Lake Erie in batteaux to demand the surrender of the French garrison and a pledge of peace from all of the Native allies of the French. Rumors abounded. Then a runner reached Detroit with word that the Ottawa War Captain Obwandiyag, called Pontiac by the French, had intercepted the British Rangers at the mouth of the Sandusky River.⁵⁶ Pontiac spoke with Rogers asking him what his business was in trespassing on Ottawa land without permission from Pontiac. There were some tense moments that followed, it was said. However, in the end Rogers allayed Pontiac's concern by telling him that he came in peace with his men only to accept the surrender of the French garrison of Fort Detroit. A pipe of tobacco was smoked whereupon Pontiac gave Rogers permission to proceed to Detroit without fear of attack.

Rogers and his men arrived at Detroit on November 29, 1760. All the tribes of the Great Lakes region were present to observe the commanding officer of the French post unequivocally capitulate, and his officers become prisoners of the Rangers. A British flag was raised over the fort to demonstrate to the Native population the supremacy of England in the colonial far west. The Wyandot and Ottawa, who were the most war-like and militant of all tribes, were outraged that the French appeared so weak as to give up without a fight. Equally, they were shocked when the British did not kill their French captives with blows of the tomahawk, as their own fierce

---

55 Aghstaghregck is referred to as a principal chief, or a nephew of a principal chief of the Wyandot. It is noted that he was killed at Niagara.

56 The exact location of the meeting is debated. Some sources say the rangers were camping at the mouth of the Cuyahoga River; others claim the Sandusky River or the mouth of the Detroit River.

warriors would have done to a captive Enemy who surrendered without a fight, White or otherwise. Their warrior spirit and code of honor would have demanded it. Many of the warriors observing the ceremony reminded themselves that it had been only a few short years past that they had raised the war cry and swung their hatchets at these hated English who had followed Braddock. To make matters worse, now the shadow of the English King was hanging over their lands. It went without saying that where the English raised their hand in professed peace gestures, soon English settlers would follow.

At the time, Tarhe watched the proceedings, deep in thought. He remembered the field where Braddock and his men had perished. Tarhe at age fourteen had proved himself in the battle by striking several of the Red Coats with the deadly aim of his bow. Both arrows found their mark and felled two soldiers. As the British line began to crumble and turn, Tarhe rushed in with war club in hand and dispatched each of his two victims with a swift blow to the side of the head.[57] His boldness caught the eye of Pontiac who initially thought the young warrior's move to be reckless. Pontiac changed his mind when he observed the painted youth of fourteen expertly remove both men's scalps while carefully recovering his arrows from their bodies and placing them in his quiver. He did this in a calm, unperturbed manner while Red Coat bullets whistled over his head. Once the battle was over, the Wyandot returned to their village across the river from Detroit. There was much rejoicing in the village and plunder to be divided up by clans so that all shared in the spoils of the battle victory.

For Tarhe, that meant admiring the two British Bess muskets with ammunition pouches and cartridges he had taken off the field and loaded onto the horse he had claimed. In addition, Tarhe displayed to his family the two English scalps he had removed from the men he had killed. He had carefully scraped the flesh from the skin before stretching the hair on hoops and then painting the

---

57 It was the practice of Wyandot warriors to quickly dispatch an Enemy wounded or unfit captive with a measured blow to the head guaranteed to immediately kill them rather than torturing the enemy victim. It was not the Wyandot warrior's way, or code, and "the burning of prisoners was an obsolete custom with the Wyandots." LD-OBOT, p. 139.

undersides in red ochre. It was a sign to everyone in the village that this youth who had gone to war had come back a man. He had proved himself a warrior beyond anyone's doubt. Though Tarhe was only fourteen then, he was more than six-foot-tall for his age, and looked every bit the part of the warrior. His new found status could provide him with opportunity, if he wished, to turn his attention to finding a suitable mate in a wife that would complement him in the years ahead.

Tarhe remembered how he had his eye on one particular young woman living at the French settlement surrounding Detroit. She was a beautiful young woman who was not a Wyandot but French Canadian. Tarhe was very modest and shy about expressing his interest in her. He had spoken to this young woman on several occasions and found her name to be Ronyouquaines, of the La Durante family of her father.[58] Tarhe was smitten by her dark eyes, black hair, and beautiful pale-skin. Her name was Ronyouquaines La Durante.[59] She was living with her father at the Detroit French settlement. Ronyouquaines believed she was born a year after Tarhe, in 1743, which made them close in age. She told Tarhe that she did not know her mother who died when she was a very young child in the Louisiana colony of New France before her father brought her north to Detroit. Some of the French traders at Detroit thought that the young girl was actually Wyandot. Some claimed that she was mixed-blood, and others said that her mother had been an adopted captive taken surreptitiously from the French. The Wyandots were on excellent terms with the French during those years and such a seizure would have been unthinkable.[60] Tarhe spoke with Ronyouquaines

---

58 It is said that her mother was possibly a Wendat woman at Detroit, but no name or proof is cited. It is likely that her mother had died by the time Tarhe met Ronyouquaines, and there is no evidence that her mother was or was not Native. Some sources speculate that her mother was a captive white woman who was adopted by the Wyandot.

59 There is much contradictory source information on the woman who would become Tarhe's wife. Some claim that they married in 1757 when he was fifteen and she fourteen, while other sources dispute that as fanciful as he had not proven himself definitively as a warrior at such a young age which was a Wyandot pre-requisite for the lead-up to an eventual marriage.

60 Wyandotte-nation.org

many times and was smitten by her, as he believed she was with him. Finally, he decided to discuss these things with his parents.

Tarhe remembered bringing the matter up to his father and mother even though the war between the French and the English still raged in 1757. Tarhe's mother had a big say in the question of the marriage of her son. A leading Clan Mother of her Porcupine Clan, marriage would likely mean that Tarhe would leave her clan lodge to live with the bride's mother. However, in this case, Ronyouquaines was living in her father's trading cabin near the fort, so that would not happen. "All of this will need to be worked out," Tarhe's mother told her son,[61] "But, first things first. We must discover if this girl is romantically interested in you." So Tarhe's mother and father, along with relatives, paid a visit to Ronyouquaines father and his relatives. It was there that Tarhe's mother spoke with Ronyouquaines and her father, and found that the girl was indeed interested in Tarhe. An agreement of a tentative coupling that could lead to eventual marriage was reached by all parties. In Wyandot culture, a man was not considered able to take a life-long marriage partner until the age of thirty. However, many young people chose to pair off before that time in the hopes that they would later cement that life-long bond as mates. So, a ceremony was held whereupon Ronyouquaines moved into the lodge of Tarhe's mother's immediate Porcupine Clan with her close kin. To Ronyouquaines, who was well-acquainted with Wyandot protocol, culture, and language, Tarhe, the proven warrior, was a greater catch than the French boys at the fort who eyed her with envy but had no standing. The partnering was consummated and soon a daughter was born who was given the Turtle Clan name Myeerah,[62] which meant Walk-in-the-Water, a reference to the bird called the crane of the lakes and marshlands. Already the French at Detroit were calling the toddler the "White Crane" because of her unusual pale skin inherited from her mother.

---

61 The name of Tarhe's mother is not known.
62 The name Myeerah belonged to one of the Turtle clans of the Wyandot. His grandmother may have been named Myeerah. It is certain that his mother was not. Tarhe-Wyandotte Nation

Tarhe shifted his thoughts from his wife and daughter Myeerah to the immediate matter at hand. With the surrender of the French, Tarhe, and many others understood that there would be no more opportunities to go to war against the English if a lasting peace were made. The Clan Mothers would not allow it for the sake of protecting the tribe from English retribution. Tarhe would have to prove his worth as a member of a war party somewhere else if he was to advance. Hopefully one day he might become a War Captain himself, like Pontiac of the Ottawa. It was for that reason that Tarhe's mind turned to the southern tribes like the Cherokee and Catawba, who were long-standing enemies of the Wyandot. The Wyandot had no kinship ties with the Cherokee that would interfere with warfare. What mattered to Tarhe right now was that he petition the young warriors to help raise a war party against the Cherokee; an opportunity that he hoped the Clan Mothers would approve of. Out of necessity, that war party would need to set out at once before the hunting season arrived.

As it happened, there were other young men in the village with the same restless idea as Tarhe, who needed no coaxing to raise the hatchet against the Cherokee. As Tarhe had never travelled the Great Warrior Paths to the Cherokee country he was not allowed to lead the war party of eight men or more. Nor did he have any experience warring against the Cherokee. Tarhe was told he would be one of the warriors. The party set out in late summer following the Great Path that led from their Detroit village to their Lower, and then Upper Sandusky kin villages where they would rest before setting out on the long journey. The warriors travelled light, covering twenty miles or more a day, from sunup till sundown. There were many paths they could take. The War Captain of the party, an experienced warrior older than most of them, chose to cross the Ohio River at the island across from the creek that the Haudenosaunee called Weel-Lunk. That trail would take them to a branch that led to the Youghiogheny Path that joined the Great Warrior's Path to the Cherokee lands.

Tarhe made a mental note of all the landmarks along the path they were following so that he would never forget the route. The path climbed the western side of the Allegheny Ridge onto the plateau whereupon it joined a branch of what their War Captain knew as the Seneca Path. This path was one that the Haudenosaunee used to make war with the southern tribes.[63] At this juncture, the War Captain decided to take the more direct route that followed the old Warrior's Path that traversed the valley of the South Potomac River since they were not going as far south as Catawba country. The Clan Mothers had warned him not to come close to the White settlers anywhere for fear of violating the recent peace agreement with the English. That meant staying out of the South Potomac Valley. However, the warriors knew that it would be easy to avoid detection if they were careful about not being seen. Also, they learned from a Shawnee party returning from the Overhill Cherokee towns near Chota[64] that the Cherokee were alerted to the presence of war parties of their enemies. The Shawnee had not been successful in their raid, and were returning to the Ohio Country with two warriors wounded. Their War Captain argued that it would not be good for the Wyandot to go there with so few warriors. The Shawnee were returning by way of the South Potomac Valley. Although more settlers were seen arriving from over the Blue Ridge, still the Whites were not as numerous as they had once been due to the previous war that had devastated the valley from Bemino's handiwork.

Tarhe's War Captain named Muskrat decided that they would change direction and head for the Cherokee villages of the Middle Towns.[65] The path they were on crossed the North Fork of the Potomac River and then reached a branch which their War Captain said would take them through a cleft in the mountains. That path led directly down to the South Potomac Valley to a place that was once a Shawnee summer camp that Whites called Old Fields. It was a spot where the Shawnee at one time

---

63 Presently the juncture is just south of the city of Oakland, Maryland today.

64 Chota was a major Overhill Cherokee town in what is now eastern Tennessee.

65 Middle Cherokee Towns were located in what is now western North Carolina.

had cleared for crops. They would not take that fork through the gap[66] but instead continue along the south path to where it met the old path following the South Branch of the Potomac.[67] From there, the valleys south between the mountain ridges would take them to the Cherokee lands that they wished to enter. Perhaps they would find an unsuspecting group of Cherokee hunters that they could attack while avoiding any White settlements of Virginia. "If we are successful," the War Captain named Muskrat told his men, "Each of you will have the opportunity to take an Enemy's scalp and perhaps capture a horse, take some captives to please the Clan Mothers, and obtain a musket and precious ammunition."

---

66 Today called Greenland Gap, WV.
67 Currently at Petersburg, WV.

Chapter Five
Pontiac's Uprising

Tarhe and the warriors returned to their Detroit village in late August from their raid against the Cherokee which had been a success. The War Captain Muskrat praised the actions of Tarhe for setting an ambush for the Cherokee warriors who pursued them after the lightning raid on the village where not one of their own people had been hurt. But the news of their success against the Enemy was overshadowed by the serious situation that they found all Natives were facing just before the hunting season was to begin. While Tarhe had been gone, the Red Coats at Detroit who were now garrisoning it had received an order from their General called Amherst to restrict the supply of ammunition and gunpowder that the English traders at Detroit could trade to the Wyandot and all others.[68] In addition, the supply boats arriving at the British post from the East were bereft of the usual gifts that were traditionally given to the tribes as a sign sealing a peace treaty that had become an institution in itself. Tarhe found that the Wyandot village was in an uproar over this shocking turn of events since the departure of the French. Gunpowder was in extreme short supply just before the warriors planned to go on the

---

68 This was a policy instituted by Amherst in the spring of 1761 in an attempt to deprive the former Native allies of the French with the ability to make war on the English in the future.

hunt to prepare for securing winter meat. Without ammunition, they would be forced to rely upon bows and arrows which made hunting much more difficult, meaning fewer deer and elk taken. Less game meant not only less meat for the pots but fewer hides that could be dressed for trade. Already, the cost of scant goods at the Detroit trading post had risen in price due to great demand and tight supply.

All of this news was troubling. Tarhe had no difficulty seeing how leaders like the Ottawa war chief Pontiac were right about the grip that the hated English were tightening around their necks. Already the wives were complaining that their cooking pots were wearing out and the blankets for the children were thin and threadbare. Pontiac had taken to actively speaking in private to the headmen of the different tribes surrounding the Detroit region. He was saying that Natives needed to meet this English threat by joining together as one to resist and expel the English so that the French would eventually return. Tarhe did not want to get involved. He wished to take his bow and arrows and leave for the hunt to provide for his family and his clan. As Tarhe prepared to set out with other hunters, word came that the English had sent Red Coat soldiers to build a blockhouse and stockade near the mouth of the Sandusky River, and one at the place the French called Presque Isle, both on the southern shore of Lake Erie. Pontiac was heard to have said, "You see, I tell you that the English are liars. They have come to our land to make slaves of us, and then to destroy us and take all of our land for themselves."

By the time Tarhe returned from the hunt, he heard from Pontiac's couriers that the English fort near the mouth of the Sandusky River had been completed and was already garrisoned with the British Red Coats.[69] This recent news of more English soldiers close to them was another shock to the tribes surrounding Detroit. It added to the evidence of Pontiac's claim of the evil

---

69 The Sandusky blockhouse was finished late in November 1761, and the officer who built it, Lieutenant Elias Meyer, had remained to command it with fifteen men.

intent of the English against all Native peoples in the area west of the mountains. Tarhe brought in a large amount of game for food that should supply his family and clan through the approaching winter. Whatever lay ahead in the coming year was not easy to see since he had scarcely enough ammunition for the spring hunt much less a renewed war against the hated Cherokee. More and more, Tarhe attended the talks that Pontiac gave as he made his rounds between the Ottawa, Chippewa, Pottawattamie, Wyandot, and any others who would listen. Pontiac was making a lot of sense to Tarhe by announcing his long list of complaints against the English. And as Pontiac called for action to be taken soon against the English, he revealed that he was sure that the French would soon return to the Canadas to aid their Native children and help them with their struggle.

When the spring of 1762 came and the snows melted allowing traders to trickle in from the East, Tarhe was shocked to find that the English traders from Pittsburgh did not bring gunpowder, lead and rum with them, on orders from the English General Amherst. What they did bring in the way of household goods had enormous price increases that most Natives could not meet with the meager furs taken over the winter. Tarhe tried to put this out of his mind and focus on a return campaign against the Cherokee. He wanted to go again since he had earned the merit of leading a war party in the coming summer, to which he privately rejoiced. While finding the warriors to accompany him would be easy, supplying themselves with ample ammunition would not. The situation was vexing. Tarhe knew how much the younger men needed an opportunity to prove themselves in battle, gain tribal and clan honor, and be seen in the eyes of marriageable women in the village as a suitable mate. To put it simply, the young men that Tarhe was about to choose as summer approached were obsessed with going into battle.[70]

---

[70] For the Wyandot, the most martial of all tribes in the Ohio Country, it was absolutely necessary for a young man to prove himself in battle if he was to be accepted as a full-fledged member of his clan and tribe without exception.

When all the necessary preparations were made, Tarhe said goodbye to Ronyouquaines and young daughter Myeerah. He set out for the southeast with enough men to split into two parties once they reached the Cherokee lands. Tarhe followed the same route as the previous year with an exception. This time, when he and his men reached the juncture with the well-worn path used by the Haudenosaunee that paralleled the west side of the Allegheny Mountains, Tarhe chose to go in that direction.[71] Once they arrived in the Cherokee land, Tarhe first surveyed the area without revealing the presence of the Wyandots who remained in a hidden camp. Tarhe then selected a village to attack. But before doing so, he split his men into two parties. One party Tarhe would take on a lightning strike against the unsuspecting Cherokee. The other men would patiently wait in ambush along the path that Tarhe and the others would return on. The Cherokee warriors were sure to follow in an attempt to catch the Wyandot raiders with whatever captives, horses, and plunder they would be burdened with.

Tarhe's plan worked to perfection. The warriors with him gathered prisoners and plunder and made a speedy escape knowing that the Cherokee had been alerted and would be hot on their heels. As Tarhe and his men passed his second group, Tarhe had two warriors secure the captives, all women and children, at a distance from the ambush site while Tarhe and his remaining warriors turned to take part in the ambush. The Cherokee, in their haste to recover their captive people, fell headlong into the trap. Several of their warriors were slain or wounded on the spot. Only a few escaped. Tarhe and his combined force had won a great victory. Some of Tarhe's men wished to strike again at another spot that was favorable, however Tarhe was not one to push his luck. He had calculated correctly and they had been very fortunate. Not one of his men had been wounded beyond a graze here or there. But that did not mean that it could or

---

71 The Seneca Trail or Path follows Route 219 from Oakland, Maryland south through Elkins, WV and beyond to eastern Tennessee, and what was the Overhill Cherokee villages.

would happen again. Now that the Cherokee had been alerted, a second attack could result in disaster if they were the ones outnumbered and ambushed. Tarhe had his men carefully strip the dead Cherokee of their weapons and the valuable ammunition they were carrying.

Soon they were back at their home village. The Clan Mothers were pleased that there were women captives of child-bearing age who could be adopted and assimilated as potential wives and mothers-to-be. The Cherokee children would be adopted into families who had lost children of their own to the White man's diseases which were running rampant ever since the English traders arrived in the spring.[72] Tarhe found that the situation at Detroit had further deteriorated to the point that there was open talk among the tribes of a coming war as the only way to break the hold of the English yoke upon their shoulders. Pontiac called for a council of headmen of the different tribes to be held in his Ottawa village by late summer. Pontiac forbade any French or English to attend the meeting. Surprisingly, Pontiac asked that Tarhe attend, even though he was not an official Wyandot Sachem or a leading War Captain. Pontiac had had his eye on Tarhe ever since his baptism under fire at Braddock's defeat. Tarhe, now twenty years old, was a proven warrior and leader in Pontiac's eyes. Pontiac believed that if war was to come with the English, that he would need someone like Tarhe to lead the Wyandot warriors. Pontiac already had an inkling that the Wyandot Sachems would not support him, as they, so far, were reluctant to do. Some of the Wyandots, particularly those living on the upper reaches of the Sandusky River were favorable to Pontiac. However, at Detroit, the Wyandots under their leader Teata, were against Pontiac's call for action to go to war with the English.

Pontiac shrewdly laid out his plans to attack the English fort at Detroit by beginning the council with a compelling story from

---

72 Diseases such as small pox, influenza, measles and a host of other fevers and coughing fluxes were particularly deadly on Native people in America as they had no immunity and suffered high death rates.

a Lenape Prophet named Neolin. Neolin had received a vision in 1761 from the Master of Life that promised an Eternal Paradise to all Natives who would reject the material goods and cultural ways of the European Whites. He advocated a return to a traditional way of living that meant abstaining from alcohol, wearing animal skins, and hunting once again with the bow and arrow. "The Great Spirit is angry with us Native people for allowing the Europeans to enter and take our lands," Neolin preached. He said that the time had come to rise up and expel the White Man forever from Native lands. Hundreds of Natives in the Ohio Country had already become followers of Neolin when Pontiac heard his message. However, Pontiac altered the Prophet's story to his own benefit, telling the tribes of the Great Lakes that the Great Spirit intended for only the English to be ousted and not the French. The Prophet's message as presented by Pontiac had the desired effect of bringing many converts to Pontiac's cause of open warfare against the English, which would begin first at Fort Detroit.

On April 28, 1763, Pontiac called for a grand council. He appeared before a large audience of several thousand warriors. Pontiac's body was painted black for war with red feathers adorning his scalp lock. He spoke at length for hours, invoking the words of the Prophet, and reminding everyone assembled of the outrages that the English had committed against each one of their people by denying them the rights to rule their own lands as they see fit. Pontiac's words were spellbinding. He was urging the warriors before him to unite together as one and to pick up the war axe against the English and strike it deep into their heads. "We must come together as one people whose common purpose must be to drive from among us the English dogs who seek to destroy us and take our lands," exclaimed Pontiac to the fevered throng. Pontiac wanted their allegiance. He promised he would show them the way when the time came to strike the first blows. When the grand council was over, Tarhe approached Pontiac and declared his unequivocal support of all the warriors he could muster to the Ottawa leader.[73] Teata, on the other hand, the leader of a neutral faction of Wyandots, retired to his village without comment. Pontiac was elated that Tarhe would support Pontiac's war.

The opening attack of the war was soon coming. On May 7th, a British surveying party of twelve men several miles from the fort were ambushed and all killed or captured. On the same day, Pontiac with a large force attempted to take Fort Detroit by a surprise ruse but was thwarted, whereupon a siege of the fort began two days later. All English soldiers and settlers, including women and children, who could be found outside the fort were killed, including the prisoners from the survey team. Tarhe was not present for the opening attack. He had left several days before with a large force of combined warriors at Pontiac's command to attack the English at the blockhouse near the Sandusky River. On May 16th, Tarhe was able to outwit the fort garrison with a ruse of his own that allowed him and a handful of warriors to enter the front gate on the request for a parley with the commander. In a matter of minutes, all the soldiers were killed on Tarhe's signal except one Englishman named Pauli, who was trussed up as a prisoner to be presented to Pontiac on their return. Tarhe's warriors took revenge on the handful of hated English traders found within the blockhouse without hesitation. To Tarhe's delight, none of his warriors had suffered as much as a scratch. In addition, a huge amount of provisions and precious lead and gunpowder were removed from the blockhouse before it was put to the torch. All of the stock was paddled by boat back to Detroit where Tarhe received the accolades from Pontiac.

The attack on the English at Sandusky by Tarhe and the Wyandot warriors was repeated again the next month against the English fort at Presque Isle on the shore of Lake Erie some 160 miles to the northeast of Sandusky. Tarhe had with him a combined force of 250 warriors made up of Ottawas, Chippewas,

---

73 In many accounts of Pontiac's Uprising, Tarhe is called Takee, however according to Wyandot sources, these two men were one and the same person.

Tarhe the Wyandot War Captain

Senecas, and his own men. The fort was a larger structure than that at Sandusky. It had a garrison of nearly thirty men who Tarhe believed had no knowledge that the English fort at Detroit was under siege by Pontiac, or that the Sandusky blockhouse had been destroyed. On the early morning of June 19th, Tarhe had his force surround the palisaded fort. He realized that the English had received word of his approach and consequently were crowded into the solitary blockhouse. After two days of battle, Tarhe used one of his mixed-blood Frenchmen to call on the blockhouse defenders to surrender in the morning or they would be burned alive once the blockhouse was set afire. He promised them they could leave without harm as the Natives only wished to destroy the fort. However, once the door to the blockhouse was opened, the warriors rushed in and took the defenders captive and divided them up by tribe. The fort was then ransacked and burned without any Native casualties.

At the same time, Seneca warriors and Ohio Valley Iroquois called Mingos by the English attacked and took two remaining outposts along the trail from Presque Isle to Fort Pitt. A few men of the garrison were able to escape to Fort Pitt, bringing word to the commander there of the new Indian war that had erupted. Soon, the Pennsylvania frontier learned of the Indian attacks and settlers fled with their children to the safety of Fort Pitt. They feared that renewed Indian attacks against their homesteads was about to begin as had happened during the earlier war with the French and their Native allies. With more than 500 settlers crowded into Fort Pitt, word reached the fort that Native warriors had cut the main road leading to Bedford in the east. Soon, several hundred warriors made up of Seneca, Mingo, Delaware, and Shawnee arrived and surrounded the fort, effectively beginning a siege to destroy it. At the same time, war parties spread out across western Pennsylvanian settler cabins and attacked those people who had not heard of the new war. Dozens of homes were destroyed and many English were killed in the attacks or made captive. Fort Pitt was bottled up. There was no way for word of what had happened on the frontier to reach Lancaster and Philadelphia for reinforcements as yet. In the meantime, the hostile tribes were turning their attention to Virginia where settlers had pushed westward over the Alleghenies.

By the spring of 1763, William Zane, now forty-eight, felt that he had endured as much turmoil as any man could in his position of caring for and raising a family of six children without their mother to help. William had tried with some success to hide his grief at Anna's death. Yet there was not a day go by that he didn't take the path to Anna's gravesite to lament her loss which he felt so deeply. True, he had the support of the slave Peggy who had done all that she could to see that the boys and the young baby girl Elizabeth were fed, washed, and tended to in only the manner a woman could. William chided himself for not taking more time to socialize with the handful of widow women in the South Potomac Valley that he might possibly find some companionship with. What always deterred him more than anything else was the loss he felt for Anna. It was that, combined with the constant heavy load of work that needed to be accomplished every day in the fields. That was the only way that William felt he was going to be able to provide his family with the things they needed above and beyond simply feeding them. The whole situation was vexing to William when he thought about it.

Silas, who was now nineteen and Ebenezer, sixteen, were old enough to help William and Luther with the field work. As far as William was concerned, their bits of home schooling down at Conrad Moore's home was over. Jonathan and Andrew, aged fourteen and twelve respectively, were assigned by William to tend to the horses, sheep, hogs and chickens. These chores relieved the two younger boys of the hard field work and allowed them an occasional chance to catch up on some badly needed schooling of their own at Moore's. Often, they took Isaac, their younger brother aged nine with them. Now that the crops of corn, squash, potatoes, and some wheat were in, William found time to teach the boys how to load and shoot a musket so that they could accompany him on the bi-monthly hunt in the upper hills for deer or elk that would provide the family with meat. William's ammunition was scarce, however he felt it an important duty that the boys learn to use the weapon that could mean the difference in surviving so many possible difficulties on the frontier. Peggy was always at baby Elizabeth's side in the home and busied herself with cooking and curing food while washing the endless amount of laundry that only a household of men could produce in the summertime heat.

There had been many good times for William and his family during the year of 1762. William had taken the boys with him to Winchester to visit with his brother Isaac and to see what a settlement community looked like, bringing awe to their eyes. He had talked to them at length about his own mother and father, and his life growing up across the river from Philadelphia which now was much larger than Winchester. William told stories about all of the things that the city boasted that he remembered. He told them about his own mother Grace, and what kind of a person she was like. There were many cold winter nights, with everyone together, including Luther and Peggy, sitting around the hearth's warm fire. William told them stories about his first wife whom he met and married before meeting their own mother, Anna. He was only seventeen, younger than Silas, when he married a Lenape woman named White Sparrow from the nearby village. "White folk call the Lenape, Delaware, but I don't." He described to them how she looked and dressed, and how she taught him words and phrases of the Lenape language which he still remembered. William taught the words to his sons, but it was only Isaac and Andrew, who were the youngest, who seemed to master the difficult tongue, although Jonathan was fairly good at it too. When Ebenezer asked his father why the marriage ended, William sighed and said, "Although I loved her dearly, the differences between us due to my civilized and her savage backgrounds was just too great, so she left me for her own people, and I never saw her again."

William told his sons how he was raised as a Quaker in New Jersey. He was taught at an early age to respect Native people as friends and equals to White people, and to cause them no harm. William explained that the Puritans of New England believed differently as did so many of the Scotch-Irish immigrants coming to

America. "The Quakers believe that every human being is born with a soul, an "inner light." They believe we must care for Native people as if they are our own, and teach and civilize them, not hate them," William added. Silas spoke up. "Pa, you're dead wrong. I've heard from the other boys what them red devil heath savages did to our people in the last war with them, and what we can expect they'll do if another war comes about. They ain't got no souls. They're nothing more than savages we need to git rid of once and for all," exclaimed Silas. "Pa, I respectfully don't want to hear another word of your Injun-loving talk even if you are my father," Silas added, to the shock of everyone listening. Isaac chimed in. "We'll teach them Injuns a thing or two if they try to attack us here, right Silas? We'll wup 'em good!" Silas glared at his young brother, saying, "Shut yer mouth, Isaac. You got no idea of what yer talking about. Let's hope we never have to find out," Silas added. William could see his sons were formulating ideas of their own. At least William could take comfort in that fact, no matter how distasteful it was for him to hear, at times.

More settlers than ever arrived in late spring from Winchester to take up Fairfax's remaining lots in the three surrounding manors that he owned. A man from Hampshire County named Daniel Perry came and looked over about 206 unclaimed acres of land on Walnut Bottom Run adjacent to William and Jonathan Cockburn.[74] It made William uneasy to think that he might have a new neighbor so close to him as he had not had before. The land of the valley appeared to be filling up, and William didn't much care for it. He had come to like his privacy. But by early June, the torrent of arriving settlers halted when word reached the valley from Winchester that a new Indian war had started. William and the boys rushed down to Van Meter's to hear the details. "The whole frontier north of the Potomac is being attacked by war parties from all the Indians. Fort Pitt is surrounded. Only a week ago did word reach Philadelphia and then Williamsburg of what's happening. It's said that everything the British built west of Pitt is gone; burned

---

[74] Perry would eventually be authenticated the claim on February 19, 1770. (Virginia Northern Neck land grants 0-256.

up; all the way to Detroit. People are saying in Winchester that it's only a matter of time before them red devils descend on you folks in the valley here," the messenger said. The thought of another Indian war sent chills through William's body.

The Virginia government in this time of approaching war, did not have the same pacifist leaning as the Quaker legislators in Pennsylvania. William explained to his sons why. The Virginians did not have any sympathies for Natives when they remembered what had happened a mere six years ago. The Commonwealth of Virginia already had an existing militia law. Consequently, the Governor and his Council immediately called for one thousand militia to be raised, with five hundred to be commanded by Colonel Stephen, a veteran of the Braddock campaign, and five hundred led by Major Lewis. Everywhere, militiamen were being called to meet the expected Native war and the Valley of the South Potomac was no exception. William, and his two elder sons, Silas and Ebenezer, were required to report at Van Meter's where the crumbling remains of old Fort Pleasant had stood. Luckily, William and Eb were allowed to work close to home on the refurbishing of the fort, while Silas, now nineteen, was to report for service on patrols. Silas went a step further and volunteered for a valley ranger detachment which would seek out the Enemy if it should come their way. It was a decision William opposed but could do nothing about as his eldest son was now becoming his own man capable of deciding what he wanted to do. At heart, Silas ached for the excitement of adventuring far and wide over the mountains, and William knew this. Ebenezer badgered his father daily to join Silas at the first possible moment, but luckily, no reports of Native warriors surfaced as the summer months passed by.

However, that was not the case elsewhere. The Commonwealth of Pennsylvania had been grossly unprepared for the Native onslaught that besieged the entire length of the province, sparing no one in their isolated cabins and sparce settlements once Fort Pitt was surrounded. Even after the Natives were defeated at the Battle of Bushy Run by Bouquet's relief force on August 1st resulting in the resupply of Fort Pitt, that only brought a temporary respite in the savage frontier wilderness war. It was only in early August that everyone in the South Potomac Valley heard of the Shawnee strikes to the west of them where settlers had surreptitiously made illegal land claims on Shawnee hunting grounds. White settlers were not allowed to settle west of the crest of the Alleghenies and violate the law of the British Crown by the terms of a treaty with Natives. Apparently, the Shawnee War Captain named Cornstalk by Whites, had taken the matter into his own hands at the urging of Pontiac. Cornstalk led a large party of sixty or more warriors across the Ohio River in early July[75] and ascended the Kanawha River.[76] There, the warriors split up and attacked every settler cabin that could be found west of the Allegheny Front. Cornstalk then took his war party up the Greenbriar River to a little settlement on Muddy Creek situated around the fortified house of a settler named Archibald Glendenning. Cornstalk's Shawnee warriors successfully took the inhabitants by surprise and killed all the men and captured the women and children to take back to their villages. When word of the attack reached the South Potomac, it was being called the "Clendening Massacre."[77] William's local militia ranger company was put on high alert. Silas was sent with men to reconnoiter the South Potomac Valley to the south. Eventually they returned without finding evidence of the presence of Indians.

At Detroit, Pontiac's siege of the English fort remained at a stalemate during the summer. The English soldiers were effectively bottled up inside the palisade, but Pontiac had been unable to force them to surrender, or to come out in the open and fight. However, everything changed in early June when alarming news reached Pontiac and his allied warriors, including the Wyandot. A sailing ship had been spotted entering the Detroit River from Lake Erie. It was an English relief ship from Niagara destined for

---

[75] Some references give June 27, 1763 as the date of the attack while others state it was July 15th.

[76] In what is now West Virginia

[77] This settlement was in the southeast corner of lower West Virginia about two miles from the modern city of Lewisburg, WV.

Fort Detroit, carrying reinforcements, provisions, and ammunition for the fort defenders. Pontiac made every effort for his combined force of warriors to intercept the ship as it lay moored in the middle of the river several miles from the fort, due to a lack of wind for the sails. Every attempt to attack the ship failed, and the ship made it to the fort to unload its desperately needed cargo. The setback irked Pontiac to no end, but he resumed the siege in spite of the English being resupplied.

More bad news reached Pontiac in the weeks ahead. His spies returned with word that a flotilla of many batteau carrying Red Coats and rangers were spotted on Lake Erie, close to the mouth of the Detroit River. These English reinforcements had stopped at the Lower Sandusky Wyandot village and burned it to the ground along with all the corn fields. In addition, spies reported to Pontiac that some of the Pottawattamie chiefs, along with Teata and his Wyandots, were privately suing for peace with the English commander of Fort Detroit. Pontiac summoned Tarhe and the other chiefs still loyal to him. Together, they devised a plan to attack the string of batteau once they came close to the Wyandot village. However, Tarhe and the other War Captains, including Pontiac, were foiled when the English in the batteaux fired grapeshot from their mounted swivel guns. Together, twenty-two batteau with over 280 soldier and ranger reinforcements made it to Fort Detroit unscathed. Each boat carried not only its complement of men, but barrels of provisions and ammunition to resupply the fort.

Within a day after the English arrival, Pontiac received word from a French spy that the English were going to attempt to sortie out of the fort under the cover of dark and launch a surprise attack on Pontiac's own village to destroy it. Pontiac called Tarhe from his Wyandot village to discuss this new development, and lay plans of his own to thwart the English. Pontiac advised Tarhe to take the bulk of his warriors and stealthily take up hidden positions outside the fort on one side of the path that the Red Coats must take on their way to the Ottawa village. Pontiac and his warriors would lay in wait on the other side of the trail from the fort. At 3:00 am in the early morning of July 31st, the gates of Fort Detroit opened and over 270 English Red Coats and rangers began their march on the trail to Pontiac's village in the distance. At a point where the vanguard of the English crossed a small bridge over a creek, Pontiac gave the order to fire and the ambush was sprung on the exposed English. Tarhe had his warriors press hard,[78] delivering volley after volley of musket shot into the silhouetted Enemy. The results of the musket fire were devastating. In a few moments, the English realized if they tried to advance any farther, they would face annihilation, so they retreated. The subsequent failed attempt to reach the Native village cost the English twenty-six dead and thirty-eight wounded, while Pontiac's warriors lost seven killed and a dozen wounded, some of whom were Wyandot who had been with Tarhe at the forefront of the ambush. Though Pontiac's ambush had been successful, Fort Detroit remained surrounded but undaunted. Pontiac had no recourse but to continue the siege.

---

78 Tarhe is referenced by the Wyandotte Nation as having taken an instrumental part in the Battle of Bloody Bridge, as the event of July 31, 1763 came to be known.

Chapter Six
Captured by the Wyandot

At Pontiac's urging, Tarhe now turned his sights on the exposed settlements along the Virginia frontier in an attempt to drive the settlers from the mountain valleys west of the Shenandoah once and for all. Tarhe had accomplished everything that Pontiac had asked of him, and more. Tarhe was not pleased with all that was transpiring as of late. He knew he had placed his family and clan in a precarious position by being constantly away at war and thus unable to provide adequately for their needs. Tarhe implicitly trusted Pontiac. However, it was becoming obvious to him that the French Father was not sending his soldiers from the Louisiana Province as he had promised Pontiac he would do when Pontiac first went to war. Pontiac assured Tarhe that the French would come in spite of the grumbling of many warriors and Sachems around Detroit after months of unending siege. Privately, the Sachems believed that sooner or later the English would arrive with an army to punish the tribes that aided in Pontiac's revolt. Many rumors abounded. However, Pontiac had more immediate things to deal with than the false talk of an English army approaching. At the moment, he confided to Tarhe that in spite of the great victories Tarhe had won earlier in the year and the vast amount of gunpowder and lead ball that had been taken from the English stores at Sandusky and Presque Isle, their ammunition was running out just when it was most needed to be able to continue the siege of Fort Detroit and provide the means for the fall hunt.

Tarhe respectfully reminded Pontiac that over one hundred English traders caught in the Ohio Country when the war began were now dead. Consequently, no English trader from the East would dare set foot in Native lands to trade, no matter what the price was paid. "Perhaps we acted in haste," Tarhe offered. Pontiac did not wish to dwell on the past. "Without ammunition arriving as yet from the French in the south, there is only one solution available to us, and we must take it, Tarhe," Pontiac insisted. "You must attack at once the settlements along the Virginia frontier and bring us back ammunition, horses, captives, and whatever plunder can be carried. That frontier is defenseless. I am told there is no English army there. Everyone knows how great a warrior you are, Tarhe. I have faith that you will be able to do this for me and our cause while I continue as best I can to conduct the siege." Tarhe nodded in agreement, and left to make preparations for the warriors he would take with him. At the same time, Tarhe suppressed the rising doubts in his mind concerning Pontiac's words. "As a Wyandot War Captain, I have been asked to once again go to war and I shall do so," Tarhe said to himself. "It is not my place to say or do otherwise."

In the coming endeavor, Shawnee, Mingo, and Delaware war parties would assist Tarhe separately in a joint autumn attack everywhere. Their warriors would continue attacks on the settlers in the valleys of western Pennsylvania to draw off the colonial militia. As Tarhe prepared to leave for the Upper Sandusky village, he received word from the Shawnee in the Scioto River Valley villages that they would also send war parties across the Ohio River. They planned to ascend the paths following the rivers called the Great Sandy and the Kanawha to their tributaries that originated in the mountain valleys where English settlers could be found, as was done at Muddy Creek in the summer. On the way down the Tuscarawas River trail that would lead to the Great Warrior Path that had been used for generations, Tarhe wondered to himself what awaited him and his twenty warriors in the Valley of the South Potomac. Surely the Virginians had heard what had happened earlier to the isolated settlements up the valleys called by the English Greenbriar and Tygart. Tarhe realized he must prepare his men for the possibility that Pontiac's vision based on what had been told to him at Detroit might not be accurate. Rather, the English Virginians could be well-prepared to meet Tarhe and his men. If they did, Tarhe knew that they would be well-armed, have plenty of ammunition, and would invariably outnumber Tarhe's warriors.

In Tarhe's mind, speed and stealth was tantamount in arriving unannounced and hitting the Enemy with lightning raids to catch them off-guard. All precautions must be taken once they reached the South Potomac. Striking quickly and withdrawing at once with their plunder must be an absolute necessity. And if they were actively pursued, Tarhe would rely on his ability to choose the right spot for an ambush. An ambush would send those pursuers reeling backwards on their heels while Tarhe and his men could make their escape. The plan was formulated in Tarhe's head as he and his warriors covered twenty-five miles a day on the paths that led to the great Allegheny Mountains ahead. Once there, Tarhe hoped to divide his men into three war parties, with each striking a different place. Then they would meet up again at a pre-arranged location far enough away from any pursuers on horseback. Tarhe talked to the warriors who would lead their own parties and reminded them of the necessity of sparing any English who did not oppose them directly. They would need adult captives to use to carry plundered goods on their backs on the return trip. Tarhe knew that this meant that scalp trophies must be kept to a minimum by orders of Pontiac and the Clan Mothers.

Soon after crossing the north fork of the Potomac River, Tarhe made camp for the warriors and went ahead with scouts along the main path to reconnoiter in the fading light.[79] Then returning, Tarhe gave final instructions to everyone, noting that they would rendezvous at this spot in the mountains where the trail forked to the south. One war party would attack the settlers living on the southern portion of the South Branch of the Potomac and then return by way of the same trail.[80] A second war party would proceed along with

---

[79] The Great Warrior Path crossed the north fork of the Potomac River close to Gorman, Maryland on U.S, Rt. 50 on the Maryland-West Virginia state line.

[80] Currently Petersburg, WV on the South Branch of the Potomac.

Tarhe's men and then break off to the north along the path that led to what the English called Patterson Creek. Tarhe and his war party would descend the main trail of the old Warrior's Path to the place that the Shawnee used to cultivate crops in the summers long ago. Whites called it the "Old Fields." If all went well, they would meet up after the raids at this camp on the Potomac North Fork before heading home. Tarhe once again urged his two Captains to strike quickly at one or perhaps two, or three cabins if they were successful, and to be sure to gather ammunition most of all. Tarhe emphasized that they were not to tarry or be distracted by anything else that might divert them for any reason. "Remember!" Tarhe warned. "There is every reason to believe that the English are prepared to meet our threat as they have had much time to consider the possibility. With that, the warriors went to sleep with no fire.

The early October morning dawned as any other for William and his family. They all arose at first light and ate a simple breakfast prepared by Peggy. William outlined the things that needed to be done that day and all of it involved laborious work. Peggy would take baby Elizabeth with her to the Van Meter's home to barter eggs for some much-needed flour. Isaac and Jonathan would later take the short cut to Conrad Moore's cabin for some schooling on how to write after their chores were done. "Pa, do we have to again?" asked Isaac. "I can already write my name and count all the numbers I need to know." "Isaac, that's my word. You don't hear your brother complaining, now do you?" countered William. Jonathan remained silent, knowing that there was no point arguing with his father. "Me and Luther, with Ebenezer and Andrew's help are going to try and get in most of the ripened corn before the deer and elk take it down. Since your brother Silas has gone scouting with the rangers up Patterson Creek Manor settlement, I know it's hard but we've all got to pull together and get these things done before winter. We might just have a little extra left over when it's all sold to take a trip to Winchester again," said William, trying to encourage his sons.

William had the two boys, Jonathan and Isaac, leave soon after Peggy was gone and their duties completed. He ordered Andrew and Eb to work the side of the field that was the furthest away from him and Luther. Several hours passed as they harvested corn. William was methodically stripping the cobs of corn from the stalks when he noticed that Luther had suddenly stopped. "Why ya all stopping Luther? Luther stood motionless, looking up in the sky. "Mr. Will, Mr. Will, do you smell dat?" Luther asked. "William stopped and raised his nose to the westerly breeze coming off Patterson Mountain. "Luther, isn't that woodsmoke? That's unusual as there's no one living above us, and it's not the time of year for natural fires of any sort," William responded. William was puzzled by it. "Maybe it's hunters we don't know about Luther," William quipped. "Maybe so, Mr. Will, but as long as I been here, I never smelled dat smoke coming from over the hills. Maybe hunters Mr. Will. Maybe trouble too," Luther exclaimed. William called to Ebenezer to come over. "Quickly saddle up a horse and ride on down to Van Meters and tell them to put out the word that for some reason there's smoke coming off of Patterson Mountain that seems peculiar. With that, Ebenezer did what he was told and rode off down the old Warrior's Path to Old Fields.

William and Luther went back to work. It wasn't but minutes later that Luther called out in alarm. "Mr. Will, Mr. Will, we's about to be getting' in a heap of trouble." William looked up and to his complete surprise he saw three Native warriors painted black coming towards them at a run. Luther immediately sank to his knees and began to sob, "Please Lord, don't let them Injuns kill me," as tears streamed down his cheeks. William yelled out to Andrew who was some distance from himself. The warriors were quickly closing the distance to William and Luther. "Andrew, Run! Run! Run with all your might and don't look back," William screamed. With that, Andrew dropped everything and disappeared into the nearby wood line. It was at that moment that the warriors pounced, striking William and Luther on the sides of their heads with war clubs that knocked both of them senseless. When William finally staggered to his feet, the warriors had tied a tether around his and Luther's neck and began pulling both of them towards the cabin.

At the cabin, all was pandemonium as the warriors and their exceedingly tall War Captain busied themselves ransacking the cabin of anything valuable, while another brought William's remaining horse out of the barn. Amazingly, no shots had been fired as yet that might alert people in the valley as to what was happening. William whispered to Luther that if they hadn't killed the two of them as yet, then it was likely they wouldn't unless the warriors were attacked. "They're likely going to take us somewhere. Maybe hold us for ransom, I'm guessing. At least no one else but you and me got caught up in this. The two young'uns are safely down in the valley with Peggy and the baby, and Andrew and Eb got away," William nervously stated, trying to control his feeling of complete dread and fear. He noticed the Native War Captain was standing at a vantage point to keep a steely gaze on the valley below. All the while the warriors piled the household goods outside the cabin that William realized he and Luther were going to have to carry. Far in the distance, William could hear the peeling of Conrad Moore's bell. "So, the alarm's been sounded. Andrew must have safely made it to the valley and raised the alarm."

It was at that moment that something caught the attention of the Native War Captain. He motioned to two warriors in the direction of the short-cut path coming up the hill from Moore's. William's heart sank when he saw the two men take off at a run. It could mean only one thing, that Isaac and Jonathan were unfortunately returning from schooling. Likely, the two boys had no idea what was happening here and who was about to meet them. He could only hope that Isaac and Jonathan would have enough time to see the Natives and turn and run. However, after a few long moments, William realized that their escape was not to be. The two warriors brought in both boys who now had their hands tied in front of them and tethers around their necks. William's eyes made contact with his sons and he whispered to them not to struggle to escape or they would be killed on the spot. William had been told by the survivors who witnessed Indian attacks during the late war with the French to not resist. With that, the Indian leader motioned to William and Luther to pick up their bundles of household items, from bedding to pots and pans. All of William's powder and lead, along with his remaining musket, were carefully carried by the warriors as special prizes.

William could hear alarm bells ringing up and down the valley as the war party moved swiftly back up the path they had come by. The last act they committed now that there was no reason for stealth was to set William's house and barn ablaze. William turned once to see the home he had built over the years become engulfed in flames. And as if that were not enough, the milk cow in the field was killed with a hatchet blow to the head. All the rest of the farm animals were likewise dispatched by a lone warrior who would serve as a rearguard for the war party, once they got underway. The climb over the rising hills preceding Patterson Mountain was uphill and rough in spite of generations of buffalo and elk that had created it during their seasonal migrations. William struggled with the load on his shoulders during the hard climb. Occasionally a warrior swatted him onward with the side of his hatchet. Luther, who was younger than William fared better due to his muscular build and stocky legs. William's knees were another matter. Instinctively he knew that if he foundered, or fell, that the Indians would not hesitate to kill him on the spot rather than stop for even a moment's rest.

When their party reached the point where the path crested Patterson Creek Mountain, William could see in the distance what he and Luther had originally smelled. Several settler cabins were ablaze there as well. What caught William's attention was that the War Captain had stopped when he heard gunshots coming from afar in the Patterson Valley. There was a look of concern on his face. To Tarhe, the gunshots meant one thing. The war party led by Spotted Elk had not only been seen but was being attacked by the English. "Yes, I was right to think that they are well-prepared for us," Tarhe thought to himself. Tarhe could not see any of his men from that war party approaching the trail ascending the creek towards the Warrior's Path that he and his men were on. Tarhe wished he could come to their aid. However, he knew that the chances of being pursued himself had just risen and he couldn't take the risk of losing everyone to try to save a few. "No! We move on," Tarhe exclaimed in Wandat language that William and the others could not understand. "If our warriors are able to, they know where to find us at the rendezvous."[81]

---

[81] The native language of the Wyandot is called, "Wandat" which is sometimes spelled "Wendat." I have chosen to use "Wandat" spelling throughout the text.

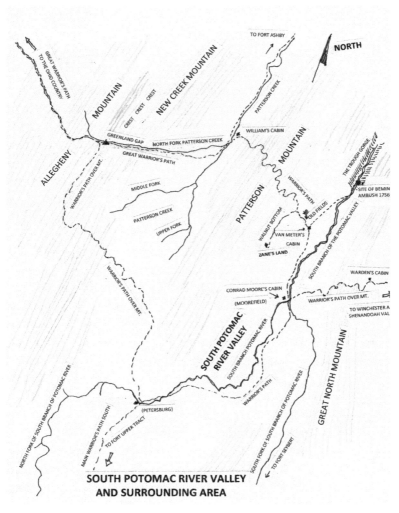

Map of the South Potomac Valley

The next climb up out of the Patterson Creek upper valley was more difficult than anything previous for William. He knew that his stamina was running out with the heavy load and the steepness of the path. William had not been this far west on the path. However, Silas had told him that the path followed the North Fork of Patterson Creek and climbed through a natural gap or notch in what some traders called the New Mountain that rose to higher sandstone heights than even the Blue Ridge.[82] That gap was narrow and very steep until it emerged to the other side of the mountain and was joined by another trail coming from the southeast in the South Potomac Valley far below Conrad Moore's. The path they were on was stony, wet, and slippery due to a lack of sunshine. William lost his footing several times to the exasperation of the warriors behind him who kept prodding him with their hatchets. Finally, William felt his legs give way. He fell to the ground, spilling the bundle of the plundered possessions he was carrying. Immediately, several warriors began kicking him violently in an attempt to force him to get up. William could not. He was spent. He was finished, and could not go on. A warrior pulled out his war club from his sash and approached the prostrate William, who realized the end had come.

It was at that moment that Isaac broke free from the warrior holding his tether, who was preoccupied watching William. Isaac scooped up a piece of dead tree limb on the ground next to him. Holding it with his two tied hands, Isaac swung at the warrior approaching his father, and then used it in a jabbing motion to prevent the warrior from getting close to his father. Isaac angrily shouted at the Wyandot in the few Lenape words he knew, saying, "No kill, no kill, Father! My Father! He had Lenape wife #1, No kill! Tarhe had been watching this remarkable outburst with a degree of curiosity. Although his warriors did not understand what the English boy was saying, Tarhe could speak Lenape. He understood the young boy's brave but pathetic motions and

---

82 Today, that gap in the mountain is called, "Greenland Gap" in West Virginia. Sandstone cliffs rise on either side of the North Fork of Patterson Creek some 800 feet.

words. When the warrior with his raised club turned to Tarhe to see if his Captain wanted the boy killed as well as the old man, Tarhe motioned the warrior away with a nod of his head, and approached this upstart himself. At the same time, Isaac realized that he was not in any position to make a demand. So, the boy of almost nine years of age motioned to the pile of goods that his father had dropped, and said to Tarhe, in Lenape, "I carry. Me and brother carry. No kill my father." And in that moment, Tarhe took notice of the boy's remarkable courage. Tarhe told the warrior to untie the two brothers and before he could motion Isaac and Jonathan to pick up the goods, the two had already begun. With that, the warrior gave William a hard kick that sent him rolling down the short embankment into the creek. He was battered but alive.[83]

Soon after everyone resumed walking up the path through the gorge, the rearguard warrior whistled to Tarhe. Within minutes Spotted Elk and his warriors came into view, out of breath. One of the warriors was being helped due to a wound in his thigh. They had one captive with them, a young girl of eleven or twelve, and one horse, but no plunder. While trying to catch his breath, Spotted Elk related to Tarhe what had happened. They had descended the creek into the valley and attacked two cabins which

---

[83] There is an interesting reference to William Zane in Blumel's book, "The Zanes: A Frontier Family." In 1777, William, who was still alive, paid a visit to his sons at Fort Henry in the Wheeling settlement. There, he wrote a letter to American General Hand at Fort Pitt on June 22nd. "He said that being more than sixty years old with a constitution much shattered by five years of captivity in Braddock's war and that the negro carried off by the Indians deprives him of means of support and he requests General Hand to secure the return of this man if the Indians made peace." An exhaustive search by this author could find no evidence of either William's service in the French and Indian War or evidence of his captivity and release in prisoner lists. Of the few adult male captives taken prisoner at Braddock's defeat, the Delaware tortured and killed all thirteen as witnessed by James Smith, himself a captive inside French Fort Duquesne. Blumel believes that William Zane was referring to Pontiac's War, however, his name is not included in any repatriated captives turned over to Bouquet in 1764 as terms of the treaty. What is most peculiar is that William, while writing about recovering his negro slave, said nothing at all about his son Isaac, who was captured fourteen years previous.

were empty. The next settler cabin they encountered had English people. Soon after taking the girl captive, their warriors were surprised by mounted Enemy English who drove hard at them before Spotted Elk and his men momentarily forced them to fall back. "We have little ammunition left, Tarhe, so we could go no further. And on our way back up this path, I could see in the distance more mounted English riding hard up the path from down in the valley. They will be here very soon," Spotted Elk exclaimed. Tarhe sized up the situation. He had a total of fourteen warriors. One of them was wounded. As to ammunition, they probably had enough to repel the English one time, unless they used the plundered gunpowder and lead meant for Pontiac. Quickly, he ordered two of his men to take the three White captives, the negro captive, their wounded man, and the horses up the path as fast as possible. Tarhe was going to prepare for an ambush with the rest of his men, and would catch up with them later.

Tarhe deployed his warriors on both sides of the narrowest portion of the gap near its top. He said that he would be with the half of the warriors in the forefront of the ambush. They would fire first on his command, and then immediately turn and run past their comrades who would wait to fire upon any mounted Enemy who pushed forward. It wasn't long till Tarhe's sentinel down the path came at a run, saying that the horsemen were no more than a minute behind him at the most. Tarhe and the warriors primed and loaded their muskets and waited from cover. Sure enough, the sound of thundering hooves reached their ears. In seconds, the armed riders came into view. Since they were preoccupied with keeping their horses from slipping on the narrow path, the first riders had their heads down as they forced their snorting horses uphill. Unfortunately, those men in the front did not see the hidden warriors and ran into Tarhe's ambush. Tarhe gave the order, and six of his eleven men, including himself, fired their muskets in unison, dropping two of the men from their saddles, and hitting another two who were in close order. Horses screamed and fell sideways over the embankment, or attempted to turn around to escape the fusillade, but couldn't.

Greenland Gap

Swiftly, Tarhe motioned the warriors who had just fired to fall back. There would be no scalp trophy taking this time. As they passed their comrades, Tarhe turned to see additional militiamen ride on through their own wounded or dying comrades in an attempt to take their revenge on what they saw of the retreating warriors. Tarhe had counted on that. As they approached Tarhe and his second line of the ambush, they too rode into a sudden hail of bullets that dropped more men from their saddles and caused complete chaos and confusion among the Enemy. Only one English man was able to get through the writhing mass of wounded comrades and panicked horses. That rider halted his horse and got off a well-aimed rifle shot at the Indians which knocked a warrior off his feet with a bullet to the ribcage before his comrades retrieved him and disappeared up the trail. William, who had seen it all unfold from his position in the low water of the creek bed knew that a ranger had fired his rifle, judging by its unique sound. That shooter might have been Silas who had found his mark, but it was little consolation to William for all the men wounded and killed that lay close to him. With the cries from the injured scattered about, the fight had gone out of the remaining militia rangers. There would be no more pursuit, at least for some time.[84]

To Tarhe's relief, the Enemy mounted militiamen did not pursue his warriors with their captives any further. Between his men, all that they could muster was enough powder and lead for seven

---

84 No records exist anywhere to confirm or deny that there was a pursuit of the Wyandot raiders in an attempt to rescue captives or exact retribution for the raid. In fact, historical fact does not exist detailing that the raid even occurred, beyond the simple statement recorded, that, "Isaac Zane was returning from school in Moorefield, Virginia when he was captured by Wyandots." It is important to note that there was no settlement called Moorefield in 1763, much less a school house. It is also noted that Jonathan may have likely been captured at the same time, however there are no facts to support or disprove this, other than the belief stated many years later by Jonathan who accompanied the ill-fated Crawford campaign in June of 1782. He was chosen as a scout by Crawford because he said he was acquainted with the area having lived amongst the "Indians" for several years, a reference to his possible captivity by the Wyandot, and subsequent adoption, and then ransoming, release, or his choice when he reached a mature age to return to white society whereas Isaac did not.

shots and that was it. What mattered now was that they move with enough speed that they could put a great enough distance between them and any possible relief force still intent on catching them. When Tarhe and his exhausted party arrived at the rendezvous point, they were elated to find that the third war party of their comrades were already there having made their escape with relative ease. But the news of their raid was as troubling as everyone's. They too had met immediate resistance after getting off one settler cabin attack of their own. The War Captain shook his head while telling the story. "We were unable to bring any captives back with us as there was none to be found at the settler cabin. However, we did secure four horses and a small amount of powder and lead, along with some meager provisions. Tarhe, it appeared to me that somehow the settlers had got advanced warning of our coming and fled the cabin, even leaving food cooking in the hearth pot. We had no opportunity to advance forward as we heard a bell ringing far down in the valley. My sentinel up a tree spied mounted Enemy in the distance with more men than my own. We were able to fire the cabin before withdrawing." Tarhe nodded his head in agreement. Silently, he thought to himself that if he had been there, he would have set an ambush for those hated mounted Enemy.

With the spare horses, the warriors were able to tie the loads of plunder taken from the Zane home, thus relieving the captive two boys, Isaac and Jonathan, of their burdens. However, Tarhe made sure his warriors tied the hands of the two once again, and secured each with a tether around their necks. He did not trust the younger of the two, who had showed remarkable courage back at the gap. Tarhe did not want to give him an opportunity to make his escape, which he was sure the youth was thinking of at every moment. Tarhe placed the young girl named Sarah between Isaac and Jonathan. Warriors followed behind her, and far out of sight, a warrior served as a rearguard to alert Tarhe if they were being pursued again. Soon, the Wyandots were across the highlands of the western mountain where the creek waters were draining away from the Potomac to the west. Here, Tarhe realized that they had finally reached the safety of the hills that led to the Ohio Country and home. They could now relax and make a more leisurely camp at night with a fire to warm them as no Enemy would come this far from their homes. Soon, they reached the shallow river crossing of the upper or Little Youghiogheny. From there, the Warrior's Path made a beeline for the Monongahela River. It was at the ford that Tarhe and his party caught up with a large group of Mingo warriors returning from their own raid on the Virginian settlements.

The Mingo War Captain told Tarhe that they had accompanied a large band of Shawnee[85] warriors by way of the Great Sandy River after crossing the Ohio. At nearly the same time[86] that Tarhe was leading his men to the valley of the South Potomac, the Mingo and Shawnee followed the Great Sandy upriver to the upper reaches of the tributaries where settlers had crossed the mountains into the valley below. There, the warriors divided into two groups and each decided to attack separate settlements. The Mingo headed towards what the Whites called the Jackson River where they had built a stockaded fort at the confluence of Dunlap's Creek and the Jackson River.[87] On their way down Dunlap Creek, the war party encountered a settler's cabin owned by a man named William Carpenter who lived a short distance from a nearby stockaded home of a White man named Brown. The warriors attacked Carpenter and killed him outside his house. There they took prisoner Carpenter's young son and two young brothers of Brown, along with a woman who was in the cabin. The adult Brown, who was working in the far fields, heard the gunshot that killed Carpenter. He immediately ran to warn those at Fort Young. The Mingo, fearing a swift pursuit, thought better of continuing on. Rather, they ransacked the house and returned the way they came with their captives, a few horses, and a large amount of plunder, guns, and ammunition.

---

85 I find this reference from American archives to be wrong as there were no Lenape (Delaware) villages that far southwest in the Ohio Country at the time. Most likely the chroniclers recorded the raid from a source who did not know exactly what Native people were involved in the raid.

86 One colonial account gives the year as 1764 which is erroneous. The raid happened in October 1763 because the raiders traded their captives with Tarhe and his returning warriors from their own 1763 raid.

87 Site today of the city of Covington, Virginia.

The Mingo told Tarhe that they found out that they were right to beat a hasty retreat. A runner from the Shawnee war party that they had originally accompanied had been attacked on their return trip at a place where they thought it safe to camp for the night. Three warriors had been killed and several wounded. Those who escaped, like the runner, told the Mingo that the Shawnee survivors had lost everything in the ambush, including their weapons, ammunition, horses, and captives. The somber news confirmed to Tarhe that apparently the English were well prepared for any attacks against them. Undoubtedly, they would be more ready than ever to confront war parties in the future. It was not a thought Tarhe wished to consider, knowing that his luck could run out at any time even with his cautious preparation and strategy. Tarhe knew that he must convey this to Pontiac upon his return. The days of raiding the Enemy frontier with impunity were gone, as was the ammunition needed to conduct it. Too, what would be missing in the future was the warriors willing to put their lives on the line when the odds had turned so dramatically against them. Disheartening as it was to accept, the war that Pontiac envisioned which would roll the English back over the mountains had failed. The only course ahead, in Tarhe's mind, would be to eventually sue for peace with the Whites and get the best possible terms. Deep in his heart, Tarhe knew that the terms of peace would favor the Whites only. Native people would be forced to give up more land. For the moment, it was a thought he wished to put out of his mind to get back home.

Chapter Seven
The Clan Mothers

The Wyandot and Mingo shared what provisions of food they had among them. The Mingo warriors admired the horses that Tarhe's men had taken for their own, finally admitting that they coveted horses more than prisoners. Tarhe sensed that his newly-made Mingo friends were asking for a possible gift from Tarhe, but he was not going to let something as valuable as a horse go to the Mingo without getting something in return. "A possible trade might be in the offing," Tarhe thought to himself. I do not want to let them know that I like the two young brothers the Mingo have made captive. To me and my people, plunder and horses are not as important or as valuable as a potential captive for adoption. While women and young girls might make good candidates for marriage, right now the Wyandot need more warriors. "Tarhe shook his head in disapproval, and motioned to the Mingo that they get some rest for the morning's journey. However, in the morning when he saw the Mingo once again looking over the horses, Tarhe matter-of-factly brought up the subject of the two captive brothers by saying, "Those two White boys look too sickly to reach your Mingo village without dying. Why don't you unburden yourself and take their scalps here and now?"

The Mingo War Captain feigned anger, saying to Tarhe, "It is you who do not see their value as I see them. Yes, they may appear frail at the moment but they will make great warriors for us one day if they make it to our home." Tarhe waited a moment before responding. "I do not think they are worth anything myself. Why, just look at them. They're not even together worth the value of one of our horses." The negotiations went on, back and forth, for a considerable time, which let Tarhe know that the Mingo were indeed interested in some sort of trade. "They are easily worth a horse each," the Mingo War Captain countered, but Tarhe responded icily, "Just look at those two. Do you really think that they will take to adoption and make fine Mingo warriors? I do not. More likely you will find a hatchet in the back of your head if they reach your village and you turn your back. The only good warriors they will make is English warriors," Tarhe scoffed with glee. "Who is of more value than those two is the young English girl we have who will make a fine wife and mother of many Mingo children." The bait was set. After more haggling, a deal was finally reached. The Mingo left with a pick of one of the horses and Tarhe's White captive female named Susan in addition to Carpenter's son, and the unnamed woman taken from Carpenter's cabin who they already had. In return, Tarhe took possession of the two Brown brothers named Adam and Samuel.[88] Also, Tarhe had the negro slave named Luther to bring back to Detroit. Tarhe knew the Clan Mothers would be overjoyed, as would his Sachem. Altogether, he had four White male captives of young ages, and an adult negro who did not harbor the same hatred for Native people as adult White men.

Tarhe's return to his village at Detroit with the captives would be the only good news that he would bring. After meeting with the Mingo, the gravely wounded Wyandot warrior Spotted Elk did not live more than two more days. The English lead ball had entered his back below the shoulder blade and broken a rib as it tore into the wounded man's left lung where the ball lodged. Spotted Elk

---

88 There exist several references to the trade of the two Brown brothers to the Wyandot by their captors, who were likely the Mingo. Some say that the deal was a sale, however, at the time sale and trade were the same thing, as goods, horses, or other captives were involved in the mutual deal.

had weakened rapidly since leaving the Gap, and could hardly ride in the saddle of a horse. His last hours were hard for the Wyandot warriors and Tarhe to take. He bled dark red blood from his mouth and his breathing was increasingly labored as the lung, Tarhe guessed, had collapsed. There was nothing Tarhe could do for Spotted Elk, his friend since childhood, but try to make him comfortable as he approached unconsciousness and then death. They could neither take his body to Detroit or bury him in the hard, stony ground. Rather, the warriors found a spot in a rocky cleft off the trail where they placed his body and covered it with enough rocks to prevent the wolves from recovering it to tear to pieces. Soon, they were crossing the Ohio River and headed up the Tuscarawas River Valley to the Wyandot village at the upper reach of the Sandusky River. There, they would rest before taking the lakeshore path to Detroit.

Tarhe knew that once they arrived, there would be much rejoicing among the families of his warriors to see their loved one's return, as much as he would be glad to be reunited with Ronyouquaines and his daughter Myeerah. Family was everything to Tarhe and his warriors. "But as I rejoice in the happy reunion with my family," Tarhe thought to himself, "So will the wails of mourning be heard throughout the village. The wife, children, family, and clan of Spotted Elk will grieve because he is not returning, nor was his body recovered for proper burial." Tarhe winced at the thought of leaving his friend's corpse along the wilderness trail. However, he knew that there was no possible way of practically transporting it to Detroit, short of jettisoning all the plunder on a horse and strapping the body to it. That, of course, would have been contrary to the command given to him by Pontiac and the Clan Mothers to bring back goods and captives, above all else. Returning to the Wyandot village at Detroit in early November, Tarhe was shocked to find that the siege of Fort Detroit was over, and Pontiac was no where to be found. Tarhe was told what had happened by the Wyandot village Sachems. Apparently, Pontiac had been visited by a party of Frenchmen and his Native allies from the Illinois Country. They were sent by the French officer named de Villiere to deliver a message to Pontiac and the English in command at Fort Detroit. The Frenchman declared in the message that they were not coming to Pontiac's aid and that he should make peace with the English, as the English now ruled the lands that were formerly French.

Pontiac, it was said, was dumbfounded by the news. He had already lost many of his allies like the Chippewa who left days earlier to go on their delayed fall hunt and into winter quarters. The words of the Frenchmen spread quickly through the villages in the area. Everyone knew now that Pontiac's war against the English at Detroit was effectively over. And with that, Pontiac realized that he had failed in his grand scheme to drive out the English which would depend, at some point, on support from the French. As a matter of fact, Pontiac had wrongly deluded himself that the French would bring soldiers to help him. It had not happened. Now Pontiac had undeniable proof that it was never going to happen. Some Wyandots heard Pontiac speak to his Ottawa people that same day. He gathered them together at their village and announced that he was leaving Detroit, never to return. He was sure that the English would sooner or later wish to exact vengeance upon him for the war Pontiac had inspired. Pontiac was not going to idly wait around for that to happen. Rather he was leaving for the Ohio Country, perhaps to a place on the Maumee River where he could establish a new village far enough away from the English. Pontiac urged his Ottawa people to join him and leave now so that they could begin building new shelters and join in a hunt before the snows arrived. When Tarhe had a chance to walk to the Ottawa village, he found the rumors true. The place was abandoned, and Pontiac and his people, gone.[89]

---

89 In fact, the war that Pontiac had begun was not over as yet, although the tribes surrounding Detroit had effectively quit with Pontiac's departure. More fighting would occur in the opening spring of 1764 by Seneca, Mingo, Delaware, and some Shawnee warriors into Pennsylvania against border settlements. From July to August 1764, the Superintendent of Indian Affairs for the British Government, Sir William Johnson, negotiated a peace treaty at Fort Niagara with about 2,000 Natives in attendance.

After meeting briefly with Ronyouquaines and his child, Myeerah, Tarhe had the important duty to perform of presenting the captives to the Clan Mothers for their inspection and deliberation of what should be done with them. The White prisoners along with Luther had been housed together in a lodge for that purpose. Tarhe made the announcement to the village that the captives were to be brought forward. Soon the Sachems, Clan Mothers, and villagers began assembling for the ancient formal ceremony. Tarhe could see that women and boys were forming a gauntlet line in anticipation that at least the Negro slave named Luther would be made to run it, however, Tarhe had other thoughts. He approached the Clan Mothers and respectfully waited to speak with them. When given the nod of approval to speak, Tarhe said, "Wise Mothers! My warriors and I have brought these captives back from the Enemy in the mountains so that you may see if they are candidates to become Wyandots. All of them are not adult Enemy. All are children, save the male with the dark skin. I respectfully ask that you consider them as possible adoptees, so that they may begin the assimilation into our clans and families, including the Negro of dark skin. He was made a lifetime slave of the Whites and he now seeks his freedom among our people. First, I will present to you the two sets of brothers."

Tarhe had the warriors bring forward the four boys. Each had been stripped naked and painted with clan designs. A belt had been placed around each of their necks to lead them to the awaiting mass of people. Tarhe paused to allow for a response from the Clan Mothers who took their time discussing among themselves the words that Tarhe had just spoken. Then, with a nod, the head Clan Mother bade Tarhe to bring the first two brothers forward for the women to look over. The elder boy, Adam Brown, was twelve or thirteen years of age, as Tarhe had been told by the younger Zane, who could speak enough Lenape for Tarhe to understand. Adam's brother was much younger. Both boys were made to stand naked in front of the villagers, not to humiliate or ridicule them, but in preparation for the adoption ceremony about to unfold if they were chosen. After some deliberation, the Clan Mothers

The Clan Mother Speaks

motioned to a family of the Wyandot Deer Clan to come forward whereupon they had Tarhe present the eldest boy to them. They family had lost several young members to disease during the last winter. With a nod from the Clan Mother of the Deer Clan, Tarhe spoke in Wandat, declaring to everyone in a loud voice, "The prisoner is going to be adopted. The prisoner is going to be adopted!"[90]

Adam did not know what was about to happen and feared for his life. It occurred to Tarhe that the youth was hesitant to go with the Wyandot family, perhaps thinking that he was about to be killed by them, not understanding the circumstances of what was really happening. At the same time, Tarhe heard the younger brother named Samuel call out to Adam in a fearful voice. He was thinking that the two of them were to be taken separately to an unknown place for execution, as they had been told by their family members back on the frontier of what would happen if they were "captured by the Indians." Tarhe intervened, and spoke to the Clan Mothers, asking them if that family could take the other younger brother also to adopt, and the Clan Mothers agreed. The boys went together with the family they were pledged to. Before they were given clothes, Tarhe motioned to them not to worry as nothing bad was going to happen to them. However, the ceremony was far from over and they were instructed to remain in place.

The adoption of the two Brown brothers had been approved by the Clan Mothers and the family that was to accept than into the Wyandot. But first they must be put through the ritual daubing of red paint on their foreheads by the Elder Clan Mother to signify that the individual was to be taken by the family for the adoption ceremony. Adam Brown and his brother Samuel were then guided down to the river by clan members of the family that was to adopt them. Both boys first had the hair on their heads plucked clean by a number of women from the family. Some of them used cold ashes on a piece of bark to dip their fingers in, in order to take a firmer hold of the hairs they wished to pull.[91] One woman skillfully used

---

90 Wyandot adoption ceremony, LD-TTIF, pages 134-35.

91 The adoption ceremony ritual in the Wyandot tribe varied from clan to clan, the author has been told.

two pieces of river clam shell to pluck the hairs. Everything was pulled out on both boys, excepting a small area about three to four inches on the crown of the head which the Native women intended to leave as a scalp lock. Jonathan, and Isaac intently watched the proceedings of the ritual. When the women were done, the Clan Mother for the family signified to the women that the two boys were ready to go to the Detroit riverbank. There they were taken naked by the hand into the icy cold water of the river where the women dunked the boys underwater and held them down for a short period of time. Adam and Sam bobbed to the surface gasping for air at the last moment as the women giggled with glee.

Tarhe now turned his attention to the two other brothers named in English, Isaac and Jonathan. He had them brought to the Clan Mothers for their scrutiny. Tarhe presented the older Zane boy, named Jonathan, first to the women. He looked to be a youth of maybe fourteen years, and stood tall and straight before the Clan Mothers and the village without any look of fear in his eyes. Yet to Tarhe, the elder brother did not possess the same fire in his eyes that Tarhe had seen in the younger boy which had caught his attention back during their retreat from the South Potomac Valley. There was something about the older brother that gave Tarhe pause. Tarhe couldn't put his finger on why this youth might not be a good candidate for adoption. Maybe it was the way the younger brother could speak and understand Lenape tongue, whereas the elder never spoke it, but seemed to understand what was being said by his brother. Perhaps he was already too old to make a good Wyandot warrior. Maybe he had some element of White hatred towards Natives inside him, and as a matter of survival, he would appear congenial towards his captors but would always have one eye towards the horizon and the woods. Tarhe remembered what an elder in the village told Tarhe about candidates for adoption. "Our standards for adoption as a Wyandot should be very high, and only the best chosen to become a citizen of our tribe. If a captive is not chosen for adoption or ransom, they would be killed on the spot with little misery and pain by a strong blow to the head."[92]

---

92 LD-TTIF, page 167.

This was different, Tarhe told himself. Though Tarhe had seen it before that an adopted captive was found to be unsuitable, this was a boy who was not yet a man. That is why the Wyandot, as a rule, refused to adopt White males whose minds were set against Natives by the time they were adults. "Time will tell," Tarhe thought to himself, as the youth named Jonathan was prepared to be adopted into a local family who had also lost a son.[93]

Tarhe went through the village and found one of the adopted White women who could speak English. Tarhe asked her to accompany him to the adoption ceremonies to speak in the English tongue to the four boys to assure them that what was about to happen, or already happening, was not to endanger their lives. Although Tarhe knew that it was not proper to have the English language spoken to White captives, which might interfere with their learning Wandat tongue, nonetheless, he felt it instructive at the moment, because the boys seemed confused as to what was to become of them. The woman, named Mary, struggled with her English. She had not used English at all since her arrival as a captive first of the Shawnee, who then bartered her to the Wyandot, but kept her two children.[94] Mary explained to the four boys that she was originally from the South Fork Branch of the South Potomac, where she had been captured by the Lenape War Captain Bemino when the Upper Tract Fort fell to the Shawnee and Lenape warriors in the year 1758. Mary explained to them that they were in safe hands with the Wyandot as long as they did not try to escape which was

---

93 There is no evidence to tell what clan Jonathan was adopted into, and what Wyandot name he was given. One account says that he was adopted by Tarhe, but there is no evidence to support this claim, and some sources do not even mention that he was adopted by the Wyandot. What is interesting is that during the 1782 Crawford campaign to attack the Upper Sandusky Wyandot and Delaware villages, one of Crawford's favored scouts was Jonathan Zane, who was picked for the campaign because he was familiar with the area having been there earlier in his life, he said, which is a reference to his time spent with the Wyandot as an adopted captive.

94 This person in question is modelled after the real person, Mary Burke, who was returned the next year during the repatriation of White captives to Bouquet as one of the terms of the peace. One of her daughters, Hannah, returned to Mary in 1771, while the other daughter unnamed was never heard of again.

all but impossible due to where they were. "You must accept your current situation as the best you have, as there is none other which any Wyandot family will offer you. You will come to find that very few White captives who are adopted as Wyandots ever leave the tribe to return home. This is a much better place to live, and you will be taken care of and loved."[95]

Mary tried with words to describe the meaning of the ceremony. "Your old clothes from your frontier life were purposely taken from you so you stand naked before the entire tribe, not to humiliate or ridicule you, but to symbolize a new birth. Submerging you in the water symbolically means that your body and your White blood are being cleansed. The person you were, the family you came from, the way you lived, and all that you understood about your former life is to be washed away. When you are taken out of the water it means that you are transformed and own nothing, just like that of a newborn child. Then you will be dressed in the finest new clothes, including a shirt, breech cloth, leggings, and moccasins, and given all the essential necessities of a new life in a new family. This is what the Wyandot call their adoption ceremony."[96] Mary finished by telling the four that they would be adopted into loving families to replace members who had perished and that they would be given new names and a new life which they would come to cherish. "Soon, your training as a warrior-to-be will begin, and along with that, you will learn the Wandat language as I have." With that, Mary smiled, and then turned and left.

After Adam and Samuel were dressed completely in the Native style, with a colonial shirt hanging down over a belted breechcloth with leggings and moccasins, Adam learned that his new name, which he could not pronounce, was Ta-Haw-Na-Haw-Wie-Te, and Samuel was given the clan name Ta-Sa-Tee.[97] These names would be finalized during the next Green Corn Ceremony, where names were given to newborns and adoptees once a year in the late summer. Both boys were formally introduced to their

---

95 LD-TTIG, page 153.

96 LD-TTIG, page 134.

97 The Wyandot meaning of these two names is not known or recorded.

new Wyandot father and mother who had not taken part in the clan adoption ceremony at the river, but had stood and watched. It was now Jonathan's turn to have his head plucked of hair, save a scalp-lock, and be taken by the hand into the water and dunked completely. Jonathan struggled immediately to raise himself from the frigid water. However, a warrior of the clan stepped out of a canoe into the water and held Jonathan down until it was apparent that the boy was drowning before the laughing warrior pulled the boy out. Jonathan was taken to the women on the shore who dressed him in new Native clothing and took him to a lodge near Tarhe's where he would meet the rest of the extended family and be fed.[98] It was now Isaac's turn to undergo the adoption ceremony that would begin with the plucking of the hair on his head which he underwent stoically without as much as a murmur. Before he was to be taken to the water to have his White name and history washed from him, Tarhe arrived with Ronyouquaines in hand. They had been talking with the Clan Mothers about what they wished to do with the younger boy named Isaac.

Since returning from his travel to the South Branch of the Potomac River, Tarhe had learned from his wife Ronyouquaines something of great importance that she was reluctant to tell him, but which she knew she must do. While Tarhe was gone, Ronyouquaines had suffered the loss of the beginnings of a child that she was carrying in her belly, which was devastating. In fact, as Tarhe knew from before, his wife had experienced a previous loss since having given birth to Myeerah. Ronyouquaines sensed at the relatively young age of twenty the terrible truth that she was likely not going to be able to give birth to any more children because of the nature of her unknown condition that was not allowing her to carry an unborn child to term. Ronyouquaines had consulted several clan healers who were unable to determine definitively what to do to treat her. A friend of her father at the English Fort Detroit who worked as the post surgeon from time to time agreed to see Ronyouquaines, but he too could not diagnose her infirmity. However, it was an elderly woman at the Detroit

---

98 It is not known what Wyandot name Jonathan Zane was given.

settlement who was of mixed French and Ottawa blood, and a recognized healing Shaman, who came to a diagnosis. She examined Ronyouquaines and determined from her bouts of internal bleeding, that not only would she likely not have more children, but that her internal distress might not heal itself, or be healed at all in the long run.[99]

Ronyouquaines knew how much her husband Tarhe wanted more children, and especially a son. Seeing that Tarhe had developed a fondness for the English captive named Isaac, Ronyouquaines suggested to her husband that they adopt him. They could take him into their household in a manner that would fulfill Tarhe's wishes but without formally taking the boy as a son. Ronyouquaines held out the possibility that she would one day be able to conceive again and give birth to a rightful blood male heir.[100] Tarhe would call Isaac his Nephew, and Isaac would learn to call Tarhe, Uncle.[101] The idea appealed to Tarhe. He consulted with the Clan Mothers of his own Porcupine Clan. He also spoke with the women who had overseen Ronyouquaines since she left her French father's household. The adoption was approved by everyone with the condition that the young boy be formally recognized as a member of the Porcupine Clan who would give him his adopted new name. And so, it was done and Isaac's adoption completed. Once the ceremony was over, Isaac was dressed in a set of clothes that reflected his newfound Wyandot standing. Before

---

99 So very little information is known about Ronyouquaines. Some ancestry sites claim that she was 100% French heritage and died in 1816, however that appears to be confused with Myeerah who died that year. The Wyandot sources suggest that after her marriage to Tarhe and the birth of Myeerah, nothing more is heard of her in any references, and it can likely be deduced that she died at an early age after giving birth to her daughter.

100 This was a common situation in Native culture across tribes. Another well-known case is that of the young English captive Simon Girty who was taken in by the Seneca/Mingo chief, Guyasuta, and raised like a son for eight years without formally calling him his son. Rather, Simon Girty, for the duration of his adoption and beyond, referred to Guyasuta as his "Uncle."

101 This form of adoption was common among woodland tribes. The Seneca adopted the captive, Simon Girty, when he was a young teen, and he was placed in the family of the Chief, Guyasuta, whom Girty called Uncle from thereon.

he could enter the lodge of Tarhe and Ronyouquaines, Isaac had to be introduced to Tarhe's extended family of siblings, parents, uncles, and grandmothers. There was much feasting, singing, and hugging of the newest member to their clan of which everyone rejoiced. It was all taken in matter-of-factly by Isaac who understood the gist of what was being said and done with him and for him. What he didn't understand, Tarhe explained as best he could with Lenape words that Isaac might grasp. What impressed Isaac the most was the genuine embrace which Ronyouquaines gave him. It was so unusual for him to feel the comfort and warmth of a woman's touch that reminded him of his own mother, Anna, who he could barely recall.[102]

When the festivities in the Porcupine clan lodge were finishing up, a Clan Mother called for silence as an important announcement was to be made concerning the newest son of the clan. Isaac would be given a new name for the time being. A hush came over the assemblage of Native faces, young and old, as the mothers stood together to proclaim that the boy would be given the name The Eagle.[103] The Clan Mother spoke. "In our clan, the eagle is a symbol of messenger. The boy will be called The Eagle, a messenger, which fits him well." Tarhe was reminded the next morning that there was still some business at hand to be dealt with that would involve the whole village. A determination of the status of the Negro captive named Luther had to be formally conducted and whether or not he was to be adopted, ransomed, traded, or sacrificed to satisfy vengeance. Tarhe knew that the Wyandot would never burn him if it came to that. But at this point, it seemed to him to be wrong to deal with the man harshly. Tarhe knew how Luther had done all that Tarhe had asked of him on the way back from the South Potomac. Nonetheless, it was out of his hands to

---

102 Anna, Isaac's birth mother, died in 1761, if that date is accurate, when Isaac was seven years old, going on eight.

103 It is not known by the author what the actual Wandat words for The Eagle are, and whether or not the name The Eagle was a name owned by the clan, which it likely could have been. Also, it is not known why he was given that name upon adoption, or if it was due to something about Isaac that inspired the people who named him to call him The Eagle, and not something else.

make that decision. All that he could do was speak to the Clan Mothers who were assembling in the center of the village. Luther was brought before them with his hands bound and stood before the women, sensing that something was about to happen concerning his fate. He shot a glance towards Isaac and asked him in English if he knew what the Natives were going to do with him, but Isaac could only shrug his shoulders. Isaac had the presence of mind to keep quiet and not rudely speak in English while the Clan Mothers were conferring with each other with an air of authority.

Chapter Eight
The Training Begins

The women each looked Luther over as they continued to talk among themselves. Tarhe requested to speak with them about the captive but they refused to hear him at this delicate moment of negotiations. One of the women said within earshot of Tarhe, "This man of the black skin is worth a lot to the English who treat such people as their slaves to own like a piece of property. He would be worth at least a horse to the English commander at the fort." Another woman, slowly shaking her head said, "He may be the property of an English man far away from here, but to the English at the fort he is just another slave that they could care less about in value. I don't think that he is worth a horse. He appears of strong build but he is older, and has been worked much during his years." Finally, the women reached the conclusion that they would see what kind of price Luther might fetch at the fort, or perhaps with one of the traders from Quebec. But first, the Negro must run the village gauntlet as the head Clan Mother daubed Luther's forehead with red and black paint. Howls of laughter and joy erupted from the villagers who ran to get themselves switches and clubs to use against the gauntlet runner. At the same moment, the Clan Mothers motioned for the warriors next to Luther to untie him and strip him of his clothes to prepare him to run as the villagers split into two lines.

It was at this time that Tarhe intervened and approached the Clan Mothers. He took the naked Luther by the shoulders and spun him around to display the man's back to the women and the rest of the village. There was an audible gasp. Luther's back was a mass of scars that were the result of numerous deep, vicious whippings that had been inflicted upon him when he was a much younger man. Tarhe motioned to Isaac to come forward to his side, and asked him in Lenape to question Luther about the scars. "Mr. Isaac, tell them when I was a young man in Virginia I was born into servitude and taken from my Mama when I was just a littlin boy, so I run away many times to try to find her and every time they sent out the dogs to brings me back, and give me a terrible whipping that I not forget ever. Dat's why I hate the English but had respect for your father, Mr. Will, who never laid a hand on me." Isaac told Tarhe what Luther had said verbatim, missing nothing. Tarhe, in turn, spoke to the Clan Mothers and the assembled village, repeating the story in a loud voice, so all could hear. Then Tarhe gave advice with authority of a War Captain. "This man of the darker skin than our own I believe should be welcomed here by the Wyandot and no hand laid upon him by the gauntlet line. I do not think it appropriate, or honorable, that we add more injury to him that our hated Enemy the English have already done to him. He has had the spirit to survive such troubles and toiled under the whip of the English. It is my opinion that this man would become a true and loyal Wyandot if given the opportunity, which I now implore the Clan Mothers to do."

Having said his piece, Tarhe stepped back and awaited the decision of the Clan Mothers who were absorbed in a heated discussion. Tarhe could hear one of the women say, "We should not miss this opportunity to trade or ransom him. He is an English slave and is worth much in goods which we desperately need." However, two of the other mature women of the village shook their heads. They pointed in Tarhe's direction, indicating to him that they were in agreement that the Negro be adopted. Tarhe recalled that the village clans in the past war had brought many captives back from the English frontiers, including a Negro woman

Luther

and her child who were adopted. Finally, a decision was reached that seemed to settle it. Tarhe told Isaac and Ronyouquaines that Luther was to be adopted, which brought a sigh of relief to Isaac's face, as he had great fondness for the man he had known since he could remember. Isaac asked Tarhe in Lenape if that meant that Luther was now a free man and Tarhe nodded yes. With that, Isaac asked to speak with Luther in English, in order to explain to him what he did not comprehend, and Tarhe motioned for Isaac to do so. "Luther! Luther!" Isaac exclaimed, "You're a free man now, no longer my father's slave or anyone else's slave. The Wyandot are going to adopt you as one of their own, or rather, one of us." Luther, overcome with emotion at the wonderful news, turned to the villagers, and the Clan Mothers in particular, and thanked them profusely in English, with words they did not understand.[104]

No time was lost in beginning the training of the adopted boys, including Isaac, to become hunters and then warriors. There was no time for the boys to reflect on their former White families and lament. The instruction began even as they struggled to speak and understand the Wandat language. First, they had to learn how to master the tools of hunting which were the weapons of war. Each of the boys was assigned an adult warrior mentor to teach them. This was Wyandot tradition. A warrior whose name was Bent Nose began by instructing Isaac and Adam together. The first steps involved how to use a bow and arrow, which neither of them had ever held prior to their capture. Hours were spent every day on learning how to string the bow with the sinew, then how to hold it and draw the sinew string back with measured strength. That was

---

[104] The Wyandot and the other woodland tribes of the Ohio Country had no prohibition about adopting people of differing skin color, such as African-American slaves who were either captured on the colonial frontier during periods of war, or had runaway from their masters on the frontier. Through adoption, they became equal members of the clan and tribe and were trained as warriors. One adopted former slave of note was Pompey, who became a Shawnee after being captured on the Virginia frontier during the French and Indian War. Pompey rose to the position of trusted advisor to the Shawnee chief Black Snake because he could speak English and translate for the chief, and he knew the habits and nature of White people from his former servitude.

relatively easy for Isaac and his brother Jonathan as they had held and used many tools on their farm, and thus already had some upper body strength. Adam Brown had no trouble with the bow, but his younger brother Sam did not possess enough wrist strength to keep it steady. Days were spent firing arrow after arrow at close targets that were moved further and further from the young archers once they had mastered the closest ones. It was laborious, and at times, boring work under the supervision of patient warriors selected by the clans to do the instruction and take their time. Nothing was rushed. Nothing was overlooked. Simply, each trainee had to accomplish the task at hand without complaint until it was done, before they could move on to the next challenge.

Bent Nose pointed out something of importance about the use of the Wyandot bow, and especially the arrows. He began speaking in Wandat which neither boy could understand. As Tarhe was busy with other matters, Bent Nose motioned for the boys to stay put till he returned. After several moments, Bent Nose came back with another warrior who appeared to be in his late teens. The two talked back and forth in Wandat till the youth, painted and dressed as a warrior, turned to the newly adopted and said, "I am Wyandot, I speak some English words to you I have been asked to do." Clearly, the warrior had not used English language for some time when he revealed to them, "My former name was Billy.[105] I now help Bent Nose teach you importance arrows." Isaac noted that the only thing about this warrior named Billy that hinted of his White heritage was his blue eyes. Billy took one of the bows and pointed out that the Wyandot purposely put a knot in the string of Wyandot bows. "Now look at arrow. The end of it opposite the head is a dimple, not a slit. Dimple fits over knot on string. This means Wyandot warrior can shoot arrows of Enemy but Enemy cannot shoot Wyandot arrow back because no have knot on bow string as Wyandot arrow not stay on Enemy bowstring." Isaac, more than the others, examined the arrows carefully as Billy spoke, and nodded that he understood. "Bent Nose says you

---

[105] William Ice was taken captive with his family on the South Branch of the Potomac River Valley in 1755 during the French and Indian War.

practice with both kinds till master both. One day you will go to war with other Wyandot boys against each other, two sides for practice, no deadly tips to arrows."[106] The talk of mastering the bow and going to war stirred a feeling of excitement in Isaac. It was a sense of freedom he had never felt before in his life back at the homestead with its drudgery of unending chores which was becoming a distant memory by each day's passing.

Because Jonathan was older than Isaac and possessed more strength in his arms and shoulders due to already entering puberty, he was the first to become proficient in the use of the bow. Jonathan improved to the point where he was assigned to accompany the hunters and learn their techniques of bringing down game, such as a deer, with a well-placed arrow. Jonathan, who had accompanied his father on a few occasions in the woodlands above Old Fields in the South Potomac Valley, had no experience hunting with a bow and arrow but he found it quick, though difficult, to learn. Approaching a deer or elk with stealth in preparation to strike them with an arrow was no easy feat. Isaac found the task easier in spite of his smaller size than Jonathan, once he had developed the extra upper body strength. Both boys noticed that most of the arrows given to them for use had flint arrowheads. They were told that arrowheads for war were fashioned from metal saved from burned out cooking pots or kettles that were beyond use or repair. The arrowheads were cut from the old pots and fashioned into a point that could be sharpened over and over by grinding a new edge on stone, which was impossible to do with a flint point.

In addition, nearly every day the boys engaged in foot races with other Native boys or long distance running through the woods to build up their lung capacity as well as stamina in their leg muscles. This was necessary conditioning for a warrior traveling on the network of trails that crisscrossed the wilderness everywhere. Tarhe explained, "Sometimes it takes many days for our warriors to reach an Enemy's land. We do so by traveling at a set brisk pace from dawn to dusk on the path with limited provision or rest. Upon reaching the Enemy's stronghold and conducting

---

106 LD-BOT-118-119.

warfare, our warriors must return as quickly as they came, often with captives, plunder, and our wounded with them, and in such a manner as to avoid a pursuing Enemy party from attacking us. Conditioning for such an enterprise is everything for a warrior. It is his duty to his family, his clan, and his nation, and to do so without complaint or shirking. Your fellow comrades will depend on you to pull your own weight and never jeopardize those in your party." Now, several months since their arrival in the Wyandot village, the boys were beginning to understand the Wandat language, even if their pronunciation of words was still awkward when they spoke. Their attempts often brought hearty laughs from the other Wyandot warriors. Isaac had an advantage over the others in learning the language. He had Ronyouquaines who spoke French, Wandat, Lenape, and some English words. Tarhe, of course, spoke Lenape also, but unlike Ronyouquaines, he disciplined himself to speak to Isaac only in Wandat.

One aspect of hunting that Isaac found particularly of interest was working with the other village boys his age and older when they were grouped together to flush out game. It was exciting for him because he had never had an opportunity to play with other boys his age in the woods back home. A plan was devised by the hunters when they found a particular area where an abundance of deer or elk had been spotted which they hoped to harvest. At some distance from that spot, the boys would spread out in positions along a V-shaped plan with the open ends of the 'V' on the far extremities. The hunters would hide themselves a mile or so from the potential game animals and wait until the boys began to advance, usually moving down a valley so that the animals would be forced to move away from the advancing line. In the process, the animals would be funneled towards the awaiting hunters. It was imperative that the boys stay in step with each other and not advance too quickly so that they ended up within the range of the hunters. This meant that Isaac had to keep the fellow to his left and to his right within eyesight at all times and move in unison with everyone else. After one exhausting yet successful hunt in which many deer were felled, Tarhe explained to Isaac that the hunting technique he had just taken part in was used with the same success in war.

"I was only fourteen, about your brother's age, when I first went to war with the warriors from our village against the English Braddock. We were allies of the Frenchmen from their fort at the Great Forks of the Ohio, but we paid little attention to their war tactics that were no different from the English. At the first encounter with the Red Coats, the Frenchmen stood upright in place to give and receive musket fire. However, our warriors quickly moved off into the woods on both sides of the path and began advancing on the flanks of the Red Coats as if they were deer. Eventually, this caused them to panic and turn, much like the deer in the woods that you helped drive today." "What happened then?" Isaac asked. "Why, we took our time and shot them down as they stood bewildered in the open ground of the trail they had just cut." Tarhe was silent for a moment. "They died in droves, not like men, not like warriors, but like helpless deer caught in a trap. Those English had that same wild look in their eyes as I have seen in deer, like those harvested today. It is the look of blind fear," Tarhe added. "No Wyandot warrior can ever possess that look, or turn their back on the Enemy and flee in panic. It is a law among our warriors that they never turn their back to the Enemy. Never." With that, the explanation was over.

Tarhe had his mind on disturbing news he wished not to share with anyone at the moment. While he knew that there were some Mingo, Shawnee, and Lenape war parties still attacking the Pennsylvania frontier in late summer, an army of English Red Coats were known to be coming to Detroit under a War Captain named Bradstreet. It was said that he was being sent to chastise those Natives who had supported Pontiac in his war against the English forts. But now, in the summer of 1764, the Wyandot were no longer supporting that ill-fated war. Yet Tarhe realized the Wyandot could be held accountable for the English deaths, since Pontiac and his Ottawas were no longer present. This army was to come by boat across the lake called Erie and would arrive in a couple of weeks, Tarhe figured. It would be impossible for the

Wyandot to oppose an army of any size that was being described by runners. The Wyandot had very little ammunition and not enough warriors to fight, meaning most would die if a fight developed. In addition, another English army was assembling at Fort Pitt in the Ohio Country. It was said that this army would be commanded by the War Captain Bouquet who had defeated the Native forces at the place called Bushy Run. Bouquet, it was told, would have not only Red Coat troops but the hated Virginian militia who were known to be demanding vengeance for the raids on their homes, much like that which Tarhe had conducted in the South Potomac Valley last year. It was said that this army was ordered to march directly into the Ohio Country across the Great Ohio River, to destroy all the Native villages they could find.

These threatening developments troubled Tarhe. What should his people do, he thought to himself? Though Tarhe was not a village Sachem, as a respected War Captain, Tarhe knew that his opinion held great weight among his people. There was much to consider, as the Wyandot people were spread out in several villages. The main village where Tarhe resided was on the south side of the Detroit River a few miles across from the fort. Teata's band of Wyandot, who favored the French Catholic priests, lived on the other side of the river in a village closer to the Fort. They had resisted for the longest time Pontiac's threats that their warriors join his rebellion or face his wrath. In addition, the Wyandot Sachem named Nicholas Orontony had taken his people's clan to the Sandusky River area and established a village many years before the war between the French and English in the year named 1747. The village was first located on land close to the lake before moving to the plains farther south on what was the upper reaches of the Sandusky River. Though Orontony had died in 1750, his Wyandot village had done more than survive. They were claiming a huge swath of land of the Ohio Country as their own and invited all Wyandot living elsewhere to join them. It was an offer that Tarhe thought to be enticing, now that more English were said to be coming to Detroit.[107] Tarhe's mind was deep in thought

---

107 LD-OBT, pages 90-92.

when Ronyouquaines entered their lodge with news. "Teata has just returned from the Haudenosaunee council at Niagara with the English man named Johnson and the huge assembly of many tribes from the Great Lakes and beyond. You should go, my husband, to hear what he has to say."[108] Ronyouquaines paused for a moment. "Teata is saying that a peace with the English has been achieved."

Teata met with the Sachems of both of the Wyandot villages in a formal council lodge. Tarhe sat listening in silence. Teata laid out before the council the terms of the treaty which were discussed at length by the Sachems. One sticking point that raised many eyebrows was the veiled threat that White captives of the Wyandot would have to be returned to the English as one of the conditions. That is when several of the Sachems requested to speak to the council, with each saying that they would never agree to that demand under any circumstances. Forcibly returning their adopted family members would never be possible. The kinship ties that had been established were too great to bend to that outrageous demand of the people the Wyandot had despised for so long. Tarhe thought to himself about Isaac The Eagle. He would never agree to returning this young man who was becoming like a son to him, and by all appearances, was embracing the Wyandot people and their way of life. "No," thought Tarhe. "I will take The Eagle, my family, and my clan and move far away from the reach of the English. Staying at the Detroit villages would only delay the English demand until they grew strong enough to destroy all of us." The discussion in council continued for several days. Every speaker had an opportunity to state their well-thought point of view for their people's future. However, the council was interrupted when a runner arrived with news that many English soldiers in a flotilla of batteaux had left Niagara[109] and were headed west following the shoreline of Erie Lake. The news was disconcerting, to say the least, and the council broke up.

---

108 This Niagara council went on for days, but primary concluded by late July.
109 Bradstreet left Fort Schlosser above Fort Niagara with 1,400 soldiers in batteaux on August 8, 1764.

The English army under their War Captain Bradstreet had stopped at the bay of Presque Isle and camped at the ruins of the old fort. There, Bradstreet had met with a delegation of Lenape and Shawnee deputies and held council for several days. He assured them that he and his army would not attack them if they all agreed to terms of peace. Tarhe and the Sachems at Detroit were kept informed of these developments from Wyandot agents who listened and watched. However, it still came as a shock on the 26th of August when the long string of English batteaux bringing reinforcements and provisions for the garrison at Fort Detroit came into view coming up the Detroit River. The Wyandot in Tarhe's village greeted the arriving English with shouting, whooping, and firing what little ammunition they could spare for hunting from their guns. However, Tarhe was not there to here the noisy salutation to the English. He, and his family and most of their clan were well on their way along the shore path to the Wyandot village on the Sandusky Plains. Being so close to more English arriving at Detroit brought a bitter taste to his mouth when he thought about it. They would be too close for comfort, and some might even seek Tarhe out to kill him for his past attacks against the English frontier, Tarhe thought. Simply, no good would come with his staying any longer at Detroit.

Isaac understood enough words of Wandat to know what was happening and why the Wyandot with Tarhe were moving, taking with them only what they could carry or pack on horses. In all, Isaac's adjustment to the Wyandot way of life was becoming easier by the day. His training lessons with his warrior mentor were something Isaac looked forward to. Playing war with the boys his own age gave him an exhilarating feeling he had never felt before whether they were hunting for deer in the woods or hunting for men of an unsuspecting Enemy. Isaac learned that the Wyandot called it "the chase." In fact, there were moments of euphoria for Isaac when he was successful at any of the tasks given him in warrior training in which he could outdo the other boys, and especially his older brother, Jonathan. No more did Isaac have to spend his daylight hours doing tedious and exhausting field work in his father's crop fields. In the Wyandot world, only the women and girls labored at farming the crops of corn, beans, and squash which Ronyouquaines said were called, "The Three Sisters." Undesirable captives for adoption were occasionally kept as "slaves" by the Clan Mothers to help with the laborious task of raising food crops. Isaac thought it odd, if not humorous, that Luther, who had spent all of his adult life toiling in the fields as a slave to the English, was now forbidden to work in the Native fields because of his newly-established identity of a warrior-in-training. "I don't know, Mr. Isaac, who or what I am at the moment, but I am so happy for my aching back that I'm not doing no more hoeing," Luther had remarked to Isaac, with a big grin on his face.

The move to the Upper Sandusky village had been an arduous undertaking for everyone, but one of necessity. The Wyandot with Tarhe knew that many more of their nation would join them as soon as the English began making demands of the Natives surrounding Detroit. Teata would not be able to resist the powerful persuasion of the English and their force of arms if needed to back up that persuasion. At least at the Upper Sandusky village, the Wyandot would be out of reach of the arms of the English. However, a new English threat reached Tarhe just as they were finishing the construction of lodges and cabins before the warriors prepared to leave for the important hunt. The rumor of an English army assembling at Fort Pitt appeared to be true. Runners brought news that the English War Captain named Bouquet had been only temporarily delayed in setting out into the Ohio Country due to a lack of enough provisions arriving from the East. This disconcerting news, which had been heard before, had been dismissed as nothing more than rumors when it failed to materialize. Tarhe was caught off-guard. He realized, in retrospect, that he should have found out the truth for himself. English traders from Fort Pitt had been bringing goods, and especially needed ammunition to the Wyandot at Upper Sandusky with regularity since the peace brokered with Sir William Johnson at Niagara in the summer. However, not one had spoken about a massive army being prepared for an invasion of the Ohio Country. This only served to remind Tarhe of why he mistrusted all English, whether trader, diplomat, or soldier.

Tarhe immediately sent his trusted scouts southeast to the Lenape and Mingo villages to find out what they could from their Native brethren and their own observations concerning the intention and strength of this English army at Fort Pitt. They were not long in returning while Tarhe was still out on the hunt and was called back to council. Apparently, in early October the huge English army had left Fort Pitt.[110] Tarhe learned with relief that the English were not headed to Upper Sandusky, but rather on a straight course for the Lenape, Mingo, and Shawnee combined villages on the Muskingum River. It could only mean that the War Captain Bouquet was intending on attacking those villages in revenge for the siege of Fort Pitt and the raids against the English frontier. A discussion was held among the Wyandot headmen. Isaac sat in the rear of the council lodge to hear what was of utmost importance to everyone. When it was Tarhe's opportunity to speak, he stood and said to the silenced council, "We must take this English threat seriously until we see what it is they are intending to do, and whether or not it involves direct war with us. It is important for our warriors to know that with the fall hunt underway. There will be little, if any, ammunition left to oppose the English if they decide to attack us once they are done with the other tribes, who have faired no better than us in acquiring the means to defend themselves."

A murmur passed through the crowded council lodge as Tarhe remained silent for the moment, gathering his thoughts for what he next had to say. "What weighs heavily in our favor is that it is very late in the season for the English to be campaigning and they still have not reached their appointed destination at the Muskingum. By the time they get there, and if they attack the tribes in the surrounding area, I believe they will have no time left to pay us a visit.

---

110 Bouquet's army was comprised of regular troops and Virginia and Pennsylvania militia, totaling 1,150 men. It left Fort Pitt on October 3, 1764 and headed along a main Native trail for the Muskingum River Valley where many mixed tribal villages were located.

By then, the weather will have turned against them. I am sorry to say that our kin brothers and sisters with the Lenape and Mingo in particular are going to feel the wrath of the vengeful English first. However, we will not be able to come to their aid even if they should ask of us to do so." Many heads nodded at Tarhe's words. "I ask our Sachems and Clan Mothers to consider our situation here with winter approaching soon upon us. I advise that we wait to see what the English will do. If the situation becomes dire for us from the threat of the English, we will retire to the Wyandot village on the Maumee River to the west. In the act of doing so, we will draw the English further and further away from the path to Fort Pitt, and their supplies of food that they must survive on. I don't believe that they would be so foolish and vengeful to pursue us there." With that Tarhe sat down as the council heads deliberated into the night. In the morning, Tarhe found his advice had been chewed over and taken.

Chapter Nine
The Shaman

Word arrived at Upper Sandusky that Bouquet's army had reached the Muskingum River after ten days journey from Fort Pitt. Once there, Bouquet marched his army down the river until an area of broad meadows was found where the English could set up a large camp and graze their cattle and horses. There Bouquet met with a deputation of Sachem chiefs and War Captains from the Mingo, the Lenape, and the Shawnee who wished to speak to Bouquet in council. It was said that Bouquet agreed to parley but kept his soldiers on alert with arms ready. The orator Guyasuta of the Mingo acted as spokesman for the combined tribes and gave a speech suing for peace with the English, saying, "We now put away all evil from our hearts; and we hope that your mind and ours will once more be united together."[111] Bouquet was unmoved upon hearing Guyasuta's words, it was reported. Rather, Bouquet replied angrily, saying, "Sachems, war-chiefs, and warriors, the excuses you have offered are frivolous and unavailing, and your conduct is without defense or apology."[112] Tarhe heard all this, but what mattered most to him was Bouquet's

---

111 Actually, Guyasuta spoke at length, giving a number of excuses for the Native participation in Pontiac's war, none of which Bouquet believed true at all.

112 Bouquet replied angrily at length, citing the numerous deadly attacks upon the frontier that occurred in the past year.

threat, which was repeated to Tarhe word for word. "I am now come among you to force you to make atonement for the injuries you have done to us. I have brought with me the relatives of those you have murdered. They are eager for vengeance, and nothing restrains them from taking it but my assurance that this army will not leave your country until you have given them ample satisfaction. I give you twelve days from this date to deliver into my hands all the prisoners in your possession, without exception." Bouquet's demand was said to have a chilling effect upon the Natives in his presence. After issuing his directive, it was said by those who brought the news to Upper Sandusky that Bouquet refused to council further. He told his men to prepare to break camp in the morning. Bouquet was moving his army further downriver to be closer to the Native villages in case he needed to attack and destroy them after twelve days.

"So that is what the English want," Tarhe exclaimed. "They want all their White flesh back which Natives have taken in war and opened their hearts to by adoption." There was a panicked reaction at Upper Sandusky once the terms of the English peace were circulated among the people by those who had attended the English council. However, there was good news also to be reported along with the bad. The English commander had been heard to say to the tribes who were present, "Your allies, the Ottawas, Ojibwas, and Wyandots have begged for peace and the Six Nations have leagued themselves with us." Tarhe realized that Bouquet was referring to Johnson's peace treaty that Teata had attended and spoke in Johnson's presence. Teata gave his assurance for the Wyandot people as a whole that they wished for peace with the English. Tarhe realized he had needlessly objected to Teata taking it upon himself to speak for all the Wyandot Sachems. Johnson, who lived in the settlement adjacent to the Mohawks on the frontier of New York colony, did not know the specifics of Wyandot protocol. He mistakenly assumed that Teata was speaking for all Wyandots when he was in fact not. That had inadvertently worked to an advantage for Tarhe and the Wyandot at Upper Sandusky. It also revealed that Bouquet, while focused on the former captives of the Lenape, Shawnee, and Mingo, had no real idea that the Wyandot possessed the greatest

The Shaman | 117

number of adopted former White captives of any nation in the Ohio Country.[113]

Tarhe wanted to see for himself what would happen at the new camp of Bouquet. He dared not take with him anyone who had been a former captive like Isaac or Adam lest they should be seen by one of the hundreds of soldiers present and seized on the spot by the Whites. Because the Wyandot had not been present at the initial Native council and been asked to turn over their captives, Tarhe determined not to identify himself but to only observe the proceedings. Day after day, Natives arrived at Bouquet's camp with weeping family members presenting their adopted White captive to Bouquet's authorities. At times the wailing of those who had lived with the Shawnee and Lenape were as loud as those village members who were saying goodbye in heart-wrenching floods of tears. It was an unbearable scene that the English seemed to be rejoicing in, and that the Natives were forced to endure. Tarhe could also see that the Virginian militiamen that he called "Long Knives" wished for nothing more than last-minute Native resistance to provide them with the opportunity to shoot down as many "Injuns" as they could with impunity. Those men knew that the return of White prisoners was little consolation to them. Many family members had been killed during the frontier attacks on their cabins regardless of the fact that the British government had mandated by law that settling west of the crest of the Alleghenies was forbidden under the official British Proclamation of 1763 issued the previous year.[114]

By mid-November, with the weather turning much colder, Bouquet, now in possession of over 400 White captives who had been turned over to him, prepared his army to break camp and return to Fort Pitt. While Bouquet knew that he did not have all of the captives held by the Natives, he did have an assurance from

---

113 It has been pointed out to the author on numerous occasions and by several individuals that the Wyandot had assimilated the greatest number of White captives of any nation.

114 The Royal Proclamation of 1763 was issued by King George III on October 7, 1763 as an attempt to alleviate the Native problem with settlers illegally entering on Native lands. Unfortunately, the British Government had no troops on the colonial frontier to enforce the terms of the treaty claim.

the Lenape, Shawnee, and Mingo, that the remaining White people would be returned to Fort Pitt in the spring. Bouquet enforced that agreement by taking with him hostages from the tribes to hold until their obligation was fulfilled. Tarhe was satisfied that the Wyandot were out of the range of Bouquet's demands. Tarhe was sure that the wily English Captain probably had heard from his spies that the Wyandot were holding a number of White people whom he believed were prisoners of the Wyandots. Tarhe thought to himself, "It is foreign for the English to ever believe that their own people would want to stay with the Wyandot and never return. They have never lived with our people. They do not understand us at all." He asked himself, "Why would an English woman who was an indentured washerwoman on the frontier, then captured by the Wyandot and adopted into the tribe as a free woman, want to return to the people who would never accept her as anything else than an indentured washerwoman?" Tarhe recalled an adopted former English servant woman saying to a newly-arrived captive, "I'm free to come and go as I wish here. I can marry who I want and divorce them if I grow tired of them. Most of all, I am beholden to no one."[115] Regardless of what the White Virginians thought about all this in relation to the Wyandot, Tarhe knew that Bouquet must return his army as soon as possible rather than visit the Wyandot to press for the return of captives. It simply was just too late in the season. Tarhe had taken the opportunity to assess the army's provisions. Soon they would be out of food.

True to Tarhe's assessment, Bouquet and his army re-crossed the Muskingum with their captives in tow and headed northeast on the trail leading to Fort Pitt and the colonial frontier. During the first night of their encampment, dozens of repatriated captives slipped through the sentries and vanished into the wilderness to return to their former Native families, much to the embarrassment of the soldiers and their commander. The English were perplexed that White people whom the army had just liberated were turning their backs on their own people to go back to the savages. It was beyond their comprehension. Tarhe learned from the Native spies shadowing the

---

115 This is an actual documented statement taken from a story-board the author viewed at the Fort Pitt Museum 2016 Captives Exhibition display.

withdrawing army, that every night in succession, captives would escape, regardless of the security measures that Bouquet tightened to prevent those fleeing. Tarhe also learned that there were many family reunions at Fort Pitt once Bouquet returned with those former captives who either chose not to escape or wished to reunite with colonials. Fathers and mothers found long-lost sons and daughters; husbands met with wives they had not seen in years who were changed in so many ways. It made Tarhe think of the Native families across the breadth of the Ohio Country who were now grieving for kin they had been forced to give up, especially children. Tarhe also heard something that reminded him of the cruel nature of the Whites. At Fort Pitt and elsewhere, any children not claimed immediately by family members were sold into seven-year indenture contracts by authorized agents of the Pennsylvania colony who did so seeking to gain profit for themselves on the backs of children's plight. The very thought of it brought a taste of disgust to Tarhe's mouth.

Upon his return to Upper Sandusky, Tarhe met with the Sachems in council to discuss what should be done once the snows of winter began to melt in the spring. It was agreed that the Wyandot Clan Mothers should go from clan to clan and ask any adopted former White captives if they wished to return. Those who voluntarily wished to do so would be taken in the spring of the coming year[116] to satisfy the English demand for the return of their flesh. However, it was agreed without question that the majority of adopted former captives not be forcibly returned. If the English Captain demanded more people be returned, then the Wyandot would move those people, like Isaac and dozens of others, to a place far beyond the reach of the English. And it went without saying that if the English marched their soldiers to the Upper Sandusky, that the Wyandot would consider that an act of war, and attack them before they ever got close. However, winter brought an end to the matter. Everyone, including Tarhe, settled into winter village life as the snows closed the paths of the Ohio Country. This gave Tarhe much needed time with Ronyouquaines who suffered from on-and-off bouts of

---

116 Bouquet requested that remaining captives who were not turned over to him in the fall of 1764 be returned to Fort Pitt by late spring of 1765.

illness. More than anything else, Tarhe wished to spend cherished moments with his only child, Myeerah, who had grown by leaps and bounds during Tarhe's constant travel the past year.

Isaac, too, enjoyed the confines of winter village life. He listened to the stories told around the lodges of the rich traditions and history of the Wyandot people. Those stories told to him by Elders traced their tribal history all the way back to many migrations since leaving the Canadas during the war with the Haudenosaunee and their Dutch allies,[117] before the arrival of the English. There were many nights of singing, story-telling, and the playing of games by clan members around the lodge fires which Isaac enjoyed immensely. Isaac heard the Creation Story of the Wyandot, which took many nights to be recited. An elderly Shaman with a wrinkled, tattooed face, told the story as all gathered about and listened intently. "A woman of the Sky People, named the Woman Who Fell From Above, gave birth to twin sons, the Good Twin and the Evil Twin. They, in turn, created the manifest world called the Great Island that to this day resides on the back of a Big Turtle that we live upon. The Good Twin and the Evil Twin quarreled over their creations, which resulted in a big fight between them. Finally, The Evil Twin was defeated and died by falling on the antlers of Deer. To honor the memory of his brother, the Good Twin restored the Great Island to a balance that contained both good and bad. This brought to the emerging Native people the balanced seasons of winter and summer, friend and enemy, and life and death."[118] It was an enthralling story that Isaac could grasp because he was constantly immersed in the language which brought the stories to life.

---

117 This occurred to the ancestors of the Wyandot in the mid-1600's in southern Ontario who were repeatedly attacked by large Iroquois war parties armed with Dutch muzzle-loading muskets against the villages and few French allies to oppose the onslaught. This was later called "The Beaver Wars" and the war was a loss for the Wyandot people who were forced to flee to the Great Lakes northwest to avoid complete annihilation. The Iroquois sought to defeat all surrounding tribes, including the French, and assume total control over the beaver fur trade for themselves.

118 LD-TTIG, pages 1-2; LD-BOT, pages 1-15.

The Shaman | 121

Around the communal fires in the lodges that winter, Isaac also learned about the clans of the Wyandot. When a person was adopted into the Wyandot people, they were chosen by a family or assigned to a family in need of someone to replace a family member who had died. That was determined by the elder women of one of the seven clans of the Wyandot, each which came into existence many generations past. There was the Big Turtle Clan, the Little Turtle, the Deer, the Wolf, the Bear, the Porcupine, and the Snake Clan. Each clan originated from a supernatural animal deity that gave the clan its name. In time, clans grew to become collections of interrelated families; a kinship which they shared with each other. Each clan was self-sufficient, with its own clan government, traditions and even religious practices. "Because the Wyandot people are created from the Mother, the clans are ruled by the mothers," Tarhe's mother told Isaac. "Clan Mothers decide so much of how we conduct our daily lives," she continued. "One woman is the head of the household, and she is always the eldest woman. She is what the English and French call a Matriarch. The Clan Mother owns all the property of the household, whether that be a multi-family lodge house or cabin. When she dies, all the property is inherited by her eldest daughter."

Isaac learned that the Clan Mother's household consists of all her daughters and granddaughters, along with their mates. The man is but a houseguest in the Clan Mother's longhouse. While the man is not submissive to her, he is nonetheless very respectful.[119] If divorce is needed to end the marriage, he is forced to leave immediately with only his clothes and hunting weapons. He goes back to the clan lodge of his own mother. His wife keeps everything else and is free to marry again. The children, if there are any, stay with the mother, to be raised under the rule of the Matriarch, and her court, without question. These Clan Mothers tell the warriors when they can go to war, and when they cannot, because the men always want to fight. The woman telling this story turned and said, "Isaac, we women know that you men do not know yourselves, or your nature. In fact, you are blind to it. You would fight your petty wars of vengeance until there was no one left in the village. It is we women who give

---
119 LD-TTIF, page 118.

birth to the warriors and mourn for them when they are killed in battle. We decide when it is time for you to go to war, and when it is time to put the war club down and go hunt." She continued. "That is because the Clan Mothers are the caretakers of our clan traditions which are law. It is we who request of warriors to bring us captives for adoption to replace our lost souls from injury, disease, and warfare. That is how you came here by one of our traditions; by one of our laws. And look at what a good fit you are. One day you will take a wife and hopefully fulfill another of our traditions. We expect you to sire many children for our clan and our people," she chuckled. "And they in turn will take care of you in old age."

Night after night around the lodge fire, Isaac learned more about the clan way of life. It was hard for him to remember it all. He was told that each clan kept a collection of clan names that were given to newborn children or adoptees during the Green Corn Ceremony, which was held once a year, usually in late summer.[120] That person would carry that name for their lifetime, and upon death, the name would return to the clan, to be given again to a new member. "Your name, The Eagle is one of our Porcupine Clan names," Tarhe's mother explained to Isaac one day when discussing the clan. "In our Wyandot tribe, which is a collection of all of our clans, the overall tribal War Chief appoints the tribal Warpole. He can only come from a War Chief Captain of the Porcupine or Snake clans. My son, Tarhe, is our Porcupine War Chief. One day he may become the overall Warpole of the Wyandot," she noted.[121] Isaac tried to remember the other important things about the clan that would guide him in the days ahead. A man could not marry a woman in his own clan under the penalty of death. An adopted White man could not actively engage in tribal politics, or become a village chief chosen by the Clan Mothers. Each clan was different in the way of doing things. They had their own traditions that other clans were not obligated to follow or be accountable for.[122]

---

120 That date of the feast, by tradition, was held in later summer, on August 15th or thereabouts.
121 LD-TTIF, pp. 108-109.
122 LD-TTIF page 29.

The Shaman | 123

Sees Many Visions

Most importantly, each clan had their own healers with their own healing practices that were protected secrets that clan members were not allowed to talk about. These healers were called Shaman, and each Shaman had their own particular expertise in some area and manner. Some were adept at curing illness with medicinal plants and herbs known to them. Others could heal spiritual and mental illnesses. Certain Shamans had the power to leave their bodies and guide the souls of the dead to find their resting place or unity with the Great Spirit. Other Shaman could defend against any sorcerers in the village who might be casting evil spells on unsuspecting people. Isaac learned that still other Shaman possessed the ability to enter the supernatural world on their own accord by detaching their spirit from the body and enter different realms of the Spirits. Tarhe's mother gave an example. "A young warrior in training from the Porcupine Clan got into a fight with another boy from the Deer Clan, and was wounded by a blow to the head. He was treated by a medicine healer and the surface wound healed in a short period of time. However, the boy fell into a deep sleep and could not be awakened. We summoned a clan Shaman who entered the spirit world by a means known to no one, to see if our boy was afflicted by evil spirits. After some time, the Shaman returned to consciousness and reported that indeed, an evil spirit from the Deer Clan offender was found hovering near the spirit of our sleeping son. After an incantation in the Spirit World, the evil spirit was ordered out by our Shaman. Within an hour, our Porcupine Clan son regained consciousness without any more troubles. That is the power of our Shaman. What is most interesting is that the practitioner we summoned was a woman. Remember, Isaac The Eagle, a Shaman can be either a man or a woman in our clan and in most clans of the Wyandot."[123]

Isaac asked Tarhe's mother about the Great Spirit and the Manitou that he had already heard spoken of, but did not know what it meant. "Isaac The Eagle, you have an inquisitive mind. It is not so easy for me to put into Wandat words an answer for what you ask. That is because the Great Spirit is a Supreme Spirit, the

---

123 LD-TTIF, page 44.

Maker of All, who cannot adequately be described. He is in that rock, and in that tree. He has created everything that we can see with our eyes and know with our minds. His greatest creation through the works of the Good Twin is the people on this Turtle Island. The Great Spirit rules over this world of his creation and all the creatures in it. I have heard that it was said long ago when our people lived to the North before the war with the Haudenosaunee that the Black Robes who called themselves Jesuits thought our Great Spirit was like their God of Jesus. Of course, that is ridiculous. The Jesuits knew nothing about our people or the Great Spirit. They only wanted to attract us with their word-books to their God that came out of those books. We had no use for their Jesus God. Our Great Spirit is right here, all around us, in all things great and small. Our one Spirit has made all things and to whom we give honor for his bounty in our feasts and dances.[124] He gives us food as a gift to all His people which is life. However, Isaac, Manitous are something different for they are energy and animal spirits that visit us and speak to us in their own way of things that are yet to come and things that will be during our life. Manitous guide us through life and into death. They point us in the direction of the Supreme spirit of all people, and of all Manitous. It is a wonderful thing to find a Manitou to guide one's way in this life.[125] I hope you find yours. This has been much for me to say to you, and much more for you to think about. So, I am done." Isaac thought to himself. "She is right. She has said much more than I can understand."

Isaac was adept at learning Wandat, and so took part in the traditional songs and prayers that were recited around the lodge fires with zeal, hoping that his pronunciations were right. Isaac and Tohunehowetu Adam Brown would sit together with Adam's younger brother Sam at their side. But Isaac made note to himself that his own brother, Jonathan, always stood or sat in the rear watching, but not taking part in the festivities. So, it came as no

---

124 LD-TTIF, pp. 131-133.

125 The idea of a Manitou spirit-guide could be considered comparable to the idea of a guardian angel.

surprise to Isaac that in the spring, one of the adopted people wished to return to the White colonials. It was Jonathan, at age sixteen, who revealed to Isaac his intention to go. "I want to return home, to see Papa and our family," Jonathan said to Isaac in English.[126] Isaac glared at his brother for the longest time before replying. He was angry that his brother was talking to him in English language about the old ways that were long past. Replying in Wandat, Isaac emphatically said, "My family is here with the Wyandot. I recognize no other kin that you talk about in the language I despise. Tarhe, my Uncle, has told me that when we come of age, if we wish to go, we can go.[127] However, know that if you go now, I will not recognize you as my brother, who you will no longer be." With that, Isaac spat on the ground in front of Jonathan's feet and then turned his head away. Jonathan knew Wandat well enough to know Isaac's state of mind and meaning, which would be an irreversible conviction.

Jonathan kept his word and left with English traders in early summer for Fort Pitt, with another former adoptee, an older woman, who wished to return. Tarhe had understood the young

---

126 Historically, the story of Jonathan's captivity and repatriation is very problematic with conflicting assumptions and no proof. Even the question of his capture by the Wyandot at the same time as Isaac is questionable with some sources saying yes and others saying no. There is also an undocumented reference to Jonathan's ransom by some unknown White person at an undisclosed time and price which has no verifiable fact to it. If it was William Zane, Jonathan's father, or his agent, how would they know what nation and what village Jonathan was living in, and then how would someone get there from the South Branch of the Potomac Valley when there are no roads, no settlers, and no one who could speak whatever language it may be to be able to communicate and negotiate for the ransom. Under such questionable circumstances, possibly a trader to the Wyandot from Fort Pitt could have conceivably negotiated for the teen, but for what reason. Part of that highly suspect narrative claims that the unnamed tribe in question was willing to part with Jonathan but not Isaac. There are authors who have claimed that Jonathan escaped his captors, thus perpetuating the widely held post-war belief that all captives wished to escape the 'savages' and waited for the right opportunity, as Daniel Boone did after his capture and adoption by the Shawnee chief Black Snake.

127 In correspondence with LD, he states that the Wyandot, in general, would not keep an adoptee against their will, and allowed them the opportunity to leave, rather than escape, when they "came of age," meaning old enough to fend for themselves and make decisions for themselves.

man correctly from the beginning. He could see that Jonathan had not taken well to adoption in spite of all the benefit of the doubt and support from his disappointed Wyandot family. However, Tarhe also knew that having a so-called warrior amongst them who's heart was not in it when others were depending upon him with their lives, would end up turning into disloyalty and cowardice that Tarhe and the other warriors could never tolerate. "Better your brother leaves now on his own accord before one of us, perhaps you, are forced to sink our hatchet in his skull for turning his back on the Enemy and his fellow warriors. It is for the best, my Nephew," Tarhe explained to Isaac. "Do not despair. Your brother is blinded by the shine of his Whiteness.[128] He is not the first one to wish to leave because they have no rapport with our Native ways. The thoughts in his head are more like that of an adult White man. It is hard, if not impossible, once the English words are rigid in the mind for adopted adult males to truly understand our Native way of life.[129] They are slaves to the English way of thinking about everything. I've watched him closely; that is how your brother thinks. He did not like the idea that a warrior, upon marriage, must go to live in the home of his in-laws. He quietly balked at the notion that Clan Mothers are women of great importance in our tribe, not like that of the English where women are the slaves of men and own nothing. Jonathan was careful about what he said so as to not betray his thoughts. However, a man's thoughts are betrayed not by his words but by his actions. Jonathan held himself back from us. It is for the best that he is gone, my Nephew. In time, you will come to see the truth of my words."

Tarhe changed the subject. "Now that peace has once again been agreed upon with the English, for the sake of our young men like yourself who wish to become warriors by proving themselves in battle, we must think of mustering our energies to go to war. We will attack the Cherokee who before too long will be coming our way to destroy our village and take our women and children

---

128 LD-TTIG page 134, an explanation in Native terms for the reason why adoption was not led to assimilation.
129 LD-TTIF page 26,

away as their captives. My nephew, Isaac The Eagle, the time has come for you to go to war." By mid-summer, many English traders from Fort Pitt were bringing their strings of packhorses laden with everything from household goods to bolts of cloth to trade. For the first time that Tarhe could remember in a while, gunpowder and lead musket ball was in copious supply, enough for hunting for meat to fill their stomachs and acquiring furs to be dressed for trade. And of course, ammunition was now ample for making war on the Cherokee to the south. Tarhe wanted to create several war parties for the campaign, so that the young men like Isaac and Adam and others could gain experience as warriors. Tarhe would spread them out amongst the veteran warriors who would be charged with keeping an eye on them on their first warrior mission. As it turned out, when all preparations were ready, there would be two parties. Tarhe would lead one of them, and Bent Nose the other.

Chapter Ten
War with the Cherokee

The chosen warriors and their young apprentices were secluded from the rest of the village after having said their goodbyes to family and clan. The first step in their preparations was for all of them to begin a fast. This was to focus their minds on the task ahead. Then, the oldest of the warriors led the others in the singing of war songs. After a night of prayers beseeching the Great Spirit and one's personal Manitou for courage, endurance, and safe conduct, the warriors arose the next morning for the war dance to be held in the village. A large post had been sunk in the center of town and painted black and vermillion. The warriors dressed in their war attire which consisted of a breechcloth, leggings, and moccasins. A blouse or a blanket could be worn over the shoulder if the weather turned cold, but otherwise, the warriors would be traveling light to Cherokee lands. Before the war dance could begin, the warriors must paint themselves in a warrior's manner. Tarhe instructed each man according to his clan. Wooden bowls of red and black powder mixed with sunflower oil were brought forward by the women for the task at hand. "Red is the color that means our life," the head Clan Mother said. "Black is the color of war and death; the death of the Enemy, and a sign that you as a warrior are prepared to accept your own death."

Tarhe had prepared them for this. He told the young warriors-to-be that they must ready themselves for going to war by painting themselves, both face and body, as warriors had done for generations in the past. The application of war paint was an important ritual and part of becoming a warrior, Isaac and Adam were told. They were handed the bowls, that contained sunflower oil mixed either with red ochre or charcoal, in which to daub their fingers. "Painting oneself is powerful medicine," Tarhe said.[130] "We paint ourselves to represent our clan, our spirit guides, and our accomplishments as a warrior. Painting one's face, one's body, and one's hair is a prelude to warfare. I will show you how to do it. However, the final painting of your war face will be done when we arrive close to the Enemy. Then we will apply our battle face meant to bring fear to our Enemy when they behold us. That final face marks our spirit transformation into the warrior state of mind that is capable of showing no mercy to the Enemy, and can take their lives and scalps without hesitation. A warrior must be prepared to fight to the death and never turn his back on the Enemy or his comrades. A warrior must remember that he is to never allow himself to be taken alive in battle. Never!" Tarhe reiterated. "If you are captured by the Cherokee Enemy, I can tell you that they will burn you slowly over a hot fire so your flesh is roasted from your bones while you are still alive. That is what awaits you if captured. To be captured in battle, or to turn your back on the Enemy and run is a sign of cowardice, and strictly forbidden. Remember that at all times, and discipline your mind as you paint yourself. To paint your war face will transform you completely to do the things of war that are terrible and unspeakable to your family. Hopefully, you will have an opportunity to see what I mean in the days to come."[131]

---

130 LD-TTIF page 148

131 There is evidence to suggest that the final painting of the face in a hideous manner was a psychological tool to affect a transformation in the person to be able to kill and maim, which they would otherwise be hesitant to do as a family man. After battle, the washing of the paint from the face was a reversal of the process, so that the warrior could be turned back into the

Next, the entire village assembled around the war post. This was the signal that the war dance was to begin. Isaac judged that the pole which was sunk upright in the ground was ten feet high or more. The bark had been carefully stripped off and the inner surface of the pole was painted black with streaks of red winding around it that reminded him of snakes. Bent Nose was the first warrior to lead the circle of warriors around the post. He began by singing his war song in which the others joined him in reciting the many deeds of Wyandot warriors in battle. Isaac and Adam imitated the cadence and foot movements of the warriors ahead of them in the circle as they brought up the rear. Then one by one, beginning with Bent Nose, the warriors approached the war post and struck it with their war club or tomahawk as if the post was the hated Enemy. Isaac took note that some of the warriors struck the post and then stabbed at it as if to run it through to show to everyone exactly what he would do to a real Enemy, when he encountered one. When it was Isaac's turn, he struck the post with the ball of his war club and made the motion of firing an imaginary arrow at it, which met with approving murmurs from everyone. This was repeated several times during the day.

The next morning, the warriors assembled with their lightweight traveling gear and their weapons. As neither Isaac or Adam had muskets, both boys carried their unstrung bows with a quiver of arrows over their shoulder. Tucked in their sashes were their wooden war clubs. Tarhe, who was at the head of the two combined war parties, gave the word to leave. Armed with his musket and iron tomahawk, Tarhe began to sing the departing traveling song. Isaac knew that song was a prayer to the Great Spirit to watch over their war party and the people of the village that they were leaving behind. Then the line of fourteen warriors followed behind Tarhe in single file. When the song was over, Tarhe let out a hideous war-whoop. Each warrior, in turn, repeated the war-whoop so that the village was informed that the warriors were departing. It was a time-honored tradition that every war party

---

family man without the reminder of what he had done in war. This process can be likened to lessening the PTSD of the returning veteran from combat.

Adam Brown Tohunehowetu

leaving their village had taken part in since time immemorial. Near the edge of the village, Tarhe let a single shot ring out from his musket and each man with a gun fired theirs once according to their position in the line. From the corner of Isaac's eye, he could see Ronyouquaines with Myeerah waving goodbye to him.

Tarhe took his men across the Ohio River to a branch of the Great Warrior Path that ran from north to south just west of the beginning of the Allegheny Mountains which some called the Seneca Warpath. This was a well-worn trail that Haudenosaunee Nation used to go to war against not only the Cherokee but the Catawba as well who were allies of the Cherokee. The path was very old. Many people, including the Cherokee war parties coming north, traveled the path. Tarhe knew that Enemy war parties could appear at any time on a twist or turn of the trail.[132] For that reason, Tarhe advised Bent Nose to scout ahead on the trail in case there were Cherokee surprises awaiting the Wyandots. Bent Nose would take an experienced warrior with him to help. If trouble was encountered, one warrior would engage the Enemy while the other would withdraw at a run to warn Tarhe. Tarhe had in mind to raid the densely populated area that the Cherokee called in English words, "The Overhill Cherokee" villages.[133] Tarhe told his men that the main Cherokee town was called Chota. It was the capital of the Cherokee nation as a whole, with many smaller villages located nearby. "It is a very dangerous mission we are upon. There are many Cherokee people everywhere, and their warriors will be looking for us or for sign of our presence. We must be very careful and patient above all else. A misstep could cost us our lives. A miscalculation will force our immediate withdrawal. The most fearsome of the Cherokee warriors will pursue to attempt to catch us and annihilate us. We will carefully scout the Cherokee warriors and pick the time and place for a lightning strike and then

---

132 This trail passed through the present town of Elkins, WV, and had many branches, including the branches that led to the South Branch of the Potomac River Valley which Tarhe had used to bring Isaac north after the Wyandot raid of 1763.

133 Overhill villages were in what is now eastern Tennessee.

we will vanish." Isaac could feel his pulse pick up at Tarhe's words. He was filled with both excited anticipation and some sense of fear, all at the same time.

The attack on the Cherokee was a success. Tarhe carefully chose to surprise a Cherokee hunting party he had scouted rather than outright attack the heavily defended villages. He knew the Cherokee method of hunting was the same as the Wyandot. So he spread his two parties carefully to allow the Cherokee to come to his men without suspecting a trap. Once the attack opened with the signal from Bent Nose, Tarhe joined his second group for a prepared ambush along the trail Bent Nose would withdraw by. It was a strategy that Tarhe had used many times in the past which always seemed to work. Luckily, it did once again. While they did not take any prisoners captive during the attack, Tarhe's war party was able to kill four Cherokee and take their scalps. Isaac and Adam got much needed experience at the same time. In fact, Isaac had wounded a Cherokee with one of his arrows that pierced the man's left thigh. However, his fellow warriors were able to extricate their wounded comrade. It was a triumph for Isaac that did not go unnoticed by his companions who bragged about him on the trip home. There would be much celebrating in the village upon their return, and most importantly, none of the warriors with Tarhe's party had been killed or wounded.

That autumn of the year 1765 and well into 1766, Isaac devoted himself to hunting with a passion previously unseen. He had become exceptionally adept with his bow and arrows. Isaac had mastered from Tarhe the method of stealth in the forest so as to be able to approach a game animal, whether deer or elk, without being detected. As a result, Isaac was able to provide Tarhe's immediate family and that of his own clan with much as much meat as they needed. In addition, the animal hides, when dressed and tanned, would allow Isaac enough trade equity in furs to purchase his first smoothbore musket, gunpowder, and lead ball from the English traders. Many traders were now arriving on a regular basis from Fort Pitt since the war was over. Soon Isaac was hunting with his gun, and able to take it with him on war parties against the Cherokee. Because Isaac was becoming known as an excellent marksman, he was chosen to accompany war parties again and again. Several times that summer, and the next, Isaac joined the Wyandot against the Overhill Cherokee who were said to be vexed by the stealth of the warriors from the north who always surprised them and managed to inflict casualties. By the early winter of the English year 1767, Isaac The Eagle, at the age of fourteen, was making a name for himself and turning heads among the tribe at Upper Sandusky for his steady hand with a gun. Isaac was quickly proving himself a man as Tarhe had done at the same age.

On that previous fall raid to the Cherokee, Isaac noticed something that disturbed him which he later discussed with Tarhe. "I thought that the English King across the great water told his English children to obey his command that White settlers were not to cross the crest of the mountains and settle on Native land to the west. But I have seen that they are doing so; far many more than I have ever seen before," said Isaac. "My Nephew, it is impossible to understand the greed of the English for land. We Wyandot do not share that greed," Tarhe explained. He bent over a picked up a handful of dirt, saying, "How can a man think that he owns this soil anymore than the bird owns the sky it flies through, or the fish owns the water it swims in? These are gifts given to us from the Great Spirit as bounty for all living things to share. But the English do not believe this. They do not understand this. Their eyes are blinded and their ears clogged with dirt. It has been that way, I am told, since they first arrived from across the waters to the Great Island. They wish to consume and destroy everything our people see and are a part of. One day I believe they will destroy us too. There was a time that the English King forbade settlers to cross the mountain called the Great Blue Ridge to the Shenandoah Valley. But they did, and he did not punish them. It is said in our traditional oral stories about our creation, that the children of the Bad Twin would one day eventually come from across the Great Waters to seek revenge against everything his brother, the Good Twin, had created." Tarhe allowed that to sink in. "You see, Nephew, the children of the Bad Twin have already arrived. They are intent on destroying the creation of their father's Good Twin brother, which is us. The Good Twin created the Native people. The Bad Children are here and they had taken the form of the English who wish to destroy us."

The situation with the encroaching White settlers on Native lands west of the Alleghenies did not improve. It actually worsened with each passing month for the tribes of the Ohio Country, which included the Wyandot. Tarhe argued before the Sachem councils during the winter and into the spring of 1768, that something must be done before a new, terrible war with the English would arise. The Sachems were not so sure. While thanking Tarhe for his insight and advice, they pointed out to him that no English settlers had transgressed on Wyandot land in the Ohio Country. Those White settlers arriving in the Tygart River Valley and the Greenbriar River Valley far to the southeast were for their nephews the Shawnee to consider how to deal with. The Wyandot were not the keepers of the peace for the entire Ohio Country. "Tarhe, we will soon receive a Mohawk emissary sent by Warraghiyagey, the man the English call William Johnson, who the English Father has appointed as his representative to all the northern Native nations. We have already appealed to Warraghiyagey to tell us what the English Father wishes for his children to do."

Big Jaw, the Wyandot Sachem visiting from Lower Sandusky rose and spoke. "Tarhe, you advise that we take this matter into our own hands. Though I believe you to be a great warrior, you speak to us like a young cub who wishes to claim his first scalp." The words stung Tarhe, but he remained silent. "You must not forget that it was the Haudenosaunee who at one time defeated us in war and drove us out of our homeland. Yes, we are now a powerful nation with more warriors than the Haudenosaunee could begin to field. However, because of our mutual shared history with them, we call them our Uncles for that reason. Warraghiyagey is the man they highly esteem, who exerts great favor over them in all matters. What I say is that while we, the Wyandot, have much influence over the western tribes of the Great Lakes and beyond, we respect the influence of the Haudenosaunee over us. The Six

Nations, as Warraghiyagey calls the Haudenosaunee, sit at the east door to our Wyandot country. By this door, and from the mouth of Warraghiyagey's Mohawk emissary he sends to us, we will know his mind in the matter of the designs of the White people. So, I advise that it is by the consent of this council that we wait and watch, even though I have no official say here." Tarhe respectfully nodded his approval of the headmen's decision, but privately he did not believe that the man called Johnson had the best interests of the Wyandot in his mind. "This Johnson rules over the Haudenosaunee like a King himself, and they his subjects," Tarhe thought to himself. "Whatever is to happen will favor his closest Native allies at the expense of the tribes living in the Ohio Country who face the greatest invasion from the Virginians who the Shawnee call the 'Long Knives.' Neither Johnson or the Haudenosaunee have the long arm of influence whatsoever over them."

Johnson's Mohawk representative arrived and met with the Sachems privately. Tarhe was not party to what was discussed, however he soon heard. Warraghiyagey first wanted the Wyandot to be made aware that the Cherokee, who had been the brunt of the Wyandot and Haudenosaunee war parties since anyone could remember, had petitioned the British Crown in Virginia to seek aid in protecting the Cherokee from further onslaught. Virginia, in turn, had turned to Warraghiyagey, the superintendent of the northern Indian affairs, and also to a man named John Stuart, who was the southern superintendent. It was said that Warraghiyagey had in fact welcomed the ancient war with the Cherokees that sent warriors south on the paths behind or west of the colonies where they could procure Enemy scalps. However, the Virginians wished to placate the Cherokee in order to prevent them from seeking vengeance against Virginian traders and settlers who had committed murders against Cherokee Natives. The Virginians had petitioned the English Father directly, and as a result, Warraghiyagey had been ordered to halt the war parties. "It would please Warraghiyagey that you Great Sachems stop your young men from attacking the Cherokee, as the Haudenosaunee, especially the Seneca, have been likewise ordered. Warraghiyagey will negotiate a peace between you and the Cherokee as soon as possible."[134]

Tarhe spat on the ground when he heard this saying, "No White man, not even Johnson, can tell the Wyandot what to do." However, Tarhe learned that there was another matter of even greater importance that the Mohawk emissary was bringing with him to the Wyandot. "Warraghiyagey is calling for a grand council with all the Natives of the Ohio Country, and with the Six Nations and their allies. It is to be convened in the fall month of October at the Great Carrying Place between the Mohawk River and Wood Creek[135] where the English had established a fort called Stanwix," the Mohawk stated. "On this belt of wampum and these strings, Warraghiyagey invites the Great Sachems of the Wyandot to attend." The emissary presented the white wampum to the Wyandot council who received it. "It is at this grand council that Warraghiyagey, speaking for the Father the King, will make a decision concerning the boundary line between English and Native territory. It will be a just settlement that all can appreciate." When Tarhe heard of the proposed boundary decision, he was aghast at the implication. He guessed that the Haudenosaunee, who had Warraghiyagey's ear, were sure to sell to the English the land which they claimed was theirs by the right of conquest that happened some eighty years previous. However, no Six Nations now lived on this land. Too, the land in question west of the mountains was the hunting grounds of many tribes, like the Shawnee, the Delaware, the Mingo, the Miamis, and even the Wyandot. Tarhe shook his head in disbelief. "No good for the Wyandot will come of this," he thought to himself.

What Tarhe had feared had in fact come true soon after the council opened on October 24, 1768.[136] With colonial commissioners from the affected colonies present, Johnson spoke before

---
134 In fact, it took William Johnson two years to negotiate a treaty that in 1768 produced an armistice, with gifts presented to all involved.
135 Current site of Rome, New York.
136 This council was officially recorded in history as the Treaty of Fort Stanwix.

an assembled audience of over 3,000 Native attendees, including, of course, the Six Nations of the Haudenosaunee, as well as a smattering of the western tribes, including some Wyandot. Tarhe was not in attendance because he was not a headman. However, it came as no surprise to him when he heard that the Iroquois, as the English called the Six Nations, had agreed to sell a large portion of land they claimed as their own though they did not live on it. The sale was to be made to the British Crown for a sum of money paid only to the Six Nations as the rightful heirs. None of the other tribes living and hunting on the land in question would be compensated. None had been consulted in the negotiations which apparently had already been completed between Johnson, the colonial commissioners, and the Six Nations. Those left out of the treaty did not comprehend its implications but Tarhe did. The most important part of the treaty was the new boundary line that affected all Native people in the Ohio Country. The line ran west from the Wyoming Valley in Pennsylvania colony to the east bank of the Allegheny River at the Native village of Kittanning. It then followed the river to its juncture with the Monongahela at Fort Pitt. The line continued southwest along the east bank of the Ohio River all the way down to the mouth of the Tennessee River. That meant that all the western lands between the crest of the Alleghenies to the Ohio River would now be given over to the English. Included in the treaty acquisition was the Ken-Tuck-Kee hunting grounds of the Shawnee south of the Ohio River. Tarhe was sure that the English would release these lands for White colonial settlement at the first possible moment.

To Tarhe, that meant one thing. The door was now officially open for the Long Knives to pour into this newly-acquired territory which he was sure the Shawnee, and likely the Lenape, would contest as it was their prime hunting lands. The anger boiled up in Tarhe every time he talked about the terms of this treaty around the winter lodge fires at Upper Sandusky. "More land has been taken from us, and this time by other Native people, the Haudenosaunee, by guile for their own profit. What do these Iroquois Sachems care about any of us? This is exactly what the French warned our people of many years ago. They said that the English, through deception and lies, would gradually take all of the land and destroy us in the process. The English will take their time with the Wyandot. We are the most powerful, but we are also the furthest from the land grab. They will use the Long Knives Virginians to wear down the Natives, beginning with the Shawnee, and then the Lenape and Mingo before they deal with us. This will give us time to decide what to do. Even now as we sit here, the Iroquois who received the silver coins from the English, have spent it all with the rum traders to get drunk and buy their wives and cousins paltry trinkets until it is all gone. It must be a sorrowful sight to behold, and I am glad that it is not the Wyandot who are the victims of this debauchery."[137] However, Tarhe mulled over other aspects of the new treaty that affected the Wyandot, which had gone unanswered. In his mind, the Wyandot were a martial warrior society where warriors became men from boys by the trial of warfare. "How are our young warriors-to-be going to prove themselves in battle if we cannot war with the Cherokee any longer?" Clearly Tarhe was vexed by this turn of events. And through it all, Isaac was beginning to understand why from the point of view of the Wyandots.

Through the winter, Isaac asked for an opportunity to speak with the head Clan Mother of the Porcupine Clan in the village. She was elderly, and very busy, with much to do in the clan affairs. However, with the winter weather, she made time to talk with Isaac over several occasions. The woman was tattooed with both clan symbols and shamanist lines inked across her wrinkled skin. While speaking over the course of many sittings, she still managed clan business by interrupting her story-telling to give instructions to one of her many council subordinate women who approached with a question. "It is one of my jobs to be the caretaker of our

---

[137] Natives of the 18th century had no means to store money or invest it for future profit, nor did they have any use for it in their dealings among themselves. The inherent value of White man's coinage was meaningless to Native people, and so the Iroquois used it to make immediate purchases in goods and drink until it was all gone, all 10,000 English pounds. It has been called one of the greatest binges in American colonial history.

Porcupine Clan traditions which go back farther than anyone can remember in our history." "What are the clan traditions?" Isaac asked. "Well, each clan has its own rules and duties that can differ. But I settle disputes that arise between the people in our clan. I see that the laws of our clan are followed by all. I represent our clan in the council of Clan Mothers that decides on an overall Village Chief after each Clan Mother's own council of women pick their own clan chief from the men.[138] Clan Mothers preside over the telling of the Oral Stories of our people. We say who can marry who, and we give the men permission to go to war, or instead, to go hunt. Why we even decide when people like yourself are to be brought back with the warriors."

Isaac didn't know what to say in response to this stunning declaration on the old woman's part. Seeing he was perplexed, she explained. "Whenever one of our clan family dies, it is the way of our people to find someone to replace that person. We request the men to replace that loss by bringing us back captives for the purpose of adoption if a natural replacement is not available. When we had several losses, I asked the warriors to bring captives to me. You were brought here to replace the unborn child that Ronyouquaines was unable to give life to. She grieved for that child as if it had been born, and had then died. Then soon after the war party of Tarhe's left I had a dream about you. I saw an image of you in a dream. It was a dream in which I was aware and saw a young boy, a White boy, soaring high in the sky like an eagle. Dreams are very important to our people, and most important to me; a gift of mind's sight from my Manitou. I awoke, knowing you would be coming, and that the name to be given to you would be The Eagle. It means the One-Who-Soars-Close-to-the-Creator. And it also means Messenger. It is your destiny to be a messenger, like the eagle. Your naming in our clan is decided, and belongs to the Porcupine Clan, not to your parents, or in this case, to your Uncle Tarhe, and his wife, Ronyouquaines. Your name is to become official in the tribe at the Feast of Name Giving.[139] You do not know it

---

138 LD-TTIF, page 64.
139 LD-TTF, page 114.

as yet, but you will bring courage, wisdom, strength to our people by this name. However, I like the English name Isaac, also. So, we will call you both, as you will need an English name if you are to benefit our people in the days ahead which the Great Spirit has decided for you, and for us. Now, Isaac The Eagle, that is enough. I am tired," the old woman said as she rose to her feet and was helped by one of her aides to her nearby lodge, leaving Isaac alone with much to think about.

By next summer of the year 1769, Isaac, aged sixteen, had come of age as a result of his new-found warrior status to seek a bride if he wished. However, that was the farthest thing from his mind most of the time. Isaac was already aware of the long Wyandot tradition concerning the taking of a mate, or wife, for life. Because the Clan Mothers knew that it took men a longer time to fully mature than women, men were considered fully competent and able to provide for a lasting marriage when they turned the age of thirty. At thirty, they were now eligible to be an integral part of tribal council, serve as a chief if appointed, officially receive a new name, and take a wife as a life-long mate.[140] However, it was much different with women, especially when they were young; especially once they entered puberty. Though the age of thirty was a time when a couple was considered fully committed as life-long mates to each other, it was not uncommon at all for a young woman, who was in love, to make her feelings known in a much more aggressive way than the man. In any case, unbeknown to Tarhe, his daughter Myeerah, almost thirteen years old, had experienced her first menses. This came as a complete surprise to Tarhe when Ronyouquaines told him because he had his mind on so many tribal problems. Tarhe had not seen that his daughter was on her way to becoming a woman. It is more of a matter to consider than you might think, Tarhe," Ronyouquaines stated. "Our daughter has her eyes set on one man only. She says she is in love with Isaac The Eagle." That startling news left Tarhe absolutely dumbstruck.

---

140 LD-TTIF, page 16

Chapter Eleven
Isaac Becomes a Father

During the autumn of 1769, many traders visited the Wyandot village at Upper Sandusky, all vying for the chance to supply the warriors with ammunition for the upcoming hunt. In doing so, they also wished to supply them with the other necessities for their families during the winter, all on credit. Most traders were bringing their wares from the growing settlement around Fort Pitt at the Forks of the Ohio. As Isaac passed a group of three English traders sitting around a fire near the council lodge waiting as protocol demanded for permission to trade, Isaac heard one of the men say the word, "Zane," which momentarily stopped him in his tracks. Isaac remembered the word he had not heard spoken in six years. He gave them a quick glance and then moved on. However, Isaac found time to locate Luther in the village, whom he spoke to in Wandat. Luther had recently become an advisor to the village Sachems who they consulted with on matters of dealing with the English, which Luther was knowledgeable. Luther had the keen ability to speak English and Wandat tongues, as well as Lenape, and some Shawnee. But more so, Luther understood the English mind having lived for years as a personal slave of the English, all the while observing how the English viewed the world and people of color in it. Isaac asked Luther to quiz the traders about why they had been talking about the name Zane, and if it applied to him whom they had somehow recognized. Luther agreed to do so, and was gone for some time before returning to tell all to Isaac.

Luther related to Isaac what he had learned. "Two of the traders are working for the third, named McCormick.[141] They say that settlers from across the mountains in the east are pouring into the unclaimed lands between the mountains and the Ohio River. They met three brothers by the last name of Zane who have arrived and made claims to land south of Fort Pitt on the east side of the Ohio River where the mouth of the creek named by the Haudenosaunee, Weel-Lunk, meets the Ohio. He remembered seeing you pass by while they were talking. He knows you're formerly of the Zane White bloodline. McCormick would like to speak with you. I told him I didn't think it was possible, but I'd tell you regardless, Isaac." Isaac mulled it over for a moment before replying. "Did you tell him anything about Zane?" Luther shook his head. "I know who you are, and you're not a Zane to me, like this McCormick thinks. But he didn't say why he wants to see you. You know that he has to be on his best behavior here in the village. He must follow our strict protocol regarding liquor, women, and adoptees. Go speak with him, it can't hurt. Maybe you'll learn something from these slippery English," Luther offered. Isaac decided he would do so. He approached the traders who greeted him with English words. Isaac refused to reply in the same, rather asking the head trader McCormick in Wandat, "What do you want to ask me?" McCormick hesitated. He was used to hearing White captives speak in English. "What is your English name, son?" McCormick questioned, "And where are you from?" Isaac paused, looking the White man in the eyes before responding in a measured tone in

---

141 Alexander McCormick, trader to the Wyandot and other tribes, was originally from Ireland before coming to work in the trading business at Fort Pitt. By 1771, he established two trading posts, one at Upper Sandusky across the river from the major Wyandot village and another at the Wyandot village on the Maumee River. At the outbreak of hostilities in the Ohio Country in late 1776, McCormick was captured by the Wyandot at a Lenape village. McCormick was given to the wife of the Wyandot Half King to replace her brother who had been killed. McCormick eventually was released, but rather than returning to Pittsburgh, decided to live with the Wyandot at Upper Sandusky as a trader.

Wandat. "I am not your son, English man, and I am no child to be toyed with." McCormick countered. "I meant no disrespect. I just know you have a name that I might recognize." Before turning his back on the traders and leaving, Isaac said, "Won-dot-n-dee. Isaac ee-jah/ht-zee."[142]

In the following year 1770, a new tribal chief of the Wyandots at Upper Sandusky was chosen by the Clan Mothers and village Sachems. His name was Dunquat; called Pomoacan by the Lenape. Dunquat was of the Porcupine Clan like Tarhe. While the Wyandot principal chief at the Detroit village was a Wyandot named Jacques Duperon Baby, Dunquat became the overall chief of the Upper Sandusky village. There were many outstanding War Captains among the Wyandot for Dunquat to chose a Warpole from. Unfortunately for Tarhe, although he was a celebrated warrior, he was not selected. Dunquat chose another equally celebrated warrior among his people from the lower mixed Wyandot and Seneca village at Sandusky. The warrior Zhau-Shoo-To would serve as Dunquat's Warpole, or overall War Chief of the Wyandot warriors. Zhau-Shoo-To had proved himself in battle many times over alongside Tarhe. However, Dunquat favored his new Warpole for one main reason and that was that Zhau-Shoo-To had taken Dunquat's daughter in marriage as chosen mates. However, what surprised Isaac more than anything else when he heard of the new Warpole, was that Isaac discovered that Zhau-Shoo-To was a White man by birth parents like himself. Zhau-Shoo-To was called Coon by the English traders because his previous name had been Abraham Kuhn. He had been captured as a young boy early in the French and Indian War in eastern Pennsylvania from a German family, and had been brought to Detroit, like Isaac. There, Kuhn had been adopted into the Bear Clan and given a new name. In Isaac's mind, it was an odd turn of events in some ways that he could not understand entirely. However, when Isaac

---

142 This is the phonetic spelling of the Wandat words, "I am Wyandot. My name is Isaac."

met Zhau-Soo-To, the warrior spoke to him only in Wandat and they did not discuss one word concerning their former birth families.[143]

In the early spring of the following year, Myeerah's mother, Ronyouquaines, announced to Tarhe and everyone in the clan that Myeerah had conceived a child through union with Isaac The Eagle, who was the father. The budding romance between the two of them had blossomed. "If the Great Spirit wishes it so, then a child will be born late in the year," she said. The news was received with great rejoicing. While the two young lovers were not committed to each other as lifetime mates yet, the arrival of a child to the Wyandot Porcupine Clan would be a blessing to everyone. A great feast was held to celebrate the occasion. Everyone knew how important it was to keep the clans and the Wyandot tribe as a whole populated in the face of so much war that resulted in the deaths of warriors. Too, the introduction of White man's diseases, like the stinking pox[144] had devastated Native communities, including the Wyandot. In addition, with the influx of White settlers to the hunting grounds on the south and east side of the Ohio River, Natives had been warned that those lands were now open for White settlement. Overall, all the tribes found that hunting game animals closer to home was less productive due to more hunting competition. The result was that tribes, like the Wyandot, began supplementing their diet with more vegetables from farming to make up for the loss of some of the meat. Clan Mothers began to notice some pregnant mothers were unable to carry children in their bellies to term. Less children born meant lower birth rates for

---

143 Zhau-Shoo-To, aka Coon, would lead many war parties against the settler frontier during the American Revolution in the west. He had a reputation as having a terrible dislike of Whites, especially the Virginian Long Knives. He was known to have fought against them, and killed many without exception.

144 Smallpox was the primary lethal disease for all Natives who did not have immunity, but influenza, measles, and a host of other pandemic-like viral and germ infections ravaged Native villages since the arrival of Europeans in North America.

Isaac Becomes a Father | 147

Myeerah

the tribe. And without war, there were no captives being brought to the villages to replace losses. It was a vexing problem in all ways.

However, a healthy male child was born to Isaac and Myeerah before the first snows. At the "Naming Ceremony of New Children" during the upcoming Green Corn Feast, the baby boy would be given a Wyandot name. His English name would later be recognized as Ebenezer.[145] Isaac remained busy throughout the spring of 1772 hunting far and wide to bring meat and hides back to the village for Myeerah to dress the skins for trading, and to cure the meat for future needs. In the interim, while the Wyandot lived far enough away from the new boundary of the Ohio River, they received plenty of word from passing traders and kin-related tribesmen of what was happening to the south. The Shawnee had been enraged when they learned the full extent of the terms of the so-called treaty that the Iroquois agent Johnson had forced upon them. The hunting grounds to the south of the Ohio River in the Ken-Tuck-Kee lands belonged to the Shawnee forever, they believed. They did not acknowledge that it was owned by the Haudenosaunee who justified their claim as the rights of conquest from wars nearly one hundred years ago. The Shawnee knew that the Iroquois, who preferred they be addressed as the Haudenosaunee or People of the Longhouse, were in no way the mighty confederacy they once were when they drove all Natives

---

145 The children of Isaac and Myeerah have presented many problems. The lack of accurate records has meant some conflicting number of children and their names, depending upon the much later attempts at documentation. That Myeerah conceived a child at the age of thirteen is of itself in question, though plausible. The child Ebenezer is stated by several sources attributed to 19th century references as having occurred in 1771. That would mean Myeerah, born sometime in 1757, was fourteen years old when she gave birth, and Isaac, born 1753, was near or about eighteen years old, which is plausible, but by today's standards, highly unlikely for a mother that young to give birth. There is also a problem with the child being given the name Ebenezer at birth. Since Isaac did not recognize his previous White family, and since Ebenezer was a brother, there was an uncle by the same name as well. It is more likely that the child was given a Wyandot clan name, and many years later, when Isaac was an older man and that child had become an adult was the name changed to Ebenezer. The clan and Clan Mother would never have recognized the name Ebenezer at the time of the birth in 1771.

out. Now they were a shadow of their former might. In the eyes of the Shawnee, the Iroquois were living up to the name the French had given them years ago, for in French, Iroquois meant "rattlesnakes."

Trouble was brewing during the year and into the next as hundreds of settlers kept entering the Ken-Tuck-Kee hunting grounds without the permission of the Shawnee. When asked to leave, the Scotch-Irish backwoodsmen from across the mountains claimed that the treaty gave them the right to not only enter the land but claim it as their own. Tarhe told Isaac of all this, and more, saying, "It is only a matter of time before war comes again to the Ohio Country, and this time, it will reach us close to our homes." This development gave Isaac a great deal to think about as he went about his daily duties to his family and clan. At the same time, many traders were arriving at the Upper Sandusky village that they were calling, "Half-King's Town." Half-King was the name given to Dunquat who had taken up residence in the village. He was called the Half King because of the old way of remembering the days when the Wyandot demonstrated fealty to the Iroquois League. Soon after the turn of the last century, the French arrived at Detroit in 1701 and established a trading center and village there. It was then that the ancestors of the Wyandot, who had been exiled after a long war with the Iroquois, petitioned the French and the Iroquois to build a village at Detroit. The Iroquois Confederacy granted them that right, and the right to settle on the south side of Lake Erie at the Sandusky River. In deference, the term Half King was recognized by the Iroquois council and given to whomever the Wyandot chose as overall chief. Of course, Dunquat felt no need now to consult the Iroquois for permission in any matter. The Wyandot were much stronger than the Iroquois alliance these days.

Isaac was now dealing directly with the English traders coming to the village to purchase his furs for trade goods. Although Isaac knew the English words that the traders spoke among themselves, he nonetheless demanded they speak to him in Wandat language. This made it more difficult for the traders to have an edge in the trade because they were not as adept at thinking trade strategy in the Native language that not all of them were fluent in. One day, a small delegation of Mingo, otherwise known as Ohio Valley Seneca and Cayuga of the Iroquois Six Nations arrived in the village on their way to visit relatives in the East. They were travelling along Lake Erie and then past Niagara to visit the man named Johnson in the New York colony frontier. With them was a White man dressed in Native clothing, who approached Isaac some time after his arrival. He addressed Isaac in Wandat which he could speak fairly fluently. "My name is Simon Girty. I know that you are Wyandot, but your blue eyes tell me that you are adopted from White birth parents, as I was some time ago adopted by my Uncle, the Seneca Mingo chief, Guyasuta." Isaac nodded in affirmative, but said to Girty, "If you have been adopted by the Seneca, then why are you speaking in English words I heard you speak to the English traders who happen to be in the village?" Girty smiled at Isaac and motioned for him to sit down so they could talk.

"I know who you are, and there's something I want to say to you, and I'll say it in English cause I have a point. I know your heart is Wyandot through and through. I spent eight years with the Seneca, and my heart is with them; they're my people." Isaac shifted nervously, signaling that he had no use for these words, but Girty stopped him short. "Just listen to what I have to say. I've been talking with your Uncle, Tarhe, one of the greatest warriors of the Wyandot. There's a war coming, and it's coming soon, and there's no way to prevent it. I'm talking about war with the Virginians. And it's a war our people, the Wyandot and the Mingo Seneca can't win no matter how hard we fight, or what's sacrificed. The Whites, our birth-people, are coming to take Native lands, one way or another. Tarhe's going to fight, and so will you I imagine to try to prevent the takeover of Native land from happening. I'm saying all this to you because I see you taking the stance of the Wyandot to fight to the death, and that's a true Wyandot warrior. But you have the choice to do more than that for your people. The Great Spirit, I truly believe, has brought you and I to the Native peoples we have come to love to be more than a good warrior who dies for his people. No matter how many scalps of the Long Knives you take, there will be more and more of them to take the place of those you kill," Girty said.

"I'm saying all this to you because you've got blue eyes, and underneath that paint, your skin is as White as mine, or any Long Knife. Your people, like mine, one day are going to need someone who can translate and perhaps mediate. They need someone who the Long Knives will listen to, but who can also speak to his own people as well, with words spoken not out of weakness, but out of knowing that the war to come cannot be won. You see, when all the Wyandot warriors are killed, it is the helpless women and children, both yours and mine, who will suffer. They will suffer for a lack of anyone who can find common ground with the Enemy to prevent a massacre that they are intent on committing for revenge. Dunquat's advisor, your Wyandot brother with the dark skin named Luther, is as skilled a negotiator and mediator as any in this village. But he is a Negro in the White man's world. No Virginian will listen to him no matter how much sense he might speak. He's nothing more to the Virginians than a piece of runaway property who needs whipped severely and then returned to his rightful owner. You, on the other hand, like Coon and Adam, are people the White Enemy will at least listen to, if given the chance. However, Coon the Warpole will not accept that opportunity to talk when he can fight. I see that you are headed down that same path as him. Isaac, you could be much more to your people and your family. Speak English to the English. One day you might need it. Fight when there is a good fight, but know that no matter how many you kill of the Enemy in battle, you can whip them but never defeat them in the long run." Isaac stared at Girty in disbelief at what he had just heard. As Girty got up to leave, he offered one last comment, "Just remember what I've told you. It's the truth."[146]

---

[146] Simon Girty is known to have made several trips with Mingo Seneca leaders at the behest of his adoptive Uncle, chief Guyasuta, to visit William Johnson at Johnson Hall in upstate New York. The purpose was to discuss the Shawnee crisis. The Shawnee were increasingly voicing complaints to Alexander McKee, Johnson's Deputy Agent of Indian Affairs at Fort

The next morning, the adopted Seneca named Girty was gone with those headed eastward. Isaac thought about Girty's words many times, turning it over and over in his head, until he thought it best to dismiss it altogether. He considered himself Wyandot in his heart and mind and that was all that mattered. Isaac decided he would not speak English to the English; not now, not ever. If war was indeed coming, as Girty predicted, then the Long Knives would be defeated in battle, contrary to Girty's belief. "It is our land, not theirs," Isaac thought to himself. "We will fight until we win, and with warriors like Tarhe and Coon, there is no question that we will not win." Isaac discussed the matter with Tarhe when he had a chance. While agreeing in principle with Isaac, Tarhe's response was more studied, and more balanced. "Isaac, we the Wyandot people know of no time when there has not been war in our history, for one reason or another. And while we have won many battles, and brought much glory to our warriors, too, we have suffered many warriors who have died as a result. You may remember when we captured you and your brother that a great warrior and brother of mine died in my arms from a bullet shot by a Long Knife trying to re-capture you. The warrior's name was Spotted Elk. I had known him since we were little boys playing at Detroit. We grew up together. Though we came from different families, we were of the same clan. We had made a vow to protect each other for the duration of our lifetime as a loved and cherished friend. And he died there, in my arms, and I could not even bring him home to his mother and wife for a proper burial. There's not a day that goes by that I do not think of him, and how I failed to protect him as he protected me. It has been a hole in my heart. Yes, Isaac, we will fight, but I shudder to think of the cost in the end. Girty is a smart man. He understands that cost all too well."

An opportunity arose for Isaac that he would have never imagined considering at any time previously. Two traders visiting the

---

> Pitt, concerning the encroachment of settlers and surveyors upon Shawnee hunting grounds located along the lower Ohio River and into Ken-Tuck-Kee which had already been sold by the Iroquois Six Nations to the British Crown, specifically Virginia.

Wyandot at Upper Sandusky named James Conner and John Gibson had let it be known that upon leaving the Wyandot, they intended on heading south to the Lenape towns on the Scioto and then east to the Moravian Christian Delaware Mission at Schoenbrunn. From there, they would stop to visit the Zanes at Wheeling and then continue on to the trading center at the growing settlement of Pittsburgh. In light of Girty's discussion with Tarhe, Tarhe told the traders that the Wyandot warrior Isaac The Eagle was a Zane by birth parents. Tarhe felt it was time to test Isaac to see if he really wanted to remain with the Wyandot or return to his Zane kin. The way for the twenty-year-old to determine such a decision was for him to accompany the traders to Weel-Lunk and pay a visit to his relatives, who were said to be clearing land. Isaac protested to Tarhe upon hearing the wishes of his Uncle. "I have a family to care for," Isaac exclaimed. "Myeerah is heavy with child again and I cannot leave her unattended." Tarhe was adamant. "I and Ronyouquaines will see to her needs. Go now and speak to the traders, and make arrangements to leave with them, as I ask."[147]

The journey by horseback with the traders from Upper Sandusky to the Scioto River Valley was uneventful for Isaac. Richard Conner wanted to visit the Shawnee village where he was romancing a Shawnee maiden, he hoped to marry one day. Conner had encountered serious difficulties because she was actually an adopted White named Margaret Boyer, however, she and her Shawnee parents considered herself completely Shawnee. Her parents were refusing to let their daughter marry a White man, especially one who was a trader. After a brief stay, Isaac and the two men headed east to the Moravian Christian Delaware Mission on the Tuscarawas River named Schoenbrunn that was being built. Isaac was introduced to the missionary David Zeisberger

---

[147] There is no factual evidence recorded by the Zanes at Wheeling, or anyone else, that this visit ever happened. However, in the fictional or factual lore written by White authors, it is suggested that Isaac did visit his brothers at Wheeling. Since there was relative peace on the frontier at this time in 1773, a visit was possible, but whether the Zanes made any attempt to prevent Isaac from leaving, is pure conjecture.

who had already attracted a number of Native converts to live at the Schoenbrunn village next to the church once the cabins were finished. Isaac took an instant dislike to the White preacher whose stern personality reminded Isaac of the traveling preacher of the South Potomac Valley he had briefly met many years ago as a child. The traders pushed on along the trail that joined the east-west path called by Whites the Old Mingo Trail that led from the interior of the Ohio Country. They headed east as it would take them to a large island in the Ohio River. On the other side of that island was the mouth of the creek named Weel-Lunk by the Iroquois many years ago. Now it was being called Wheeling Creek by the handful of White people settling there, including the Zane brothers, Isaac was told. Upon reaching the Ohio River, Isaac surveyed the large island and announced to the traders that the island was as far as he wished to go. Since the traders were going to cross the shallow ford on the south end of the island and then proceed to the Wheeling settlement within eyesight, Isaac asked them to tell his birth brothers that he would speak to them if they came to visit him at his camp on the island, but no closer to their settlement.

Within several hours, Isaac saw the trader Gibson return with three other men, one of whom Isaac recognized as Jonathan. It had been ten years since Isaac had last seen two of his three elder brothers, so it was difficult to remember what they looked like to be able to identify them. Silas and Ebenezer approached Isaac with open arms, expressing their profound joy of seeing their younger brother again. They were not at all shocked by Isaac's appearance with a shaved head and scalp lock, nor the fact that he was dressed in Native clothing, which some traders on the frontier had adopted as their own. "Well, if it ain't my kid brother! Look at you! My, have you ever grown more than I could ever imagine," said Ebenezer. "Jonathan, here, told us all about you from the time you two were taken by the Injuns back at Old Fields, but I never thought much of what you'd look like since you were a young'un then." Isaac turned his attention to Jonathan who was standing aside, silently glaring at him. "Why you still dressed like an Injun, Isaac?" Jonathan questioned in a mocking tone. "Why are you dressed like one of them murdering Long Knives?" Isaac shot back, clearly angered. "Ain't you had enough of them heathen red devils?" Jonathan countered. "I thought you might come here to redeem yourself and come to your senses. Or maybe that little squaw you had your eye on has got you all fit to be tied so you can't come to your senses?" Isaac instinctively touched his tomahawk in his sash, ready for whatever action might happen with this brother-turned-Enemy.

Ebenezer intervened. "That's enough, the both of you. Isaac, we're so happy to see you again, beyond belief. Pa is back on the South Potomac. Andrew's there, and so is Elizabeth, who is growing into a fine young woman. She looks so much like Mama. And Pa, the last time I seen him, asked me if I had seen you, or knew your whereabouts, and that of Luther. Pa misses that slave so much with all the work that needs done around the farm." Isaac cut Eb off. "That slave you're referring to is a free man now with the Wyandot, a trusted advisor. He's never coming back here into servitude for no one, not even Pa." Eb looked down at the ground, gathering his thoughts. "Isaac, we came here for a better life than what Pa has. There's no quit rent to be paid here to someone like Fairfax which is like slavery also. We're free men, trying to carve something out of the wilderness for ourselves and our families. You could be doing that too." Isaac quickly confronted his brother, saying, "This is not empty land for the taking. This is Native land you're squatting on, driving off the game, cutting down the timber, and bringing your cattle and horses to graze on, none of which is rightfully yours, no matter what the Crown says."

Eb chose his next words carefully. "Isaac, this land you're talking about was rightfully purchased by the Crown from the Six Nations up north who claim it as their own to sell if they wished. They were legally paid for the land, and the Crown is opening it up to settlement without someone like the pompous ass Fairfax grabbing it first for his own to rent out. As long as we stay on our side of the Ohio, we've done nothing wrong. You say that it's Native land, but I have not found any evidence of any villages here or close by to show me that this land is their home. There's not even any abandoned cleared fields like you can find at Old Fields that the Shawnee claimed they cultivated corn on. We're not here to deprive any Native or his family of their home. You know me, Isaac, I've always been very respectful of Native people, knowing what Pa taught us about his first wife who was Lenape. It's just not true what you're saying," Eb finished. There was an uneasy silence between them, until Jonathan spoke up. "I know why you're here, Isaac. Them Injuns are giving you a chance to redeem yourself as a White man, if you wish, like they did with me, and I'm telling you, you should take it. There's nothing about them savages that is right. They're not God-fearing Christians, they let women tell the men what to do, and they're letting the land go to waste and just sit there. I'm telling you; they'll be your undoing if you go back to them red rascals and no one here will be able to help you then, cause it'll be too late if you take their side."

Isaac studied his brother thoughtfully, and then spoke. "I don't know why you're so hateful, Jonathan. The Wyandot treated you fine. They never hurt or mistreated you, and your Wyandot mother loved you dearly, and wept for days when you left and never came back. Whatever has hardened your heart to fill you with this hate, you are now misplacing it on me. I'm guessing you've always disliked me. Perhaps you thought our Mama loved me more than you as I was the youngest boy. I'm sure she loved you too, as I once did. But I am not coming back to the White frontier. My life is with the Wyandot." Hearing this from Isaac, Ebenezer softly replied. "Isaac, I can speak for everyone to say we all love you, and now seeing you alive and with us again, we love you only as blood kin can. It would be mighty sorrowful if you didn't soften you heart a little and stay with us awhile. For God's sake Almighty, give us a chance Isaac. You've been gone a long time and we've missed you dearly. Come across and stay with us a while before you make any decision about returning. We're not the bad people that Jonathan says the Injuns have told you. Your mother, if she was alive, would have wanted you to give us all a chance to get to know each other again and be as one family. You're one of us, Isaac, not really one of them."

Chapter Twelve
War with the Long Knives

After several moments, Isaac arose from where he was sitting and without saying a word turned away from his birth brothers. Isaac saddled his horse, and then mounting it, he rode across the river shallows to the west side of the Ohio River to the head of the Mingo Path. Behind him, Ebenezer, Silas, and Jonathan stood motionless. Silas had a disgusted look on face. The eldest Zane brother had remained silent the whole time, just observing. Now Silas finally spoke. "There's not a thing we can do about him, Eb. He's gone over to the Injuns, that's all. Jon said so when he first returned from the Wyandot. I've heard it said among many settlers, especially those who tried to reclaim their captive children when they were turned over by the Injuns to Bouquet back in '64. It's really simple Eb. Isaac was too young when the Injuns got him. Now there's just too much Red Niggar in him that can never be taken out. I heard said by a fella back in the Potomac Valley, a fella named Renick who observed a neighbor's boy when he came back briefly from the Injuns. The words were something like this," Silas recounted. "It is easy to make an Injun out of a White man, but hard, if not impossible, to reclaim a White man after being converted."[148] Silas paused for a moment to let that sink in. "Isaac has been converted, that's all. We should be glad that Jonathan was old enough not to swallow Injun life whole."

Isaac wanted to take the shortest route to the Upper Sandusky from the Wheeling frontier. At a juncture with the Mingo Path several miles from Wheeling, Isaac took the creek path to the northwest that would lead him past Schoenbrunn Mission and the major trail following the Tuscarawas River to the north. That path to home at Upper Sandusky met the Tuscarawas Trail north of the Moravian Mission. Isaac skirted the Christian preachers and their Lenape brethren. The meeting with Isaac's Zane brothers had disturbed him. He remained deep in thought as he rode; mulling over what had transpired at Wheeling, especially with Jonathan. Isaac didn't wish to talk to anyone, or have to explain himself more than he already had to White people. They couldn't or wouldn't understand why he was returning to his Wyandot home and his family he missed. It was not that Isaac was troubled by any conflict concerning his identity. Isaac knew who he was. He had made his choice. What bothered him on the return to the Upper Sandusky village was the thought that his brothers, especially Jonathan, considered Natives to be nothing more than two-legged deer of the woods taking up valuable land that all the Virginians wanted. He could see in their talk that they believed Native people had no legitimate right or ownership to the land that White people coveted. Native people were simply something to be dispensed with to get that land, and any means would justify that end.

This realization was a deep shock to Isaac; that his own blood family was party to stealing the very land under the feet of Natives for their own. But as he thought about it, it occurred to him that his disappointment with his Zane blood family ran deeper than that. Except for possibly Ebenezer, it was apparent to Isaac that Silas and Jonathan had nothing but contempt for him. He was sure

---

148 This is an actual quote from Felix Renick that was recorded from his observations of a neighbor's child who returned from captivity as an adult teen, but who was unable to assimilate back into colonial society, and eventually returned to Native life. The boy that Renick was talking about was John Sea, who had been captured in 1763, and returned in 1765, but had promptly ran away back to live with the Shawnee.

that they looked down upon him as a fool to be despised for not returning to White people. They were holding the view that there could not be anything of value that a White person could find that would make him turn his back on his own people and live with "Savages." Isaac could see that there was nothing he could say that would ever convince them otherwise. Isaac mulled over what had happened; lost deep in thought. "It is just as the Porcupine Clan Mother told me about White People before I left." She said, "Look into their eyes. Watch their faces. How cruel the Whites appear. Their lips are thin, their noses sharp, their faces furrowed. Their eyes have a staring expression. They are always seeking something. The Whites are always uneasy and restless. We do not know what they want; we do not understand them. We think that they are mad because they say that things they want come from their head, and not their heart. What they want is never enough and never pleases them. They want more and more. What is it they want more of? Our land. They truly are the children of the Evil Twin, come to destroy us," Isaac remembered her lamenting.

Isaac had felt that animosity most from Jonathan, of all people. "He was insulting," Isaac recounted. "Perhaps I was right to think that he always felt that way towards me, and I never saw it for what it was. I wonder if Tarhe had seen this about Jonathan? I wonder what had turned Jonathan's heart so hardened towards me, and the Wyandot?" Isaac asked himself. "How could someone ever change Jonathan's mind to believe anything else than hate?" Isaac's thinking turned to the words Simon Girty had spoken, giving advice that "the power of mediator and translator would be needed one day by someone like him. Isaac questioned Girty in his own mind. His advice seemed impossible in the face of people like Jonathan, his birth brother. These questions, and more, troubled Isaac as he reached Upper Sandusky. There were just no answers he could find to reach any conclusion. Arriving in the village, he found few people to greet him. "Something terrible must have happened," Isaac thought to himself. It didn't take long for Isaac to discover that Ronyouquaines, the wife of Tarhe and mother of his own wife Myeerah, had died while Isaac was gone.[149] Every one of the Porcupine Clan was in mourning. Tarhe was in isolation, and would not speak to Isaac for the time being. He found Myeerah in Tarhe and Ronyouquaines' lodge, taking care of their young son, Ebenezer, and the new baby born only three days ago, a boy who would be named Samuel.

Isaac felt exhausted from the ordeal visiting his Zane birth family combined with the death of beloved Ronyouquaines. Most of all, the thought of Jonathan and the things he had said when they met filled Isaac with rising anger that he could not relieve himself of every time he thought of him. Myeerah was preoccupied with the newborn baby and so unable to know what was troubling Isaac, who seemed to grow more and more out of sorts as each day passed. The anger eating inside him over Jonathan's words kept Isaac upset until he lost his appetite and refused to eat what Myeerah had prepared for him. The following morning, Isaac attempted to rise from his sleeping bench, but could not. His face was flushed. Myeerah was alarmed when Isaac tried to speak because he sounded delirious. Soon, Myeerah was unable to rouse Isaac at all. He was fevered, and appeared to be unconscious, which some kin said was like a coma sickness to which he could not be awakened. Fearful that Isaac might die, Myeerah called upon the old Clan Mother for advice. After she examined Isaac for herself, the old woman came to the conclusion that a tribal Shaman needed to be called upon to determine what to do. Finally, the elderly Wyandot Shaman named, "Sees Many Visions" arrived.

The first thing the wizened healer requested was that Isaac be taken to his lodge away from Myeerah and the children who he did not wish to be party to Isaac's treatment. This was accomplished with the help of several warriors who carried the unconscious Isaac to the appointed place. The old man ordered that he was not to be disturbed for any reason until he was finished, which was understood.

---

149 There is no exact date of death of Ronyouquaines, or cause. The fact that she disappears from Wyandot oral history lends itself to the Wyandot belief that she died at a relatively early age, most likely from a deadly physical ailment. If she was born about 1743 and died in 1773, she would have been thirty years old, possibly. That she died at such an early age, after having had only one child, lends to the idea that she had some internal ailment like possible cancer.

"Sees Many Visions" would tell Isaac after he recovered that his examination revealed to him that Isaac's ailment had to do with the Spirit, and not a specific physical trouble. To reveal the source of the Spirit problem, the skilled Shaman would have to put himself into a trance and leave his own body to visit the Spirit World. How he did this was by means known only to him and his Manitou, which he would never reveal to anyone. To provide the correct conditions for the onset of the trance, "Sees Many Visions" first made an offering of cedar smoke to fill his lodge. This was followed by the burning of strong tobacco which was important in creating the right conditions for opening his mind to the Spirit World. As the tobacco burned, the Shaman recited words to the tobacco smoke, saying, "A man is sick. The Great Spirit has informed me of your virtues. I rely on your assistance in effecting this man's cure."[150] "Sees Many Visions" then took his rattle and began to sing a song known only to him, while rhythmically shaking the rattle, invoking the Spirit Door to open.

By next morning, Isaac's fever had broken. At noonday, his eyes slowly fluttered open and gradually adjusted to the dim light inside the strange lodge. Finally, Isaac noticed the old man sitting off to the side who was watching him in silence. Isaac asked, "Where.... where am I? I do not recognize this place, or you." The Shaman was slow to respond. "I am called, Sees Many Visions. I am a Shaman. I have been tending to you since Myeerah and her Clan Mother requested my services." "What happened to me?" asked Isaac. "I don't remember anything except for a great pain in my head." "You will be fine now, my son. I discovered that you were troubled by a Shadow that was hovering over you in the Spirit Realm. I believe that it became attached to you through the door of anger; your anger. I saw the face of a Shadow man in the Spirit World. Your anger in this world attracted the Spirit which was feeding from your life energy. Normally you would be protected from such a Spirit, but this one lured you through the door of your empathy to someone else who did not appreciate your empathy. Perhaps that empathy was for one of your White birth kin you recently visited. I chased it away so it will not bother you again by

---
150 LD-TTIF, page 55.

an oath that I said to cast it out and away. Now, go to your wife. She is anxious to see you. Oh, do not discuss what I have told you with anyone; not Tarhe, or Myeerah. And bring me two deer skins when you can for my troubles." Isaac, a little dumbfounded by what was said, nodded in agreement, knowing he would be quick to pay that debt, as he felt so much better.

Myeerah was overjoyed to see Isaac had recovered. While he was gone, she had covered her face with ashes to mourn the loss of her mother, who had already been buried. With autumn winds blowing off the Great Lakes, Isaac took to hunting after doing all that he could for his wife and their newborn. Isaac knew that the grieving among Tarhe, his daughter, and their clan kin would go on for weeks possibly. It was tantamount that he should not interfere with this sacred tradition when someone close has died. Isaac remembered what he had been told by the Clan Mother. "When a chief is in mourning no complaint can be brought before him and no advice asked in any affairs."[151] It was only when the first snows began to fall, that the Porcupine Clan families began to return to some normality and Tarhe was able to continue his duties as Clan Chief for the training of the youth of his clan as young as the age of ten in the art of conducting war.[152]

Eventually, Tarhe resumed his discussion with Isaac on everything from Isaac's visit to the Zane birth brothers, to Jonathan's inherent nature. "Nephew, your birth brother Jonathan was not a good choice for adoption. I remembered when you and him were first brought to our village. I was reluctant to accept him for adoption. The Clan Mothers are usually right about who is adopted and who is ransomed to the Whites or traded away to another tribe. In Jonathan's case I think that they made a misjudgment, believing that his youth would make him a good candidate to become one of our people. In reality, he possessed an imperfection in his character that prevented his accepting us. It was a state of mind, I believe, already having its hold on him, common to so many White adult men, which is very difficult to detect in a youth. Regardless, it is for the best that

---

151 LD-TTIF, page 159
152 LD-TTIF, page 69.

he is gone." The talk about Jonathan stirred many thoughts in Isaac's mind in regards to what the Shaman had told him, which he could not discuss with Tarhe. Did his blood kin Jonathan have an evil spirit he sent to Isaac? Isaac realized that it was best to put it out of his mind, lest dwelling on Jonathan could arouse the situation again.

Gradually, talk turned to the continuing rumors arriving with traders concerning trouble between the Shawnee and Virginian Long Knives south of the Ohio River into Ken-Tuck-Kee hunting grounds. Tarhe could see no resolution of the troubles in any other way but war. It would be a war that would put the Long Knives in their place, but likely cost the Shawnee a great deal of suffering. "I am glad we live at a long arm's reach of the Long Knives to our villages. The Shawnee think so too about their villages, but I am not so sure. However, with the coming of winter and the snows covering the paths, all Native peoples of the Ohio Country can rest easy that the problems with the Long Knives will be put off till the coming spring, and then we shall see," Tarhe remarked with apparent satisfaction. However, that was not the case as Tarhe had predicted. The winter of 1773 into early of 1774 was fitful on the frontier along the Ohio River to the south. Periods of milder weather allowed both Shawnee warriors and Virginian trappers and explorers to roam the paths of the Ken-Tuck-Kee lands. Confrontations occurred when the two antagonists met, as was told to the Wyandot at Upper Sandusky.

To make matters worse, the British garrison at Fort Pitt was withdrawn earlier the previous year which left no clear authority to keep order over the Virginians who did as they pleased in "Injun" country. Tarhe was informed of an incident in early October where Shawnee warriors attacked Long Knives interlopers, killing many of them. This heralded difficult months ahead with sniping by both sides which sparked fear among the White population of a new war about to start at any time. By late February, the continuation of isolated Shawnee attacks against parties of arriving Virginians into the Shawnee hunting grounds caused the local inhabitants along the frontier of Virginia and then Pennsylvania to begin "forting up." Local militia officers thought it wise to send scouts to search for evidence of approaching war parties. Tarhe had seen and heard of this kind of tension before. He knew that all it would take for war to break out would be a precipitating incident for the Natives that would tip everything towards bloodshed from which there would be no return.

That incident was not long in coming by the late spring of 1774. The Mingo War Chief known by his English name Logan was away hunting when his family was massacred across from the mouth of Yellow Creek on the Ohio River by roughshod frontiersmen itching to kill "Injuns" and start a war. When Logan returned, to his shock he had to bury his scalped, dead relatives, including his pregnant sister and his brother, along with several others from the village. Logan's sister had not just been killed and scalped. Her unborn child was cut out of her belly, killed, and scalped as well. Logan had always been a friend to White people. He had fed them when they were hungry and did not take up the hatchet during the war with the French and their Native allies. But now Logan vowed revenge against Virginians whom he was told had committed the murders. His runners went out on paths to the surrounding villages in the Ohio Country with the shocking news. Logan called for a council with those warriors who would support him. Since Logan was a Mingo with many kin in the Mingo villages to the south and east, the Mingo warriors he appealed to decided to join him at the first possible moment. Within days, factions of Shawnee agreed as well to fight with Logan. However, the Lenape counseled to remain neutral in what they believed would be a war that they wished to avoid due to living so close to the White frontier. A runner came from Yellow Creek to the Upper Sandusky Wyandots with a request from Logan to join him in attacking the Virginian frontier settlements. The tribal council of the Wyandot sent a message back to Logan that they had to discuss going to war and that would take some time. Hearing that, Logan, and all the warriors he could muster headed for the Long Knives settlements east of the Ohio River, making sure to avoid Pennsylvania settlers whom Logan did not wish to harm as they had not been involved in the massacre of his family.

Logan's Lament

The late spring turned into early summer as Logan, with his Mingo and Shawnee war parties, intensified their raiding against the Virginian frontiers until the borderlands became depopulated. Many settlers were either killed, burned out, or fled east. The Wyandot council could not come to a quick decision. Past wars with the Whites had shown them the jeopardy of going to war which always ended to the detriment of the Wyandot. Too, war was not an easy thing to decide upon, knowing that Wyandot warriors, once committed, would never back down from an Enemy. This had caused a lot of needless death in the past. Tarhe told Isaac that it would take the whole tribal council to declare war. Once the council committed the tribe to war, the Head Chief and his Warpole had the sole right to command the warriors without exception.[153] All Wyandot citizens were obligated to obey the commands of the Head Chief and his Warpole during war, and they were accountable to the tribal council. In the Wyandot world, Tarhe explained, "Warriors cannot just go to war on their own without tribal approval and the council of Clan Mothers when their advice was required. "Going to war is not a light matter; not an easy thing to decide since every Wyandot's fate hangs in the balance," said Tarhe, "including the fate of our women, children, and elderly."

By mid-summer, the devastation wrought by the Mingo and Shawnee was prompting the Long Knives to plan a response by putting into place a course for war on their own part to be taken to the Shawnee, in particular. One of the many things precipitating this was the words spoken by the Shawnee War Chief named Cornstalk to the Pittsburgh authorities. The Wyandot got word of Cornstalk's rebuke to the White leader at Fort Pitt[154] who asked Cornstalk to "not take amiss the Act of a few desperate young men," meaning the party that had massacred Logan's family, and the other depredations of other Long Knives on the Ohio River. Cornstalk had replied, "Virginians should likewise not be displeased at what our Young Men are now doing, or shall do against

---

153 LD-TTIF, page 69.

154 Virginian John Connolly, provisional commander at Fort Pitt under the order of Virginia Governor Lord Dunmore.

your People." The head man at Pittsburgh named Connolly was said to be enraged at Cornstalk's reply. Tarhe exclaimed, "The Whites expect that we should overlook what the Long Knives have done to Natives, but our warriors should be held accountable for retaliating." At the same time, an emissary from the Six Nations arrived, saying that William Johnson had died suddenly on July 11th while negotiating with a council of the Iroquois Confederacy to help preserve the peace on the northern frontiers. His last words were that all the tribes, including the Wyandot, should refuse any alliance with the Shawnee in their war in the Ohio Country. He had advised the Iroquois council that they send emissaries to the Wyandot, Ottawa, and other western tribes urging them to remain neutral in the war raging to the south. It was strong words for the Wyandot to listen to. They remembered how the same Iroquois had driven them from their Huron homelands more than a hundred years ago. The Wyandot had long memories, and none of them good about their eastern so-called brothers.

The Wyandot tribal council, including Clan Chiefs and Clan Mothers decided unanimously. There would be no war with the Long Knives and no alliance with the Shawnee or Mingo. The Wyandot would fight when the situation warranted it, but this was not a time like that. The Long Knives were not marching against Wyandot villages at this time. The council understood implicitly how important it was for their friend Logan to seek and fulfill vengeance for the murder of his family. Now they heard that his tomahawk was red with the blood of the Long Knives he had killed, and Logan was satisfied to withdraw from the war that he had started but had no intention of continuing further. Word was spreading quickly that the Virginians were sending two armies against the Shawnee and Mingo villages to the southern Ohio Country with the intent of destroying them in their own act of vengeance. Cornstalk planned on meeting the Long Knives' army that was descending the Kanawha River from the White settlements before they could join with the other soon to come down river from Pittsburgh. Cornstalk sent an emissary to the Wyandot council imploring them to send him warriors, however, the council overruled any support of the Shawnee. Officially, the tribal council thought it wise to remain neutral and state that to all involved. Tarhe, though he had no authority to speak for anyone but himself, asked to talk before the council.

"As one of your Wyandot War Captains, I accept and obey your wishes in this matter. I am not speaking to you to question your authority. I dislike the Long Knives as much as any man here, and I realize this is not the fight of the Wyandot Nation. I simply wish to remind the council that we have many warriors who have not proven themselves as men in war due to the lack of opportunity to attack the Cherokee any longer. It is for their benefit that I speak. I ask that you approve sending a party of our veteran warriors with our novices to support Cornstalk. These warriors would remain under the command of our own War Captain, and not the Shawnee and Mingo. I would gladly serve in that capacity if asked. That is all I have to say," Tarhe stated. The tribal council asked Tarhe to leave while they deliberated. Finally, after all of the members had spoken their minds in turn without interruption, as was tribal tradition, Tarhe was called back in, and Dunquat rose to speak to him. "What you say, Tarhe, are words of wisdom spoken by the great War Captain that you are, knowing that our strength as a nation depends on our warriors being ready to fight when the time comes. So, we grant your request with one exception. It is the opinion of the tribal council that the War Captain Chiyawee[155] will lead the party of several dozen warriors, and you will be his second-in-command. Choose those warriors carefully and prepare to leave as soon as possible," Dunquat ordered. Tarhe nodded that he understood without complaint. Later, Tarhe explained to Isaac that Chiyawee was a great warrior and captain with much more influence with the tribal council and Dunquat than Tarhe. Privately, Tarhe thought that perhaps Dunquat and the council thought him to be too brash which might cause unnecessary casualties if the situation arose.

---

155 According to Wyandot history, Chiyawee was a Wyandot War Chief at the Battle of Point Pleasant. He was not Principal War Chief, but influential.

With goodbyes said, Chiyawee and Tarhe led over thirty warriors south from Upper Sandusky to the Scioto path that led to the Shawnee villages where Cornstalk was assembling his warriors. Tarhe had personally selected the warriors with Chiyawee's approval and made sure they had workable weapons and ample ammunition. Isaac The Eagle and Adam Tohunehowetu were among the novice warriors selected. Arriving at Cornstalk's massive camp, the Wyandots were surprised to find that warriors from other nations who had also declared their neutrality were present as volunteers to aid Cornstalk, just like the Wyandot party. There was a band of Ottawas who came in shortly after Chiyawee's men. The Ojibway had sent warriors as well, and to Tarhe's surprise, Lenape warriors were already in camp, led by their War Captain Buckongahelas. In addition to Mingo warriors under Plukkemehnotee, named Pluggy by Whites, there was a band of Miamis from the west. Cornstalk received word from his scouts that the Long Knives army under the command of a Virginian named Lewis had just reached the mouth of the Kanawha River on the Ohio, where the roughly 1,100 militiamen made camp. Another army under the command of Dunmore had left a day ago from Weel-Lunk on the Ohio River to link up eventually with Lewis.

There was no time to waste, in Cornstalk's mind, if his warriors were to defeat the first of the Long Knives army before the second joined up with them. Cornstalk called for a council of war with all the respective War Captains. Their Native army would leave as soon as possible for the Ohio River and plan to cross the river there once rafts were built. With that, all of the more than 700 mixed warriors prepared to leave by stripping to the barest of clothing, and painting their bodies for war. After a hard, quick march, Cornstalk's force arrived on the Ohio, unseen, about seven to eight miles upriver from the Enemy's camp. There, they crossed the river, and camped for the night with no fires. The next morning,[156] the warrior army rose before dawn and silently approached the unsuspecting Long Knives camp. Cornstalk asked

---
156 October 10, 1774

Chiyawee to have his Wyandots take the far-right flank and protect the Ohio River shoreline from any Enemy who might attempt to flank the main body once the battle commenced. It did not take long to start. Two militiamen out hunting stumbled upon the advancing warriors and sounded the alarm. Immediately, the Long Knives camp was abuzz with activity as militiamen formed up and advanced to meet Cornstalk's warriors coming towards them. Within a short time, the battle was underway in full force as both sides exchanged heated gunfire. Tarhe wanted both Isaac and Adam to stick close to him as the two sides were about to meet in close combat. Bullets flew everywhere from the roar of muskets, causing casualties, especially among the militiamen. Within the first couple of hours, many Whites were hit when they dared show themselves in the open, whereas Native warriors used the cover of trees to protect themselves.

Isaac proved to Tarhe and those warriors around him what a good shot he was, having hit several Long Knives at nearly one-hundred yards. However, Tarhe would not let Isaac crawl forward to retrieve the Enemy scalps, knowing that if he was hit and captured by the Virginians that they would skin him alive for fighting with the "Injuns." The battle see-sawed back and forth through the midday. However, by early afternoon, it was becoming apparent to Chiyawee and Tarhe that the main body of the Shawnee and Mingo warriors under Cornstalk and Pluggy were not making progress at breaking the Enemy line and forcing a rout. The Long Knives were now fighting in pairs to avoid more casualties, where one man fired while the other loaded. By mid-afternoon, the Long Knives had been able to gain the ridge of high ground on Cornstalk's left side and were getting dangerously close to flanking the Native army. The only attempt by the Enemy against the Wyandot holding the right flank against the Ohio River had been stopped cold. It had been broken up, thanks again to the accurate gunfire of Isaac and those warriors around him. As the afternoon lengthened, Cornstalk received word from his scouts afield that a Long Knives army was advancing quickly down the Kanawha River to reinforce their beleaguered army.[157] Cornstalk considered all the possibilities and realized that with ammunition running low and many wounded warriors to tend to, it was time to give up the battle and withdraw without a victory in hand.

A less disciplined War Captain might have tried to fight on. However, Cornstalk knew that though his warriors had killed many Enemy, so too had many of his own men been killed and wounded. He sent word to Chiyawee to have the Wyandot be the last to withdraw and hold the Enemy in place while continuing to face them. Warriors were designated to carry their wounded from the battlefield and take as many as possible aboard the rafts to the other shore. In the meantime, Cornstalk signaled the extended line of his fighters to slowly shorten up and take steps from the field, with the Wyandot moving from the right flank to the center as they too withdrew. Tarhe could see that the Long Knives were in no hurry to pursue them. As the Wyandot warriors gradually withdrew, they passed over the bodies of those White men killed in the early morning exchange. On Chiyawee's order, Tarhe thinned his men so that some could help their own severely wounded be carried to the river, along with the Wyandots who were lightly hurt. Isaac spotted a militiaman's discarded rifle, powder horn and bullet bag which he stopped to pick up. As he did, an Enemy bullet grazed his hand but did no serious damage. The dead warriors had to be left on the field of battle with the knowledge that the Enemy would scalp and mutilate them beyond recognition. Bringing the wounded back on litters would be challenging enough on the twisting path back to the Shawnee Scioto villages. Some, who had more serious wounds would likely die along the way, unfortunately.

The returning warriors were sullen. They knew, as Cornstalk did, that they had not defeated the Long Knives army who would soon cross the Ohio River and follow them to their villages in a few days. The ammunition was largely spent with no way to replace it in the short term to defend against the two Enemy armies that were sure to come seeking revenge. In addition, Cornstalk

---

157 This was the reinforcement of 200 men under Colonel Christian of the Fincastle County Regiment who arrived after dark.

estimated that close to forty warriors had died and were left on the field. What was equally worrisome and disheartening was that more than seventy warriors from all the tribes had been wounded, of which almost half of the wounds Cornstalk considered severe. Chiyawee and Tarhe decided to leave immediately for the Upper Sandusky now that the battle was over and they had no further reason to stay longer. Tarhe had the satisfaction of knowing that his youngest warriors had proven themselves in the battle and garnered for themselves much honor, and necessary valuable experience to be considered Wyandot warriors and men. Isaac, on the other hand, had no Enemy scalps to display as trophies to his marksmanship. However, the rifled gun he had found was an extraordinary prize that he would cherish from hereon. Once the Wyandot war party reached the Upper Sandusky village now called Half-King's Town, Chiyawee and Tarhe presented themselves before the tribal council and gave an accounting of the battle and its disappointing results. They noted that inevitably, two Enemy armies would soon march unopposed into the Ohio Country bent on the destruction of all Natives, regardless of who was neutral or not. A decision was made that Dunquat must call together all his War Captains under his Warpole Coon and prepare for any future Enemy onslaught headed towards the Wyandot. They would fight if attacked, but otherwise, not.

Chapter Thirteen
The Gathering Clouds of War

In a matter of days, word reached Upper Sandusky that the English Captain Dunmore and his army had marched to a point near a cluster of Shawnee towns on the Pickaway Plains of the Scioto River Valley. Here, Dunmore stopped and made camp in preparation for war once Lewis's southern army joined with him. It was told by Native runners that Cornstalk had approached Dunmore under a flag of truce and sued for peace with the Long Knives rather than see his people destroyed by the overwhelming numbers of their soldiers. Dunmore, it was said, agreed to terms of peace that highly favored his conquering army. All hostile Natives were to agree to make no further war. They were to stop all war parties from raiding the Virginian frontier any further. In addition, the Shawnee must agree to completely forfeit any claim to the Ken-Tuck-Kee lands across the Ohio River and must not allow their hunters on those lands. All White captives taken since the end of the war with Pontiac had to be returned. All horses, valuables and household goods of the Long Knives taken during the raids against the Virginian backcountry settlements were to be restored. The Shawnee and Mingo must promise that any boats of settlers passing down the Ohio River would not be molested. The worst part of Dunmore's treaty was aimed directly at the Shawnee. They must provide some of their chiefs as hostages who would be held over the mountains at the place called Williamsburg until Dunmore was satisfied that the Shawnee were in compliance with his terms.[158] "All in all," Tarhe explained to Isaac and Adam, "While the terms are favorable to the Shawnee in that their villages and women and children will not be attacked, nonetheless, the directive that the Shawnee give up the Ken-Tuck-Kee hunting grounds is a serious injury to their Nation for which I think they will never comply with in the long run."

Isaac was ecstatic to spend time with Myeerah and the children after so long an extended absence. With winter about to set in, Isaac took his new rifle out hunting and found it to be more accurate than the smoothbore trade gun he had always used. Although it took longer to load due to the need to wrap the smaller-sized lead ball in a piece of greased cloth patch, it took less shots to bag the same number of deer. That was because he had no misses due to the erratic smoothbore musket ball once it left the barrel. The winter and spring of 1775 were some of the happiest moments Isaac had experienced with his young family. Ebenezer, the toddler was now walking, and Samuel was crawling. To add to the joy, Myeerah announced when the snows began to thaw that she was pregnant again, and would give birth in the fall of the same year. As soon as the paths from the east were open, traders from Pittsburgh returned with goods and Isaac provided Myeerah with many gifts of beautiful cloth, silver earrings, and a looking glass from the trade hides he had been able to amass from the last fall's hunt.

One morning when he was about to set out on the chase, as the Wyandot called the hunt, Isaac heard the voice of the Shaman, Sees Many Visions, call out to him. "Isaac The Eagle, come visit me first before you leave for the woods. I have something important to tell you. Isaac set his rifle and pouch down inside his lodge and followed the old man to his own. He seated himself across from the Shaman who spoke after several moments of silence. "I have something to

---

158 Officially called the Treaty of Camp Charlotte, the terms were agreed upon in late October 1774, thus ending what came to be called, "Lord Dunmore's War."

tell you. I had a dream that concerns you. In the dream, I saw you looking for your Manitou but not being able to find it and I could not see what it was, or looked like. You did not know who and what it may be, and you did not know where to look. However, then I heard a voice calling to me, coming from a small white Spirit stone. It said to me, 'I know where The Eagle can find his Manitou, however, he needs your help to find me, as I am hidden from his eyes."

Well, I awoke and thought about this for some time, as to what it meant. But I put it out of mind and went looking for herbs along the path that leads to the northeast away from our village. It was there, along the rocky defile where the path descends to the creek, that something caught my eye by the glint of sunlight upon it. It was the very stone that I saw in my dream. I picked up the stone and held it in the palm of my hand. I could feel its Spirit echoes. I knew that it was telling me that I must find you to give it to you. Here it is." Sees Many Visions opened the palm of his hand and uncovered a small smooth white stone the likes that Isaac had never seen before. "This stone, Isaac The Eagle, will lead you to your Manitou, as I have been told. It has Spirit in it to guide you to your Manitou, or rather, your Manitou will find you at the same time. Fashion a leather pouch to keep it in, and string that medicine pouch around your neck so that the stone is close to your heart. Do not show it to anyone. It is for you only. It is powerful. When it leads you to your Manitou, you will have a Spirit guide for life in this world and into the next." With that, the conversation was over, and Isaac left on the hunt with much to think about.

Days later, Isaac heard news about the activities of his Zane birth family. The brothers Silas, Ebenezer, and Jonathan had helped a Pennsylvanian militia officer named Crawford build a frontier fort at Wheeling the past year prior to Dunmore's departure with his army for Shawnee country. That fort sat on the crest of the hill overlooking the Ohio River, on land that the brother Ebenezer had claimed for himself.[159] Ebenezer had gone on to

---

[159] That structure was named Fort Fincastle for Viscount Fincastle, Lord Dunmore, Royal Governor of Virginia. It was completed in 1774 under the supervision of Colonel William Crawford, and the labor of over four hundred militiamen and regular troops from Fort Pitt.

serve under Dunmore's division of the army that eventually met with the Shawnee at Camp Charlotte. Jonathan was known to have been a scout for a detachment of over four hundred militiamen from Fort Fincastle under the officer named McDonald that descended the Ohio River in late July and then headed inland up from the mouth of Captina Creek on the west side. The little army headed towards the cluster of Mingo and Shawnee villages at Wakatomika on the west side of the Muskingum River. The villages there were attacked and destroyed by McDonald and his men. The women and children had escaped unharmed, and only a few warriors were killed while inflicting similar casualties on the Long Knives. This had all happened unbeknownst to Isaac. The news confirmed in his mind that his blood brothers by birth had been lying to him all along when they met at Weel-Lunk previously. They were not simply the settlers from across the mountains come to claim land for a homestead. Isaac's brothers had now picked up arms against Native people, demonstrating that they were no better than the rest of the Long Knives who wished to destroy the Shawnee, and then Wyandots.

"It is not that simple," Tarhe argued. Not all Virginians think and act the same as you would believe. Those men that killed Logan's family for sport are one kind of Long Knife. Once they committed their cowardly deed, they left the other Long Knives on the border with us to suffer from Logan's retribution which the perpetrators knew would follow. Some Whites hate us more than others, and some do not hate us at all. You must be able to see that with those Whites who come to our village. They are not bad men. In the White man's world, Whites must obey an order from a Military Captain, just as I must obey an order from Chiyawee in battle, or from the tribal council, more so in times of war. Cornstalk ordered us Wyandot to protect the flank of his Shawnee fighters because he knew that Wyandot warriors never shirk a duty in battle, once given. And so, we did, at great peril to all of us. Likely, your birth brother named Ebenezer was ordered to build the fort and then to serve his Captain Dunmore. He could not refuse any more than I could refuse Chiyawee. It is Jonathan who is the one to really take up the war axe against us with enthusiasm. He is a different Long Knife from Ebenezer or the cowardly killers of Logan's family. Jonathan is cold and calculating. He volunteered as a scout because he wanted to, not ordered to. He was like a Wyandot hunter seeking out his prey in a cold and calculating manner. Give thought to it, Isaac, and you will see that I am right," Tarhe stated.

The summer of 1775 held no new developments for the Wyandot. However, they increasingly heard word of great upheaval among the colonials on the other side of the mountains. Rebellion had broken out against the King of the English, first with the Bostonians[160] and then throughout the colonies. Shots had been fired and the city of Boston was besieged. Natives throughout the Ohio Country did not know what to make of this. Many said that the English King across the Great Water was being chastised by his rebellious American children. Word spread from village to village that Dunmore had been deposed and his representatives at the Fort Pitt settlement were appointing their own officials and calling themselves "Patriots." By mid-summer, Tarhe and the tribal council heard that the rebellion had not been resolved peacefully. Instead, war between White brothers supporting the English Father and those against the English Father was increasing. Since there was no longer English rule at Fort Pitt that Virginians needed to abide by, settlers, surveyors, land claimers, and fur hunters were pouring into the Ken-Tuck-Kee lands in alarming numbers. In addition, with Dunmore gone, the peace accord that he had fashioned the previous year with the Shawnee, in particular, was being completely ignored. In Tarhe's mind, that could only mean one thing to be sure of. Sooner or later, war with the Whites would come when they wanted more land.

In early fall, a delegation of English Red Coat officers from Detroit in the company of French mixed-blood translators visited Dunquat's village requesting an audience with the chiefs and tribal

---

160 Bostonians is a term used to denote the colony of Massachusetts people who began the rebellion at Boston against the British Crown which quickly grew to include the rest of the colonies on the Atlantic, in 1775.

Jonathan Zane

council, which was granted. The council listened as the English explained to the Wyandot headmen and Clan Mothers that the English King was quarreling with his disrespectful children in America who wished to sever their ties to their rightful Father, King George. King George was worried that his Native children in the Ohio Country might listen to the lies being spread by the Rebels and take their side in the quarrel. The English were here to tell the Wyandot to remain neutral in this family dispute. An officer asked them to remember that though the Wyandot and the English had fought against each other because of Pontiac, that war hatchet had been deeply buried. Their English Father loved his Red Children and would protect them from the Rebels who wished nothing more than to dispose of all Native people. The Rebels wanted to take all the land for themselves, as they were attempting to do in Ken-Tuck-Kee. To show their good faith, the English commandant in his Red Officer's Coat had his men unload from the pack horses a load of provisions, household goods, and precious ammunition for the Wyandot to distribute among themselves as gifts from their English Father. Tarhe could see what was happening, and it worried him to no end. Both sides of the quarrel would eventually attempt to woo the Wyandot to their side to fight in their war.

The English visit from Detroit stirred much debate among the Wyandot headmen. While they held no love for the English, the Wyandot tribal council new that the growing threat to them was not the English but the Rebel Long Knives calling themselves Americans. What was increasingly troubling was that with each passing week, fewer and fewer traders from Fort Pitt were coming to Upper Sandusky. When they did, they had meager trade goods and no ammunition at all. Tarhe was told that this was because most all of the trade goods that had been stored in the trading company warehouses in Pittsburgh were gone, and no goods were arriving from Philadelphia. That was due to the fact that those goods were imported from England, and the provisional Rebel officials had no money or credit to buy anything even if the English would sell to them. Apparently, the English at Detroit had some inkling of this, having distributed gifts without hesitation. Then runners arrived from the Mingo villages to the south with word that two emissaries from Fort Pitt were on their way to Upper Sandusky to council with the Wyandot, as they had with the Mingos, and the Lenape before them. It was led by a man named James Wood, an army veteran of Dunmore's War and McDonald's campaign.

Wood would have never been allowed to speak on his own due to his past service fighting against the Shawnee. It was possible that he would have been killed by the Mingo if it were not for his traveling companion, a man known to all the tribes, and a friend to the Wyandot. Simon Girty was accompanying Wood on his mission to the tribes to deliver peace messages from the Patriot Americans, as they were calling themselves. Girty was said to be in the employ of Virginia. They hired him because he spoke all of the Native languages which Woods did not speak. Also, the Long Knives knew Girty was a capable guide who knew all the paths and the personalities in the Ohio Country. Most important of all, Girty knew the necessary protocol needed with each tribe to be able to enter the village and speak before their council. He and Wood made camp outside Dunquat's town and waited for the Wyandot to greet them. The next day, several warriors arrived to summon the two men to the Wyandot council lodge where Dunquat and his headmen were waiting to hear what Wood had to say. Wood stood up and spoke while Girty translated to the Sachems. When Wood was finished, the Warpole Coon rose and told Wood and Girty to return to their camp where they would await an answer from the council concerning the petition Wood had made asking for peace and neutrality.

It was there that Isaac took the opportunity to talk with Simon Girty who remembered him from his last visit. Isaac was taken aback when he saw Girty working on the side of one of the Enemy Long Knives, the emissary named Wood. "Why are you working for this man who is our Enemy?" Isaac asked Girty in private. Girty responded, "It is so good to see you well, Isaac. I am employed as a translator for this man, in that capacity only. The Virginia government is paying me for my services. You know I am no longer living with my brothers, the Seneca. I am standing in both worlds, Isaac, Red and White. I see both sides, and though I am at the moment in the employment as a translator for the Virginians, I am trying to help all as a negotiator, when that opportunity arises. My presence does not mean that I have chosen one side over the other, as you might think," said Girty. It was during their conversation that the Wyandot Warpole Coon arrived in the company of several warriors. He confronted Wood on the hostility of the Americans towards their own Father the King across the Great Water. Coon wished to know why. Wood replied through Girty that the matter was between the King and the Americans only. "We do not need or desire any assistance from the Wyandot or any other nation. We wish your people to continue in the peace and friendliness with us by observing a strict neutrality, as we have not the least doubt that all differences between ourselves will be soon accommodated." Isaac was not so sure to believe this White man's words.

In the morning, Wood and Girty were summoned back to the Wyandot council lodge. In that council, Coon openly confronted Wood with news that the Virginians were building posts and forts in Ken-Tuck-Kee in preparation to drive off all Natives in the Ohio Country and claim the land for their own. This accusation was well-worn, and dated back to Pontiac's time, and before with the French. Wood replied that he knew of no fort, and no plans of the Americans to attack Fort Detroit. In the heated exchange, it was apparent to Girty that the Wyandot council members were hostile to the American emissary and his assurances to keep the terms of the Treaty of Fort Stanwix and remain on their side of the Ohio River. Wood and Girty were treated with cool respect, but it was apparent to both men that Wood had not won over the Wyandots to the American cause. Nor had the Wyandot Sachems even promised to remain neutral in what seemed to the headmen to be an approaching war in every quarter. As a last request, Wood asked the Wyandot chiefs to attend peace talks at Fort Pitt in the coming months. The tribal council agreed to consider the invitation but gave no indication they would come. As they prepared to leave, Girty pointed out to Wood his observation that the

Wyandot appeared to be well-supplied. No doubt the kegs of gunpowder Girty had spied in the village were gifts from the British agents working from their Detroit post. As they rode out, Girty saw Isaac watching him and gave Isaac a nod of friendly recognition.

A grand council for peace talks was opened on October 7th at Fort Pitt. Present were headmen and warriors from the Lenape, Shawnee, Mingo, Ottawa, Seneca, and Wyandot Nations. Though Tarhe was not a headman, he and Isaac accompanied the Wyandot Sachems and War Captains headed by Dunquat and Coon. The council opened with the Virginia commissioners explaining to the Natives how all of the thirteen American colonies were now one family with a "great fire" at the Philadelphia town. Guyasuta was the designated spokesman for the Natives as a whole, with Simon Girty translating for both sides, as he knew the language of all the tribes present. Again, the request was made of the Natives of the Ohio Country to acknowledge the terms of the treaty signed with Dunmore the previous year and abide by the boundary of the Ohio River. The commissioners promised that if Natives, including the Shawnee, remained neutral in the American conflict with the King, that they would see to it that the Virginians stayed on their side of the river. When the treating was over, the Natives were given a paltry amount of gifts. This revealed to everyone present that the Americans, who were claiming superiority over the English, were too poor to provide the necessary protocol to prove their words were truly spoken. Many warriors went home with nothing in hand. Many more, including Tarhe, noted that the garrison troops at Fort Pitt were dressed in ragged threadbare uniforms, another indication that the Americans were so poor that they could not dress their own men in proper clothes.

As predicted, Myeerah gave birth to a child in winter; a boy who would be named William, after Isaac's father. By late spring of the following year of 1776, word reached Upper Sandusky from several sources that the war between the King of England and his rebellious colonials was intensifying across the breadth of the colonies. Many loyalists from the frontiers of the Six Nations Confederacy were fleeing to Canada as a result of the attempted arrests by the Rebels, as the English were calling them. Word from the Six Nations told the story of their six tribes questioning in council their previous decision to remain neutral and not ally with the British. This came at a time when their loyalist friends were being persecuted, especially in the Mohawk Valley. Even Sir John Johnson, the son of the deceased great superintendent of the Natives, Sir William Johnson, was forced to abandon all his possessions and estate and escape to Canada over the Adirondacks to avoid arrest for his loyalism to the Crown. In June, from Canada, Johnson received orders from the Commander-in-Chief, General Carleton, to begin recruiting men from the hundreds of refugees driven out by the Rebels. Johnson was to organize the men into loyalist provincial regiments which would return to the colonies and aid British regulars in waging war. However, even with that news, it appeared to the Wyandot council that the Six Nations, while upset over the treatment of their White friends, were not ready to budge from their avowed neutrality, at least for the moment.

Wyandot runners from the village at Detroit made their way to Upper Sandusky in early summer with news that a new Captain of the British had arrived to take command of the Detroit post and the surrounding settlement. His name was Lieutenant Governor Henry Hamilton. After meeting with the immediate chiefs of the tribes in the area, Hamilton asked that the Upper Sandusky Wyandots come to Detroit to receive gifts from the King their Father. In return, he asked for assurances that they would remain steadfastly neutral in the conflict enveloping the colonies in the east. By the time that Dunquat, Coon, and many Sachems of the Upper Sandusky clans arrived for the council with Hamilton, the Governor's message had changed since they first heard his invitation. What the Wyandot did not know was that Hamilton had received an urgent message by express from the British Commander-in-Chief at Montreal, General Sir Guy Carleton. In the letter addressed to Hamilton, Carleton advised, "I include the Indians, who should be kept as strongly attached to the King's intent as possible, and ready to act upon any occasion, when called upon. You must therefore defer all other matters for the present."[161] Hamilton was taken by surprise by the request. He realized that he must address the Wyandot in their upcoming meeting with a different approach to begin securing their potential alliance. In addition, plenty of gifts must be prepared for the Wyandot from the stores at Fort Detroit. Hamilton knew that gift-giving was a time-honored tradition. In this case, it would be used to ensure that his request for Native support in the future against the Rebels was not a mere empty gesture.

While the thirteen colonies on the eastern seaboard declared their independence from Great Britain in a declaration signed on July 4th, word of it did not reach the western frontier settlements and the Native tribes of the Ohio Country till almost a month later. In the meantime, Hamilton at Detroit was actively soliciting the support of the Native Sachems in a series of councils held at Detroit. However, Isaac heard from Tarhe that the Americans were likewise petitioning the tribes of the Ohio Country to treaty council with them. Beginning in early June of 1776, the Americans sent a former trader acquainted with the tribes between the Ohio River and Detroit, named William Wilson to visit each nation to deliver an invitation. Dunquat sent word requesting Wilson meet with him in person to explain the American request. By the time Wilson arrived at Upper Sandusky, Dunquat was no longer there, having traveled to Detroit. Wilson boldly made the trip to Detroit in the company of friends to deliver his message to the Wyandot Sachems, but once there, his presence was betrayed to Hamilton who demanded to speak to Wilson. The treaty peace belts Wilson had given to the Wyandot were returned to him whereupon Hamilton harangued Wilson and denounced him in front of the Natives in council, calling him a traitor to the King.

Hamilton wrote to Carleton later detailing his actions after listening to Wilson's Rebel lies. "I tore the Messages, letter and speeches of the Virginians, and cut their Belts in the presence of two hundred Indians, deputies from the Ottawas,

---

161 Letter from Carleton to Hamilton, July 19, 1776, Haldimand Papers, National Archives of Canada.

Chippewas, Wyandots, Shawanese, Delawares, Cherokees, and Poutawattamies. I told the Savages assembled at the Council to content themselves with watchfully observing the Enemy's motions and that if the Virginians attacked them, I should give notice to the whole Confederacy, and that an attack on one nation should infallibly be followed by the united force of all to repel or as they term it, Strike the Virginians."[162] Hamilton, though angered by Wilson's presence among the Natives, respected Wilson's character and gave him safe conduct through Native country back to Fort Pitt. While in the company of Dunquat, Wilson stopped briefly at the Upper Sandusky village, and then continued further to the home of an unnamed "Indian friend." It was there that Wilson was met the next day by Isaac The Eagle in the company of Tarhe, who came to see Wilson. Tarhe discussed with Wilson his visit at length and what had transpired at Detroit, which Tarhe had been party to. Isaac translated in Wandat Wilson's words. Wilson asked Tarhe what the Wyandot had to gain by supporting the British? "They might furnish your people with clothes and such like, but if the Americans are successful in the war, they will be so incensed against the Indians who fought against them, that they will march an army into your country and destroy everyone, and take your lands from you."[163]

Tarhe was quiet for a very long time before he finally spoke, with Isaac translating. "What you say is very true. I do not dispute it." Then reaching for his tomahawk in his sash, Tarhe placed it upon the crude table saying to Wilson, "There is my tomahawk. I will never lift it, nor shall any of my family fight against the Big Knife, if I can help it, unless they come into my

---

[162] Letter from Hamilton to Carleton, dated September 2, 1776, Haldimand Papers, National Archives of Canada.

[163] This encounter has been recorded in American Archives with much confusion associated with it. Wilson stated that it was the "chief" he questioned, not Isaac. However, American post-war writers attributed Tarhe's response as that of Isaac, which it clearly is not. This is a case where a primary source document was read incorrectly, and then a false interpretation made from it, that it was Isaac saying that he would never go to war against his own people. Reference to History of the Panhandle, page 96, printed 1879.

own house." Wilson departed for Fort Pitt, reporting to Morgan that it appeared that many of the Natives would likely side with the British if war came. Regardless, in spite of Hamilton's opposition, Sachems of the Lenape, Wyandot, Ottawa, and Shawnee attended a council held at Fort Pitt in late October. Lofty speeches were exchanged with vows of neutrality from all parties that ended with presents given to all the tribesmen this time. George Morgan was convinced that war was averted, however, Tarhe knew that Morgan was deceiving himself. Many of the same Native emissaries met again with Hamilton soon after the council with the Americans where he spoke to them. His words were soothing to those tribes most affected by the friction with the Long Knives. The Wyandot from Upper Sandusky were equally satisfied with the results as well. They gladly took home with them plentiful gifts and much needed ammunition for the coming fall hunt, which had been reduced to a trickle from the Pittsburgh traders.

Carleton, in command at Quebec, was party to word reaching him from England that a military campaign was planned for the upcoming year, the details of which he was not, as yet, informed. Nonetheless, he wrote to Hamilton at Detroit on October 6th, saying, "You must keep the Savages in readiness to join me in the Spring, or to march elsewhere, as they may be much wanted." By the end of the year, with war raging in the East, the Mohawk War Captain Thayendanegea, known by the English as Joseph Brant, had just returned from visiting England and King's George's court. Knowing that a British campaign was planned for the spring which would involve Native warriors, Brant made his way to British Fort Niagara to meet with the loyalist commander John Butler. From there, Brant sent a message to the western tribes, anticipating Carleton's demand for participation of the warriors. "I do not think it right to let my brothers go to war under the command of General Carleton as General Carleton expects and tries to have the Indians under the same command as the regular Troops, but it will be the best method for us to make war our own way." Brant was one of only a handful of Natives who could read, write, and speak English. He had learned this during his childhood schooling at Reverend Wheelock's Native school in Connecticut. While the Wyandot agreed in principle with Brant's message when it was read to them, at the same time they disagreed with Brant himself, who wanted the Wyandot warriors to serve under him, if war in the West should result. Brant, after all, was Iroquois; the same people who had treated the Wyandot badly over the years, as the tribal council reminded everyone.

Unbeknownst to anyone in the colonies or the wilderness beyond, King George III of England had not been sitting idly by during the onset of winter in late 1776. King George believed that he had acted towards the rebellious elements of his colonies with too much military restraint until now, hoping that they would become convinced that their differences with the Crown could be worked out. It had not happened and the King had run out of patience. He realized that he must stop this rebellion with the full force of His Majesty's military might. King George turned to his minister of war, Lord George Germain, to devise a strategy for ending the American rebellion and restore peace. Germain, in turn, met with his advisors and planned an expeditionary army under General Burgoyne to arrive in Canada, and then to advance south from Montreal and head for Albany. There, his army was to link up with a British force headed north up the Hudson River from New York. At the same time, to distract the Rebels and draw off some of their forces sure to oppose Burgoyne, Germain would send a second, smaller army departing southeast from Oswego on Lake Ontario. That army under Lt. Col. Barry St. Leger would advance to the headwaters of the Mohawk River and attack the Rebels down the Mohawk Valley. Upon reaching Albany, St. Leger was to link up with Burgoyne. Both of these British invasions needed to be supplemented with Native allies, in Germain's mind. Thus, as the massive British armies were assembled in England for the trip over the Atlantic in the upcoming spring of 1777, Germain penned orders for Henry Hamilton at Detroit that were sent to Carleton first.

Hamilton at Detroit received Germain's orders in Carleton's letter that arrived in late May. Hamilton had been a career military officer who had resigned to take the political appointment of Lieutenant Governor at Detroit. He was shocked at what was being ordered of him to do, as he had little expertise when it came to Natives. "Sir, you have herewith enclosed a copy of a letter from Lord George Germain which is sent you at full length, for your Instruction and Guidance," Carleton wrote on May 21st 1777 from headquarters. It was Germain's words that shocked Hamilton. "It is His Majesty's Resolution that the most vigorous Efforts should be made, and every means employed that Providence has put into His Majesty's hands for crushing the Rebellion, and restoring the Constitution. It is the King's Command that you should assemble as many of the Indians and employ them in making a Diversion and exciting an Alarm upon the frontiers of Virginia and Pennsylvania."[164] Germain included a list of names from the Pittsburgh area that Lord Dunmore, who was safely back in England, had provided Germain from memory. This "list of persons well disposed to His Majesty's Government, living on the Frontiers of Virginia," contained not a single person that Hamilton knew personally, such as the names Simon Girty and Alexander McKee, nor where he might find them. Yet, Hamilton knew he must come up with a plan to execute what seemed to him to be an impossible task. He was at a great disadvantage since he knew few of the Native chiefs around Detroit, nor could he speak the many diverse languages. Yet orders were orders, and something must be done, and done immediately.

---

164 Letter to Hamilton from Carleton, forwarding Germain's orders. Haldimand Papers, National Archives of Canada.

Chapter Fourteen
Ambush at Fort Henry

Dunquat and the tribal council at Upper Sandusky received an official invitation from the English Captain Hamilton to attend a Grand Council at Detroit. The council was to be held in mid-June for all the concerned tribes of the Ohio Country and the Great Lakes region. Hamilton wished for all Natives to hear the words of the English King from across the Great Water. Isaac watched the excitement grow in the village as word of the pending Grand Council circulated from clan to clan and lodge to lodge. Everyone knew at this point that the English would provide the upcoming assemblage with gifts of all kinds as well as food and drink from the King's larder at Detroit. Isaac asked Tarhe what he thought was to happen at this Detroit council called by the English if the Wyandot decided to attend? "It is a forgone conclusion that the headmen, and most all of the warriors and their families will go to Detroit. I already can guess, from what I've heard from our brothers at the Detroit village what is going to happen. The English are going to encourage us, along with the other tribes of this so-called Western Confederacy, to pick up the hatchet and go to war against the Rebel American Long Knives. The English Captain Hamilton will say so with flowery words of flattery followed by fiery threats to punish the Long Knives for stealing our land. Then he will bribe us with shiny new hatchets for the warriors and bolts of colorful cloth and copper pots for our women. This will be washed down our full bellies with British rum to seal the agreement of alliance from our Sachems and War Captains."

Isaac noted that Tarhe ended his assessment by staring for the longest moment into the distance before speaking again. "You must know, my Nephew, that I have witnessed this happen before when I was a young warrior. I gave the war whoop with other warriors before a similar council at Detroit, however not to the British, but to Pontiac. Then it was to affirm war against the English; now we are about to become allies with them. What does not change and which aches my heart more than you can know is that we, the Wyandot, will be coerced to fight in another White Man's quarrel. It will not be of our making, nor with it bring about any good for us as a nation. I fear it will be but another step on the road to our destruction by the Whites. When I raised my tomahawk high in the air for Pontiac, I did not see the dead and wounded warriors nor did I hear the wailing of the families for their lost ones. War is war, Isaac; a terrible thing. We have been on a continual war footing as a people since our eviction from our ancestral home in the Canadas by the Iroquois Haudenosaunee and their Dutch allies more than a hundred years ago." Isaac remained silent as Tarhe gathered final thoughts. "I remember clearly Pontiac's words. If we destroy the English in war, the French King will come back and help us regain our lost lands. That did not happen. Now it will be the English, I predict, who will tell us if we destroy the Long Knives Rebels, it will be the English King who will help us regain our lost lands. It is a lie we suckle like a babe on its mother's teat."

On the morning of June 17th, Isaac arose from the temporary shelter he had erected for him, Myeerah and the children they had brought with them to Detroit. Spread out across the meadow before the fort was a sea of Native lodges populated by hundreds, if not thousands of Natives from all directions. There were tribes that Tarhe named that Isaac had never heard of such as the Fox, Sauk, Wabash, Mascoutens, and Kickapoos from the Illinois Country. There were Chippewa from Saginaw and Chippewa from Ousahtanon, with all their War Chiefs and Village Chiefs present from their clans. Mohawks and Senecas arrived from the Six Nations Confederacy with other Iroquois tribes said to soon follow.

And of course, the Lenape, Poutawattamies, Miamis, Shawnee, and Mingo were already counseling in their respective temporary lodges in advance of Hamilton who was to begin his oration. It was mind-boggling to Isaac. He was awed by the sight of so many Native people gathered together in one spot for the same reason concerning their futures. Added to the din of so many Native voices that Isaac did not know and could not comprehend were other noises rising above that. There were the shrieks of hundreds of children at play, the murmurs from throngs of Native women working over cooking pots preparing food, and the barking of dozens of Native dogs as they ran wild throughout the extended temporary camp with impunity. "It is truly a sight to see," Isaac thought to himself.

Shortly after midday, the English commander Hamilton made his appearance leading an honor guard of several dozen Red Coats who marched in unison behind him to a cadence set by a drummer. Hamilton was dressed in a resplendent British officer's Red Coat trimmed in white lace with silver buttons. Slowly, a hush came over the throng of Natives as they realized that Hamilton was about to address them. Hamilton motioned to his interpreters to come forward and take position in front of the dais that Hamilton climbed up on so all could see him. Tarhe commented, as he pointed. "There, Nephew, is William Tucker interpreting for the Ottawa, Charles Baubin, for the Miamis, Pierre Drouillard for our own nation, and next to him is Duperon Baby, one of Hamilton's captains of the Indian Department at Detroit and a Sachem of the Wyandot at Detroit. Those other interpreters I know only as Kissinguaa and Piaiyash.[165] Hamilton began to speak by greeting the tribes present by name. "Let us before all things return thanks to the Great Spirit above, who has permitted us to meet together this day, and to assemble round this Council Fire! Children! I bid you all welcome War Chiefs, Village Chiefs, Warriors, Old Men, women and children. With these strings of wampum, I open your eyes that you may see clear, and your ears that you might listen to my words since I speak by order of the Great King, my Master, who is Father of us all!" With that, Hamilton proceeded as Tarhe had

---

165 Haldimand Papers, list of Nations at council held at Detroit, National Archives of Canada

predicted he would by complimenting the warriors present from each tribe. He commended them for their courage and bravery in facing their Enemy, the Long Knives, who were now the Enemy of their Father, who had not forgotten his Red Children's prowess in war.

The council went on for more days, before ending on the 30th of June when the tribes readied to disperse. Hamilton, in his last speech, told the tribal headmen that the King had not forgotten their plight, and wished to strengthen the bonds between them in light of what was happening in the Ohio Country. "Your Father, the King, knows that the rebellious and disobedient children of his wish to destroy all of you and take your land for themselves, just as they wish to dissolve the bonds of kinship with him. It is his earnest wish that his Red Children will help him chastise severely those who will not abide by the Father's will. Together, we must sweep away all obstacles between us so that we have a clear road of mutual understanding that will forever brighten the chain of friendship between the King and his Children. Therefore, the King, your Father, has authorized me to put this War Hatchet into the Hands of his Indian Children, so that you can dull its shine with the blood of your Enemy, in the manner that you see fit." With those words, Isaac was astonished to see the English officer Hamilton descend from the dais, and with his deputy agent of the Indian Department, Jehu Hays, began to sing a war song, which all of the nations took up singing in accompaniment.[166] When done, Hamilton called on Dunquat, the Half King of the Wyandot, to come forward. Then, in front of all the tribes, Hamilton handed the war hatchet to Dunquat which signified that the Wyandot were appointed to be guardians of the hatchet. It was a great honor bestowed on the Wyandot, and Dunquat in particular. However, Tarhe pointed out to Isaac, "As guardians of the war axe from this Council, it is now a foregone conclusion that the Wyandot have been chosen by Hamilton to be the nation to strike the Rebels first. Our neutrality is effectively over from this moment on."

With the council done, Tarhe, Isaac and their clan families prepared to leave for Upper Sandusky. However, Hamilton intervened,

---

166 This reference is not from the Haldimand Papers, but an account relayed to Draper in the Draper Papers.

making sure that the Wyandot had an ample supply of everything needed to make war in the upcoming months. Horses on loan were loaded with kegs of gunpowder and lead for bullets. Each warrior who needed a new hatchet was given one without obligations to pay for them. Families, like Isaac's, were provided with salt pork provisions, a new cooking pot, English wool blankets, and assorted trinkets for the women folk. It was nothing less than a small treasure for everyone who had been in much need since the past winter. However, the warriors, especially Tarhe, knew that it came with a price. That price was going on the war path against the Pennsylvania and Virginia frontier. Back at Upper Sandusky, Isaac sensed a new mood in the village. Everyone busied themselves for a collective mission that would come sooner than they thought. Dunquat, with his Warpole, Coon, and all the War Captains of the clans discussed strategy into the nights. Frenchmen of mixed blood sent from Detroit counseled with Dunquat on where they thought was the best objective to strike first, and when. Individual warriors were busy sharpening knives and axes. The gunsmith at Detroit, Jacques Chauvin,[167] arrived in early July to spend several weeks repairing the muskets and rifles of Wyandot warriors who had broken mainsprings and jammed musket balls in the breach. And most important of all, warriors began meticulously plucking the hair on their heads save for their scalp-lock in preparation for battle. Many were occupied with painting themselves in a manner only known to them, in light of personal Manitou instruction and clan symbols. Isaac could see it was the face of a Native nation going to war, and Isaac heeded the calling as well since he was a warrior too.

It was in middle August that word was sent to Isaac that Dunquat, the War Chief of the Wyandot wished to speak to him. Isaac did not know the reason, and speculated on several possibilities. When he entered the council lodge where Dunquat was seated, Isaac The Eagle found Tarhe there, as well as Adam Tohunehowetu. Adam's brother Samuel was present, along with several other White adopted men who were now warriors. Seated

---

[167] Reference from Roll of Officers, Interpreters, and Others employed in the Indian Department at Detroit, drawn for pay, Haldimand Papers, National Archives Canada.

next to Tarhe was Coon, the Wyandot Warpole. It was evident to Isaac that Tarhe knew what this meeting with Dunquat was about. Dunquat spoke directly to all, but Isaac sensed it was directed to him in particular. "As keeper of our English Father's war hatchet, I have given our solemn oath that we will strike the Enemy, and we will. There is a battle coming; I cannot say where because there are spies present among us who would tell the Long Knives and prepare them. Regardless, you must know that it is our tribal tradition that we do not allow you, even as the Wyandot warriors that you are, to go into battle against your White birth family. This applies more so if they now are your sworn Enemy, just as our clans would not go into battle against each other. That tradition will be strictly followed.[168] As it would be unjust for warriors like yourselves to remain in the village while we make war, I will allow you to accompany the warriors, but you must follow my instruction. Since Tarhe has trained you, you will remain under his command at all times without question. Do I have an assurance from each one of you that you understand my orders?" Dunquat asked. Isaac, without comment, nodded his head, along with the others. However, he left the meeting still puzzled. He did not know where they were going, but somehow, he felt that Dunquat was speaking to him more than anyone else in the lodge, and that could mean only one thing.

Isaac The Eagle did not have long to find out. Dunquat ordered the assembled force of three hundred and eighty-nine warriors, most of whom were Wyandot, to set out south from Upper Sandusky. They arrived at the Moravian Christian Delaware Mission at Schoenbrunn on the 8th of August. Dunquat believed that the Christian Delaware at Schoenbrunn were neutral in the growing frontier war between hostile Natives and the Long Knives. He used the mission as a stopping off point on the way to the White frontier as a place where he knew his warriors could rest and be fed by the Moravian minister, David Zeisberger. Dunquat ordered his warriors to behave themselves

---

168 This tradition not only prevented adopted White warriors from facing their old relatives in battle, it made sure that they would not be taken captive by their former kin so as to be repatriated, or, as was more likely, killed out of hand for being captured while fighting with Natives against Whites.

and not plunder the Delaware congregants. Also, he forbade the non-Moravian Delawares in a nearby village from bringing rum to his warriors while they were there. Further, Dunquat chastised several Mingo warriors who went out in the Moravian fields and killed several of the settlement's pigs on their own accord. Two Shawnee visitors who happened to be staying the night at Schoenbrunn and planned to go on to Fort Henry in the morning were detained by Dunquat. He did not want White people to get the news of his plan to attack Fort Henry, as he had not yet disclosed this to anyone. Unbeknownst to Dunquat, the pastor David Zeisberger had already sent word to Fort Pitt that a large party of Wyandot were on their way to the American frontier with big plans to attack somewhere.

Dunquat spoke to Zeisberger the next morning before leaving, and Isaac had an opportunity to listen in to his reply to Zeisberger's avowed neutrality. "My Cousins, I am very glad and I am very happy that you have cleansed my eyes, ears, and my heart of all the evil the wind had blown in during this journey, because the journey I am on is not a common one. I am a man of war and am going to war. Therefore, many things come over me and many bad thoughts go through my head and probably also into my heart. I am happy that my eyes are now bright and I can look at my Cousins with clear eyes. I am happy that I can listen to my Cousins with open ears and can take their words to heart."[169] With that, Dunquat excused himself and left to see that preparations were being made for his warriors to leave at the first possible moment. Tarhe turned to Isaac and said, "Dunquat does not trust the White Preacher Zeisberger. Privately, I believe that the Black Coat is a two-faced liar. While he professes neutrality, he is sympathetic to the Long Knives. I have heard that he sends them messages that are brought to him by Lenape spies in the Ohio Country. Dunquat has spies of his own, too. He knows the faces of the possible carriers of information to Fort Pitt. One is a White trader you met named Richard Conner who wishes to gain Zeisberger's favor so that he and his Shawnee wife can come live here with Zeisberger's Lenape and become praying Indians." "Tarhe,

---

169 From David Zeisberger's diaries, August 8, 1777, Schoenbrunn Mission, page 397.

why might Dunquat go through the pretense we just observed with Zeisberger and his leaders, if he already guesses the man's treachery?" Isaac asked. "It is simple, my Nephew. Dunquat knows that there is no harm that the White Preacher can commit against us, at this moment. Dunquat could order us to slay every one of them and burn the village to the ground, if he so wished. However, Dunquat wants the Black Coat to lie to us in front of all his people, for the future. And Dunquat will not forget."

Isaac had no doubt where the massive Wyandot war party of Dunquat's was headed. It all made sense, and confirmed to him the meaning of the conversation back at Upper Sandusky with Dunquat. They were headed for the settlement at Weel-Lunk; the place Isaac's birth family called Wheeling, which now had a fort built to protect it named Fort Henry. Dunquat had taken every precaution possible for his large force to remain undetected upon their approach to the Ohio River. Because of the time of year,[170] Dunquat had the warriors cross the river above the island in the middle of the channel opposite the fort on the bluffs. The crossing was ideal because the island screened their movements at dusk. Wyandot spies had arrived several days before and scouted the movements of settlers around the fort and the militia garrison strength. They reported to Dunquat that there appeared nothing out of the ordinary to indicate that the settlers were expecting an attack. In fact, the authorities at Fort Pitt had sent a message to the Zanes at Wheeling a week prior, urging them to prepare for a possible attack as reported by Zeisberger. But because Fort Henry was recently garrisoned with two companies of Virginia militia, and no sign of Natives had been discovered by scouts, the warning was discounted as improbable. "The residents of Fort Henry were oblivious to the approach of an Indian army who made a war party look laughable."[171] In fact, Dunquat was able to place hundreds of warriors across the river and distribute them around the fort and throughout the surrounding corn fields without being seen by anyone.

---

170 September 1, 1777, the Ohio River was low, and fording the channel without rafts or canoes was entirely possible.

171 LD-BOT, page 126.

Ambush Sentinel

Tarhe was instructed to take his band of warriors to the top of the hill opposite the fort and surrounding settlement to keep an eye on any Enemy approaching on the path from the east that was visible in the distance from where they were posted. Tarhe spread everyone out in an arc as well in case the unexpected happened, and mounted Enemy, for whatever reason, climbed the hill.[172] An ambush was prepared by Dunquat in the cornfields to the southeast bordering the path that led to the interior. As dawn broke on the foggy morning of September 1st, two men from the fort were seen leaving. They followed the path to the creek trail to round up stray horses. At some distance from the fort, the two men bumped into six warriors who fired on them. One man was instantly killed; however, the other was purposely allowed to escape to sound an alarm at the fort. From his vantage point on the hill, Isaac could see what happened next. A Long Knives militia company of fourteen men trotted out from the fort along the path through the cornfields to confront what they believed were six Natives. They entered Dunquat's L-shaped ambush whereupon dozens of warriors fired a volley into the militia line and then rushed in with hatchets to finish them off. Hearing the shooting but unable to see what was happening due to the low fog, another group of militiamen followed the path of their previous comrades into the same ambush with the same results. Very few men survived. Those few hid themselves as best they could. Above the noise, Isaac was sure that he heard the voice of his birth brother Ebenezer calling for the gates of the fort to be closed and no one leave again to attempt a rescue of those ambushed men. Apparently, Ebenezer was the only Enemy to realize that there were more warriors surrounding the fort that anyone imagined.

With the ambush over, Dunquat ordered his men to begin firing sporadically on the fort to keep everyone bottled up. He knew that there was no way to attack the fort without sustaining unnecessary casualties. And it would only be a matter of time before reinforcements arrived from the eastern posts, which negated the opportunity to wait and starve out the defenders. Rather, his

---
172 This hill is referred to today as Wheeling Hill.

warriors had successfully killed many of the hated Enemy and taken their scalps. The random shots from the warriors allowed the settler cabins to be meticulously plundered of all valuable household goods which had been left in haste, including horses and livestock. Field animals of the settlers were killed and all cabins and buildings burned. In the middle of this task, a relief force of mounted riders arrived along the river trail from the north. All the riders entered the fort except one man who was cut off. Isaac pointed the rider out to Tarhe as the lone militiaman drove his horse up the hill in the direction of the hidden Wyandots. At the last minute, Tarhe gave the word to rush the rider as he reached the crest of the hill with no place to escape. Isaac got a good look at the rider's face. Several warriors were within an arm's reach of pulling the Enemy rider from his horse before he forced the animal over the cliff's edge and rode it down the steep hillside on its belly. Isaac raised his rifle to take a shot at the man, but Tarhe lowered the barrel with his hand. "That White man is a brave warrior who has earned the right to escape imminent death with his life in hand. The Great Spirit would not wish for you to kill him."

With the battle over, the Wyandots withdrew across the river with their wounded. They had killed twenty-one[173] of the Long Knives with only one of the Wyandot warriors killed in the cornfield ambush. However, there were half a dozen wounded, one of which was likely not to survive the arduous trip back to Upper Sandusky. Though the Moravian preacher Zeisberger had asked Dunquat to take another road when they returned from where they were going, "so that White people would not follow you into our Town putting our women, children and us in danger,"[174] Dunquat ignored the preacher's request. On September 10th, Zeisberger wrote, "The Wyandot Half King, who came up with the wounded by water, came with his Captains to visit me and says he was happy to see me again." Dunquat was secure in the knowledge that he had struck the first major blow in the wilderness war as was prom-

---

173 The number of Whites killed fluctuates between fourteen and twenty-one, according to multiple sources.
174 Quote by David Zeisberger from the Zeisberger Diary, August 13, 1777.

ised to the British Captain Hamilton. However, as always was the case when the Wyandot went to war, Dunquat and Tarhe silently tallied their casualties in a dispassionate manner. First, the life of a valued warrior had been lost, and possibly another, with several more irreplaceable men wounded. On the other hand, the settlement at Wheeling had been destroyed as far as its material wealth, but the fort itself still stood. Twenty-one Enemy militiamen had been killed. However, Dunquat knew that there would be another twenty-one to replace them within a few days. The lives of Long Knives were expendable and of little value; the lives of Wyandot warriors were not.

Dunquat was not finished. He told no one what he planned as he and his men passed through the Moravian settlement on their way to Upper Sandusky. Dunquat waited until things had quieted down on the east side of the Ohio River, especially at Weel-Lunk. Secretly, Dunquat took a much smaller army of about one hundred warriors, including Tarhe, but not Isaac or Adam this time. By avoiding the Moravian settlement, the force made their way to the Ohio River whereupon they traveled down the west side river path several miles below Wheeling till they were opposite the Virginian blockhouse and cabin on the east side. Scouts crossing the river returned with news that the small Enemy settlement at Grave Creek which Dunquat hoped to attack was deserted. Dunquat was aware that there were still militiamen at Fort Henry that he wished to somehow lure out of the fort. He devised a plan whereupon several warriors crossed the Ohio River and set the abandoned blockhouse and cabin on fire, sending clouds of smoke into the air that could be seen for miles. A scout from Fort Henry spied the smoke to the south and alerted the fort who sent out a militia company under a Captain named Forman. Forman marched his men down the east path along the river to find out what the smoke was about. One of Forman's scouts in their camp that night at Grave Creek thought he heard a noise coming from the river that sounded like paddling. On the next morning's march back to Fort Henry on September 26th, the militiamen had to pass through a narrow part of the trail where the steep hillside met the river. There they were ambushed by hidden Wyandot warriors, save for the militia scout and a handful of his men who took a high ridge. Forman, his son, and twenty-five other men were killed outright and one man was captured, with one Wyandot warrior killed in the melee. On the 4th of October, Zeisberger got a surprise visit. "Dunquat personally came with the entire Company, which consisted of about 100 men, and he and his Captains visited me. My children [Wyandots] are doing very badly, because they have killed another 27 White men. One Wyandot was killed and some were wounded and had to be carried the whole way. We gave them food to eat because they were very hungry."[175]

---

[175] In David Zeisberger's hand in his diary, October 4th, 1777.

Chapter Fifteen
Attack on Fort Randolph

Over a month after returning to the Upper Sandusky village, a disheartening piece of news reached Dunquat, the tribal council, and the War Captains of the clans, including Tarhe. Their mutual Shawnee friend and tribal chieftain, Hokolesqua, whose named meant Stalk of Corn, or Cornstalk, had been murdered by the Long Knives while he was on a diplomatic mission. Cornstalk wished to speak to the Captain at the fort called Randolph which was recently built on the site of the Battle of Point Pleasant, as the Long Knives called it. Cornstalk had always been a friend to the Wyandot in spite of the council's refusal to officially support Cornstalk's cause during the past war with the Long Knives on the Kanawha. It was a shock to hear what had happened. Cornstalk's sister Nonhelema, called the Grenadier Squaw by the Whites, was still held as a hostage by the Long Knives. She had gotten word out describing how her brother Cornstalk, Red Hawk, and Cornstalk's son, Elinipsico, had been brutally murdered by Long Knives militiamen while being held as prisoners inside the fort.[176] In fact, the three Shawnee had not been captured by the Enemy which led to their cruel fate. Cornstalk had entered the fort to explain to the fort's commander that while he could hold his own clan's people

---

176 Cornstalk and his two companions, one of which was his son, were murdered inside a jail cell room inside Fort Randolph on November 10th, 1777.

close to him from going to war, there were many more Shawnee warriors who were not inclined to act on Cornstalk's advice to keep the peace. Captain Arbuckle decided to keep Cornstalk, Red Hawk, and Elinipsico as hostages, which ultimately led to their deaths. They were shot to pieces in their jail room by angry militiamen seeking revenge on these three Shawnee who were unable to defend themselves.

Dunquat's grief for the death of his friend led quickly to anger. However, with winter about to break in late November, most of the warriors were out hunting and too scattered to be called back to the village to prepare to attack the Long Knives again. No attack could be mounted at this time to the relief of many Wyandot warriors who had been gone from the families and the village for so long. In particular, home was where Isaac wished to be more than anywhere else when the first snows fell. Myeerah was about to give birth once again, and hopefully add a fourth child to the other trio of brothers, Ebenezer aged six, Samuel aged four, and toddler William, aged two. It was a difficult delivery for Myeerah that lasted a day and into another. Finally, the child emerged to everyone's delight, a healthy baby boy, who would, in time, be named Isaac, after his proud father. There was much laughing, singing, dancing, and feasting in the village that winter. Everyone was glad for a respite from the war footing they had all been put on since the council held in the spring at Detroit. The village had not received much in the way of presents from the English since then. With the warriors constantly away, they had been unable to hunt enough fur-bearing animals to be used in trade for pots and blankets. All the replacement blankets and pots that they had was the plunder taken from settler cabins, most of which came from Weel-Lunk. Yet, the Wyandot were happy. They had their families, and few casualties of war so far. Isaac considered himself, Tarhe, and Adam fortunate to be unscathed from battle.

Even with the weather turning colder with much snow, it was still a good opportunity for Isaac to leave on short hunting trips that were usually successful. He would take with him a toboggan upon which he could strap the butchered carcasses of deer

Nonhelema

and pull the load back to the village even when he occasionally needed to use snow shoes. Isaac usually ventured along the main trail out of the village that headed to the northeast. After several miles, he would leave that trail and descend into the many sheltered valleys that had streams, now frozen, which emptied into Lake Erie to the north. It was on one of his hunting excursions up a side valley where he had not travelled before that Isaac became caught in a blinding snowstorm. The blizzard reduced his visibility to near zero for hours on end. Heavy woods surrounded him. The utter grayness of the sky matched the deep snow on the ground making it difficult for Isaac to know which way to go in the fading daylight of the late afternoon. The temperature turned colder at the same time causing Isaac to be unsure as to what he should do. Instinctively, his mind told him he must find shelter while he still had light so that he could wait out the storm till morning. With luck, Isaac was able to crawl beneath the snowy limbs of a spruce tree, and blocked the wind with his sled.

Isaac was worried as he lay there in the darkness. He had already eaten the last of the food he had brought with him. Now he had nothing to eat, and there was no wood to be found beneath the tree that could be burned for warmth. He could not sleep in his present condition though he was exhausted. As he listened to the wind whispering through the leafless limbs of the trees above, the words of the Shaman, Sees Many Visions, came back to him. "Isaac, there is Spirit all around us. You can hear the Wind Spirit as it moves through trees, you can see the Spirit of Nature in the trees around you, you can feel the Spirit of Water as it flows down the streams' courses. Everything is Spirit that you are not separate from, for you have been created by Spirit. Do not be afraid. Spirit finds you, sees you, guides you. Embrace Spirit, it is your Soul." Isaac relaxed when he recalled the old wise man's words. He reached into the leather medicine pouch that he had dutifully created to hold the white stone given to him by Sees Many Visions. Putting the stone into the palm of his left hand, Isaac let his worries evaporate, and fell into a deep sleep.

In the morning, when Isaac awakened, the storm had passed but the sky was still overcast. The pangs of hunger and the chill throughout his body told him that he must somehow soon find his way back to the main trail and home before he perished from the penetrating cold. The problem was that he did not know from which way he had come, nor which way would lead him back. The heavy snow of the previous day had erased all traces of his tracks, and now nothing looked familiar in the sea of white. Isaac stood for moments, looking around him with uncertainty. In his hand was the white stone he held tightly in his grasp. His inner voice said to him, "If you do not move, you will die. But move where?" he silently asked himself. It was then that a distant movement in the upper branches of the trees caught his eye. It seemed to be a big bird coming closer and closer to him. As it passed over his head flying above the upper limbs of the forest, Isaac saw that it was an eagle, an eagle with a white underside. The bird made a sound as it flew past him; a high-pitched whistling call, like a screech. Instantly, Isaac intuited that the bird was calling to him. "Is it calling for me to follow it in the direction it is flying? Isaac asked himself. Isaac grabbed his sled and gun, and headed in the direction the bird had flown. He knew that to stay where he was, he would freeze to death. Although he could not see the bird any longer, his ears could hear the call of the bird in the distance. "Screeee, Screeee," it called. Isaac followed, and soon reached a point where he recognized the landscape around him that he had originally passed through the day before. By late afternoon, he arrived back at the village, and told Myeerah and Tarhe how he had become lost during the snowstorm. However, he did not mention the White Eagle that guided him. For Isaac knew beyond any doubt that he had found his Spirit Guide, his Manitou.

The spring thaw of 1778 came early, opening the paths for travel throughout the Ohio Country. Dunquat held many meetings with the tribal council, the Clan Mothers, his Warpole, and War Captains like Tarhe. Dunquat proposed an ambitious campaign to attack the Enemy at their fort called Randolph on the

Kanawha, in reprisal for the murder of Cornstalk.[177] Dunquat believed that the fort defenders could be ambushed much in the same way that Fort Henry was surprised. He hoped to lure a militia party out of the fort and then spring an ambush. With luck, the warriors might be able to enter the fort gates in the process. Since Dunquat did not have the support of the Wyandots at Detroit, he sent runners to the Mingo villages to the south and east, asking for warriors to accompany his own force. Tarhe was asked to take part in the attack. In all, over two hundred[178] warriors assembled for the campaign. Where Tarhe, now aged thirty-five, went, so did Isaac, a mature warrior aged twenty-five. Dunquat knew from scouts that the garrison at the fort numbered about one hundred men. His Shawnee informants told him that the Enemy had many men sick, and all were undernourished. He hoped that would give his warriors an edge in the coming battle. The force set out in early May for the Kanawha on the Ohio River. On the 5th, they arrived at Zeisberger's mission at Schoenbrunn, traveling part of the way by canoe on the Tuscarawas River. It was a convenient place for Dunquat to stop again, and seek food for his warriors from the Moravians, even if they were reluctant to do so.

On the morning of the 7th of May, Dunquat left with his large band of warriors, but not before Zeisberger learned of their intention to attack Fort Randolph. Zeisberger noted, "The Half King informed us that they would not come here on their return march but would take another way instead."[179] Dunquat was able to get his warriors to the Ohio and cross the river as Cornstalk had done several years before. However, to Dunquat's surprise, someone had brought word to the fort that an attack was coming. Dunquat suspected one of the Moravian preachers, or more likely, a Christian Lenape who happened to be at Upper Sandusky when the warriors were making their preparations. Regardless, the fort did not

---

177 Fort Randolph was built in 1776 by Virginian militia on the spot of Lewis's camp at the mouth of the Kanawha River and the Ohio River.
178 Some references say 300 warriors. Capt. William McKee inside the fort reported near 400.
179 Zeisberger diary entry, May 7, 1778.

allow anyone to leave through the main gate, so the possibility of an ambush was negated. Said Captain William McKee from inside the fort, in a letter to Fort Pitt, "Their scheme appears to have been to draw a party out, who they must inevitably have cut off, being very advantageously posted in ambush. I having had previous notice of their intention of attacking us about that time with a large party did not send any out, so their scheme was defeated."[180] Once Dunquat realized what had happened, he ordered his warriors to kill all the 150 head of cattle grazing around the fort, and take the horses across the river. A siege of the fort was begun by the warriors that lasted several days. An attempt to call on the fort to surrender during a half-hearted parley failed. Dunquat decided it best to call off the siege. He split the warriors in half, with Tarhe taking the horses, and several wounded men, back to Upper Sandusky. Dunquat and the others would bypass the fort and head up the Kanawha River to the Greenbriar Country. Revenge for Cornstalk's murder drove him.

Isaac helped Tarhe with the wounded who had to be taken across the Ohio River on rafts, just as was done during the previous battle several years ago. It was an arduous task because the river was high, and some of the rafts used to cross days before had been accidently washed downriver. Isaac was one of the last of Tarhe's band to cross. He had purposely lagged behind to make sure that they were not followed by the Enemy from the fort. As Isaac reached the north shore of the river, he heard a familiar sound he had not heard since winter. Somewhere above him, an eagle, perhaps his eagle Manitou passed over him, headed downriver. Isaac scanned the sky but could not see it. In the distance he heard the distinctive call, "Screeee, Screeee!" With that, Isaac began walking the downriver shoreline, not knowing if there was something the eagle was calling him to find. After some distance, Isaac was about to give up when he spotted the head of someone in the water, hanging onto a waterlogged tree branch. Quickly, Isaac plunged into the water. A warrior named Two Hawks who was wounded, had accidentally rolled off one of the rafts when

---

180 Letter, McKee to Hand, Fort Randolph, 21st June, 1778.

being taken across. Isaac helped Two Hawks to the shore and got help to assist the wounded warrior, who thanked Isaac profusely.

Lenape Christian brothers brought news to Zeisberger at Schoenbrunn of the Wyandot incursion. "We received news that the Wyandot Half King and his men had attacked the Fort on the Canhawa, but did not fare very well, and that many of his people were wounded. Half of them are turned back, but the rest of them went further on into the country."[181] It wasn't until June 16th that Zeisberger heard news of the disastrous raid on the small frontier settlement at Donally's Fort[182] settlement near the headwaters of the Greenbriar River. The warriors attacked the fort to no avail due to the stubborn resistance of the Virginians. Many warriors were killed and wounded during their fruitless frontal assault on the fort which was unsuccessful. The fort had not been taken, and worse than that, ten Wyandot warriors were killed, and many others wounded. "We received news that the Company of Wyandot who had left the fort of the Canhawa and gone further into the country had suffered a serious defeat, and that 10 Wyandot, including 3 Captains were killed and others were wounded. Some warriors who had been there brought this news here," wrote Zeisberger.[183] Word of the devastating defeat reached Tarhe at Half King's Town before the last party arrived with their wounded. Tarhe was shocked at the number of dead and wounded, but said nothing. When all added up, these casualties from the two attacks were something that the Wyandot had not previously experienced since Tarhe could remember. And to make matters worse, there was little to show for their costly effort, save a few Enemy scalps and some horses.

Isaac could read the look on Tarhe's face. This was not the kind of warfare the Wyandot meant to wage, nor, apparently one they could win. The village was filled with the wails of the women lamenting the recent deaths of loved ones. It seemed to Isaac that

---

181 Zeisberger Diary, June 9th, 1778.

182 The attack commenced in early June, and by June 16th, Wyandot warriors returned by way of Schoenbrunn.

183 Zeisberger Diary entry for June 16th 1778.

no lodge had been spared a death or wounded warrior save his own, for which he was thankful. It was said that Dunquat and Coon spoke with the tribal council before retiring in seclusion. It was tragic that the bodies of the dead warriors from the attack up the Greenbriar River Valley could not be brought back to their families for proper burial which would provide, at least, some sense of closure. But the sight of so many wounded men was equally tragic. Warriors would yet die from their pierced bellies or lungs. Tarhe knew that they would suffer immeasurably during the last days or hours of their lives. That would be balanced by the warriors who would recover, but be unable to walk, carry a gun to go to war or to hunt, and be an invalid the rest of their lives due to permanently injured limbs. Isaac now could see the real cost of war; he reflected that he was not merely aiming and firing his rifle at someone else. These dead, dying, and permanently wounded warriors, many of whom Isaac knew, were irreplaceable losses. The Wyandot had no reinforcements like the Long Knives did to take their places.

Governor Hamilton at Detroit prepared for the new Grand Council of the Natives of the Western Confederacy to be held on June 14th 1778 at Detroit.[184] However, at the appointed hour that Hamilton was to speak before 1600 Natives from all nations, he was surprised to learn that the majority of the Wyandots from the Upper Sandusky village were not in attendance. When he asked his Wyandot advisors what had happened, Hamilton was appraised of the latest events that had occurred far to the south at the Rebel forts. "Yes," Hamilton told himself, "The Hurons[185] whom I placed the war hatchet for keeping have done as I've asked. It's a pity that they have suffered a defeat at the hands of the Rebels. In all likelihood they will be reluctant to lead attacks against the frontier in the very near future." Hamilton noted that the Wyandots from

---

[184] Simon Girty, Alexander McKee, Matthew Elliott, and several other men of like mind escaped pending arrest at Fort Pitt on March 28th, 1778, and made their way to Detroit to offer their services to the British and Natives in the Ohio Country in their war against the Rebels.

[185] In almost all 18th documented references, the Wyandots are referred to as the "Hurons."

Detroit villages were present. A few War Captains from Sandusky that he had not heard of, namely, Grip, Koniongerie, Kionquaan, and Lohongetton,[186] had been sent by the tribal council. After the usual greetings and salutations of the Nations, Hamilton moved on to the business at hand. "Simon Girty was then brought forward, and declared an interpreter, as having escaped from the Virginians and put himself under the protection of His Majesty after giving satisfaction assurances of his Fidelity," Hamilton exclaimed, to the delight of many warriors and chiefs who knew Girty personally.

Hamilton exhorted the assembled War Captains and warriors with the following words, "Children! I beg your attention, You have succeeded in almost all your enterprises, having taken a number of prisoners, and a far greater number of Scalps. You have driven the Rebels to a great distance from your hunting grounds, and far from suffering them to take possession of your lands you have forced them from the Frontiers to the coast where they have fallen into the hands of the King's Troops as I had foretold you would be the case, for which good service I thank you in the name of the King, my master." Hamilton let that sink in, and gave his translators a chance to catch up with him. Continuing, Hamilton added, "The King has ordered me to give you an Axe,[187] he has not as yet told me to bury it, whenever he does, my children shall know it immediately." It was Hamilton's attempt to urge the warriors to continue to attack the Rebels. As he signaled his troops to bring out the huge quantity of food provisions, clothing, and ammunition, there was one final message Hamilton needed to convey. He motioned for Alexander McKee to mount the dais and join him. "Children! I have good news to communicate to you; this is Captain McKee, who has escaped from Fort Pitt to join his hand to ours." Hamilton related to the throng before him that McKee was the man Hamilton had appointed to be the Captain of the Indian Department at Detroit. McKee would oversee not only the conduct of the war in the Ohio Country for Hamilton, but manage the

---
186 These are phonetically spelled names entered into Hamilton's record of the Grand Council, Haldimand Papers, National Archives of Canada.

187 A war axe, otherwise known as a war hatchet, or tomahawk.

distribution of provisions and ammunition in the future to each of the tribal villages as they were sent by the Detroit garrison.

Hamilton's choice was a wise one from his point of view. McKee was a former deputy of Sir William Johnson's Indian Department, so he knew all the Sachems and War Captains involved. McKee was multi-talented in that respect. He could speak many of the Native languages, so he did not need an interpreter to accompany him. McKee would serve from the field, so to speak, as he had a Shawnee wife at one of the Scioto River villages, and claimed his mother was Shawnee herself. McKee knew the trails throughout the Ohio Country having travelled them all many times, during his duty prior to the war with Johnson's Indian Department at Fort Pitt soon after it was built. McKee also served in the past as a trader. As such, he knew what goods the various tribes wanted and needed most of all, and the value of the goods at market prices. McKee was liked by most of the tribal chiefs, and especially the Shawnee, who Hamilton rightly figured were in the most important place to confront, or be confronted, by the Rebels from the Ken-Tuck-Kee lands. Most importantly of all to Hamilton, McKee had one outstanding ability that surpassed everything else about him, or any other man of equal standing. McKee was literate. He could write English. Near the close of the Grand Council, Hamilton made note to the assembled warriors of the need to assist the Wyandots, without speaking of their recent defeat at the hands of the Rebels. "I think my children are sufficiently numerous to go and assist their Brothers the Hurons and Shawanese…. The Great Spirit has given us but one mind, I hope he will continue his fondness to us."[188]

In fact, Hamilton was wrong about his idea of Native cohesiveness and their being of one mind. At worst, his thinking was sheer fantasy, and at best, necessary propaganda he believed he needed to say to bind the various tribes together to facilitate wilderness warfare. What Hamilton did not know was the fact that if it were

---

188 Hamilton quotes from recorded speech given June 14, 1778 at Detroit, Haldimand Papers, National Archives Canada. When he uses the word 'Huron', he is referring to the Wyandot.

not for the ties of kinship between tribes in the Ohio Country, they could very well have been warring with each other than with the Long Knives. Clan Mothers in all the tribes had a great hand in keeping the peace that Hamilton thought was a foregone conclusion. Hamilton was simply another Englishman and White man who did not understand Natives, or their way of doing things. He did not comprehend that intertribal grievances were no small thing to be overlooked or minimized. Native people kept grudges forever, it seemed to those White men who had lived with Natives for any length of time. As McKee had many friends he could count on, he also had made enemies over the years, like the Wyandot in general, and Dunquat in particular, who did not like McKee.

"Hamilton is an idiot," Dunquat exclaimed upon hearing of McKee's elevated position in the Indian Department. "Another typical English who knows nothing about Natives like us, and yet wishes we do his bidding and overlook his self-serving dog called McKee. McKee has always had one interest in Native people, and that has been Shawanese. It is a well-known fact that the man named William Johnson allowed McKee to serve the Shawanese with the best of provisions and gifts from the British larders at Fort Pitt before the Long Knives took over. McKee became wealthy raising the prices of trade goods while keeping a portion of the returns for himself and his hand-picked traders. McKee bragged to everyone that he had Johnson's ear because McKee, like Johnson himself, took a Native wife when most English do not. However, I know McKee is untruthful when he claims his own mother is Shawanese. In reality, McKee is really the spawn of a White woman who was captured at a young age by the tribe. She may have become a Shawanese by adoption, but her skin was that of a White woman, and so is McKee's. Not a drop of Native blood runs through his veins. McKee served to do Johnson's bidding. He was Johnson's instrument to chastise us with insults for supporting Pontiac that I have never forgotten. McKee hopes by sitting at the feet of Hamilton to make a fortune for himself at our expense, as he did with Johnson. McKee is no friend of the Wyandot, I am sure. We will see what happens from hereon, but I suspect that he will influence the naïve Hamilton, who is our friend, to move away from our needs. That is all I have to say."

The Wyandot warriors at Upper Sandusky were ordered by the tribal council and the Clan Mothers to stay put, and in effect lick their wounds. No war parties ventured afar, yet Dunquat made sure that he had intelligence from all quarters on any movements of the Enemy. A small party of warriors visited Schoenbrunn in late July with a White prisoner taken by Mingo warriors who had attacked the frontier, but little else was happening. It was not until early August that word reached Upper Sandusky from Mingo runners that the Long Knives Captain Clark had taken a small army of men from the growing Ken-Tuck-Kee settlements and successfully attacked the isolated British posts in the Illinois Country to the west. Kaskaskia and Vincennes had fallen, and all the Red Coat garrison soldiers made prisoners. Clark was bragging to the Miamis and Wabash tribes in the area that he soon would raise a larger army to march on Detroit. Hamilton was taken by surprise with this news that the British Native allies in the Illinois Country were changing their allegiance or avowing neutrality. It was the unexpected development that Hamilton had always avoided thinking about. In the back of his mind, he worried that the Rebels would take the offensive, and that was what had happened. Hamilton perceived that everything he had worked so hard at, to forge a Native alliance for the British cause, was falling apart, which Lord Germain had ordered him to complete.

Word of another setback in early August reached the Wyandot at Upper Sandusky first before arriving on Hamilton's desk. It was the worst kind of news that the Wyandot could ever expect. Even Isaac could feel an invisible noose tightening around the necks of his adopted people when he heard that a new General named McIntosh had taken command of the Rebel Long Knives at Fort Pitt. Neutral Lenape reported to Dunquat that McIntosh had received orders to raise an army to attack Detroit from Fort Pitt, but his orders had been changed recently. McIntosh was to prepare an army to attack the Wyandot specifically to, "chastise and terrify the savages, and to check their ravages on the frontiers of these states."[189] It was said that McIntosh was meeting with the neutral Lenape faction to seek their approval to allow the passage of his army through their lands. This was a blow to Dunquat, the tribal council, and everyone in the village. So many women, children, and elderly, along with the wounded who were recovering but could not be quickly moved were at risk. "Nephew, you know what will happen if a Long Knives army comes here to this village," Tarhe warned Isaac. "They will hope to find our innocents who cannot defend themselves to kill and scalp, like Myeerah and your children. We cannot let that happen. We will have to fight them until not one warrior is left." Isaac had no words to speak. He sat in stunned silence at the prospect of an Enemy direct invasion, which he had never really considered.

Hamilton received "Secret and Confidential Orders" from the new British Commander at Quebec, named General Frederick Haldimand. Hamilton was to quickly assemble a strike force of regulars and militia to head to the Illinois company at the first possible moment and re-take the fort at Vincennes. On September 24th, Hamilton set out with over 100 men by batteaux. McKee assured Hamilton that he could rally a substantial body of warriors to meet him along the way. In the meantime, McKee made sure that the Shawnee, Wyandot, and hostile Delaware were supplied with provisions and ammunition while McKee was gone. Then, in late September, the Long Knives McIntosh had a small army of men build a forward base fort on the bluff overlooking the Ohio River some twenty miles below Fort Pitt, that was called Fort McIntosh. The Wyandot tribal council met to discuss this development while the warriors disbanded to commence their fall hunt except for a few scouting parties. It was then, in late October, that a large Long Knives army was spotted leaving Fort Pitt downriver.[190] Scouts shadowed the army of over 1,200 men as it slogged its way past the fort and on its way to the Tuscarawas River Valley. There was foreboding in Half King's town at this ominous news. Warriors were called back from hunting, and everyone made preparations for an

---
189 Haldimand Papers reference, National Archives Canada.
190 McIntosh's army left on October 23, 1778.

Attack on Fort Randolph

impending attack. There were many discussions between Dunquat and his War Captains about what should be done, considering that they could never oppose such a large army if it reached their village, and the Lenape village of the nearby Wolf Clan.

Some War Captains were of the opinion that they should strike the Enemy army in small hit-and-run attacks to wear them down. Others opposed this idea, and thought it best to withdraw the entire village closer to the Maumee River thus forcing the Enemy to extend their supply lines much further. Isaac was with Tarhe when he spoke before the assembled councils. "Dunquat, Warpole, Captains, Clan Mothers, and Warriors. It is now the beginning of the month the English call November and already we have seen the weather turning for the worse for us. So, it is as worse for the Enemy. They have only managed some twenty miles from their fort, with many, many more to go if they are to reach here. Our scouts have counted the cattle they are bringing for food to feed 1,200 mouths. It is my belief from what I have learned from our scouts that it is too late in the season for the Enemy to reach us here. We have noted that they are not wearing warm clothing. Nor have enough cattle to feed them all the way to here if they should come this far. I do not think they will come, and if I am wrong about this, one thing I know for sure. It will be after the snows have begun to fly, and their men will be starving. They will be on our ground which they do not know their way, and we will make short work of them. It is my opinion then, let them come. All we need to do is watch and wait, and be sure to have enough ammunition." The counseling continued, but it would be proven in short order that Tarhe had been right, once again.

Chapter Sixteen
The Enemy Prisoners

The Enemy army of McIntosh did not come. The harsh weather and lack of supplies forced McIntosh to stop on the west bank of the Tuscarawas River where he had his army build a stockade fort he named Fort Laurens. With food nearly gone, McIntosh left a garrison of 150 men with most of the remaining provisions. It was commanded by Colonel John Gibson. McIntosh left with the rest of his army for Fort Pitt, on December 9th. When word of this development reached Half King's Town, everyone was overjoyed at the good news. Simon Girty arrived at Upper Sandusky soon after McIntosh's army left Fort Laurens. He had with him two dozen Mingo warriors. Girty announced that he intended to go with a war party to this new Enemy fort on the Tuscarawas and attack it. Several Wyandot warriors sought and were granted permission to accompany Girty and the Mingos. Their war party arrived on snowshoes around Fort Laurens in early January without the fort garrison knowing their presence. It was there that Mingo scouts reported that an Enemy relief party from Fort McIntosh was almost to the fort, allowing the Mingo no time to prepare an attack. However, with the help of Girty, an ambush was planned for the moment when the Enemy returned to Fort Pitt.

A successful ambush of the relief party was sprung by the hidden warriors only three miles from the fort as it was returning. The

American losses were two killed, three wounded, and one man captured who was carrying Gibson's dispatches to McIntosh. Girty returned to Upper Sandusky with those dispatches where Dunquat summoned Isaac to read the letters before the tribal council.[191] Girty then went on to Fort Detroit with the intelligence. He met with the British commander in Hamilton's absence, Captain Lernoult. Girty pressured Lernoult, in the presence of the Mingo warriors with him, to commit Red Coat soldiers to accompany a Native attack on Fort Laurens at the first possible moment. Girty reminded the British captain that Hamilton had previously promised to send soldiers. Reluctantly, Lernoult turned to his second in command, Captain Henry Bird, and ordered him to select a small force of men that Lernoult could spare to accompany Girty and the Mingos back to the Upper Sandusky Native towns, which now included the Lenape village of Captain Pipe's people. However, when the mixed force arrived at Half King's, they found a large crowd of Natives in the village center watching some sort of event that was about to take place. Captain Bird, dressed in his British light infantry uniform, pushed his way through the Wyandot, with Girty close behind to interpret. There, a warrior held a Rebel prisoner who was recently taken in the ambush by Girty and the Mingos. The warrior was preparing to kill the pleading, distressed man who begged Captain Bird to come to his aid. Bird later wrote, "I found everyone preoccupied with enjoying the immediate prospect of torturing a prisoner at the stake to the exclusion, in their minds, of all else." Bird immediately intervened to save the prisoner.[192]

Isaac and Tarhe watched Bird's efforts unfold. Bird reached the Rebel prisoner and put a hand on the man. Then Bird turned to the throng of Natives and said, "This man is now under the protection of the Great King, your Father. I, as his representative,

---

191 Pieper, in his book, "Fort Laurens" states that the letters were read by an interpreter to the Wyandots, page 52.
192 Bird's account betrays his erroneous assumption that the prisoner was to be burned at the stake, when in fact, the Wyandot had ceased to do so many years prior.

will take custody of him." As Girty translated, a hush fell over the warriors. Isaac could see a look of utter shock, and then contempt on their faces. All eyes focused on the British officer for a moment who was speaking, until finally they ignored him altogether. No one moved to release the prisoner. "Girty, I order you to tell these savages again what I have just said. I order them to give me the prisoner." Girty swallowed hard before answering Bird. "You don't order these people, Captain. That's a grievous insult they'll never forget or forgive, I can assure you." Angrily, Bird replied, "Damn you, Girty. Aren't you a White man? Can't you see these bloodthirsty savages are about to murder this man right in front of us?" Girty reluctantly turned to the warriors who were glaring at Bird, so as to repeat Bird's last commanding words. It was at that moment when the initial warrior pulled his knife and grabbed the prisoner by the hair before Bird could stop him. Seeing this, Bird shouted at the warrior to "Wait, I'll buy him!" to no avail. Instinctively Isaac made a motion to do something, but Tarhe put his hand on Isaac's shoulder saying, "Nephew, this is not your business. There is more to this than meets your eyes, I tell you." Isaac caught himself and stepped back, just as the warrior began dragging the bound prisoner who was screaming, away from the crowd.

The warrior then expertly removed the man's scalp and in the next move, slashed his throat open with his knife. With several slashes of his tomahawk, he severed the prisoners head, ending Bird's emphatic attempts to order the warrior to stop. The warrior busied himself mounting the head on a post. When done, he wiped the blood off his weapons and returned to the crowd of people as if nothing had happened. Bird, who had planned to speak to the mix of Upper Sandusky warriors about the upcoming campaign against the Enemy at Fort Laurens was beside himself. In a rage, he angrily denounced the warriors as nothing but animals, and made sure Girty translated his words verbatim. Isaac could see the warriors leaving the circle around Bird one by one until the British officer was alone. "Well, Captain, your Native army has just deserted you because of your scolding, if you didn't notice, and so will I go too." Bird stood there, alone with his own men, not comprehending what had just happened. Girty spied Isaac and Tarhe, and sauntered over to say hello. Shaking his head, Girty said, "That idiot English man Bird thinks he's in England. What a horse's ass he's just made of himself. He's lost all respect in the eyes of the Wyandot, if they had any at all for an English White man. Bird don't know, like Tarhe does, what the Wyandot did to the idiots in Red Coats at Bloody Bridge or Braddock's, eh Tarhe," Girty directed to Tarhe with a wink. "It'll take me days to try and patch this up so we can have a war party, and in spite of whatever I can do, Tarhe, you know as well as I do that your people will never forget. It wasn't even one of their own who Bird was railing at."

Isaac did not understand what Girty had said. Girty explained what Tarhe already knew but had remained silent about. "What happened here to that unfortunate Long Knives prisoner was a matter of personal vengeance. Personal. If I could have delayed Bird's arrival in the village, this all could have been avoided. That Virginian prisoner is the man we captured a few weeks ago during the Mingo ambush outside Fort Laurens. He was taken by the Mingo and belonged to the Mingo, not to me, Bird, or anyone else. That warrior that you saw ignoring Bird was Mingo, not Wyandot. He was intent on satisfying vengeance upon his prisoner, here and now, for the killing of Logan's family some years back at Yellow Creek. You see, that Mingo is related to Logan by kinship marriage. The Mingo never, I mean never, forget a grievance that has gone unpunished. I remember my Ma telling me when I was kid about an eye-for-an-eye story in the Bible, and I'm sure Bird's heard that story too. But Bird didn't see what his own White people did to Logan's family and how they gutted and scalped his own sister's unborn baby in front of her before she died. So much for civilized White people. Bird would have been the laughing stock of Detroit if he had brought that Rebel prisoner in under arrest. Now he's the laughing stock of the Wyandot. Bird don't even know what would have happened to him if he had put his hands on that Mingo. There would be another pole put up with his head on top of it, and those of any of his men who tried to intervene. You saw the warriors slowly putting their hands on their hawks, Tarhe. You know what I'm talking about. Those Wyandot warriors who Bird insulted will never forgive or forget. I know, as Tarhe does, that they will not rest until they fully satisfy the passion to seek revenge in some way, upon that idiot. He will find out that he made a mistake to wrong a Wyandot."[193]

Girty had been right about everything. The next day, he managed to talk to all parties involved at Upper Sandusky in private councils. Girty was successful in getting the Wyandot to join the Mingo, along with Bird and his men, to attack Fort Laurens. The Wyandot ignored Bird during the entire course of the campaign, as Girty had predicted. Tarhe went along in his capacity as War Captain. However, he urged Isaac to remain in the village and tend to Myeerah as she recovered from the recent birth of their baby, a girl to be named Nancy, which Isaac did. The attack was successful in the beginning, but turned into a drawn-out stalemate in which the Wyandot finally gave up and returned to Upper Sandusky, leaving off the fight. They now knew without question that to take an Enemy fort by assault would result in unnecessary casualties, unless they had artillery with them. Artillery, of course, was impossible to transport in the wilderness on narrow paths. In addition, the provisions and ammunition that Bird's men had brought with them for the campaign were nearly gone, and no new provisions were forthcoming from Detroit. This was due to McKee's insistence that everything be sent southward to the Shawnee who were to rendezvous with Hamilton. The final straw was when a relief force of 150 Enemy men arrived unexpectedly at Fort Laurens with packhorses of food and ammunition, thus breaking the siege. Soon after, Bird and his men, with food and patience running out, turned to the path leading to Detroit, leaving Girty with a small band of Mingos to do what they could. However, to the Wyandot, the attempt to take the crude frontier fort of the Enemy had ended in failure.

---

193 LD-TTIF, page 152.

Myeerah and Child

Then came the shocking news of Hamilton's capture at Vincennes by the Long Knives General Clark. Word reached Detroit at the same time as runners arrived at Upper Sandusky in late March, just as spring was breaking. It was disconcerting to everyone, especially the Wyandot, who immediately counseled. Hamilton had been the champion of the Wyandot, giving Dunquat the War Axe to take hold of during the first Grand Council ceremony at Detroit. With him gone, who could tell what might happen, especially if the Long Knives at Fort Laurens and Fort Pitt renewed their efforts to attack the Upper Sandusky villages. There were some voices of the tribal council who were of the opinion that going to war for the English King instead of remaining strictly neutral was appearing to be foolhardy, in light of the past year's setbacks. Some said that now was the time for the Wyandot to approach the Americans and sue for peace before they came with an army to destroy the Wyandot once and for all. Tarhe, always the cautious counselor, spoke before the council saying, "I think with Hamilton gone, it is likely that our Shawnee friend, McKee, will exert more control than ever over the necessities given to the Wyandot. More than likely, our share of the things we need to conduct war will likely decrease in the long run. As we have little faith in the English to support us, at the same time we do not want their White Captains like Bird to order us about. We are alone in our endeavor to preserve our people. We must withhold our warriors from supporting McKee just as he would advise the Shawnee War Captains to withhold their warriors from supporting us. It is not war between the two of us. Simply, the preservation of his villages is not our fight, nor is ours his. I counsel that we wait and see what happens. If worse comes to worse, we can always withdraw to the Maumee Valley villages to the west," stated Tarhe, before thanking the council and leaving.

Isaac could see that Tarhe's advice held weight. The tribal Sachems overruled Dunquat's appeal to take warriors in renewed warfare against the Enemy frontier. Too, the tribal council believed that until the question of the Enemy fort on the Tuscarawas was dealt with, it was too risky to have war parties afield in the event an

Enemy army marched to Fort Laurens and then turned to Upper Sandusky. The Wyandot could not have their scouts everywhere at all times, it was noted. So, the Wyandot would remain on watchful alert. News was brought in to Upper Sandusky by runners from the Shawnee with word that a small army of mounted Long Knives from Ken-Tuck-Kee had crossed the Ohio River undetected and moved up the Little Miami River, arriving at the Shawnee village of Chillicothe by surprise on May 29th.[194] The villagers had managed to escape in the nick of time. However, all the lodges were plundered and burnt before the Enemy retired back across the Ohio. McKee sent a perfunctory message to Dunquat asking to send warriors to come to the aid of the Shawnee, knowing full well that Dunquat would likely not agree. In August, Dunquat and the tribal council were visited by a delegation of neutral Lenape emissaries who wished to speak to the Wyandot, but not their hostile Lenape kin at Pipe's Town.

Their orator stood before the council and began. "Now Uncles, we once more speak to you to inform you, if you have a mind to take hold of the chain of Friendship, you must come without delay. We are still waiting for you to attend a council to be held at Fort Pitt." Their intention was to request the Wyandot to desert the British. Dunquat put them off, saying he would think about their speech and counsel privately.[195] Soon after, word reached Dunquat from his own scouts that an Enemy force of about 75 men had left Fort Pitt for Fort McIntosh,[196] and then moved in the direction of Fort Laurens. Dunquat prepared the warriors for action, in case the Enemy army, though small, turned towards the Upper Sandusky as a vanguard of more to come. However, they did not. Finally, the intention of the Enemy was known as scouts returned

---

194 Colonel John Bowman's raid occurred on May 29th. He had nine men killed and several wounded, whereupon his militia, burdened with much plunder and 180 Native horses in their possession refused to attack the next Shawnee village at Piqua.

195 William Arundel, British trader at Lower Sandusky in a letter detailing the conversation to Captain Lernoult at Detroit, Haldimand Papers, National Archives Canada.

196 Colonel Richard Campbell left on July 1st, 1779 for Fort Laurens.

with word that the force had gone to Fort Laurens and appeared to be preparing to abandon it, which was finally completed on August 2nd. On that day, all the Long Knives were seen returning on the trail to Fort Pitt. Immediately, Mingo warriors set the empty fort ablaze after plundering anything of value that had been left.

Momentous military action was being taken against the Six Nations by combined armies of the Rebels along the frontier of New York colony. Two armies sent by Washington moved slowly and methodically against every village of all the Iroquois Nations hostile to the Americans. As the Native warriors could not mount any sizable defense against the huge invasion, they abandoned their homes and headed to the safety of British Fort Niagara to the west. The American invaders burned the villages to the ground and cut down fields of ripening corn and all fruit trees, thus scorching the land of the British Native allies. Tarhe swallowed hard when hearing this particular news. He feared that it would only be a matter of time before the relentless Americans turned their attention to the Wyandot and Lenape villages at Upper Sandusky and destroyed them too. However, there was also good news reaching Upper Sandusky. As autumn advanced, a flotilla of Long Knives boats was ambushed coming up the Ohio River, loaded with gunpowder, lead, and food purchased from the Spanish on the Mississippi. Three large keelboats were manned with sixty-three men. Simon Girty, his brother George, and Matthew Elliott, were accompanying about sixty-five Shawnee and Mingo warriors. With them were a few young Wyandot men who were defying Dunquat. An ambush was sprung, with only one Enemy keelboat getting away. The other two were overrun by warriors, who killed at least forty of the Enemy, with only five being taken prisoner. The boats were plundered of a wealth of kegs of gunpowder, lead for bullets, new flintlock rifles, provisions, kegs of rum and a chest of Spanish silver. "It was quite a haul,"[197] the new commander of Detroit, Major Arent DePeyster, was heard to say upon getting the news.

---

197 Girty and Elliott letters to Detroit detailing the attack. (Girty was illiterate but always had someone who could write for him.) Haldimand Papers, National Archives of Canada.

Only one of the five Enemy prisoners was alive after everyone arrived at the Shawnee villages on the Scioto. The prisoners were repeatedly made to run successive gauntlets until they fell and were killed. Only one of the prisoners did not falter. It was said his name was Lieutenant Abraham Chapline, and though terribly bruised, he had run the many gauntlets very well. The Shawnee informed Simon Girty, who had spared Chapline from being outright killed in the ambush, that they were considering adopting the young man because of his courage.[198] However, during the winter months, Chapline was determined by his Shawnee captors to be unamenable for adoption for the same reasons that Daniel Boone's adoption after his capture led to his escape. Boone initially was adopted by the Shawnee chief, Black Fish. Boone's eventual escape was a blow to Black Fish's pride; a loss of face. It served as a warning to all Shawnee that every adult White man taken captive was irresolutely an Enemy, and unlikely to ever take to adoption. Chapline's captors decided to burn him in a fire for revenge. However, McKee, living close to the village, intervened, and offered Chapline's captor a fine horse of his own in trade for the condemned White man. After some haggling, McKee acquired Chapline, and decided for Chapline's own good to send him bound with a returning party to Upper Sandusky and then on to Detroit. The Rebel officer would likely fetch a profitable ransom for McKee. The party got as far as Dunquat's village before the weather turned ugly, so Chapline was turned over to the Wyandot for safe keeping through the winter months.

In the meantime, much had been happening to Isaac in recent weeks. Dunquat conferred with Tarhe about Isaac. He wished to use Isaac on a regular basis as an interpreter in tribal proceedings because Isaac could not only speak English but had a rudimentary understanding of how to read and write which Luther did not have, nor did anyone else. Dunquat was inundated with dispatches

---

198 This is referenced in Hoffman's book on Simon Girty, with no source for the Shawnee adoption suggestion. There are confusing and contradictory claims about Chapline's connection to Isaac Zane in 1780 that will be discussed.

from Fort Detroit that were written in English by the Major there named DePeyster. Too, he had messages coming from McKee who was passing information to Detroit via Dunquat. That intelligence was obtained from Shawnee scouts on the Ohio River who were watching the movements of the Long Knives. Isaac turned out to be a great help in that respect, honestly translating for Dunquat, as well as conveying to English traders and emissaries what Dunquat wished them to know. In addition, with the growing number of White captives coming to the Upper Sandusky villages of both the Wyandot and Lenape,[199] Dunquat wanted prisoners interviewed to find out where they were from, and what was going on with the Long Knives. Most important of all, Dunquat wished to know from the prisoners anything in regards to future planned campaigns to invade the Wyandot homeland. Adam Brown Tohunehowetu had recently moved to the Detroit Wyandot village. Although he was older than Isaac and had more schooling before his capture, he was not available now to translate or write English. Isaac agreed to question the captives for Dunquat, in between hunting meat for his family and clan. Food had again become scarce as many of the warriors were out on the paths, constantly scouting for the approach of the Enemy, and could not hunt as adequately as possible. Too, English provisions from Detroit had been reduced to a trickle because supply ships from Niagara were few and far between due to inclement weather on the Lakes.

A White captive was brought to Half King's Town by a party of Mingos in early winter. Isaac learned he was sixteen years old, and originally captured by the Shawnee in Ken-Tuck-Kee as a member of Boone's salt-making party at Blue Licks.[200] The youth had been traded to the Mingo who had treated him very poorly. Isaac guessed that they eventually intended to burn him in a fire for vengeance reasons. Isaac told Tarhe what he wanted to do. "Uncle, I

---

199 The Lenape or Delaware village at Upper Sandusky was called Pipe's Town, after the Lenape Wolf Clan War Captain, named by the English, Pipe, who was the hostile faction of the Delaware.

200 One of several men captured along with Daniel Boone at Blue Licks, Kentucky, in February 1778.

wish to have someone much like a slave to help me with the hunt. It is one thing to kill a deer, and another to dress it and drag the meat back to the village by myself. That White prisoner would be of great help to me if I can purchase him from the Mingo."[201] Tarhe could see the sense of that, since his nephew was a great hunter, and needed help. Isaac approached the Mingos who were in need of ammunition and deer hides for trade. In the end, Isaac took possession of the Enemy youth, and the Mingo went on their way. "What is your name?" Isaac asked. "George Hendricks" the scared youth replied. "Good. I will call you George. You must understand something. I now own you. I bought you to help me, but we are not equals. I am Wyandot, and you are my possession. If you give me trouble, lie to me, refuse to work, or try to escape, I can just as easily turn you back over to the next Mingos who visit. They were going to burn you slowly over a hot fire. The Wyandot do not do that to prisoners any longer. However, I will not hesitate to sink my hawk in your skull for any trouble you cause me. Understood?" Hendricks, shaking, nodded his head, and uttered, "Yes Sir."

Soon after Hendrick's arrival, a mixed party of Shawnee and Mingo arrived at Upper Sandusky on their way to Detroit with a militia officer prisoner named Chapline who McKee was sending to the British for ransom. The weather made it impossible to go on any further the closer they got to Lake Erie. An agreement was made for the Wyandot to temporarily take possession of the prisoner. Isaac learned that the man was named Abraham Chapline.

---

201 The captive's name was George Hendricks from Botetourt, Kentucky. From the Shawnee, he was traded several times, and according to Draper, was bought by Isaac Zane for $100. The price is absurd, since in 1780, no one had coin in their pockets on the frontier or Native villages, and if such were indeed available, it would be in the form of British coinage from Detroit. What is more likely is that Isaac purchased the boy in a trade deal. The implication in the post war writings was that Isaac Zane was a friend to Hendricks, and all White captives for that matter, because he himself was White, and not really Wyandot. This is simply a lack of understanding that adopted captives like Isaac and Adam Brown were completely assimilated by their Native family, clan, and tribe. In war, they viewed White captives like Hendricks for what they were at the time, enemies of their own Native people who were part of the move to destroy them.

He was one of the survivors of the attack on the Ohio River the past October in which Simon Girty had participated. Girty had wanted to keep Chapline for himself to ransom at Detroit, but the Shawnee overruled him, and almost killed Chapline, making him run several gauntlets. Now Chapline was here, and Dunquat wanted to know everything about him. Especially of importance, was to find out what was transpiring to the south of the Wyandot as it pertained to them. Isaac met the bound Chapline and opened a conversation in English. "Who are you?" Isaac asked. Chapline looked up at Isaac with an intense gaze. "Why, you're a White man, aren't you? I've heard of people like you; you're called White Indians. My name is Abraham Chapline." Isaac studied Chapline for a moment. "You were captured on the Ohio River I have been told." Chapline responded. "I'm a Captain in the Virginia militia. Tell me something before we go any further. What are you doing here dressed like an Injun? Obviously, you've turned your back on your own people, ain't you?" Isaac looked Chapline over, and responded accordingly. "My name is Isaac The Eagle, and I am Wyandot. These people you see here are my people. Your people will always be my Enemy. I've seen how you God-fearing Christians have slaughtered Native women and children so that I will never call Whites "my" people again." With that, Isaac left Chapline shaking his head in disbelief.[202]

---

[202] This relationship between Isaac Zane and Abraham Chapline is one of contention. Post war writers have conjectured that the two men developed a friendly relationship that portrays Isaac as a pacifist unwilling to raise a war hatchet against White people all the while he is living with the Wyandot. In actuality, there is no possible way, not even a chance, that an adopted White captive of the militant society of the Wyandot at the time, would allow him to be a pacifist. Nor is there any possibility that Tarhe, a War Captain of the Wyandot, would allow his only daughter and only child to marry an adopted White male who had not proven himself in battle. Writers obviously did not understand what adoption meant for males, nor did they want to believe that Isaac Zane actively and willfully went to war against his own birth people, which in fact he did. Fancifully, White writers projected qualities upon Isaac to apologize for his reluctance to return to White society, intimating that it was his love for his Native wife that kept him from leaving the Wyandot, and not his own willful decision to never return, as if he had no kinship ties with the Wyandot at all.

There was bristling animosity between the two men that made Isaac understand why the Shawnee decided that Chapline would never take to being adopted. He hated Natives, pure and simple, and in a way, he reminded Isaac of Jonathan. If the man wasn't under McKee's care and the hospitality of the Wyandot, Chapline would have perished a long time ago. Isaac told Tarhe about the nature of the hostile conversation. "Chapline is why we are fighting for our lives. Put him amongst his own people and he would not hesitate to kill our women and children. The Long Knives from the Ken-Tuck-Kee settlements who are attacking the Shawnee villages have already proven this. It is people like him who want to be rid of us, so he can take our land. It is that simple, my Nephew. Try to find out what he knows," Tarhe added. Isaac met with Chapline again, in fact, many times through the winter. Isaac learned from Chapline that he was born in Shepherdstown, Virginia, close to the area where Isaac was originally from. He was a year older than Isaac, and had been at the Battle of Point Pleasant, as it was now called, as part of the reinforcements under Colonel Christian that joined Lewis's men near dark, after the battle ended. A year ago, Chapline volunteered to be part of a small expedition of forty men under the command of Colonel David Rogers. They left Fort Pitt to begin a long and dangerous voyage by boat south on the Ohio River to the Mississippi. There, Rogers obtained desperately needed supplies of gunpowder, lead, and provisions destined for upriver. Chapline said they stopped at George Rogers Clark's post called Fort Nelson at the Falls of the Ohio to briefly rest and pick up a reinforcement of men for the trip upriver, whereupon they were ambushed. When Isaac asked Abraham how many men Clark had at the Falls, Chapline just smiled at him and spat on the ground.

The winter months were brutal for everyone at Upper Sandusky, including the captives. A cabin with a fireplace was provided for them in the village. In the beginning, the captives had to remain bound through the night so that escape was all but impossible. As the winter progressed, the captives were allowed to remain untied at night, however the cabin door was secured tightly. The

Wyandot kept many dogs in the village out of necessity, using them for food only in the most severe circumstances of hunger. Unlike settler dogs who were usually brought inside frontier cabins at night, Wyandot dogs were purposely kept outdoors. They prevented any Enemy from attacking the village at night. Isaac usually freed George Hendricks during the day to accompany him on hunts, and occasionally allowed the youth to stay in Isaac's cabin with Myeerah and the children during the coldest nights. Isaac met often with Abraham Chapline, who was warming up to Isaac as the days passed by. He had a less contentious attitude and had settled down to a routine in the village. War seemed a distant memory to both Isaac and Abraham during the winter interim, allowing the two of them to talk at length.

"You don't understand me, Isaac. This is not my war. I didn't cause it, or bring it. I'm against it, at least, I see no reason to be fighting you. All I ever wanted was a chance to find a piece of land of my own, so I can raise a family. My folks came from back East to Shepherdstown because my Pa said there's not an inch of dirt that's not owned by somebody else in Tidewater Virginia. The rich gentry own everything. Pa was paying rent to an Englishman named Fairfax who never even seen the land," explained Chapline. Isaac remembered that name from his own birth father in the South Potomac Valley. "Does it make sense to pay another man rent for developing his land and never getting to keep it for yourself? I'm more convinced to fight them damn Red Coats of the King of England than anything else. Maybe then, when its done, I can claim a piece of land for myself." After listening to Chapline's declaration, Isaac responded. "The Great Spirit gave us this land to be shared equally between all of us. How can you think you can own it anymore than that bird owns the sky that it flies through, or the fish owns the water in the stream it swims through? This world we see is the bounty that his been given to us as a gift to be shared, not coveted by any one man, not Fairfax; not you," Isaac responded.

"Well, there's a whole lot of difference between our God and your Great Spirit. Our God tells us that this land is a bounty for us to make something with for our people. This great wilderness of the Ohio Country is our God-given destiny to own. We are God's children whom he wishes to conquer the wilderness and that's done by people like me on the frontier, who can tame it. You can't just let it go to waste as it appears you Injuns are doing. We want freedom from the King, and his Red allies so we can accomplish this destiny." Chapline stopped himself, realizing he had offended Isaac with Injun talk. Isaac responded in kind. "So that means that hundreds of White squatters can enter Native lands without our permission? They cut down the trees and plow up the soil, and then say the land is theirs without ever considering that it is someone else's land first? Do Native people not count as real people in your White world? You say to me you are a God-fearing Christian, and yet you and I both know that your God does not include Native people in their churches unless their skin has been turned White enough? You know that if our situation was the opposite, and I was your captive, you would have slain me a long time ago. Neither adoption or captivity is an option for Native people in your world. Look what we have done with you here? You are still alive. You are being fed. You will be spared injury so's to be ransomed. Is not our Great Spirit a more compassionate and forgiving God?"

Isaac went on. "Because we are pagans to you, White people feel entitled to do with us as they wish in war, without being held accountable to your God for your actions. You don't adopt Native people ever; you kill them out of hand as easily as I kill a deer. If I had the means of publishing to the world the many acts of treachery and cruelty committed by White people on our women and children, it would appear that the title "Savages" would with much greater justice be applied to White people than us. Your people have no intention of living in peace with Native people. You lie about it insomuch and claim that treaties bring peace. However, I see that treaties are but a respite White people take before the next war for our land. You think I am being duped by siding with the Wyandot. I say you are being duped by the gentry like Fairfax who push you onto the frontier with us to do the fighting, bleeding, and dying for their land speculators." Chapline countered in the argument. "There is a lot of truth in what you say, Isaac. But I know you have not seen the millions of people over the mountains to the east who intend to come here. There is no way the Wyandot, or any Native tribe is going to win this war. Everyday, Whites in the Ohio Country grow stronger from reinforcements. Every day, Wyandots grow weaker. You have no reinforcements. Soon, an army will be sent here from Fort Pitt to destroy this place once and for all, I am sorry to say, Isaac."

Chapter Seventeen
To Remove the Black Coats

When spring broke in the Ohio Country, the Wyandot got word from Detroit that Major DePeyster, the new commandant of the English, decided that the best way to protect Detroit and its surrounding Native villages was to go on the offensive in the continuing war. DePeyster aimed to send an army of Red Coat soldiers with Native allies to attack the Rebel settlements in Kentucky, specifically Clark's post at the Falls of the Ohio River. DePeyster summoned his Indian Department officers and agents like Alexander McKee, Simon Girty, Matthew Elliott, and others. He ordered them to petition all the tribes of the Ohio Country to pledge warriors for the upcoming expedition slated for early summer. This invariably caused consternation for the Wyandot who began meeting in council to discuss the matter in early April. Girty arrived at the same time with provisions and ammunition to be distributed to the Lenape and Wyandot whom he assumed would join without question. He was wrong. It was such a big issue that the tribal council wanted to hear from Clan Mothers and War Captains alike, in addition to Dunquat and Coon, his Warpole. That was because the council was split on what to do. The biggest obstacle, Girty found, was the old unresolved grievance the Wyandot unanimously held against the Red Coat Captain Henry Bird whom they heard was going to lead the expedition. That insult of Bird's was still unpunished.

Many voices spoke against Bird. However, when it came to whether to join the war effort, some counseled that the Wyandot must overlook their animosity towards Bird. Others argued that the Wyandot would never forget the insult from this White man Bird that happened in the near past. Now, regardless of the war situation, that insult must be avenged, they argued, and now was the opportunity. Too, there were concerns surrounding Bird's second-in-command, Alexander McKee, who had, in his own way, slighted the Wyandot at every turn. McKee had favored the Shawnee with plentiful ammunition, provisions, and goods at the expense of the Wyandot. This issue split the council. Many Sachems did not want to anger the British who might take their own revenge on the Wyandot and abandon them. Still others, like Dunquat, held the most influence in the council. "I ask this council now, when have the Shawanese supported the Wyandot in our fight? Did the Shawanese support us when we accompanied Girty to the Enemy fort on the Tuscarawas? Not one. Have the Shawanese sent their warriors to aid us in scouting the frontier adjacent to our lands in search of the Enemy armies' movements? Not one. The fight against the Enemy in the Ken-Tuck-Kee lands is a just fight, but it is the Shawanese fight, not our fight. I cannot believe that our warriors should fight and bleed so far from home and leave our own women and children defenseless at our village if the Enemy should launch a surprise mounted invasion as they have done with the Shawanese already. To call in our warriors from scouting the frontier and send them south is to blind our eyes and close our ears. It would be disastrous. That is all I have to say."

The council debated day after day without a clear decision either way. In the meantime, Chapline and Hendricks watched the preparations going on in the village with apprehension. Even though they were not told what was happening, they could see that warriors were arriving daily from every direction due to Girty sending runners to distant villages. Half King's Town was to be the assembly point for DePeyster's Native allies, according to Girty. It sat on the crossroads of so many paths through the wilderness. George Hendricks overheard Isaac talking with Girty in English one day. From the conversation, he was able to determine where the warriors would be eventually going. Hendricks passed the information on to Chapline, who thought it over. Chapline realized the need to somehow warn their comrades at the Falls of the Ohio, many miles distant through hostile country. One night in late April they made their move. Something odd woke Isaac at first light the next morning. He realized the dogs in his part of the village were silent. Rising, Isaac went to check on the prisoners and found Chapline and Hendricks gone, having fed part of their evening meal to the dogs that morning to silence them. Isaac called out an alarm to the village, and prepared to go after the two men. Tarhe, who was alerted, stopped Isaac.[203]

"Nephew, I have told Dunquat what has happened, and he wishes you to wait until he tells you to pursue. I know that he has something in mind that I will share with you as soon as I can." Isaac prepared himself to take to the warpath south. He was filled with rage for

---

203 History writers of several generations later, have taken this incident and written a fanciful fictional account that Isaac was sympathetic to the two captives and aided them in their escape, providing them with guns and ammunition. First of all, if Isaac had done so, and aided the Enemy in escaping by his own hand, he could have been killed by the Wyandot, and in the least, would have never retained Tarhe's trust or backing on anything in the future, which was not the case. If, in fact, he had aided the two men to escape, it would have been on the direction of the Wyandot council, including Dunquat, who would have planned it. Secondly, if Isaac had armed the two men, he would have done so in the belief that they might need to kill other Natives on their trip south which was absolutely against any Native's wish, that is, to arm an Enemy to kill a Native. No possibility. What is most likely is the two men escaped at a propitious time, witnessing the great assembly of warriors soon to leave against the Kentucky frontier, where their own kin and friends lived. Many years later in old age, Abraham Chapline made a statement saying that Zane was very friendly to him and aided in his successful escape, providing guns and ammunition. They may have stolen the weapons from the village at night before escaping. They may not have had weapons at all, and only much later, in 1800, claimed to have had. The reference Blumel uses in his book to Chapline, is a petition dated February 1st, 1800, called "The petition of Isaac Zane." Zane was 47 years old at the time, trying to secure a land claim in Ohio having been given to him by the Wyandots. However, that land was ceded to the United States by the Treaty of 1795 following the defeat of the West Confederacy tribes by Mad Anthony Wayne in 1794 at the Battle of Fallen Timbers. Hoffman, in his book on Simon Girty, makes reference to the two escapees successfully "eluding pursuers." The author believes that the whole Chapline account in post-war writings was fanciful fiction to portray Isaac Zane as a reluctant adoptee of the Wyandot and a man sympathetic, at heart, to Whites.

relaxing his guard with Chapline, which caused a great deal of loss of face, meaning shame, in facing Tarhe, Dunquat, and his clan. Obviously, he had been outwitted. Isaac was disgusted by the fact that he had let his people down. Tarhe returned in a few moments with Dunquat. Isaac felt a pit in his stomach and realized that he must take whatever punishment that was decided by the headmen without comment. Dunquat spoke. "I never cease to be amazed at how the Great Spirit works in ways we cannot see or predict. Isaac, the escape of the two Long Knives prisoners has been unexpectedly fortuitous in a way that I could not have conceived myself. By their escape to warn their comrades of the coming offensive, the many contentious issues plaguing the council and myself have been remarkably resolved, which I know you had no intimate knowledge of."

"We will let them go," Dunquat continued. "By their timely escape to warn the Long Knives Clark, they do us a great service, if they are able to succeed. We will not be ordered about by a man like Red Coat Captain Bird who insulted us in the past when he angrily berated our warriors in front of our own people. That insult was grievous and injuring to our pride. If it had been anyone else, they would have paid with their lives. However, Bird's words have not been forgotten. If Clark is waiting for him on the Ohio, he will have to face a real Enemy in battle himself and not have the Wyandot whom he has insulted to do his bidding. That insult will be avenged whether he knows it or not. The Red Coat English, like Bird and his captain DePeyster, believe all Natives are the same tribe. They are White people no different than the Long Knives, in this respect. They regard us as savages to be used for their own ends. But we are not the same people as the Shawanese. Yes, we have kinship ties with them, however one cannot overlook the fact that we are our own people, with our own language Wandat, and with our own clans and customs very different from the Shawanese. We are not the same people as them, and we make our own decisions for the best interests of our own people."

Dunquat continued. "The same complaint can be said of McKee. McKee, of all people, knows that we are not the same as the Shawanese. Yet he demands the Wyandot do his bidding when it is in his interests, which is to fight and die for the Shawanese, in spite of his disregard of our needs from the British at Detroit. We have secretly kept watch over the goods and ammunition that McKee's agent Girty has been told to allot to us. It is far less than what is going to McKee's Shawanese. I will send a party of warriors eventually to McKee, but not anytime soon. When the Shawanese and Mingos discover that Clark has been forewarned of the attack if that should happen, they will not go any further to attack the Long Knives fort, as I have learned from the past years is not a wise thing to do. They will come to their own conclusion with or without the Wyandot warriors being present. The Wyandot will not play the fool for either Bird or McKee. By sending a party of warriors to arrive late, McKee will be unable to say to Bird that the Wyandot refused his request. McKee knows that everything I am saying is truth. He simply has no love for the Wyandot; not even affection."

What Dunquat predicted, is in fact, what happened. The two escapees reached the Falls of the Ohio unscathed with the warning of a pending attack. However, it was discounted by Clark and his officers who did not believe the British would be launching an attack so early in the season. At the forks of the Big Miami River, Alexander McKee rendezvoused with Bird and his men, bringing the attacking force to nearly 400 Shawnee warriors with Lake Indians, to add to Bird's force of regulars and militia. On June 3rd, McKee informed Bird that he had not heard as yet from the Wyandot. "There has been no satisfactory answer from the Hurons, notwithstanding that several messages have been sent to them to expedite their joining us."[204] Soon, a runner came into McKee's camp with important news, which he related to Bird. "I am told that about the time we were on our way here, that a small party of Hurons was stopped by the Wakatomika village Indians from going to war, which those Indians declare was far from their design, having on the contrary, called upon them there several times since, for their assistance in the present undertaking." McKee continued. "The Hurons, glad of the opportunity,

---

204 McKee correspondence, June 3rd, 1780, Haldimand Papers, National Archives Canada.

returned, but have, though repeatedly invited, refused to join our Confederacy."²⁰⁵ Bird took McKee's information at face value. "Whatever the problem is with the Hurons, perhaps due to some sort of jealousy or a long-standing enmity with one of the other tribes, I cannot figure it out, nor care to," said Bird. It was beyond his comprehension that the Indians continued to squabble amongst themselves, even under the current conditions that they faced with a common Enemy threatening them all.

McKee received more bad news as Bird's force was making ready for the Ohio. A Shawnee runner arrived with news of the escape of two Rebels from the Wyandot. McKee told Bird, "I have just received an account from a prisoner of the Shawnee who had lived with the two escapees at Half King's Town during the winter. He says that a White Indian of the Wyandot named "Zeans"²⁰⁶ had directed the two men to the Miami River to a Frenchman there who would assist them in getting clear. As it was, when the entire force reached the Ohio River, the Natives called for a delay of several days to council with each other. There, they decided to strike several smaller Enemy settlements up the Licking River, rather than accompany Bird on his mission to attack Clark in his fort. Their decision, they told McKee, had everything to do with the fact that they were now at a great distance from their own villages, making it impossible to return in time if the Long Knives chose to attack their women and children from another direction. McKee tried to explain this to an enraged Captain Bird. "The Indians determine to proceed to the nearest forts by way of Licking Creek, giving for their reasons that it could not be prudent to leave their villages naked and defenseless in the neighborhood of those forts."²⁰⁷

---

205 Ibid.

206 A phonetic spelling of the name Zane in McKee's letter to Detroit, Haldimand Papers, National Archives Canada. From McKee's letter, it is apparent that Girty and others had told McKee that the two prisoners held by the Wyandot through the winter were seen talking with Isaac Zane. Likely it was known, certainly by Girty who frequented Half King's town, and others, that Isaac had purchased Hendricks as a personal slave to do work. It was always in McKee's interest to negatively portray Wyandots in his correspondence.

207 McKee correspondence, Haldimand Papers, National Archives Canada.

McKee finished by reminding Bird of the destruction wrought by the Kentucky Rebel named Bowman on the Shawnee village of Chillicothe the previous year when the warriors were away. "It should be expected that the Shawnee would be reluctant to campaign so far from their villages," McKee told Bird. However, Captain Henry Bird in command of the expedition would hear none of it. Frustrated, Bird attempted to order the Natives to no avail. As the warriors crossed the Ohio and headed up Licking Creek, Bird had no choice but to accompany them. Two forts, Ruddell's Fort, and Martin's Station were successfully besieged, and forced to surrender. All of the Virginian men, women, and children were taken captive. A huge amount of plunder from the fort's interior and surrounding cabins was divided up among the warriors before the structures were burned. Bird, through McKee, made another appeal to the Natives to now attack Clark, but again they ignored him. What was foremost in their minds was returning as soon as possible with all the prisoners and plunder before Clark and his mounted militiamen gave pursuit. The campaign was effectively over.

With the onset of winter, Myeerah gave birth to another child, a healthy baby girl who would be named Elizabeth. Although the Shawnee had devastated the two settlements in Kentucky during the Bird campaign, they were met with a reprisal from Clark soon after. Clark mounted a major retaliatory raid with almost 1,000 mounted Kentucky militiamen against several Shawnee villages. The move into Shawnee territory again caught the villages almost by surprise. A deserter from Clark's army, "a Tory sympathizer, sneaked off into the night and gave the Shawnee notice of Clark's approaching army."[208] Consequently, the village at Chillicothe was found abandoned on August 1st. However, at the next village, called "Pekawee, or Piqua," a limited number of warriors gave battle until being forced to withdraw. Clark had his men burn both villages to the ground along with all the ripening corn in the surrounding fields. Although few Natives were killed or wounded, the loss of their crops that they were depending upon

---

208 Reference from correspondence, McKee to DePeyster, Haldimand Papers, National Archives Canada.

for the winter was devastating. Isaac knew what that meant when he heard what happened. There would be little or no provisions for the Wyandot from Detroit. McKee would demand all of it for the Shawnee who were genuinely distressed. Tarhe learned that the war party that Dunquat had sent to accompany the Bird campaign had arrived in time to accompany a force of almost 200 Shawnee and Mingo warriors with McKee. They had hoped to catch up to Clark, but reached the destroyed village of Pekawee too late. The warriors already there brought their casualties into the ruined town, amounting to, "six killed and three wounded, but that of their own will be a very distressing one to their families," wrote McKee to DePeyster. With no Enemy to fight, the Wyandots headed back to Upper Sandusky to report all of this to Dunquat, Coon, and Tarhe.

In September, Isaac heard the news from Tarhe that a Long Knives army was being assembled at Fort Pitt to campaign against the Wyandot and Lenape at Upper Sandusky. Dunquat immediately sent scouting parties in that direction to see if this was true. At the same time, he put all the warriors in his village on alert to be ready if an invasion should come. While waiting, Isaac put what time he could into hunting meat for his family and clan, since provisions from Detroit were scanty. With many warriors gone from the village and unable to hunt, their situation was worsening. However, in the first week of October, Dunquat's spies reported that the planned campaign had been called off because of objections by Enemy militia officers who pointed to worsening weather and lack of provisions. This was good news for everyone finally. Warriors returned to go out on the much-needed hunt. As the fall gave way to winter, at Detroit Major DePeyster thought it best that his Indian Department agent, Simon Girty, agree to "take up his residence at Upper Sandusky among the Wyandots, sent thither from the Mingos because his services would be greatly enhanced."[209] This, of course, came as a surprise to Girty, who had no previous constraints put upon him until now. DePeyster explained to Girty. "I want you to help bring the Upper Sandusky

---

209 Haldimand Papers, National Archives Canada.

Wyandots more closely into the British fold." DePeyster felt the Wyandots appeared to be reluctant to fully join the British cause. "Their warriors are more numerous than the Mingos of the Ohio Country. Go to Upper Sandusky and interpret for them, and go to war with them when occasions are offered."[210]

"I'll do as you order, Major, but you need to know something. First, while I can speak the Wandat language, I'm not as fluent as I am with the Mingos, who consider me an adopted blood brother that goes back to my years with the Seneca who they are related to. Secondly, because I'm not adopted by the Wyandot, they do not consider me as one of their own. While I have some standing with them that I believe I can count on, the Wyandot do as they please, as they have always done in the past. What I'm saying is that I'm doubtful that they'll give me much of an ear, however I'll try," Girty offered. Girty then prepared to set out from Detroit at the first possible moment. Through the winter and into the spring of 1781, the Wyandots, and all Natives for that matter in the Ohio Country struggled to obtain food. Provisions from Detroit were not forthcoming due to no schooners arriving from Niagara. Girty arrived at Half King's Town and took up residence there. He asked Dunquat for permission to accompany the small war parties prowling the American frontier, which was granted. Everyone was taken by surprise in April when a force of more than 300 regular and militia troops from Fort Pitt attacked the Lenape village at Goschachgunk[211] and destroyed it, killing fifteen warriors who were believed to be hostiles, and taking women and children prisoners back to Fort Pitt.

Girty met with Dunquat, the Warpole Coon, and the War Captains of the Wyandot, including Tarhe. The attack had been very close to home for the Wyandot, who wished to retaliate, but had no food and little ammunition to do so, Dunquat explained to Girty. As Girty could not write, he summoned Isaac to pen a note he dictated to Major DePeyster at Detroit,[212] in the presence

---

210 ibid

211 At the current site of the town of Coshocton, Ohio.

212 Simon Girty was illiterate all his life, and needed someone else to write for him.

of Dunquat and the others. "I have 160 Indians at this place. Their provisions are all gone; and they beg that you will send them some. Your children, the Wyandots, will be very glad if you will send those people you promised to send to their assistance."[213] Dunquat had not revealed to Girty their true strength, hoping that the man sent to assist them might be of use in procuring what the Wyandot needed by going around McKee. At the same time, Girty knew very well that the Wyandot were holding back, and that his letter was a mere formality. The British at Detroit had nothing to send at the moment. The British fleet, it was said, had not arrived as yet at Quebec from England with supplies. Simply stated, both men knew that any action against the Long Knives would require provisions and ammunition. However, in the weeks ahead, some supplies arrived as Girty had requested. Now it was up to Dunquat to fulfil his part of the agreement that Girty had brokered and go back to war. Several Enemy prisoners brought in by scouting parties on the Ohio River said that Clark was back East trying to raise an army and had not as yet returned to the Kentucky lands. Dunquat decided that now was the time to take the offensive as Girty was asking him to do.

Dunquat planned for his Warpole Coon to take more than 100 Wyandot warriors along with Simon Girty, to join McKee at the Shawnee village of Wakatomika. However, when they arrived in late August, they learned that a combined force of Natives under the leadership of the newly-arrived Mohawk War Captain Joseph Brant had ambushed and defeated a Rebel detachment on the Ohio River by luring their boats to shore. The Rebel commander named Lochry and thirty-seven of his men had been killed, and the rest taken captive, along with the sizable loot in the plundered boats.[214] With the battle over, many of the Wyandot immediately left for Upper Sandusky as Girty was unable to convince them to stay so far from home for more warfare. A handful of Wyandot warriors remained, and traveled to the Ohio River. In early September, it was decided by all the combined War Captains that it would be

---
213 Girty to DePeyster, Haldimand Papers, National Archives Canada.
214 August 24th, 1781, Colonel Archibald Lochry and his men in twelve boats were attacked on the Ohio River.

best to return home, contrary to McKee and Girty's pleas to continue to pursue the Kentucky Long Knives. One night in camp on the path to Wakatomika, Simon Girty and Joseph Brant the Mohawk, got into a drunken argument. Neither man liked each other. After trading insults, Brant struck Girty on the head with a sword he was carrying, almost causing a battle between Brant's Mohawks and the combined Wyandot and Mingo warriors. Girty was severely injured. He was carried on a litter while unconscious all the way to Half King's Town where a prominent Wyandot Shaman and healer attended to him night and day, preventing his untimely death, to the relief of everyone. Brant, fearing for his life, traveled directly to Detroit to catch the next sloop to Niagara.

At nearly the same time, Dunquat and the tribal council had been busy with another pressing matter that would directly involve Tarhe and Isaac. Matthew Elliott, deputy agent of the British Indian Department at Detroit had arrived in early August at Half King's Town with orders from British Major DePeyster at Detroit to request a force of Wyandot warriors to join him. He wanted Elliott to proceed to the Moravian mission towns to arrest the White pastors there and bring them to Detroit by whatever means possible for examination and possible trial on charges of treason. Since Dunquat had recently sent a message dictated by Isaac affirming the Wyandot support for the British war effort, DePeyster thought it prudent to call upon that commitment in this time of need. DePeyster had mounting evidence that the preacher David Zeisberger was passing critical intelligence to the Rebels at Fort Pitt. In fact, Zeisberger was "suspected as early as July of 1779 by McKee of passing intelligence on the Indians to the American authorities at Fort Pitt."[215] DePeyster intended on ending this perfidy now. So, Dunquat gathered a body of some 250 Wyandot and Lenape warriors to accompany him and Matthew Elliott, along with the Lenape Wolf Clan War Captain named Hopocan, or as he was commonly called "Captain Pipe." Tarhe was to lead his clan's warriors, and Isaac was going along to interpret and write messages, if called upon. By August 10th, the entire force was only a couple of days march from the Moravian missions.

---

215 Reference from a "Man of Distinction Among Us."

David Zeisberger

Zeisberger received word in advance of the approach of the hostile Natives. Instinctively, he knew the frontier was in for trouble, and perhaps trouble for his own congregation. Quickly, he wrote a dispatch to Fort Pitt, saying, "I received notice that a party of some 250 Indians led by Matthew Elliott would probably advance on Wheeling, Fort McIntosh, and Fort Pitt." On August 24th Captain John Boggs received the warning from Fort Pitt to prepare for possible hostile attack. What Zeisberger did not know was that Elliott, Dunquat, and Pipe were coming to take him and his clergy into custody. The entire Native force stopped first at the Salem Mission to talk to the preacher John Heckewelder. The next day they proceeded to the Gnadenhutten Mission where Zeisberger resided. After resting, on the morning of August 20th Dunquat called for all the Delaware converts to assemble. In the presence of Zeisberger and his Moravian brothers, Dunquat gave the following speech, that was translated by Isaac, even though Zeisberger understood the Wandat tongue fairly well. "I see you live in a dangerous place. Two powerful and mighty spirits or gods are standing and opening wide their jaws toward each other to swallow both. And between them, are you placed. You are in danger, from one or from the other, or even from both. Therefore, I take you by the hand, raise you up, and settle you down where I dwell." Isaac heard the distinct gasp arise from the throats of the Native converts. Dunquat was demanding that they leave their homes and personal property at the missions, and settle at Upper Sandusky whether they agreed or not. The painted warriors were present, not to attack the White frontier as was anticipated, but to enforce Dunquat's words.

Chapter Eighteen
The Battle of Upper Sandusky

Zeisberger promised to have an answer by the next day. In the morning, he told Dunquat that his Moravian Christian Delaware flock would discuss the matter in the upcoming days and give him a definite answer before next spring. The reason for the delay was that the crops needed harvesting and stored so that the women and children would not perish over the winter. Dunquat acquiesced for the moment, even though he believed the Moravian Black Coat was, in all likelihood, passing information to the Long Knives, and now stalling for time. Perhaps Zeisberger had requested the Long Knives to send him help. Dunquat did not like being put in the position of enforcing the will of the English. He realized that DePeyster was using him to do the dirty work for the British, as usual. However, Elliott interceded. Not happy with Zeisberger's evasive answer which to him was simply a stall for time, Elliott pressed Dunquat in private. "If you go home without these ministers, expect no favor from your English Father; if you fail to seize them, I will leave this place and report your faithlessness. Then you will not have a Father, but a powerful Enemy at Detroit; and the English and the Americans both against you, what awaits your tribe but destruction."[216] Dunquat counseled with the

---

216 Reference from "Matthew Elliott, Indian Agent."

War Captains he had with him, and with the Lenape leader, Pipe. In the morning, he called the Moravians together and had his warriors plunder their cabins. The warriors stripped the Delaware households of their clothing and practical goods while singing their war songs. It was enough to convince the terrified ministers and their congregation that the end had come. On the morning of September 11th, nearly 400 Moravian Delaware converts and their White preachers began their trek to Upper Sandusky, leaving everything behind that they could not carry. Fortunately for everyone involved there had been no blood shed.

Soon after leaving, a body of the Lenape and Wyandot warriors separated from Dunquat and Pipe with the intent of attacking Fort Henry on the Ohio River. Dunquat was against it, but he knew that many of the warriors were young men who had not as yet gone to war themselves. They needed to prove their worth as warriors so as to gain valuable experience and honor in their home villages. Unfortunately, the warriors found the Fort Henry defenders prepared for an attack, and could not be taken by surprise or by the guile of ambush. Consequently, the warriors raided the surrounding neighborhood in search of plunder, horses, scalps, and prisoners. "Young men have to fight, slay the Enemy, and return with captives," Dunquat told himself. "It has always been that way." All the cattle and hogs were slaughtered before the settler cabins were set ablaze, whereupon the warriors re-crossed the Ohio River for the path leading to Upper Sandusky. It was now early September along the White frontier when word reached Dunquat from his surviving son that the other two sons were dead. They had been leading small war parties across the Upper Ohio River when they were killed in a skirmish with Long Knives. Upon receiving word of this personal tragedy, Dunquat was overwhelmed with grief. Isaac was deeply touched by the sad, mourning wails of Dunquat's wife for the loss of her two adult children. However, soon enough Dunquat angrily vowed he would seek vengeance. No more White captives were to be brought to the Clan Mothers for the consideration of adoption, regardless of what the women said. All Whites taken in battle, whether men, women, or children were to be put to death on the spot. That vow, which was passed from warrior to warrior in the village, stunned Isaac.

    The late winter of early 1782 had been particularly harsh on the Christian Delaware converts who made the trip to the Native villages at Upper Sandusky. They were living in crude shacks in a new community named, "Captive's Town" a short distance from Dunquat's town. The Christian Delaware had little food left and were near starving for lack of something to eat. Since Zeisberger and the other preachers had been sent on to Detroit on DePeyster's orders, food rations for the Moravian converts were practically non-existent. Isaac asked to hunt some meat for them, however Tarhe advised him to feed his own family and clan first, before anyone else. Dunquat relented, and allowed over one-hundred Delaware men, women, and children to return to Gnadenhutten to harvest whatever corn they could find standing in the fields whenever the weather broke. In late February, they did so. However, while they were busy in the fields surrounding Gnadenhutten, a mounted party of several hundred militia volunteers from east of the Ohio River, discovered the Christian Delaware on the morning of March 8th. The militiamen were actually following the trail of a fleeing hostile war party when they came upon the pacifist Delaware converts. The Moravians were rounded up, bound, and executed one by one with mallet blows to the head to save ammunition. Eighteen militiamen stood aside, calling what their comrades were doing outright murder. However, that did not stop the killing which took all day. Ninety-six Christian Delaware men, women, and children were brutally executed. Over thirty of them were children, some only babies. They were methodically scalped and then the bodies were burned while many were still alive. Two boys managed to escape, and bring word of the Moravian massacre to Upper Sandusky. Now it was the turn for Captain Pipe to grieve. Many of those Christian Delaware were his relatives from the Wolf Clan. Pipe, too, vowed bloody unrelenting vengeance on the Long Knives.

    Isaac could see that this prolonged war was devolving into bloody reprisals which the Wyandot could never win, given their slowly dwindling number of warriors fit to fight. For the first time since he had married Myeerah, he feared for her life and that of his children for what might happen if and when an Enemy army would come to their village. Even Tarhe's assurances were sounding hollow. Isaac remembered the words that Simon Girty had spoken to him some time ago about the role of translator and mediator that he might play one day. He wondered what Girty had foreseen. Isaac could not see any treaty-making of consequence with the hate-filled White Enemy in the days ahead. However, at the same time, there was some good news. Simon Girty had recovered consciousness and was up and walking again since his severe injury. However, when Isaac went to visit Simon, he did not appear to be the same man as before. Even he spoke words of revenge against the Long Knives and Joseph Brant, the Mohawk, in particular. Girty complained of constant headaches, and Isaac could see that he was drinking rum heavily.

Word reached the village of the usual threat from the Americans that was heard every spring for the last few years. However, this threat was different. It was not long in coming soon after Dunquat and Pipe sent their warriors in parties across the Ohio to spare no White settlers they could find. Soon, report after report was brought to the commander at Fort Pitt, General William Irvine, in early May of 1782. Native war parties were slipping across the Ohio River unnoticed and striking isolated settler cabins before anyone could stop them or give ample chase. Scouts, like Jonathan Zane from the Wheeling settlement told Irvine that the tracks of the war parties all led to the same place, the Upper Sandusky villages. Irvine thought about it long and hard. His orders from Washington forbade him from allowing Continental regular troops to leave Fort Pitt. However, the militia units in western Pennsylvania and surrounding the Wheeling area were available for action. Irvine consequently conceived a plan to attack the British at Fort Detroit in the coming months using the militia. However, his militia officers pointed out information from Jonathan Zane that the Native war parties were coming from the villages at Upper Sandusky and not Detroit. Upper Sandusky should be attacked. Irvine agreed, and finally gave the order in the first week of May for recruiting to begin in the local Pennsylvania counties for a mounted all-volunteer force to leave at the end of the month. It didn't take long for word to reach the Wyandot of the planned expedition from the captives taken for intelligence by war parties. Isaac had the task of questioning each captive separately before they were put to death with a couple of sharp blows to the head and then scalped. Dunquat had Isaac send written word to DePeyster at Detroit requesting men and ammunition. He had runners leave to all the surrounding tribes, and even swallowed his pride and had Isaac write a friendly letter to McKee at the Shawnee village of Wakatomika, requesting the aid of the Shawnees.

Meanwhile, Wyandot warriors were in the hillside trees overlooking the Mingo Bottoms that lay on the east side of the Ohio River.[217] That was where the militia were assembling for the campaign. The Native scouts kept count of the Enemy horses. That told them how many militiamen were gathering in the camp. That information was sent by runner to Upper Sandusky. It appeared that the Long Knives would number about 500 mounted men, many of whom were riding farm draft horses unfit for the long, hard trip of many miles to Upper Sandusky. Also, of importance was that there was no artillery to be seen, and few Enemy scouts. One was recognized by the observers. It was the former Wyandot captive, Jonathan Zane. Irvine put two men in co-command of the expedition. One was Colonel William Crawford and the other was Colonel David Williamson who had commanded the infamous militia massacre of the Christian Moravian Delaware, as it was now being called back East. On the morning of May 25th, the expedition crossed the Ohio River and took a path leading to the interior of the Ohio Country and the Tuscarawas River Valley.

Strung out in a long line of riders on the narrow path, Williamson complained to Crawford that the whole militia force was moving too slow, covering only a few miles a day. Several miles ahead, Jonathan Zane with two scouts were keeping an eye out for any Native ambushes. However, unknown to Zane or anyone else, Wyandot and Delaware spies were sending constant reports on the Enemy's progress to Dunquat and Pipe. Together, they gathered

---

217 On the west side of the Ohio River was a former Mingo village, and today is the site of the town of Mingo Junction, Ohio.

their War Captains to devise a battle plan. They were now convinced more than ever that the campaign to attack the Upper Sandusky villages had begun. Orders were given for the warriors in the towns to help all the women, children, elderly, and invalids to evacuate immediately for the path north along the Sandusky River. Dunquat needed an advantage. He planned to delay meeting the Long Knives in outright battle at the village outskirts. Rather, he knew that reinforcements were already on the way from Detroit and would arrive within a few days at most. Hopefully, McKee and the Shawnee would arrive with warriors too. So, the plan he devised was to withdraw everyone northward, and leave the villages abandoned. Hopefully, the Enemy would pursue them into a trap of Dunquat's design where the Long Knives could be destroyed.

Half King's Town was bustling with frenzied activity as the women and children were preparing food and necessities for the trip. Warriors were busy checking their guns and ammunition, as well as painting themselves in their best warrior faces to meet the Enemy. Dunquat asked that all warrior-aged males down to the age of ten prepare themselves for battle, including those warriors still recovering from previous wounds who were able to shoulder a gun. For Isaac, that meant that his eldest son, Ebenezer, aged eleven, was going to accompany him. Samuel, aged nine, would not be allowed, to the dismay of the boy. Myeerah wept as her eldest son prepared to leave with his father, who had given him his old smooth-bore musket. After months of accompanying his father on the hunt, Ebenezer at his young age, was an old hand at shooting the gun. As final preparations were being made, word arrived from scouts that the Enemy had been spotted entering the Sandusky Plains, a large grassland area several miles to the south of the village. With that, the women and children said their goodbyes and took to the trail to the north, as the warriors followed behind at a distance. Captive's Town was evacuated and soon after, so was Half King's Town. Dunquat assigned his War Captains to areas north of the village, but still within the grasslands. They were to take their men to positions where they could be hidden in the tall grass. Isaac and young Ebenezer went with Tarhe's clan warriors.

To the south, Jonathan Zane remembered Half King's Town as he entered it. He did not like what he saw. The well-established village was deserted with not a Native in sight. That meant only one thing to him; that the Wyandot were well-aware of the approaching army. They were massed somewhere ahead, preparing to launch an attack. Zane spurred his horse back to the militia who had stopped to rest and drink from a spring. There, he asked Crawford to hold a council of war with all the militia officers. Zane relayed to Crawford and Williamson, and their captains what he had just seen. Crawford asked Zane for his opinion. "The fact that the villages are abandoned, and none of the Injuns, as yet, have been discovered on the plains is sure evidence to me that they're concentrating at some point not far away for a determined resistance. To me it don't look good. We should turn around immediately and skedaddle for home while we can," said Jonathan. Many militia officers disagreed with his assessment, offering that the Injuns were just running away in fear. A vote was taken and it was decided to mount up, and go several miles further to reconnoiter. Within a short time, the vanguard of scouts including Jonathan was surprised by a volley from hidden Wyandot warriors. Crawford sent everyone forward to support the beleaguered retreating men. Eventually the whole militia force took to the shelter of a large isolated stand of trees on the grassland. The battle was now on. Dunquat had his men spread out in an arc to the north of the woods while keeping up a continuous fusillade of bullets towards the Enemy.

The Lenape warriors under Pipe were closing the ring around the woods when Matthew Elliott with a large band of Lake warriors, Canadian militia, and two companies of green-clad uniformed Butler's Rangers from Detroit arrived and took to the far flank of the Wyandot. During the afternoon firefight, Isaac crept forward in the high grass to take accurate rifle shots against the Long Knives. He was sure he felled several men without injury to himself. Isaac allowed young Ebenezer to occasionally pop up and fire his musket at the woods so as to participate in the battle. Tarhe was everywhere along the line of warriors, encouraging them to take heart and hold steady. Tarhe knew that the copse of woods had no source of water. Soon the men and horses contained within it would be out of the water they had brought with them. The gunfire from both sides slacked off at dusk. Elliott saw to it that water, food, and ammunition was distributed to everyone in the fading light. Isaac brought up to Tarhe's position a horse with food, water, and ammunition strapped to the carry-all wooden saddle. As he began to untie the load, Isaac's attention was attracted to the sound somewhere above him he recognized as the screech of an eagle. Isaac turned away from the horse momentarily to look in the direction of the scree-sound that he might identify the bird. In that same instant, an Enemy rifle-ball fired from the woods splintered into the wood frame of the carry-all on the horse's back, in the exact spot where Isaac had been standing.

Ebenezer had seen what had just transpired. Isaac caught the look of utter shock on his son's face, who realized that his father had barely missed being hit by the fatal rifle shot by only an instant. Isaac realized the same thing too. However, he instantaneously realized that it was his Manitou-Eagle who had saved his life only because Isaac had chosen to follow its heeding sound; its voice. Isaac instinctively reached for his spirit bag around his neck and clenched it tightly for a moment, without saying a word to his son about the significance of what had just happened. Isaac knew that he could not reveal anything, other than the few words, "Well, son, that was close. I made the mistake of standing too tall and making myself a target even when the battle was done for the day!" Tarhe came by to speak with each of the warriors and encourage them to hold their positions and give warning if the Enemy should decide to sortie out. It was in the fading light of the evening that a runner arrived while Dunquat, Simon Girty, and Matthew Elliott were conferring. They brought news that McKee, with a party of over 150 Shawnee warriors were no more than twelve miles away, and would arrive midday on June 5th.

The battle was resumed at daylight. The warriors kept up steady gunfire into the woods where the Americans were, causing them additional casualties. Soon after noon, the Shawnee reinforcements were spotted by everyone, including the bottled-up militiamen. The Long Knives were coming to the realization that they were surrounded and now outnumbered. Crawford and Williamson faced the dire situation with no good strategy to be found. The summer heat was intense, and there was no water left. Many of the wounded men could not be moved, and soon the thirst-stricken horses would begin to die. Consequently, a decision by the militia officers was made to breakout in the evening once darkness had fallen and head south along the path they had come from. The wounded would be taken on litters strung between two horses. However, anxiety and then panic began to set in among the militiamen as the hour of breakout approached. When the order was finally given, the planned, orderly breakout by the mounted men devolved into a mad rush to escape with every man for himself in the pitch-black night. The wounded were abandoned. To the south, Lenape warriors fired point-blank into the militia men as they passed by in the darkness, dropping many from their horses. At first light, the Rangers along with Mingo, Lenape, and Shawnee warriors gave pursuit. Since the Wyandot had opened the battle, and taken the brunt of the initial gunfire from the militia, they had the rights to the scalps and plunder in the copse of woods. Warriors went from body to body, plunging knives into Enemy wounded still alive and taking a great number of Enemy scalps. Everywhere scattered about in the woods was equipment, discarded guns, ammunition, cookware, and stray horses to be plundered to the delight of the Wyandot warriors.

Tarhe, Isaac, and young Ebenezer walked through the body-strewn woods to take a count. "Nephew, this has been a great victory for our people against the Whites. I believe they shall not come again to pay us a visit such as this. They first went through our abandoned village, as you saw. They were looking for more women and children to butcher as was done at Gnadenhutten. It was here that they met real warriors in battle," Tarhe exclaimed. Isaac knew his Uncle was right. But it was unsettling for him to see, for the first time, the naked White skin of so many men, with their torsos disemboweled,[218] their mouths agape, and their eyes open, looking to

---

218 There is reference to believe that the disemboweling of a dead Enemy was a Native ritual that separated body parts and would prevent the soul from transmigrating to the heavenly place of the Great Spirit. This would force the soul of the dead to wander the netherworld for eternity, therefore causing a "fate worse than death itself."

the skies. Within a day, it was learned from the Lenape that thirteen militiamen had been captured, including the Enemy Captain named Crawford. They were all in the possession of the Lenape who were promising vengeance upon them for the killing of their Moravian Delaware kin. "What do you think will happen to them, Uncle?" Isaac asked. "If it were entirely up to us, the Wyandot would likely take the captives to Detroit to fetch a handsome price for ransom. Their captain alone named Crawford would be worth a large sum of goods and provisions from DePeyster. However, it is not up to us. I am guessing Dunquat will stay out of it, and defer to Captain Pipe with Wingenund, his second in command of the Lenape warriors, to make a decision." That decision was not long in coming. Pipe let it be known that they were taking the captives to his village, Pipe's Town, several miles downriver where it would be decided what fate should befall them.

True to his word, on the path outside of town, Pipe had two of the thirteen men separated from the rest to continue on the path to the village. At points along the trail the other captives were methodically stripped, sent through a gauntlet of angry women who beat them mercilessly. Then, each man, one by one, was hacked to pieces while alive, until there was nothing left of them but chunks of flesh for the dogs to devour. Those women who did the slaying were relatives of the ninety-six Moravian victims. The two Enemy spared at this point, were Colonel William Crawford and Dr. Knight, a medical officer on loan from Irvine. Once in the Lenape village, Pipe let it be known to the crowd of villagers that Crawford was to be condemned to death and burned slowly at the stake to satisfy vengeance for the Moravian killings. This was to be done even though it was not Crawford, but Williamson, who had led the militiamen at Gnadenhutten. Isaac quizzed Tarhe about the burning of a man as a reprisal. "Our people long ago used to do the same practice upon our Iroquois captives during the war in Canada. We gave up that practice many years ago and have not indulged in it, although Dunquat's own wife wished to burn a few Long Knives after the death of her two sons last autumn. Dunquat forbade her, and the Clan Mothers agreed without exception."

The Battle of Upper Sandusky | 261

Vengeance is Mine

Tarhe added, "However, the Lenape, the Shawanese, the Mingo, and the Ottawa, for that matter, still burn prisoners as a way of washing away the tears of a family or clan's grief through the suffering of an Enemy prisoner. This alleviates the suffering and pain of the family and clan. We will not interfere with Pipe's wish to do so. His grief is very deep, for one of the Christian converts murdered was his own sister, I have heard.[219] I will not attend the burning of this man nor should you Nephew." Isaac had already made up his mind upon hearing what was about to unfold. He remembered a conversation he had with Simon Girty who told him about witnessing the burning death of his step-father, John Turner, at the Delaware village of Kittanning, soon after his capture in 1756. It was a horrible visage for him and his two younger brothers to watch. Upon his adoption by the Seneca into Guyasuta's village, Girty said he saw several White prisoners burned to death over the years, however never was it commonplace to him. No, Isaac would not go to watch the death of Crawford by slow fire.

Soon after that event, the Wyandot people returned to occupy their village at Upper Sandusky, finding it had neither been burned nor pillaged by the advancing Enemy. A sense of relief was in the air. The constant threat of attacks against them had lifted, even if it was only momentary. Young Ebenezer had gathered some Enemy items to give to his mother, who was overjoyed to see him unharmed. In spite of the light casualties from the fighting, there were new wounded warriors to tend to and alleviate their suffering, if possible. Elliott met with Dunquat, Coon, and Tarhe to discuss the invitation to a new council of war to be held at the Shawnee village of Wapatomika in the days ahead. Captain Caldwell of the Rangers was recovering at Lower Sandusky from his battle wound and was soon back on his feet. Caldwell was requested to bring his Rangers to the council to discuss a planned attack on the Rebel fort at Wheeling. Dunquat, on the other hand, listened

---

219 There is reason to believe that this conjecture, in some written sources, is true, however, as with many Native stories, we do not have a source on the White side to substantiate the likely claim.

intently to what was proposed, but stalled in giving a response for the moment without consulting his own tribal council. With that, Elliott left with Caldwell and his men for Wapatomika. The headmen of many tribes discussed possible attacks against the Enemy following their great victory against Crawford's army. McKee, the Girtys, and Elliott gave their advice. While the Shawnee were adamant on attacking Kentucky again, the Lenape prevailed. The call from their chiefs for revenge was strong. Caldwell and the Indian Department officers began sending messages to the surrounding warriors to meet them at Wapatomika in early July.

With nearly a thousand warriors pledged to Caldwell who was to lead his Rangers in the foray, word came from Dunquat that the Wyandot would be unable to send the bulk of their warriors due to a renewed threat from Fort Pitt to retaliate against their village. Instead, a small band of warriors would soon be sent to join the Lenape. On July 15th, Caldwell and his men left with a sizable Native army of nearly one thousand warriors on the trail from Wapatomika to Wheeling. However, soon after leaving, they were met by Shawnee scouts arriving from the Ohio River near the mouth of the Little Miami River. They brought disturbing news that the Long Knives captain Clark had been seen on the Ohio River with an army in riverboats. It was obvious to the scouts that Clark intended on attacking the undefended Shawnee villages again. The Shawnee War Captains with Caldwell stopped to counsel on this alarming news. A decision was made to immediately leave for their villages on the Scioto and Miami Rivers. When that happened, it cut the bulk of the Native army severely. The Lenape angrily decided to return to Wapatomika. Caldwell knew that he could not attack Fort Henry now. So instead, he took his fifty Rangers and close to 300 Lake Indians[220] along with a small band of Wyandot across the Ohio River to the Rebel fort at Bryan's Station which they attacked without success. Calling off the futile assault, Caldwell proceeded to the Blue Licks on Licking Creek, knowing that he would be pursued by mounted Kentuckians. It

---

220 Lake Indians was a term for Native tribes living near Detroit. Warriors would have been Ottawa, Chippewa, and Pottawattamie.

was there that Caldwell devised an ambush into which he successfully lured 182 dismounted Kentucky militiamen, with devastating results. Casualties for the Rebels were 72 killed and 11 captured.

When the disgusted Lenape reached Wapatomika, they found that another Ranger company commanded by Captain Andrew Bradt had just arrived with orders to join with Caldwell. The Delaware War Chief Pipe convinced Bradt and his men to accompany him and his warriors to attack Fort Henry, which they did without success on September 11th and 12th. On the following day, the entire force of 238 Natives and 50 Rangers gave up the siege. It would come to be known as the last battle of the American Revolution. Bradt returned to Wapatomika and the warriors broke up into smaller parties to ravage the frontier settlers east of the Ohio River. By the time Bradt's men united with a returning Caldwell, a runner from DePeyster at Fort Detroit was waiting for them with word that they were to return at once to Detroit, and refrain from any offensive actions. An armistice was being called between the British and the Americans.

At nearly the same time, Dunquat, the tribal council, and War Captains at Upper Sandusky received a message from DePeyster which Isaac translated for the council. "Major DePeyster wishes to inform the Wyandot that their Father the King advises that all his Native Children hold themselves ready for offensive action against the Long Knives, but to not attack unless attacked, or until I give you an indication to do so," Isaac reported. The message was brief without explanation. The council agreed to discuss this news more fully while spreading the word for any war parties currently on the White frontier to return to Upper Sandusky. Isaac was perplexed by the message, and said so to Tarhe. "I do not understand what this means, since we have finally won a battle against the Enemy in a most decisive way." Tarhe responded. "Nephew, there are things happening out of our control. I talked with a Virginian trader from Fort Pitt who is a friend whom I recently saw. He has always spoke honestly to me. He told me that over the mountains in Virginia, an entire British Red Coat army surrendered to Washington's army at a place called Yorktown almost a year ago. He went on to say that the English are suing for peace with their rebellious American children. Soon this war will end, and I predict it will not bode well for our people if the Red Coat Generals make concessions to the Americans. We will be the ones to pay, I fear. We will have to see."

Isaac did not like the sound of that. Yes, the Wyandot warriors had won a great battle. But the costs of being on a constant war footing month after month had taken a toll upon the nation that even Tarhe was reluctant to talk about. Even with the light casualties of the last battle, there were fewer warriors in the village due to the loss of irreplaceable men due to the constant attrition. Fewer warriors meant less men to hunt when there was no battle, and fewer men to defend the land and villages when battle did come. Gone were the days of the Wyandot always taking the offensive against whatever Enemy threatened. Isaac had seen that come about in the twenty years he had spent with them. He could look around the village and see many maimed invalid warriors who would never fight or hunt again, and yet needed tended to. Also, the Clan Mothers who had held so much power and influence to keep the clan traditions alive when Isaac first arrived to the Wyandot, were now largely silenced. Because War Captains needed to make critical decisions about surviving Enemy attacks, the Clan Mothers had no authority to speak about this unending war. Isaac worried about the elderly of the village who held the oral history and stories of their people. They were sickly now due to reduced food rations. Many were dying as a result. What would his own children know of the wonderment of those Wyandot clan stories, feasts, dances, songs, and age-old traditions if there were no one to pass this on to them. Isaac shuddered at the thought. Myeerah, who was pregnant again, was soon to give birth.[221] Their Clan Mother who was a healing Shaman had died with no one to replace her. All of these thoughts swirled in his head, and continued to trouble Isaac in the days ahead.

---

221 She would give birth to a seventh child, a girl, who would be named Sarah.

Chapter Nineteen
An Uneasy Peace

It was apparent to everyone as autumn set in that the wilderness war in the Ohio Country was inexplicably winding down by all accounts passed along from scouts in the field returning to Upper Sandusky. Isaac was not sure what it all meant. While there were many threats of impending invasion of the Wyandot homeland by Enemy armies preparing to set out from Fort Pitt, none materialized. Instead, runners from the Shawnee brought news of Clark. He had taken an army of Long Knives from Kentucky and attacked the villages of Chillicothe, Pekawee, and Lorimer's trading post. All had been plundered and burnt in a lightning strike by 150 mounted militia. DePeyster at Detroit tried to dissuade the Ohio tribes, especially the Shawnee from retaliating, and to await further instructions from him. DePeyster was in a tough position, Tarhe told Isaac. He had to face the demands of the Natives, especially the Shawnee, while obeying his General named Haldimand. Tarhe related to Isaac that he had heard the orders given to DePeyster which said, "For the present, your Attention must be employed to Restrain the Indians from every Act of Hostility except in their immediate defense."[222] That was a tall order for DePeyster to follow, considering the demands from Natives. On December 1st, a

---

[222] Haldimand to DePeyster, November 20, 1783, Haldimand Papers, National Archives Canada.

Mingo chief named Ay-on-ini-amsh, travelled to Detroit requesting to speak to DePeyster immediately. "Father, I must remind you of your promises, at the time you first engaged us to espouse the King's cause, you told us that not only the wants of the warriors but those of our families should be supplied in great profusion, which has not happened. Now you forbid us to treat our prisoners with cruelty. You will recollect that we have injuries to revenge and although you protect the Enemy from the Stake, you shall not leave our people defenseless in the face of the Enemy who continues their incursions into our lands and shows our women and children no mercy."[223] DePeyster remained silent for a lack of what to say, knowing that the complaint was largely justified.

DePeyster, McKee, Simon Girty, and most of the men in the Indian Department knew that something big was afoot east of the mountains, and perhaps as far away as England. The men who had lived and fought the war on the ground with the Natives had no clear idea what it was. Some, like Tarhe, guessed that negotiations were underway, as rumors coming from Fort Pitt suggested. Everyone hoped that the Native lands would be preserved. They wished that the Ohio River would remain the boundary between the new United States and the Western Confederacy of tribes. By the spring of 1783, the armistice in the Ohio Country was holding. But the tribes of the Ohio Country wondered aloud why the English were not arming them from Detroit with ammunition to continue the war that they felt they were winning, since the defeat of Crawford the previous year. No aid was forthcoming to their collective disappointment. Simon Girty, at Half King's Town continued to advise Dunquat to keep his scouts on the move along the west side of the Ohio River. However, Girty also advised Dunquat not to let them attack the settlements across the river until he received that dispatch from Detroit. Dunquat agreed to Girty's advice, but did not like the looks and sound of it. Privately, Tarhe told Isaac that they should expect some sort of peace terms with the Americans in the coming days. "Things are moving fast around us, Nephew. We must brace ourselves for the days to come."

---

223 DePeyster to Haldimand letter, Haldimand Papers, National Archives of Canada.

Isaac Zane

However, far to the northeast at British Headquarters for all of Canada at Quebec, General Frederick Haldimand realized it was time for him to break the most unfortunate news that lay in the letter from England on his desk. The dispatch had arrived on April 25, 1783, in a top-secret packet from England. What Haldimand read shocked him. The contents detailed a proclamation by King George ordering an end to the war in America and a cessation of arms. A preliminary peace treaty had been signed on November 30, 1782 in Paris, France. America was granted its independence. A new boundary line was to run through the middle of the Great Lakes, between British held Canada and the United States. No provision had been made for the Natives whatsoever to secure the lands of the Ohio Country for them. Haldimand wrote to a friend, "My soul is completely bowed down in grief, at seeing that we, with no absolute necessity, have humbled ourselves so much as to accept such humiliating boundaries. I am heartily ashamed, and wish I was in the interior of Tartary."[224] Through the summer of 1783 and into the fall, unofficial word concerning the shocking new peace treaty reached the tribes of the Ohio Country. The news came not from British-held Detroit, Niagara, or Quebec. The news arrived with Fort Pitt traders who were now gingerly venturing to the many Native villages of the Ohio Country, including Half King's Town. They were bringing goods for trade. Along with goods, they brought word from American authorities that the peace established between the new United States of America and Great Britain did not include the Natives. In fact, the traders said that the English had sold them out, giving the land to the Americans as one of the terms of what was being called, the Treaty of Paris.

On September 1st, 1783, Dunquat and many of the Wyandot War Captains and Sachems arrived at Lower Sandusky from the upper village at the request for a grand council by Alexander McKee, speaking for the English. McKee had just come from Fort Niagara with instructions from the Indian Department.

---

224 Haldimand to Riedesel letter, Haldimand Papers, National Archives of Canada. By Tartary, Haldimand meant the barren steps of what is now Russia.

Both Tarhe and Isaac attended, along with 300 warriors. McKee opened the council with obligatory greetings and then got to the point of why he was sent to speak to them. "Although the King, your Father, found it necessary to conclude a long, bloody, expensive and unnatural War, by a Peace which seems to give you great uneasiness on account of the boundary line agreed upon between His Majesty's Commissioners and those of the United States; yet you are not to believe, or even to think that by the Line which has been described, it was meant to deprive you of an extent of Country, of which the right of Soil belongs to you." McKee paused for effect, before continuing. "Therefore, I do in the most earnest manner recommend to you for your own advantage to bear your losses with Manly Fortitude, forgiving and forgetting what is past, looking forward in full hopes of peace."[225] McKee's Native audience murmured; some in approval of McKee's words, but many rejecting what he had said. Dunquat and Tarhe both shook their heads in silent disbelief. However, it was Isaac who whispered to them, "I have seen McKee talk before to Natives. He may be many things to the Shawnee, but one thing he is not is a good liar to us."

In early January, a copy of a speech to the Six Nations from the American General Phillip Schuyler, U.S. Commissioner for Indian Affairs, was circulated to the tribes of the Ohio Country, not from Detroit, but from Fort Pitt. Dunquat called upon Isaac to translate the letter in the Wyandot council, which he dutifully did. The crux of what the American said was, "Congress, with a magnanimity and generosity peculiar to a free people are willing to forget injuries and give peace to the Indians. The terms have not yet been communicated to us, but they will doubtless be such as the Indians ought thankfully to accept. However, if the English have informed that the Indians were included in the peace, which is concluded between the former and us, they have been deceived. The Treaty does not contain a single stipulation for the Indians. They are not so much as mentioned in the Treaty.

---

225 Reports on Indian meetings, treaties, etc., Haldimand Papers, National Archives Canada.

They are therefore left to settle matters with Congress."[226] The words stung the Wyandot headmen. "It appears we are informed that instead of continuing to prosecute the war, we are to give up our lands to the Enemy as an inevitable term of this treaty," exclaimed a Sachem. "We have wrought our own ruin in listening to the English King, just as our former Fathers the French warned us would happen." Soon, they would hear of Joseph Brant's speech that he delivered to Haldimand at Quebec. "Wherefore Brother I ask in behalf of all the King's Indian Allies, whether they are included in this Treaty with the Americans as faithful Allies should be, or not? And whether those lands which the Great Being above has pointed out for our Ancestors and their Descendants, and placed them there from the beginning, and where the bones of our forefathers are Laid is secured to them? Or whether the Blood of their grandchildren is to be mingled with their bones, through the means of our Allies for whom We have often so freely bled?"[227] It was said that Haldimand was unable to answer, other than silently shake his head.

Soon after, the Wyandot headmen received notice that it would be in their best interest to attend a counsel with the Americans to be held at Fort McIntosh below Pittsburgh during late January to negotiate a new boundary line for the Ohio Country that was being proposed as part of the peace treaty. Dunquat, Coon, Tarhe, and several other Sachems and warriors would attend for the Wyandot. Present too, were the Lenape, called Delaware by the Americans, the Chippewa, and the Ottawa. One of the American commissioners was George Rogers Clark, the hated Enemy of the Shawnee. Another was the American General named Richard Butler, who came with his deputies and a contingent of soldiers. Because of the delay in the arrival of all the Natives, the garrison at Fort McIntosh did not have enough provisions to feed everyone for long. Word went out to those already in attendance requesting hunters to bring

---

226 Letter by Schuyler, recorded in Haldimand Papers, National Archives Canada.

227 Speech of Joseph Brant to Haldimand, May 21, 1783, Haldimand Papers, National Archives Canada.

in some much-needed game. Isaac, who accompanied Tarhe to the council, was present and had his rifle with him. With the approval of Tarhe and Dunquat, Isaac volunteered to Butler to hunt as long as he had some of Butler's men help him with bringing in the animals he downed, which was agreed to. Butler could see that the Wyandot named Isaac The Eagle, had White skin, and was an adoptee. In a few days, Isaac enamored himself to Butler, who noted in his journal, "By hunting, a number of buffaloes, bear, and deer he killed made him a very useful man to us."[228]

Finally, the negotiations began with the American commissioners setting the terms. In retaliation for fighting against the Americans in the late war, the tribes were to give up lands in southern and eastern Ohio Country. A new boundary line was to be drawn by the Americans that began at the mouth of Cuyahoga River on Lake Erie, and then ran southerly to the Tuscarawas River. From there, the new line was drawn on paper across wilderness land from the site of the former Fort Laurens to a point southwest where the line ran to intercept the Miami River, and then down to its mouth on the Ohio. The Americans promised that they would prevent settlers from entering and squatting on the tribal lands outside the boundary line, however, no one believed it. The land within the new boundary line, which was largely imaginary to the Natives present, was to be opened up for White settlement. The Americans were calling this new land acquisition the Northwest Territory of the United States. Dunquat, and Coon, also known as Abraham Kuhn, put their "X" marks on the treaty next to their names. Captain Pipe signed as well, using his Delaware name Hopocan, as did Pipe's sub-chief Wingenund. No one believed the pact which became known as the Treaty of Fort McIntosh 1785 would hold for long. The Shawnee, who were not invited to the council, rejected the treaty immediately when they heard the terms of it.

On the way home, Dunquat expressed his belief that the war would soon continue, as it must. He pointed out that he knew very

---

228 Reference from "History of the Panhandle," as quoted in Blumel's book, page 74.

well the extent of the land that the Americans were grabbing, having traveled extensively over the Ohio Country. "More than half of the land they take belongs to the Shawanese, the Mingo, and the Miamis. However, those tribes who had the most to lose were not invited to the treaty, by design. These treaty papers are meaningless. The only reason I signed them is to give us a respite from the Americans so that we can adequately prepare for their next attack upon us. We need guns, ammunition, provisions, and most of all, more able warriors for the coming battles. Once the Shawnee get word of this worthless treaty that has given all of their lands to the Enemy, war will break out again, I am sure," Dunquat stated.

Isaac had other things on his mind through the spring and summer of 1785. He had a growing family with many mouths to feed. While dedicated to helping Tarhe, Isaac knew that he had neglected Myeerah and his children by being away so much as a translator for Dunquat. Isaac occupied himself with hunting for meat and furs for trade, as he always had. Myeerah was happy to have her husband back home. Nancy, now aged seven, was old enough to help Myeerah tend to the corn, squash, and beans in the fields, while Elizabeth, only five, was still a toddler at play. Things were peaceful enough that Isaac felt like he once had before he had gone to war with Tarhe on the Kanawha. From time to time, word would reach the village of the troubles to the south between the Shawnee and the Americans. The Enemy were crossing the Ohio River in droves to occupy land they felt was rightly part of the Northwest Territory as they had been told. An American fort was built during the summer at the mouth of the Muskingum River where it meets the Ohio to protect settlers with a modest garrison of troops. Small Shawnee and Mingo war parties were known to attack the settlers every so often. American reprisals against the Natives were once again promised and only averted at the last minute by calls to counsel to renew peace. Slowly but surely, every Native knew that the Americans were advancing into the Ohio Country without respite. All of this seemed far away to Isaac at the moment, who relished the pause in Wyandot involvement in the conflict which he knew would engulf them sooner or later.

As it happened, Isaac and Myeerah conceived another child that was due to be born in the late fall. Myeerah endured periods of mild sickness that would come and go during the summer as the child inside her was growing. On one particular night, she experienced enough distress that Isaac called the Clan Mother to examine Myeerah. The elderly woman prescribed a specific herb that she had prepared for women such as Myeerah who were having difficulty with a pregnancy. The herb she gave Myeerah had the desired effect and calmed her, bringing much needed sleep. Isaac and one of the clan mother's kin took care of the children and took them to their bed cots in the lodge. With that done, an exhausted Isaac laid down himself and soon was asleep. Early in the morning before first light, Isaac was dreaming. In the darkness of the dream, a little girl appeared to him, standing before him. In the dream, she said nothing, but stared upwards at him with unblinking eyes. Then, in the dream she slowly shrank in size until she was nothing more than a white stone in the palm of his hand that looked like the stone in his medicine pouch. As he looked at the stone in the dream, it disappeared too, jolting him awake with a start. Isaac reached for the stone in his medicine bag to make sure it was still there, which it thankfully was.

Isaac looked around him in the semi-darkness of the lodge-cabin, trying to shake off the remnant of the dream that had startled him. It was at that moment that he realized Myeerah was not on her cot where he had last seen her. Alarmed, Isaac quickly dressed himself and headed for the doorway. His eyes told him that the sky was lightening, and dawn would soon come, but no where could he see or find Myeerah. She was gone and he did not know where to begin to look to find her. It was a rare moment of fear that crept over him; fear that she was in grave danger. As Isaac walked through the deserted village looking for Myeerah, he heard a familiar sound. Somewhere in the distance Isaac heard the "Scree" of an eagle. He turned his head to the direction that the sound was coming from, knowing that it was a call to him which might help him find Myeerah. After walking a short way towards the "Scree" Isaac came to an area of thick growth close to the shore of the Sandusky River. There, he found Myeerah sitting alone in the reeds on the riverbank. She was weeping. The front of her long colonial shirt had blood on it. "My husband, I have lost the baby that has expelled from my body. It was a tiny baby girl. She is gone."[229]

The time came when the young men of the Wyandot wished to go to war to prove themselves in battle, as had always been done in the past. However, there was no place to go without causing repercussions for everyone. By summer, the young men's petitions to Dunquat were unrelenting, and he could hardly say no. For Isaac, this meant that not only Ebenezer, now fourteen, wanted to go, but so did his younger brother Samuel, now twelve. Even William, ten, was protesting his desire that he be included after being told no. Isaac tried to put them off, knowing that Myeerah was beside herself with apprehension. She understood the ramifications if Isaac gave his permission. Against Dunquat and Coon's will, many young warriors were slipping away during the night to raid settler cabins across the Ohio River. This would undoubtedly provoke a military reaction against the Wyandot who had largely been successful in keeping the peace, while settlers flocked into the lands east of the Cuyahoga River. However, late in the fall, word arrived that the Shawnee had been summoned to counsel with the Americans again, to quell, at least temporarily, warriors from raiding the frontier. Isaac admonished his boys. "Now is not the time to go to war to prove manhood, as in the old days. We must abide by the treaty, and see what the Shawanese do in their council."

On January 31st, 1786, the council between the Shawnee and the Americans began at the mouth of the Big Miami River. As in the past, the American commissioners dictated the terms. Richard Butler addressed the Shawnee headmen, saying, "We plainly tell you that this country belongs to the United States—their blood hath defended it, and will forever protect it. The government's proposals are liberal and just; and you instead of acting as you have done, and instead of persisting in your folly, should be thankful

---

[229] It is unknown whether Myeerah had a miscarriage during her lifetime. However, it is known that miscarriages happen to Native people.

for the forgiveness and offers of kindness of the United States." When Tarhe heard of the arrogance of the Commissioners, he predicted to Isaac that the Shawnee likely would react with war, even if their elder Sachems cried for peace. Through the summer, Shawnee war parties struck into Kentucky again and again. In October, the Americans retaliated with two invasions of their own. The attack on the Shawnee towns on the Mad River was a success. Eight towns were destroyed along with their future winter's supply of standing corn. Hundreds of Native cabins and lodges were plundered before set ablaze. Twenty warriors were killed and eighty villagers captured. All in all, the Shawnee had been dealt a devastating blow, but as a whole remained steadfastly hostile to the Enemy.

By the following spring of 1787, hundreds of settlers were coming down the Ohio River from the growing settlement at Pittsburgh to settle in the Kentucky lands. They also chose to land wherever it was safe to lay claim in the Northwest Territory on the north side of the Ohio River. Settlers were traveling with the families in flat boats, and bringing with them all their possessions without any plan to return to the East. The Native tribes petitioned the American government representatives to consider their complaints that the previous treaty was being violated by the influx of settlers. It was to no avail. Dunquat had Isaac write several letters to Richard Butler, the American Superintendent of Indian Affairs, concerning Whites crossing the Cuyahoga River into Wyandot land. There was no response in return. As the many headmen of the tribes across the Ohio Country looked to keep the peace, while hoping for some resolution to their problems, the gradual encroachment by settlers continued unabated. Finally, almost a year later, Butler responded to Dunquat with a curt reply that the chief had Isaac read to him. "Brothers, I advise you to mind your cornfields and hunting and to take care that your young men do no mischief to our people. I expect to have orders to call the Nations together in a short time to Council. I therefore wish you to sit still till you hear from me again." Dunquat was resolved that this letter was nothing more than a stall by the Americans, as they had done in the past. Dunquat wanted to immediately dictate a reply back to Butler, but told Isaac he must rest first. The cough and a growing weakness in his chest were stirring up inside Dunquat again.

Finally, Dunquat was ready to have the letter written on September 2nd. "Brothers, I have kept all our warriors at home from doing mischief to you. We expect you will follow our example in the same manner as we have." Dunquat stopped to catch his breath and gather his thoughts, as Isaac waited with quill in hand. Dunquat then went on to detail the complaints of his people to the encroachment of settlers, and the violence of Whites against Natives, summing up with the words, "Brothers, your people have struck ours—I mean those Wyandots that resort to the southward. We take it very hard that you allow us to be cut to pieces by your people. Call your people together and tell them not to do so anymore.... It is our intention that peace shall continue between you and us as long as the world shall stand, if possible. We show it very plain that we wish to be at peace with you." Dunquat signed the letter and included Captain Pipe's signature for his Lenape Wolf Clan. He then turned and left to lay down. Within at few days, Dunquat, the War Captain called the Half King Chief of the Wyandot was dead. There was great mourning in the village that went on for days. A burial was prepared for the man who had kept the Wyandot people together through so much continuing conflict and travail. Isaac was filled with sadness, as was Tarhe. Isaac had come to understand the man who so bravely and selflessly put the welfare of his people ahead of all else.

A successor had to be found. The Tribal Council and Clan Mothers reached a consensus that Tarhe was the best man for this important position of head Sachem for the Wyandots. Traditionally, Sachems had always come from the Deer, Bear, and Turtle clans. Tarhe was from the Porcupine clan. He was considered their choice because he, like Dunquat, had put the needs of the Wyandot first. But it was more than that about Tarhe's character that influenced the councils' decision. Tarhe was well-respected by the other tribes of the Western Confederacy. He was known by every British and American diplomat in the Ohio Country, just as

An Uneasy Peace | 279

he had been with the French many years previously. However, the title of Half King ended with the death of Dunquat. Many younger War Captains of the Shawnee and Miamis tribes were busy rallying warriors and headmen to the Native cause of resisting the Americans, which was gaining widespread support. Tarhe was not one of them. He upheld the Wyandot policy of Dunquat, continuing to think it best that his people remain on as friendly terms with the Americans as well as they could. Tarhe knew that somewhere in the future, more fervent actions would be required. Tarhe, with Isaac at his side, sat in on councils with the other tribes, and with the Americans. Often Tarhe gave his opinion or advice when he was asked to, because of his reputation as a counselor. Tarhe's Shawnee critics pointed out that Tarhe had the luxury of taking the stance of peace because the Wyandot, as yet, had not been openly under attack by the encroaching frontier of the Whites.

Soon the actions of the Americans betrayed their treacherous lies, showing that they had no intention of abiding by any treaties they had made. By their actions, the Americans had every intention of moving into more Native lands outside the previously agreed upon treaty line. A new fort was built on the high bank of the Ohio River opposite the mouth of Licking River and adjacent to the Big Miami River. It was called Fort Washington. The stockade was begun in the summer of 1789, and completed and garrisoned by late fall.[230] It was apparent to the Shawnee and Miami of the southwest region that the fort was built for one reason. It was to be a staging area for troops and supplies in preparation for an invasion northward to attack their villages and destroy them once and for all. Word reached all the tribes that the American General Harmar arrived on January 1, 1790 with more men and provisions for a campaign against the Natives. They had been lied to by the American commissioners. In the brief interim of peace, the Americans had obviously been planning an expedition, of which Harmar was to lead. At the principal Miamis village of Kekionga,[231] many miles north of the fort, the head Sachem and

---

230 Built at the current site of downtown Cincinnati, Ohio.
231 Present site of Fort Wayne, Indiana.

War Captain of the Miami, named by the English, Chief Little Turtle, sent out messengers as soon as the winter snows had melted. Word was taken to each of the surrounding tribes of the loosely-held Western Confederacy. Little Turtle asked for warriors to support his Native alliance in the coming battle which was certain to happen. At the same time, he sent emissaries to the British at Fort Detroit requesting much-needed ammunition and provisions. Tarhe responded to Little Turtle with the promise that he would lead the Wyandot warriors to Kekionga, as soon as he received word from Little Turtle that the Americans were beginning their march. On September 30th, Harmar's army of 1,450 soldiers, comprised of three hundred regular troops, and the rest, militia from Pennsylvania and Kentucky, set out for Kekionga.

Chapter Twenty
Fallen Timbers and Beyond

Kekionga was a collection of eight distinct villages surrounded by nearly 500 acres of cornfields. Traders called the place Miamitown which meant "blackberry bush." When the American army got close to these towns, a series of ambushes by Native warriors[232] forced Harmar to withdraw or face annihilation. American casualties were high with 183 men killed along with thirteen officers.[233] Isaac had accompanied Tarhe and almost 200 warriors. He carried with him his prized rifle, and made sure his four sons at his side, William, 15, Isaac, 13, Eb 19, and Sam 17, were armed as well with trade muskets. When the final battle was over, the Miami warriors who had done the bulk of the fighting, were calling it the "Battle of the Pumpkin Fields." That was because there was steam rising from the scalp-less heads of so many of the Enemy which reminded them of squash steaming in the autumn air. Native casualties were counted, too. Together, there were over 100 killed and wounded. As it was apparent that the American retreat would not result in another attempt of invasion before winter, Tarhe and the Wyandot headed for home after fashioning litters to carry those wounded warriors who could not walk. The elation of their victory soon wore off with the realization on the path to the northeast.

---

232 The series of battles occurred between October 7-22, 1790.
233 LD-BOT, page 156.

Several of the wounded died along the way. These men killed were losses that Isaac knew were irreplaceable.

The stark reality set in for everyone during the winter. The Wyandot people realized they were back at war, aided again by the British. It was understood by Tarhe that as soon as the spring came, the Wyandot and the other tribes could expect retaliation from the Americans. That did not take long in coming. It was said by traders from Pittsburgh that General Washington was sending a new army to Fort Washington with a new General named St. Clair to command the Americans and destroy the Native Confederacy. Throughout the summer, Little Turtle of the Miami, Blue Jacket of the Shawnee, and Buckongahelas of the Delaware assembled their warriors while sending out runners to the various surrounding tribes for their support. Tarhe received the summons from Little Turtle. In turn, he gathered his War Captains and their warriors to prepare to leave in the fall months to go to war. Those warriors killed and wounded at the previous battle with Harmar had not been replaced. It was essential that the sons of the Wyandots take those empty places and gain for themselves experience as warriors-in-training. This was to the dismay of the mothers, one of whom was Myeerah. As the appointed time approached, Tarhe could count on no more than about 180 warriors at best to set out with him. Coon, who was living at the Lower Sandusky Wyandot village joined Tarhe with additional warriors. When they arrived at Little Turtle's camp, both Tarhe and Isaac were surprised to find that a huge throng of warriors from many tribes were already present. "There must be over a thousand warriors here alone, not counting women and children who have come along," Isaac commented to Tarhe after he finished a rough count. Among the warriors in camp, Isaac spotted Simon Girty. Isaac and Simon greeted each other as old friends.

Tarhe was told by Girty that the American army had set out from Fort Washington with roughly 2,000 men, however desertions had reduced the approaching army to about 1,100 soldiers, many of whom were militia. When the Americans made camp for the night near the headwaters of the Wabash River,[234] Little

---

234 Present day location of Fort Recovery, Ohio.

Turtle's force set out in the darkness towards the encamped Enemy. By dawn, they had completely surrounded the unsuspecting Americans. Little Turtle met with Tarhe and asked that Isaac, who was armed with his rifle and known to be an excellent shot, join a group of sharpshooter warriors. Once the battle began, they were to kill the artillery crew stationed at the two cannons on a small bluff overlooking the American camp. As Isaac left, Tarhe placed his four adopted grandsons with him, two on each side.[235] Simon Girty accompanied a group of Wyandot warriors whom he knew and was accepted by.[236] Little Turtle opened the battle at very first light against the surprised Enemy, who were cut down in their camps, largely before they could get organized to

---

235 There is no proof to this contention, just as there is no proof that Tarhe's adopted grandsons were not there as armed warriors. White historians of the time period have repeatedly forwarded the erroneous idea that Isaac Zane did not fight against the Americans during his lifetime. The statement attributed to Isaac was actually spoken by Tarhe in Wilson's presence. This is simply their attempt to apologize for Isaac not returning to White society. They were unable to accept, because of their extreme racial prejudice against Natives, that a White man would turn his back on his own people and fight against them, as in the case of Simon Girty. Tarhe was now head War Chief of the Wyandot, the most martial of all Ohio Country tribes. Would he allow Isaac's four sons, who were, by tradition, old enough to be warriors in battle, and skilled enough in the Spartan-like Wyandot society, to sit home with their mother? It is inconceivable. These were not teenaged boys as White society likes to think of. They had begun training in the warrior society from the time they could hold a bow and arrow in their hands. They would be expected to fight in battle, and would have demanded to do so, if it was suggested otherwise to them. It was simply a rite of passage in manhood.

236 Hoffman, in his book "Simon Girty" declares on page 232 that, "Wyandot leaders had just awarded Simon one of his greatest honors-bestowing upon him full battlefield command of their warriors (400) in the coming fight." He does so without any reference to this conjecture. It is most unlikely that at the last moment before the battle that Tarhe, overall chief and War Captain of the Wyandot, and Coon, former Warpole of Dunquat, would hand over to Girty their leadership, much less to anyone else. First, while Girty was well-respected and liked by the Wyandot, he was not a Wyandot! And as such, he was in no position at any time to command Wyandot warriors, as many White writers have conjectured erroneously. Little Turtle, while in overall command of the Natives, let each tribe present be commanded by their own leaders. This is wishful thinking on the part of Hoffman to declare such an impossibility—again, with no references to support it.

repulse the warriors. After three hours of fighting, St. Clair called his remaining officers to organize a breakout to their rear, so as to escape or be annihilated. The wounded were left behind, along with the supplies, and the camp followers. The breakout turned into a rout that cost the Americans 920 killed and 264 wounded, including nearly all of the 200 camp followers who were butchered mercilessly. Isaac could count at least a dozen shots from his rifle that hit their mark in Enemy flesh. His own sons added to that tally with several kills of their own. What followed was hours of scalping and mutilating the dead and wounded. Too, everyone busied themselves with plundering the huge supply of food provisions. Many warriors consequently ate their first meal in days from the captured food stocks. Among the goods in camp were kegs of gunpowder and new shiny weapons of the Enemy that had been discarded during the day as men were killed. It was a lopsided victory that elated everyone. Even Tarhe remarked, "I have not seen anything like this in my life since I was a young warrior at the place called Braddock's defeat." As Isaac walked over the corpse-strewn battlefield to return to Tarhe and his sons, one body caught his eye. It was that of Richard Butler, the hated American commissioner whom Isaac had met, and hunted meat for during the negotiations that took place years before at Fort McIntosh.[237] Butler lay there with his eyes open; his skull partially cleaved apart from a Native war axe. Butler's mouth was wide open revealing it stuffed with soil. Isaac knew the implication. To a White man who spent his adult life trying to acquire Native soil, now he had earned some. On returning to Tarhe, to his surprise, Isaac found that three of his younger sons each proudly displayed an Enemy scalp from the waistbands. Ebenezer, the eldest, had two.

On March 5, 1792, the United States Congress appointed General Anthony Wayne as Major General of the new, improved, and expanded army that he was to fill the ranks with recruits

---

[237] Blumel in his book on the Zane family quotes from sources in General Butler's journal of the 1785 expedition, that Zane had 'acted as a hunter' in supplying Butler and his men much needed meat while the treaty counseling was underway.

and thoroughly train for a decisive campaign against the tribes of the Western Confederacy. Wayne set about the task by allowing himself two years to complete the training before taking to the field. In the meantime, Tarhe at the Upper Sandusky village had taken a new wife at age fifty.[238] In addition, a final child was born to Myeerah the following year, a girl who would be named Catherine[239] to replace the previous child lost. Near the same time, Tarhe and the Wyandot Tribal Council saw fit to give to Isaac a gift for his service in translating. He was granted a tract of land outside the American boundary agreed upon in the Treaty of 1785, which the Whites called a 'pre-exemption right' from the Wyandot. It was on land in the Mad River Valley near the headwaters of that river which eventually flowed into the Big Miami River that the Wyandots claimed as their own. Isaac visited the land which was near the Shawnee village of Blue Jacket, and a day's travel from Upper Sandusky.[240] The wilderness tract was roughly four miles square; called Big Bottom. It had been said that a Native village had once been there, but was now gone. Isaac hoped to move there in the future, or at least clear and build a cabin when time allowed, and war was not eminent.

However, with each passing day, more and more reports came from Fort Pitt that the American General Wayne was ready to move his large army and force a final confrontation with the hostile allied Natives. In the spring of 1793, Wayne moved his men to Fort Washington on the Ohio River. From there, they continued north to the site of St. Clair's defeat and gave the bones of the men who were killed in that battle a proper burial. Instead of returning his army to Fort Washington, Wayne had his men build a new fort near the battle site, calling it Fort Recovery. Wayne continued drilling the soldiers throughout the winter without let up. At Fort Recovery, Wayne decided to send scouts to Upper

---

238 The name of this woman is believed to be Sally Sharpe, however the date of this event is guessed at since there is no reference date found.
239 There is confusion and contradiction to the number of children born to them. Some sources claim eight, and some say seven.
240 The land is currently located at Zanesfield, Ohio, which is named after Isaac Zane.

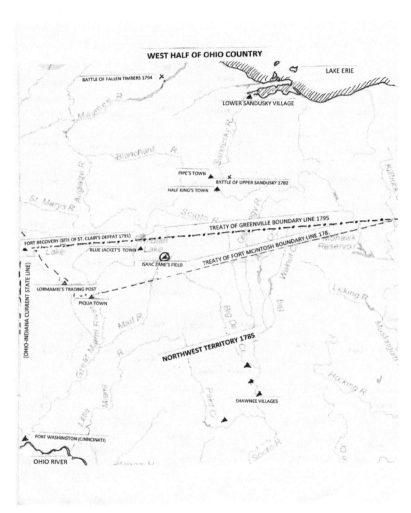

Map of Ohio Country

Fallen Timbers and Beyond | 287

Sandusky to bring back a Wyandot prisoner for Wayne to interrogate. He wanted to find out more about Wyandot warriors. One of his scouts named Captain Wells said to the General that bringing back a prisoner would not be possible. When asked why, Wells, who had been a White captive for many years, replied, "General, Sir, I am well-acquainted with the character of Wyandot warriors. I can tell you with absolute truth that Wyandots will not be taken alive."[241] Undaunted by any obstacle, General Wayne and his army departed Fort Recovery on August 17th with about 3,000 troops which included over 1,000 Kentucky militia, many of whom were mounted veteran militiamen. The Natives warriors numbered less than half that of the Americans, and were comprised of all the tribes of the former Ohio Country. Tarhe arrived a few days before the battle with the Wyandots, including Isaac and his four sons. Coon and his Wyandots came soon after.

Present with the Natives were a contingent of nearly fifty Detroit militiamen under Captain William Caldwell, formerly of Butler's Rangers in the previous Revolutionary War. A majority of the rank and file were Ranger veterans. In preparation for battle, everyone took up positions that Blue Jacket, now in overall command of the Natives, designated for each tribe. On the morning of August 20th Wayne began moving his army forward over rough terrain where a storm had blown over many trees.[242] Though the warriors remained hidden in the heavy underbrush to attempt an ambush, Wayne's two mounted columns on each flank neutralized the ambush attempt. For a time, the battle seesawed back and forth, but gradually the Americans gained the upper hand. Many Native War Captains were wounded or killed, like Egouishawey leading the Ottawas who was shot through the eye. Slowly, under the heavy fire from the Americans, the Native center began to give way. That was when Wayne sent in his troops with fixed bayonets, while other troops fired volley after volley into the warriors. At this point the entire Native line collapsed with only the Wyandots and Caldwell's men holding their positions on

---

241 LD-BOT, page 162.
242 The major engagement became known as The Battle of Fallen Timbers.

a flank. Seeing the collapse happening and warriors turning their backs and running, Tarhe motioned the Wyandot warriors to form a rear guard to prevent the Kentucky mounted militiamen from riding down the retreating Natives. As a result, the Wyandot suffered terrible losses as they stood their ground and refused to turn their backs and run.[243] Nine out of the ten Wyandot War Captains on the battlefield were killed while holding their position. Sensing his own impending death, Isaac told his sons to leave him so as not to see their father and Tarhe slain before their eyes, but they would not. Suddenly, Tarhe was hit by a bullet in the elbow, which spun him around and knocked him down. Quickly Isaac and his sons grabbed Tarhe and carried him as best they could to the rear with the last of the Wyandot warriors who were making a fighting withdrawal while facing the Enemy. Isaac knew that if Tarhe was taken alive, the Kentuckians would most certainly skin him alive before killing him. Caldwell's men who kept step with the withdrawing Wyandot likewise suffered many killed and wounded. One former Ranger, it was said, who was recognized as a former Butler's Ranger was captured after being shot in the knee. He was cut to pieces with tomahawks by the Kentuckians for his presumed role in the Battle of Blue Licks, which the Kentuckians had never forgotten.

The defeat was decisive. It ended for good the dream of the Western Confederacy of tribes to salvage their homeland in the Ohio Country. Native casualties had been heavy, with Wayne's men counting 30-40 dead, and twice as many warriors wounded. However, during the retreat, many of the dead and dying warriors were carried off, knowing that the Enemy would scalp and mutilate any Native corpse they came across on the field. After the battle, Wayne put his army to work destroying acres of cornfields and lodges that were close by. The British, who had supported the Natives materially with food and ammunition, refused to help militarily from their nearby Fort Miami. They shut the gates when the retreating warriors tried to enter to escape the pursuing mounted Kentuckians. Eventually, the British evacuated their people to

---

243 LD-BOT, page 163.

Detroit. The exact number of Native dead was never accurately accounted for. Tarhe survived the battle but was severely wounded in the right elbow, which was completely shattered. As a result, he would never again be able to raise a musket to fire it. The trip back to Upper Sandusky was agonizing for the survivors. Aside from the severely wounded who could not walk and needed to be carried on litters, Isaac knew without a doubt that the morale of the Wyandots had been broken by the battle, as well as everything else. No more would they be able to field warriors to face the devastating fire power of the Americans. The only bright side of things that Isaac could see was that he and his sons had not been killed or wounded, and would live to see Myeerah, his wife and their mother, again.

Isaac reviewed in his mind all that had happened. He realized he and his sons had come within a hair's breadth of being killed, much like what had happened to so many other Wyandots that Isaac knew and liked. They had been shot to pieces in front of his eyes. Isaac forever would be haunted by the memory of leaving them behind, some still alive, to a vengeful Enemy who would kill and mutilate them beyond recognition. He remembered the one thought which had dominated his mind at the close of the battle and that was Tarhe. Tarhe needed to be extricated before he was captured. Tarhe was the man who Isaac and the Wyandot at Upper Sandusky had come to revere over the years. Isaac entrusted his life to Tarhe, as Tarhe had done with Spotted Elk. Now Tarhe was grievously wounded. Isaac considered Tarhe to be more than an uncle to him, or a father. He was a friend who had guided Isaac much like a Manitou.[244]

By December of the year 1794, word reached the Wyandot that many of the tribes were suing for peace with General Wayne who had returned his men to Fort Washington, after building and garrisoning more forts across the northwest frontier. Tarhe, who was recovering, had Isaac write a letter for him to Wayne. Tarhe wished to say to Wayne that the Wyandot wanted to bury the

---

[244] It was a long-standing tradition in Wyandot culture of the 18th century that a person finds a life-long friend who cared and protected for each other's interests and entrust your very life with. LD-TTIF, page 164.

hatchet once and for all with the Americans. Other tribes would follow suit. Word came in the spring from General Wayne that he required the Wyandot to attend a grand council of all the tribes to be held in the upcoming summer at Fort Greenville to discuss a treaty in which the Natives knew they had no recourse. On June 15th delegations began arriving until there were 1,130 headmen and warriors present. The council, once begun, continued for over two months through August 17, 1795. Tarhe made his presence known as the acknowledged leader of the all the tribes present. He was chosen to speak for them. Isaac was at Tarhe's side, as he had always been, first as a warrior, and now as a principal interpreter. Tarhe rose and spoke at length several times during the council, with Isaac translating his words to English. Tarhe stated the case of the tribes in their pursuit for preserving their lands, but acknowledged that the time had come to accept the fact that they could no longer oppose the Americans, and must accept their fate as their cause was truly lost.

"Brother!" Tarhe addressed General Wayne. "We speak not from our lips, but from our hearts, when we are resolved upon good works. I always told you that I never intended to deceive you when we entered upon this business. It was never the intention of us Indians to do so. I speak from my heart what I now say to you. The Great Spirit is now viewing us, and did he discover any baseness or treachery, it would excite his just anger against us." Tarhe discussed the former boundary of 1785, before saying to Wayne, in a closing note, "Brother, listen! I have told you that I speak from the heart; you see the speeches I have delivered. Peruse them and see whether or not I have spoken with sincerity. This is all your brothers of the different nations present have this day to say to you."[245] When it was General Wayne's turn to speak, he did so with the authority of a leader of a conquering army. Wayne presented the Treaty of Greenville to the Natives, which dictated that they give up 25,000 square miles of northwest land to the Americans without gaining anything in return but a promise from Wayne and the American army to not destroy them

---

245 A quote from Tarhe in Charles Buser's writings on Tarhe.

or their villages. A new boundary was authorized that ran from the site of St. Clair's defeat north in a straight line, and then east to the former site of Fort Laurens, making the lands north and west of that line the only land available for the tribes to live on.[246] Natives would have to comply and move, as the territory ceded was to be opened for White settlement. The Wyandot alone would be allowed to live restricted to a reserve of land surrounding Upper Sandusky village.

The new treaty, signed on August 3rd 1795 dictated harsh terms for the tribes. Many Native leaders opposed it, but at the same time they knew that they could never again mount an army of their own capable of facing the Americans on the battlefield. When Tarhe and Isaac reached home, it became apparent to both of them that the horrendous defeat of a year ago was being deeply felt in their own village. The old ways of the Wyandot were changing more rapidly than they ever thought possible. Many years had passed since the Wyandot were ascendent in the Ohio Country, and feared by most. Those days were simply gone. Isaac was now forty-two years old, and Tarhe, fifty-three. They both realized there would be no more going to war for either of them. Tarhe, the Crane, War Chief of the Upper Sandusky Wyandots, could not lift a rifle or musket with his disabled arm. It still bothered him greatly, due to the shattered bone mass beneath the skin that caused him pain with the slightest movement. Isaac realized that the man he had spent most of his adult life with, steadfastly at his side, had now sized up the situation for his people and realized that he would change course to protect his people from anymore ravages of war, if possible. Isaac, too, would follow that course that Tarhe was formulating.

In the meantime, both men had the welfare of their immediate families to think of. Tarhe wished to get away from the Upper Sandusky village for the time being, due to the influx of Whites ignoring the latest treaty line. Settlers, preachers, and traders were arriving at Upper Sandusky without asking permission first. Worst

---

246 Part of that boundary today is the current border between the state of Indiana and Ohio.

of all, the rum traders from Pittsburgh were bringing kegs of liquor into the village and exchanging them in trade for any valuables the warriors possessed. The drunkenness of so many idle warriors was unnerving to Tarhe. While intoxicated, warriors fought with each other and traded away even the clothing on their backs for more liquor. There was no way to stop the trade in liquor without using violence, and that would likely bring military retaliation. "Nephew, let us take our families to the land given to you at Big Bottom on the Mad River. I will help you as best I can to build a cabin there and when done, I wish to visit some kin who live at a Shawanese village on the Hockhocking River.[247] Perhaps the time away from here will refresh my mind, and with the help of the Great Spirit, direct me on what should be done for our people," Tarhe offered. It was a good plan, and Isaac, as always, agreed to the thoughtfulness of his Uncle.

The land given to Isaac by the Wyandot was beautiful, wooded, and fertile where it lay closest to the river. With the help of his boys, Isaac erected a sturdy cabin within a short period of time, large enough to accommodate everyone by the onset of winter. Hunting was good and plans were laid to begin a spring plant of corn, squash, and beans, as had been traditionally done. Isaac found it was a relief to be away from the strife of the last years at Upper Sandusky. At the same time, he deeply missed his clan kin, and joined with Tarhe on many visits back to Upper Sandusky over the coming years. Too, there were always visitors from all the tribes who stopped by on their way through the country. It had been rare to see a passing White man taking trade goods to the Shawnee on the path. Gradually, that was replaced with a trickle of settlers who were stopping by and asking where there was choice land to claim. Isaac always politely told them he had an immediate claim where he was that was inviolate. One day, a party of surveyors stopped by to talk with Isaac. They brought with them disturbing news.

---

247 This village remains unnamed in references, which only state that Tarhe went to live there some time after the Treaty of Greenville. Kennedy, in his article on Isaac Zane, calls the place, Tarhe's Town, and placed it on the Hockhocking River at a crossing, however, no reference can be found to this place as yet.

Isaac's cabin, and so-called land that he and his family named Zane's Field, was sitting on United States soil. According to their survey charts, Isaac had no ownership rights to it, as all Native land within the new treaty boundary of 1795 had been appropriated by government law.

This was a quandary that caught Isaac by surprise. It had never occurred to him that the United States would take his land in this manner without first informing him of the treaty obligation and he being able to respond. What was he to do? The surveyors had no idea, other than saying to him that they guessed he would need to petition the government back East. In the following weeks, Isaac schooled himself in what would be needed to send a petition by mail to the fledgling government of the United States in Philadelphia. It would take months of work from his home, preparing the petition. Then, Isaac realized he needed to travel to the White settlement at Fort Washington that was now being called the town of Cincinnati. Wisely, Isaac chose to wear colonial clothes rather than a breech cloth and leggings that was his usual garb. He let the shaved parts of the hair on his head grow out enough before leaving, so as to not attract attention to his Wyandot Native heritage. Not knowing what he might find, he didn't want to attract attention to himself which would come in the form of trouble with White men who identified him as a warrior they fought against. Isaac realized that he was most fortunate for the opportunity that Tarhe provided him years ago to improve his English writing skills which he now depended upon for this critical petition. Having made the trip and sent the petition, Isaac went home to await whatever outcome, having been careful to not include anything about his having served alongside the Wyandot warriors on the battlefield on many occasions.

Unbeknownst to Isaac, on January 7, 1802, the U.S. Congress received his petition and referred it to a committee for review on the 11th. The congressional report opened with this statement, "That the petitioner states, that he was made a prisoner by the Wyandot Indians when an infant of nine years of age, with which nation he has ever since remained, having married an Indian woman, by whom he has many children. That his attachments to the Whites has subjected him to numberless inconveniences and dangers during the almost continual wars which existed between the United States and the Indians, until the peace of Greenville, in 1795. That previous to that period, a tract of land, on which he now lives, had been assigned to him by the Wyandot Indians, and that no idea was entertained when that treaty was made, that the land which had been given him would fall within the boundary of the United States, (which now appears to be the case) and of consequence, no provision was made in his favor by the treaty; all of which the committee have reason to believe is perfectly true: - And it further appears from two certificates, one given by five Indian Chiefs, at a place called Big Rock, on the sixteenth day of September, 1800: - That the Wyandot nation of Indians allotted the said Zane a tract of Land of four miles square on Mad River, and that the said Zane had pre-emption right, ever since the year 1758, to the lands of the Wyandot nation."[248] The second certificate was from Abraham Chapline, whom Isaac was able to locate twenty years after his captivity.[249] Chapline's certificate certifies that he was a prisoner of war in the year 1780, by the Wyandot Indians, and that the said Zane was very friendly to the prisoners in general. The committee recommended that there be a bill authorizing the President of the United States to convey six sections of land, one square mile each, to Isaac Zane, within the Northwest Territory. That never happened.

However, more than a year had gone by since Isaac sent his petition because the government committee considering land grants had voted to table Isaac's petition, apparently indefinitely.[250]

248 Quote from Brumel's book, page 75.
249 It is not known how this came about. Whether Chapline happened to be traveling in the new addition to the Northwest Territory, or whether Isaac had met his old friend and adversary at the Treaty of Greenville council in 1795 which is quite possible. Chapline was known to be living in Kentucky at Harrodsville.
250 It is unclear to the author exactly what happened except that by tabling the petition, it was to be ignored. Brumel, in his book, states, "For some reason he (Isaac) did not actually receive this land. It appears that at the time he preferred to remain at the present site of Zanesfield. He later purchased

While Isaac was awaiting a response, Tarhe arrived with news of new Native trouble brewing. The great Shawnee Chief Tecumseh and his Native alliance were calling for a new war against the United States. Tecumseh did not have a consensus of opinion among the nations. So far, the Wyandot was one of the tribes who were against joining Tecumseh. When questioned, Tarhe openly opposed his Wyandot support for another war, under any conditions. By 1812, the situation had worsened, and the likelihood of war involving the Natives seemed imminent. Tarhe asked Isaac to accompany him to Detroit to negotiate with the Detroit Wyandot. He wanted to persuade them to reject Tecumseh's demand for their complete allegiance. Isaac served as one of the translators during the counseling with all of the assembled tribes. Tarhe, and the Wyandot chief Walk-in-the-Water were asked to "take hold of the British hatchet." "No, we will not take up the hatchet against our Father, the Long-Knife." The British officers were angered by Tarhe's words and demanded to know why. Walk-in-the-Water responded, with Tarhe at his side, and Isaac interpreting for them. "We have, and we believe it is best for us and for our brethren to remain neutral. We have no wish to be involved in a war with our Father, the Long-Knife, for we know by experience that we have nothing to gain by it, and we beg our Father, the British, not to force us into war. We remember, in the former war between our Fathers, the British and the Long-Knife, we were both defeated, and we, the red men, lost our country; and you, our Father, the British, made peace with the Long-Knife without our knowledge, and you gave our country to him. You still said to us, my children, you must fight for your country, for the Long-Knife will take it from you. We did as you advised us, and we were defeated with the loss of our best chiefs and warriors, and or our land. And we

---

from Lucas Sullivant two pieces of property amounting to 1,800 acres. Later the government gave a patent for two sections of land in Champaign County" for his translating services rendered to Tarhe in 1812, to advise the Wyandots to remain neutral, page 74. How Isaac gained title to the original Wyandot grant is unknown at this time for sure, however Kennedy in his article states that the 1,800-acre purchase was the Wyandot land that had been given to Isaac, of which he was defrauded of by the U.S. government.

still remember your conduct toward us when we were defeated at the foot of the rapids of the Miami.[251] We sought safety for our wounded in your fort. But what was your conduct? You closed your gates against us, and we had to retreat the best way we could."[252]

And that, as they say, was that. Tarhe was adamant; his reasoning sound. He would not take sides in what surely was a coming war, and he would not fight in it, or allow his greatly diminished warriors from Upper Sandusky to be sacrificed again. Some young warriors would desert Tarhe's side in the hopes that they could attain some victory in battle that would enhance their warrior status. However, Tarhe knew those days were over. That time was long gone.[253] He and Isaac went back to the Big Bottom home on Zane's Field, content in the knowledge that the two of them, one speaking, and the other translating, had done all that they could in their lives, for the good of the Wyandot people.

---

251 Reference to the Battle of Fallen Timbers, August 20, 1794.
252 At the close of the Battle of Fallen Timbers, when the Natives and Canadian militia were routed and fell back to the British Fort Miami, the British commander of the fort had explicit orders to not engage the Americans, so he closed the gates thus preventing entry to the mass of British-allied Natives.
253 I am including these words as a reference to the "old ways" of the Wyandot, and it is also the title of Lloyd Divine's second book, "That Time is Gone."

Epilogue

In 1815, the beautiful Myeerah with the pale skin inherited from her French-Canadian mother for which she was called the "White Crane", passed away at the Zane home at Zane's Field, at the age of fifty-seven. The cause of her death is not known. The "White Indian" Wyandot Warpole named Coon, derived from his former name Abraham Kuhn, was said to have died in 1808 of smallpox at his home in the village at Lower Sandusky. Tohunehowetu Adam Brown, after his adoption by the Wyandot, went on to live with the Wyandots at Detroit. Years later, he moved to a village south of Detroit named after him called Brownstown. There, he became a Wyandot of considerable influence. Adam was placed in charge of treaty belts and tribal archives to oversee for his people. Adam married a Wyandot woman, had many children, and lived to the age of 75.[254] Simon Girty died in February 1818 at his home in Malden, Upper Canada, at the age of 77.[255] He was completely blind by then, and during his last hours, was surrounded not only by his immediate family, but by Native warriors who took turns holding his hand.[256]

Tarhe, known as "At the Tree" or "The Crane," Chief of the Wyandots and Myeerah's father, died in November 1816, at

---

[254] Reference from L. Divine's "Adam Brown."
[255] Present Ontario.
[256] As referenced in "Simon Girty, Turncoat Hero," page 286.

Cranetown near Upper Sandusky village. It is said by the Wyandot that the funeral for this 76-year-old man was the largest ever known for an Indian Chief. The mourners were without paint or decorations of any kind and their countenance showed their deepest sorrow.[257] Isaac would surely have been at the funeral of the man who regarded him as the son he never had. Undoubtedly, Isaac would have spoken about the man he called "Uncle" whom he had followed all his life since the age of nine.

However, Isaac, The Eagle of the Wyandot, known to some as "The White Eagle," had taken ill earlier that year at his home. He lingered for several days before "passing away." Perhaps he lay in his bed with his eyes closed, remembering all that had happened to him during his life since leaving the South Potomac Valley. While reminiscing, he heard the murmurs of his adult children and their families in the other rooms of the cabin. The chortling of babies, the voices of children playing games outside his window, and the yaps of dogs as they raced about with one another like they did at the Grand Council at Detroit. These sounds were the soft echoes of the present and past seamlessly intermixing in the distance of time. The wind whistling in the trees above the cabin caught his attention. Isaac listened intently. He found himself under the spruce tree in the winter wilderness again, listening to the wail of the snowstorm, and wondering which way he should go. And as he listened, he heard that familiar sound that was calling to show him the way. "Screeee, Screeee, the White Eagle called, reassuring. It had come to guide Isaac, as it always had; this time to a shore beyond the banks of the Mad River and to an eternal home of the Great Spirit.

Isaac passed away at the age of sixty-three, surrounded by his sons and daughters who had followed their father's footsteps to Zane's Field. It is said that his four daughters "became civilized and married White men, in consideration of the opportunities that they could have for improvement." However, true to the nature of the Wyandot warrior that their father was, Isaac's sons were reported to be, "all Indians in their habits and dispositions."[258]

---

257 Reference from Buser's "Tarhe" for the Wyandotte Nation.
258 Blumel, "The Zanes: A Frontier Family," page 71.

Epilogue | 299

White Eagle

In 1843, the remaining Wyandot people living on what was called the Grand Reserve surrounding the village of Upper Sandusky, were forced by the American government, under the previous leadership of President Andrew Jackson, to forfeit all their land and be transported to the Indian Territory west of the Missouri River. That territory was the endpoint of what would be called, "The Trail of Tears" for all the remaining Native tribes east of the Mississippi River. It had begun on May 28, 1830, with the passage of the Indian Removal Act that Jackson, an avowed "Injun hater" had lobbied for. The last of the Upper Sandusky Wyandots boarded a steamboat at Cincinnati on July 21, 1843. The legacy of Isaac The White Eagle, Tarhe The Crane, Dunquat The Half King and many other notable Wyandot, lay behind them. Ahead, lay a new life that was yet to be known.[259]

Isaac Zane's descendants would go on to claim Wyandot land allotments in what is now the state of Kansas and Oklahoma.[260]

---

259 LD-BOT, page 224.
260 Special thanks to Lloyd Divine for providing these land allotment records in his book, "On the Back of a Turtle," pages 264-265, and pages 293-294.

Isaac Zane Descendant Names

1855 Kansas Allotments
Jane S. Zane, Ebenezer O. Zane, Louiza Zane, Sarah Zane, John Zane, Theresa Zane, Jefferson Zane, Noah Zane, Margaret Zane, Ebenezer Zane Jr., Isaac R. Zane, Hannah Zane Jr., Hannah Zane Sr., Susannah D. Zane, Isaac W. Zane.

1888 Oklahoma Allotments
I.R. Zane, Mary Ann Zane, Isaac Zane, Ethan Zane, Jane Zane, Alexander Zane, Oella Zane, Maggie Zane, Buchanan Zane, Susan Zane, Eli Zane.

Bibliography

Brumel, Benjamin E., "The Zanes: A Frontier Family," iUniverse, Inc., Lincoln, NE, 2005.

Buser, Charles A., "Tarhe," Wyandotte Nation website, Wyandotte, OK., posted 2010 by L. Devine.

Butterfield, Consul W., "History of the Girtys," Log Cabin Shop, Lodi, Ohio, 1995.

DeHass, Wills, "History of the Early Settlement and Indian Wars of WV," McClain, WV., 1960.

Devine, Lloyd, "Adam Brown," Wyandotte Nation website, Wyandotte, OK., 2010.

Devine, Lloyd, "On the Back of a Turtle," Trillium Press, Columbus, Ohio, 2019.

Devine, Lloyd, "That Time is Gone." Devine Publications, 2020.

Eckert, Allan W., "That Dark and Bloody River," Bantam Books, NY, 1995.

Fitzpatrick, Alan, "Captives and Kin in the Ohio Country," Fort Henry Publications, Wheeling, WV, 2020.

Fitzpatrick, Alan, "In Their Own Words," Fort Henry Publications, Wheeling, WV., 2009.

Fitzpatrick, Alan, "The White Indians," Fort Henry Publications, Wheeling, WV, 2016.

Fitzpatrick, Alan, "Wilderness War on the Ohio," Fort Henry Publications, Wheeling, WV, 2003.

Gray, Gertrude, "Virginia Northern Neck Land Grants, Vol. II, Clearfield Publishing, Maryland, 2008.

Hoffman, Phillip W., "Simon Girty, Turncoat Hero," Flying Camp Press, Franklin TN, 2008.

Kennedy, Robert, "Isaac Zane: The White Eagle of the Wyandots," Ohio Magazine, 1907.

Parkman, Francis, "The Conspiracy of Pontiac," Volume I & II, University of Nebraska Press, 1994.

Peckham, Howard, "Pontiac and the Indian Uprising," Wayne State University Press, 1994.

Pieper, Thomas, "Fort Laurens, 1778-1779," Kent State University Press, 1976.

Phillips, R.W. Dick, "Arthur St. Clair," iUniverse, Bloomington, IN., 2014.

Spencer, C. Allan, "They Gave the Scalp Halloo, Vol. 1-4," Studitchulon Press, Wheeling, WV, 2013.

Steele, Ian K., "Setting All the Captives Free," McGill University Press, Montreal, 2013.

Thom, James A., "Warrior Woman," Ballantine Books, NY, 2003.

Thwaites and Kellogg, "Documentary History of Dunmore's War," Heritage Books, 1989.

Thwaites, R., "Frontier Defense on the Upper Ohio 1777-78," Wisconsin Historical Society, 1912.

Williams, Glenn F, "Dunmore's War," Westholme Publishing, Yardley, PA., 2017.

Winkler, John F., "Point Pleasant, 1774," Osprey Publishing, Great Britain, 2014.

Withers, A. Scott, "Chronicles of Border Warfare," McClain, WV, 1961.

Zeisberger, David, "The Moravian Mission Diaries," Pennsylvania State University Press, 2005.